**The Loveless Brothers**

Enemies With Benefits

Best Fake Fiancé

Break the Rules

The Hookup Equation

One Last Time

**Wildwood Society**

The One Month Boyfriend

The Two Week Roommate

The Three Night Stand

**Dirtshine Series**

Never Enough

Always You

Ever After

**Standalone Romances**

Ride

Reign

Torch

Safekeeping

The Savage Wild

Convict

# The THREE NIGHT Stand

USA TODAY BESTSELLING AUTHOR

# ROXIE NOIR

*For anyone who leaps without looking*

# ONE

## JAVIER

FOR THE RECORD, I know better.

I know it's not polite, proper, or possibly even legal to have your hand up someone's skirt in the third row of a massive SUV while she bites your bottom lip and the rideshare driver stares out the windshield and blasts country radio. I know that Madeline and I should be making awkward small talk while the car crawls past all the grime and neon of Atlantic Avenue on a Saturday night, counting down the minutes until we're at her place.

I should probably know her last name, or what she does for a living, or literally one thing about her besides her first name and the fact that she's got bright pink hair that smells like roses and bright red lips that taste like lime. The second we made eye contact across the bar, my entire fucking brain shut down. Madeline is, without a doubt, the hottest person I've seen in my entire life, and the skin on her upper thigh feels like warm, soft silk.

But learning her last name would require talking, and we haven't talked much at all past basic introductions. Not since I dared her to dance on the table in the dive bar and

1

she said *Not in these shoes, but you can give me a show if you'd like*, and the next thing I knew we were making out in a dark corner, and she was palming me through my jeans and saying *I live twenty minutes away.*

She lied, because it's been fifteen and we've gone about seven blocks, and every moment we spend like this erodes my impulse control a little more.

"You said you lived close," I tell her, digging my fingers into her inner thigh.

She squirms and her breath catches and her hand currently grasping my belt tightens. "You said you could wait."

"I never said that. I'd remember."

"It was implied," she says, and her head falls back against the headrest, and her eyes lower to half-mast. Her bright red lipstick is barely smudged in one spot, and I can't stop staring at that tiny break in a sharp line.

"I implied wrong," I say, and she's got one foot in its glittery high-heeled shoe on the back of the row of seats in front of us, and she rolls her hips so her panties brush my finger. They're smooth and silky and body-heat warm, and my brain goes completely blank.

After a moment, I realize she's staring at me, wide-eyed, chest heaving. She flicks a glance toward the driver—right, *fuck*, the driver, Jesus Christ—and as I move my hand, she grabs my wrist and guides it to her waist. I pull her in and kiss her again, both of us straining against our seat belts.

"I almost let you," she murmurs against my lips.

"You almost made me," I murmur back.

She's wearing a cropped black tank top, and there's an inch or so of skin showing between it and her electric-blue skirt. My hand is on fabric, then under it. Madeline makes a noise and grabs the front of my shirt, pulling me closer as my thumb traces skin and underwire.

The car stops suddenly, jostling our mouths apart.

"Dammit," Madeline hisses when she looks around to see that we're *still on Atlantic Avenue*, holy shit, though since I can see the Atlantic Fun Park out the back window we're nearly to the southern end. "It's twenty minutes most of the time."

I move my thumb higher and stroke it over her—well, her bra, but it's probably where her nipple is, and she swallows hard. I do it again, and it's fine, it's nice, but it's not—

"Take your bra off."

"We're in the back of an Uber," she says, one side of her mouth already curving upward.

"I know where we are."

Madeline wriggles, smirking, arching and pressing into the seat belt. Her eyes don't leave mine and the smile doesn't leave her face as she wriggles more, bites her lip, then sits back to pull the straps over her shoulders and the bra out through one armhole. She stops looking at me long enough to shove it into her purse, then grabs the headrest with her left hand and puts her right on the bare thigh, exposed by the high slit in her skirt.

"Anything else?" she asks. She sounds breathless, the seat belt over her chest pulling her shirt tight over the hard points of her nipples. I circle a thumb around the left one, dragging the fabric with me. She inhales softly, watching me.

The SUV stops again, *in* the crosswalk this time, and a swarm of people move past the tinted side windows and the un-tinted back window.

She glances out at them, and I slide my hand under her

shirt. Madeline makes a noise and her eyes go to half-mast again. She swallows hard, her throat working in the dark.

"Just don't get me arrested. I'd be bad at jail."

"At worst they'd hold you overnight for public indecency." I pinch her nipple, making her gasp. "It's Virginia Beach. I see worse every day."

"I wouldn't be any better at a holding tank."

"Then keep still and don't make too much noise," I say, and try to position myself so I can use both hands. Right now, I'd give almost anything not to be buckled into a car.

Her shirt rides up until the lower curve of one breast peeks out below the hem. I pause to stare before pulling it down. There's still a driver in this vehicle, even if he couldn't be paying us less attention.

"Javier," she says into my mouth a few minutes later, because we're suddenly kissing again, both my hands under her shirt while I swallow her tiny sighs and moans. "You, um, don't have to be this gentle."

It feels like something opens in my hindbrain, a secret trapdoor to the night sky. I pinch her nipples harder, and she squirms against the seat belt, sliding one hand around my upper thigh. My dick twitches at the proximity.

"Like this?"

"Yeah," she says. "Or...more, if you wanted."

"More?" I say and pinch harder. Madeline drags a breath in, her fingers tightening. I can feel her nails through the denim, and the feeling goes straight to my dick. "Tell me."

"Fuck, that's good," she whispers. "Can you—a little harder—"

I squeeze my fingers together harder, and my dick *throbs*. Madeline bites her lips and muffles a moan, and I haven't come by accident since I was a teenager but I'm starting to worry.

We're past the lights of Atlantic Avenue, and it's not dark—we're still in the city—but now it's streetlights instead of neon. Dark storefronts, then houses, then empty sidewalks.

Jesus, we have to be close.

In a moment of inspiration, I scrape both my thumbnails across the flat surface of her nipples. Madeline's mouth falls open, and her head tilts, her throat bared. She squeezes my thigh, and then we're kissing again and *fuck*, she's massaging my dick through my jeans and there's no way this doesn't end—

The dome light of the SUV comes on, and we both jerk away. Madeline tugs her shirt down, face flaming red.

"We're here," the driver says.

· · * * ★ ★ ★ * * · · ·

THREE MINUTES and one massive tip later—probably too massive, but my bank balance is a problem for tomorrow; I'll pick up some extra shifts, I don't fucking care—we're inside Madeline's apartment, her shoes kicked off, her skirt around her waist, her shirt pushed up over her tits, her panties around one ankle.

I've got her up against the wall, my mouth on her neck, my hand between her legs, my fingertips stroking slick, wet heat, my palm cupped over her clit. I think. I'm, like, ninety percent sure about that last one, but she's panting and swearing and trying not to moan and both of her hands are bunched in my shirt, so I feel pretty good about my guess.

When I bite down on that soft spot between her neck and shoulder—not hard enough for teeth marks tomorrow, probably—a moan breaks through before she swallows it. I lick the spot and tighten my grip on her, the tip of my middle finger nudging between her lips and against her entrance.

"Shit," she hisses, head back, neck still bared for me.

"What are your neighbors like?" I ask, lips against warm skin. I can feel her swallow.

"What?"

"C'mon," I say, bite her again, then kiss it. "Are they loud? Quiet? Early risers? Complain a lot?"

"They're, um. Fuck. Twenties, maybe? They had a big Halloween party last year."

"Are you gonna get a noise complaint if I make you come against this wall?"

Madeline exhales hard and smiles. She's rolling her hips against my hand—or trying to, at least. "I don't care."

"You should be a better neighbor."

"You should..." she starts, but I flatten the palm of my hand against her clit mid-sentence and she inhales sharply.

"Hm?"

"Do you even know where my clit is, or are you just guess—"

I *am* guessing, but it turns out I'm a good guesser because I slide my hand back until I've got one finger on either side of her clit, then squeeze them together.

Madeline cuts herself off again and shudders. I think her fingernails might rip through my shirt.

"*Fuck*," she whispers. "*Fuck*. Okay. Oh—fuck."

"They're not noise-complaint neighbors, are they?" I ask, right into her ear. I'm pressing her to the wall with my other hand, her rib cage heaving under me. I'm so hard I'm dizzy. "They gonna call it in if they hear me tell you to work your pretty little clit against my hand?"

She does, her hips rolling. Her eyelids flicker. "You can't even see it," she says, voice low. "How do you know it's pretty?"

"It's a good guess. The rest of you is." I move my other hand, skating it up over the curve of her breast, softly circling the pad of my thumb over her puffy pink nipple, warmer to the touch than the rest of her. "Think you can come like this?" I ask.

She huffs a noise that might be a laugh, but her head's back against the wall and her eyes are closed, her hands fisted in my shirt as she works her hips against my hand, her clit sliding between my fingers while she makes tiny, aborted noises. The heat of her bare skin soaks through my shirt, my lips still on her ear.

"Well?"

"I think so." She's moving faster now, harder, and I'm fucking laser-focused on my hand between her legs, putting the exact right amount of pressure on her clit, pushing back just enough that she can feel it. It's small and careful and oddly precise for how messy sex is, and I focus on it to shut out the way my skin feels overheated and stretched too tight, every seam in this shirt suddenly scratchy and uncomfortable, or the way my dick is trapped between my pants and my hip and I'm afraid that tiny pressure might be enough.

I'm holding it together. I am. I am. Even if this feels like some sort of wild, wonderful dream and I'll wake up any second.

Suddenly Madeline grabs my wrist and arches her back, and before I can say anything or even react, her whole body shudders and she's coming. It's not loud, but it's obvious, panting and groaning and shaking until she finally goes still against the wall, eyes closed, head back.

I stare. I think I'm slack-jawed, holding my breath,

praying that I don't come myself. My brain tries to catch up to what's happening because these things might happen to other people, but they don't happen to *me*.

Holy shit. Holy *shit*.

"Good?" I ask, like I need confirmation. I've still got her clit between two fingers, and I give it a soft squeeze, just because I can. She gives a whole-body twitch, but she doesn't pull my hand away.

Madeline nods, then clears her throat and swallows. "Yeah," she finally says. "Good."

Then she finally moves my hand and drags me in for a hard kiss.

Javier is kissing me, tongue deep in my mouth, his hand still holding my face. His spit-slick cock rubs against my thigh, and fuck, I bet right now I could turn around and brace myself against the wall and—

"Bedroom?" I say, blinking water from my eyes a few times. "Please?"

Javier's breath catches, his pupils are blown wide, his black hair wild around his face. He's looking at me like he wants to take a bite. I'd let him.

"Go," he says, and I duck under his arm and lead the way. I lose my shirt in the hall and my skirt next to the bed, my phone thunking against the floor. Oops. Javier backs me up and against the bed, his shirt already off, then hoists me onto it before leaning down, one knee between my spread legs, and kissing me.

"Condoms are in the drawer," I tell him, my heels on his lower back.

"You read my mind," he murmurs.

Moments later he's fully naked as well. His eyes never leave me as he pulls the box of condoms and also a bottle of lube from my drawer. I let one hand drift down my torso, between my breasts, over to one inner thigh, just to watch his eyes track the movement.

"What?" I ask, after I've done it twice more.

"Just thinking about how I want you," he says, ripping open a condom and rolling it on. "We could fuck like this, but nobody likes missionary best. And you could turn over, but I think I'd rather see your face when you come again."

I prop myself up on my hands, stretch out a foot, and plant my toes against his thigh, warm and muscled and lightly furred. He drops a hand to it and strokes my instep lightly, and it makes me shiver.

"Tell me how you want me if you've got so many opinions," I say. I'm going for lighthearted and seductive, but my heart's going a million miles an hour. I'm breathing too hard, and it comes out ragged and throaty.

Javier lets out a careful breath and his hand stills. "Move the pillows."

I reach over and toss them off the bed. Moments later he's sitting up against my green velvet headboard and I'm on my knees, watching him pour lube into his hand and then stroke himself. I've got a thing for nice hands and also appreciate a nice dick, and lucky me, Javier has both. I might be staring a bit.

"You can watch, if that's what you want," he says. "Or you could come over here."

I crawl. It's two feet and it's the obvious way to get there because I'm already on my knees, but it's still—it's something. I'm probably going to feel weird about it in the morning, but he'll be gone by then, so what does it matter?

It's probably fucked up that it feels easier this way, being some guy's one-night vacation fling. If I'm never going to see him again, it doesn't matter if I act like the horny slut I apparently am. In the morning he'll be gone, and I'll be my normal self again.

I kneel over his lap and lean in to kiss him. He's still got one hand on his dick, but he anchors the other in my hair and he doesn't *pull* but he does hold on, fingers threading through the strands and closing. I make an embarrassing noise into his mouth, and he tightens his grip the tiniest bit and scrapes his teeth along my bottom lip.

"You ready for me?" he asks, and then his slick fingers are between my legs, the pads against my opening, drifting back to circle my clit. *Now* he pulls with the hand that's in my hair, just enough to tip my head back, exposing my throat, and I rock toward him. "Bad question. You've been ready and eager since you got into the back seat of that car, haven't you?"

I swallow hard, my head still back.

"Before that," I say, and slide onto him all at once. Javi gasps and his eyes go wide, then flutter to half-mast, his chest heaving, both his hands like iron on my hips. He's holding me in place, fingers digging in so hard they'll leave marks.

I hope they leave marks.

"Stay still," he murmurs, head back against the headboard. "And tell me when you first wanted to fuck me."

"When you first kissed me against the wall, maybe," I murmur, clenching around him on purpose. He makes a small sound.

"You liked that?" he asks, throaty and wrecked. "When your friends were all there, drinking and laughing? You wanted to fuck me then?"

I did. God help me, I did. From the second I glanced across the bar and saw him staring at me, tall with shoulder-length dark hair, dark eyes, coppery skin, and ripped jeans. He looks Latino, maybe?

He rocks slightly, still pulling me down onto him, and my memory goes hazy.

"I wanted to pull you into the bathroom and bend over the sink," I say, words spilling out of me without much intention. "I didn't care if people saw."

"I think you'd have let me do it," he grinds out, and now we're moving together hard, his hands still on my hips, his eyes locked on my face. "I think you'd have liked letting people watch you come on my cock in a bar bathroom. I think you'd have liked watching yourself in the mirror. But I wanted you before that."

I grab the top of my headboard, grinding down hard, and

try to focus. "When I told you my name was Madeline? Like the kids' books with the nuns?"

Javier tongues one nipple, scrapes his teeth over it. Sucks it into his mouth until I moan.

"Before that," he says, and gives it another hard suck. "I saw you across the bar and wanted to go ask if I could eat you out under the table."

"Next time," I say, and my goddamn phone *rings*. It rings so loud we both jump, and then I laugh. "Fuck. Sorry," I murmur into his hair.

"Do you need to answer?"

I stop moving and look at him. With me on top like this, I'm an inch or two taller, so I'm looking down.

"Are you serious?"

"Just making sure."

"I'm *busy*."

The ringing stops, then starts again a moment later.

"Persistent," Javier says. "Someone really wants to talk to you."

"Do they." Fuck, this is the perfect angle. Every roll of his hips drives him deep into the exact right spot, shooting pleasure through my limbs. "They can—"

Three things occur to me at once.

One, my phone is on vibrate twenty-four seven and only *rings* if someone on my "important contacts" list has called at least three times in a row;

Two, when I left with Javier, I waved at Emily and then pointed at the door, which in retrospect is not the clearest of statements; and

Three, I have literally watched my drunk friends call the cops when they can't find a member of their party.

"Fuck. They're gonna call the police," I say and drag

myself off of Javier. He makes a surprised noise and lets me go, chest heaving, hair wild.

"The police?" he echoes.

"I didn't tell Emily and Theresa where I was going when I left," I say, pawing at my discarded skirt, phone still ringing, pussy throbbing mournfully. "They're drunk, I've seen them do it before. I'm sorry, just give me a—hi, Emily?"

"MADELINE!" she shouts over the din in the background. "ARE YOU ALIVE? YOU DISAPPEARED!"

"Sorry—I left the bar. I thought you saw me. I really can't ta—"

"WITH THAT GUY?" She confers with someone in the background, loudly. "THE ONE WITH THE HAIR?"

*That guy with the hair* is still sitting in my bed, and now he gets a hand back on himself and starts stroking. I try not to think about how much I'd rather be sitting on that than yelling at my drunk friend.

"Yeah, him," I say and walk forward. I plant one knee on the bed. Javier raises an eyebrow.

"HE LOOKED SKETCHY," Emily goes on. Javier rubs his thumb over the tip of his cock, and it makes his hips flex. Fuck. "PAM SAID HIS CLOTHES HAD HOLES? DO YOU NEED US TO COME GET YOU?"

"*No!*" I yelp, and now I'm kneeling on the bed, sliding my other hand up Javier's thigh, and oh my god, I need to get Emily off the phone in a way that doesn't make her worried. "I'm fine. I'm totally okay."

"What's the password?" she asks, and Javier crooks a finger at me to come closer. I stare at him, eyebrows raised, and bite my lip. He gives a tiny shrug, hand still moving on his dick.

"Madeline!"

"What?" I swing a leg over until I'm straddling Javier, almost as close as we were before. He reaches out to toy with a nipple, and I have to clench my jaw so I don't make a noise.

He leans forward until his mouth is right by my ear. "Shhh."

My whole body shudders.

"*Madeline,*" Emily is saying, and shit, now she sounds a little worried. "Password."

I've somehow slid forward on Javier's lap, even closer, the tip of his cock teasing against my clit as he holds it still. Fuck, *fuck,* I'm on the phone and shouldn't grind against it, even a little, but—I do.

"Giraffe," I guess, because I have no fucking idea what the password is. I roll my hips, and the head of Javier's cock slides from my clit to nestle between my lips, and fuck, I could—I could just—

"No, we changed it last month, remember?"

"What did we change it to?" Javier's not moving, it's just me, rubbing myself on his dick like I'm in heat or something, and thank *fuck* I'll never see him again because this is embarrassing.

"I can't tell you! That nej—nef—negates the whole point of having a password!"

This time I let myself sink down onto him, just a little. I let the fat head of his cock breach me, and then I clench around him to watch his eyes close.

"Emily," I beg. I pull back and grind my clit against him, and this time I take the head and another inch, and it's not enough, but I can't—I shouldn't—

"Please," I say, looking Javier right in the eyes. "Come on. I can't—please?"

"I just want you to be safe," she's saying, and then I've given up and Javier's bottoming out while she yells something about sticking together and watching out for each other, and I'm biting my fist trying not to whimper while I get fucked.

"I know," I manage to get out. "Thank you."

Javier smirks at that, then pulls me down by the hips and thrusts so hard my eyes roll.

Emily sighs.

"Don't call the cops," I babble. "God. *Please.* I'm fine, I'm good. I'm *so good.*" Deep breath. "I gotta go."

She says something else, but I'm already taking the phone away from my face and staring at it like I've never seen one before. Javier grabs it, stabs the red button, and watches until it's fully disconnected.

"You were that desperate?" he asks, and he's pushing my thighs wider around him, hauling me in, nails scraping up my sensitive skin. I have to arch backward and anchor my hands right above his knees, somehow even more on display than before. "You couldn't wait one more minute?"

He sounds wrecked, pupils blown wide, voice soft. "Or did you like having to stay quiet while you got fucked?"

I'm going to feel so guilty about this in a couple of hours, but right now every word out of Javier's mouth rolls along my skin like ball lightning while he grinds into me at exactly the right angle and fuck, *fuck.*

"Maybe," I breathe. "A little."

"Only a little?" he breathes, his voice hitching. "Would you like it more if you called her back so she could hear how good you are at it?"

He finds my clit again and a noise escapes me, small and desperate. I bite my lip and keep grinding against him. "Of course I wouldn't like that," I murmur.

Javier's looking at me like he can see past my skin, and I

watch him swallow. I slide a hand into his hair, smooth and a little damp. His eyes are wide, his cheeks flushed.

"No," he says. "But I *could*. Phone's right there. We could call anyone, and you could chat about the weather while I see how long I can take to make you come. You think they'd guess what you were doing?"

I have to close my eyes and bite my lip, but I still make a noise that's somewhere between a sob and a gasp. If I could speak, it might be *please*.

"Maybe it wouldn't take that long," he amends. "God, I'd fucking love that. Watching you try to stay proper and polite while you hold off coming for as long as you can. It was..." Now he's on my neck, teeth scraping along skin, one hand in my hair, the gentlest of pulls. "So fucking pretty earlier," he says. "You think you can do it again?"

"You talk *so* much," I whisper.

"You want me to stop?"

I shake my head.

"How much do you think you could take?" he asks, voice low, stroking my clit in time with each thrust, and I'm *so* fucking close. "How long could you ride me while I played with you before it was too much? I think you'd wear me out."

And it's—the thought of being here for hours, of sitting on his dick and getting off again and again, of Javier coaxing one more after one more orgasm out of me that does it. I shudder and shout and grind down as hard as I can onto him. I take him deep and rock my hips and chant "Fuck, fuck, fuck," and even when I've finished he doesn't stop moving. He pushes up and grabs my hips and kisses me hard, then pulls me down, still rocking up into me while I gasp with oversensitivity that makes my legs twitch.

"Fuck, Madeline. I felt that."

"Same," I manage to say, and he grins and then bites my collarbone, still rocking us together, aftershocks still vibrating through me.

"Good." He pulls me down hard by the hips, his eyes rolling closed. "Jesus Christ, I think you were made for me."

I'm still catching my breath, but I put one hand on his chest, push him backward, and start riding. Javier babbles and fucks up into me, hands still tight on my hips, saying shit like *so fucking good* and *look at you* and *fuck me harder*, and then he's coming, holding me so I'm practically split open, gasping while he twitches inside me.

He kisses me again when it's over, and then I manage to roll off before the condom can get weird. We don't touch except for our hands, which we manage to half tangle together before we're too tired to give up on it. My phone's by my shoulder, and after a few minutes, it buzzes. I glance at the screen.

"They're not actually gonna call the cops, are they?" he asks, sounding wrung out.

"She's probably forgotten about it by now."

"Here's hoping," he says with a funny little half smile, his face smushed into a pillow, and I snort.

# THREE

## JAVIER

I GRAB the edge of the sink in Madeline's bathroom, the cool edge of the countertop biting into my palm, close my eyes, and try not to think. I breathe in. I breathe out.

In theory, I know fifty breathing exercises, a hundred ways to calm myself down, and two hundred fucking platitudes about taking things one day at a time, but I can still feel her hands on my chest like they're burned in, and it makes everything else irrelevant.

"It's fine," I whisper, because I guess I talk to myself now. "It's fine. You're fine." There's no rule that says *No sex,* after all. There's no rule that says *Don't meet new people* and there's no rule that says *Don't derive some pleasure from life.* There's a rule that says *Don't lie,* though, and I'm smart enough to know it includes *to myself.*

It always happens like this. It's easy to make promises—No big changes for a year! No triggering situations! I'll keep my head down and work hard and live with my mom and stay sober this time!—and so much harder to turn an old buddy down when he asks *Hey, want to go get a drink?*

And yeah, I did want to go out, even though it's

Recovery 101 that Alcohol Is Not A Great Idea, Usually. Even if booze was never my main problem, it's sure never helped me make good decisions. Even though I had a soda— great work, me, nice job just barely not fucking it up—I still *went to a bar,* lied to someone, then went back to her place and fucked her.

And it was so good my fingertips are still tingling. But that doesn't matter, that's not the *point.* The point is I swore to myself—and my mom and my siblings and everyone who matters to me—that I'd give it a year. A year of no big changes, no big events, just tackling life and getting my shit together.

This doesn't feel like tackling life. This feels like acting on impulse and looking before I leap and an infatuation I can't afford right now. This feels like I'm months away from screaming her name on my knees in the rain or building her a surprise house or challenging her brother to a duel. Does she have a brother? I don't know. I don't know anything about her. *Fuck.*

Well—I know she's got her own place in a normal neighborhood, a cozy little one-bedroom apartment on the second floor. I know she's got a fake-fur throw on the back of her couch and a neatly organized shoe rack in her entryway, and I know her bathroom is small and full of hair stuff and skin stuff and makeup that's all lined up on racks. I know there are no toothpaste dots on the sparklingly clean mirror and there's framed art of an ocean-dwelling dinosaur on the wall and her shower curtain has a giant squid sinking a ship on it.

I take my hands off the counter because I'm probably messing it up somehow.

· · · · ★ ★ ★ · · · ·

WHEN I HEAD BACK OUT, I can see her in the kitchen. She's drinking a glass of water and wearing a short robe with leopards on it and huge fuzzy purple slippers. I'm still naked, and now I feel like it. Exposed and awkward and like I've got too many hands. My dick is just *out*. I find my clothes and pull them on before I head into the kitchen, which is dark except for the light over her stove.

She fills a glass and hands it to me. I thank her and drink and try not to look at her standing there, barefoot in that loud robe, her makeup off and her hair still practically glowing. I try not to want to take her back into the bedroom and do it all again.

"So," she says after I've put my glass into her sink. "You're heading back to New York tomorrow?"

"Yeah," I say, and why the *fuck* did I tell her I'm from New York of all places? I've been once in my entire life. "We were only down for a couple days. My friend's aunt has a condo."

That's not true, either. Fuck.

"Sounds fun," she says.

"I had a good time."

She snorts, crosses her ankles, and pushes a hand through her hair. "Glad I could help."

"Are you kidding? That was the highlight of my trip."

Madeline looks away and blushes so hard I can see it, even in the low light. I have to fight the urge to reach out, take her chin, turn her face to mine again and—what? Kiss her? Ask if I can stay?

Tell her that I'm not on vacation, I'm not staying at my friend's aunt's condo? Tell her I'm six weeks out of rehab and living with my mom while she sorts through the rubble of her marriage to my dad and I sort through the rubble of my life, all of which is my fault? Or do I tell her that I should go because my shift at the tourist-trap candy store near the beach starts in a few hours and I've gotta make sure my hairnet is on straight? Or maybe I tell her that this was the third time I went to rehab, and no matter how desperately I want this time to stick, number four sometimes feels inevitable? That fucking up and relapsing feels like a matter of *when*, not *if*, because I've known myself for twenty-eight years now?

I don't say any of that because I know, thanks to plenty of trial and error, when something is too much.

"I should get going," I tell her instead. "We're supposed to hit the road pretty early."

There's a long moment where she looks at me like she's expecting something else. But then she nods. "Right, yeah. Did you order an Uber yet, or..."

Then I'm doing all the business of leaving: requesting a car and putting my shoes on, making sure I've got my wallet and my phone and the keys to my mom's house, and then we're at her front door.

"It was nice meeting you," she says, then covers her face with her hands. "Wow."

I snort, despite myself. "Should I say the pleasure was all mine?"

"It wasn't."

"I'm glad to hear it."

Madeline sighs into her hands.

"This was fun," I say—the understatement of the year. "I'm glad we met."

She takes her hands off her face, and it's hard to tell because it's dark, but I think she's bright red.

"Me, too," she says, and there's that pause again, this loud silence. I bite my tongue and pray she doesn't ask to see me again. Then I pray a little harder that she does.

23

She doesn't. The hardest thing I do all night is not ask for her number.

Neither of us says anything. But I can't end it here, can I? Not like this. So I lean in and kiss her, quick and chaste, and the last thing I see is her smile as she closes the door behind me.

*Maybe someday,* I tell myself. In six months or eight, once I've stopped holding myself together by my fingernails. I'll get my shit together and find her, somehow. Ask her on a real date.

It's easy to believe in a future version of me who's capable of all that, so I hang all my hopes on that guy and wait for my ride.

# FOUR

## JAVIER

### Two Years Later
### August

I MIGHT NEVER GET USED to the country at night. Not the deep country, up in the mountains, right off a highway that's nothing but two lanes and a dirt shoulder. Not after midnight, when even the crickets have gone to sleep. It's too dark, even with the moonlight, too quiet, too *still*.

I don't exactly miss the city, all that light and noise, but I think I'll always expect it. The country silence makes the back of my neck prickle in a way that city hubbub never could, and I look over my shoulder every thirty seconds or so, convinced that some enormous, silent, backwoods creature is lurking right behind me. Or, worse, a sheriff's deputy.

Wyatt, on the other hand, is fully focused on the task ahead of us.

"You didn't mention the seven-foot fence," he hisses.

"I definitely mentioned the fence," I hiss back. I may have forgotten to mention the fence.

"No. If you mentioned a fence, I would have been

expecting *a fence*," he says, voice still low as he looks up at it. "All you told me about were cameras on the driveway and floodlights in the parking lot. You didn't mention seven feet of..." He gestures, and I can tell he wishes he could say *razor wire* or *electrified steel*, but unfortunately for his dramatics, neither of those things are true. "Chain link," he finishes. He seems slightly offended that it's not even barbed.

"Sorry. An insurmountable obstacle," I say, slinging my pack to the ground and crouching. I got overambitious packing, so it's too full of things we probably won't need: several flashlights, headlamps, a length of rope, a length of chain, WD-40, a hammer (a hammer?), pliers, some clamps, several granola bars, a charging cable, two batteries that don't fit into anything in this backpack, and a pair of night vision goggles that I borrowed from our friend Silas.

We also borrowed the all-terrain furniture dolly—which has large rubber tires instead of standard dolly wheels—from Silas, who wouldn't say why he had it.

"Okay, you don't have to insult me," Wyatt says, and I can hear that he's grinning. "I'm not saying the fence is a problem, I'm saying next time, mention the fence. Thanks," he finishes as I hand him a pair of wire cutters.

The fence is unserious, and we both know it. It's constructed of chain link unspooled around eight to ten metal fenceposts, and it's sagging. The posts are leaning because they weren't put in deep enough, and there are at least three holes under it, dug by enterprising animals. At best, it's the suggestion of a fence.

Unserious or not, we're definitely not supposed to cut all the links along one pole and roll it back on itself, nor are we supposed to walk through the hole and trespass. I can't help but think *What if there are tripwires, what if there are hidden cameras, maybe this was all an elaborate sting setup by the*

*Burnley County Sheriff's Department and a whole SWAT team is about to jump out at us*, but none of that happens. It stays dark and quiet, the only movement from the breeze rustling the forest behind us and the weeds in the badly mowed back lawn.

"Did you and Josie manage to figure out where they put it?" Wyatt asks as we step through. "When you were on your recon mission?"

"No," I admit, though we sure tried. "We didn't breach the perimeter to look through any windows. It seemed too risky in the daylight." Wyatt snorts and mutters *breach the perimeter* to himself. "Also, I didn't want to get Josie in trouble if we got caught."

"Wow, thanks."

"Okay—one, I've seen you get yourself out of trouble, and two, this is much lower risk," I point out, even though I'm not sure it's true. "Josie only volunteered to be my decoy white lady, not help me steal a motel sign."

Technically, what Josie said was *I'll come with you, and if the cops ask what we're doing, I'll hold a map upside down, act super confused, and giggle a lot*, and then her boyfriend, Wells, said *Don't forget to also twirl your hair*, and anyway, no one stopped to see what we were doing, so it was all moot.

"If it's even here," Wyatt sighs as we stop behind a building, the pool of shadow around us even deeper than the dark. "Who's to say every motel-sign connoisseur in the Blue Ridge hasn't already broken in and whisked it away right under our noses?"

"I'm being optimistic," I tell him, strapping on a headlamp. When he found out what we were doing, another friend, Gideon, rolled his eyes, sighed, and told us this was a dumb, risky thing to do. Then he gave us headlamps with red filters on the lights so our eyes wouldn't have to adjust and we'd be less likely to be seen.

Gideon wasn't wrong. This is dumb, risky, and technically, I think it's burglary. Or larceny, maybe. Silas told me the difference once, and I promptly forgot it. Anyway, it's illegal for sure because all this still belongs to someone and that someone isn't me, even if it's hard to feel bad about this crime because the whole motel is getting razed in two days. *Literally* no one is going to miss this sign.

"Ready for your weird quest?" Wyatt asks.

I hand him a pair of thick gardening gloves because there's probably broken glass everywhere. "One man's trash, blah blah blah," I say. "Thanks for coming with me, by the way. I probably couldn't swing this alone."

"Breaking into an abandoned motel in the middle of nowhere at midnight? How could I say no?"

"You love it."

"I also have an uncle who's a judge, so if we get caught, he probably knows people."

"I knew I invited you for a reason. Which side do you want?"

"You think we should split up?"

"It's a search-and-recovery mission, not a horror movie," I point out. "And if you start screaming, I'll be, like, a hundred feet away."

"Better not be a horror movie," Wyatt mutters, glancing around the corner. "If I see even one creepy doll, I'm *out*."

"Why would there be a creepy doll here?"

"That's what would make it creepy."

"So, any doll."

"Here? Yes." He adjusts the straps on his pack, tightening the one over his chest like he's about to run through enemy fire or something.

"If you see a doll, we can leave," I promise.

"Or the desiccated corpse of the owner's mother in a rocking chair."

I don't bother answering that one.

"Or one of those weird stick figures that they kept finding in *The Blair Witch Project*."

"I *told* you not to watch that," I say, adjusting the strap on my headlamp. I should've done this before I put the gloves on. "Or any of the other shit Lainey's been talking you into lately."

"She's not *talking me into* it—I like horror movies," declares Wyatt, who I have personally seen scream and knock over a chair while watching *The Conjuring*. "We're going through all the classics for a month. It's fun."

Because I'm a nice person, and because I have other shit to do right now, I don't say anything about why Wyatt would be so willing to sit on a couch in the dark and watch something he doesn't like with his *very good friend* Lainey.

"Right. Headlamps indoors only, and try to stay out of the parking lot where the floodlights are."

"Should I make a lot of noise?" he asks, because now he's being a dick.

I ignore that. "I've got Silas's night vision goggles in my bag, but they're probably more trouble than they're worth. If anything happens, I don't know—hide. Unless it's an animal, and then either run away or punch it if it corners you."

"Punch the raccoons," he says. "Got it."

I turn the corner and look out over the cracked, grayed asphalt of the parking lot one more time. At the single-story buildings that have stripes where the fake logs used to go, at the boarded-over windows and room doors that open onto the parking lot. I take a deep breath and crack a knuckle and let the thrill of rule breaking settle into the pit of my stomach. It shouldn't be as much of a rush as it is.

"Meet you in the middle," I say, and we nod at each other, then skulk in different directions.

· · * * ★ ★ ★ * * · ·

I'VE SEEN pictures of this place in the 1960s, not long after it was built, during the brief moment of optimism that this part of the Blue Ridge could be the next Berkshires. Full of kitschy motels with heart-shaped hot tubs and neon signs that flashed long into the night.

That never came to fruition, but the Lost Mountain Motor Lodge stayed open for four decades. Even as the fake log siding crumbled off the outside, the wallpaper tore and yellowed from cigarette smoke, and the parking lot cracked and grew choked with weeds. It only closed a decade ago, glory days long over.

I think I find the sign at least twice, but both times when I get close to a dark, hulking rectangle, it turns out to be a twin mattress leaning against a wall. The wallpaper is lurid and unsettling in the red light, there's not much furniture in these rooms, and what's still there is broken. I walk carefully because I don't trust the floor. There are mattresses everywhere but less trash than I expected.

I only see one needle, in a porcelain bathroom sink that's got a chunk missing from one corner. The mirror's gone, shattered out of its frame, but at least I don't see any blood.

It would be a good place to stay, if you needed one. I know—used to know—people who'd sleep here in a heartbeat, and with good reason: the roof isn't collapsing, the floor isn't falling in, most of the doors still close. There's no one around, so you wouldn't get harassed too much.

I'm standing inside a room, by a boarded-over window, looking at where the curtains used to be when I hear Wyatt.

"*Javi!*" he's whisper-hissing from somewhere outside.

I lean through the doorframe, wary of going too far out lest a car drive by, and see Wyatt doing the same, two doors down.

"I think I found it," he says. "C'mere."

Thirty seconds later, I'm standing in the bathroom of another motel room. This one doesn't have a mirror, either, and the toilet tank is missing a lid but the sink is in one piece, and best of all, there's a dark, looming rectangle in the bathtub.

"Ta-da," Wyatt says, looking extremely pleased with himself. "One weird old motel sign."

"Holy shit," I whisper, reaching one gloved hand out to touch it. "This is amazing."

I can feel Wyatt giving me one of his *if you say so* looks, but I'm an expert at ignoring those. Instead, I run my gloved fingers over rusted metal and flaking paint—I think it's forest green, but it's hard to tell in the dark—and marvel that not only is this thing here, it's intact. It's on its side in the bathtub, with LOST MOUNTAIN on the right side in big block letters and *Motor Lodge* below that, to the left, in script. Hand-painted mountains line the bottom. All the glass is long gone, but the anchors and sockets that held the neon tubes are still in place.

"How the hell is this still here?" I wonder aloud, tilting my head. "Look, you can see brushstrokes. This was hand-painted! Who took all the TVs and shitty chairs and left *this?*"

"Should I go get the hand truck and leave you two alone?"

"I'm not gonna fuck the sign," I say, though it's half-hearted because I'm poking at the anchors for the neon tubing.

"I didn't say you were gonna fuck it. Maybe you just want a private, intimate moment with the brushstrokes." Wyatt is already at the bathroom door. "I don't judge."

"Liar," I call.

"Your preferences are none of my— Uh, shit. Javi. *Javi.*"

There's the crunching sound of tires on old asphalt, and then white lights flash through the door and move along the wall, briefly picking out dark spots on faded wallpaper, and then they're gone and I can't see shit.

Without thinking I press against the bathroom wall, with a hand clapped over my headlamp, a towel rail in my back, and my pulse thudding through my veins. Suddenly I'm sweating. I breathe so loud I may as well have airhorns for lungs.

And then: nothing. I listen so hard my ears might start bleeding, but when I can't hear anything but wind and trees, I finally whisper: "They see you?"

"I don't think so." I can hear Wyatt swallow, then the quietest creak of a floorboard. "It's a car. They stopped." He takes a slow, measured breath. "Turning around in the driveway, maybe?"

"Hopefully," I add and close my eyes, resting my head against the wall behind me. It occurs to me, hours too late, that there are plenty of people out here in the wilds of Virginia with a *shoot first, ask questions later* policy about trespassers. It's not like this is someone's home, though. It's an abandoned commercial property that wound up being auctioned by the county a few months ago, and bought for cheap by—

"I think they're leaving," Wyatt hisses.

I grit my teeth because I can't see anything from this

angle, just the ugly wall where the beds used to be. Maybe the way the light changes, a little.

"Did anyone get out?"

"I didn't hear a car door."

"Sorry for making you come."

Wyatt sighs at that, and neither of us says anything until the light on the wall shifts, slows, shifts again. Then the danger passes and there's the sound of an engine whooshing past on the highway.

"If I hadn't wanted to come, I wouldn't have come," Wyatt says in his normal voice. I blink at the dark, now that I'm not used to it, and the pale circle of Wyatt's face appears in the doorway. "What else was I gonna do around here on a weeknight?"

"Dunno. Not get shot and or arrested?"

He runs one hand through his hair, makes a face, and shrugs. "Probably not shot," he says and nods at the motel sign in the tub. "How are we getting that back to the truck?"

· · · · · ★ ★ ★ · · · ·

THE ANSWER, it turns out, is *with a lot of sweat and swearing*. It's hard to get it out of the tub—why the *fuck* was it in the tub, and how did someone even get it in there in the first place? —and hard to maneuver out of the bathroom, hard to get onto the hand truck, and extra hard to wheel back through the woods to where we left Wyatt's truck.

When it's finally secured, held in place by bungee cords we're trusting too much and covered by a tarp, we flop into his front seat and look at each other. It's almost two in the morning, and we're both covered in grime, sweat, flaked-off paint, and something that had better be pine sap.

"Next time I'm bringing pulleys," I say.

There's a long silence before Wyatt says, *"Next time? Also where would you put them? They've gotta be, like, anchored."*

It's a good point, since this may well be my first and last motel-sign burglary. I'm not even sure why I want it so much, other than sheer, sudden impulse. I heave another breath, then straighten up in the passenger seat, twist, and look through the rear window.

"It still there?" Wyatt asks, slowly pushing himself upright.

I can't help but grin at the shape under the tarp, at the prize I rescued from certain destruction. It's so *pretty*.

"Yes," I say, and Wyatt rolls his eyes, but he's smiling a little, too. He gets a thrill out of this shit, and we both know it.

"What are you even going to do with it?" he asks, starting the truck. "Is it for a project, or...?"

"I'll figure it out."

He snorts. "All that and it's not even *for* something?"

"It's for my personal enjoyment, okay? I like it, and now it's mine."

"You're so weird," he says, but he's grinning and shaking his head, and I snort. There's way weirder shit in the world, and we both know it.

"Takes one to know one," I say, because when I'm this exhausted I revert back to third grade apparently. In the cupholder, my phone buzzes, and I pick it up. "If I ever make something with it, I promise to put you in the artist's, uh, notes. Shit."

We're back in range of cell service, and I've missed six calls and about a dozen texts from Admiral Lopez. It's never a good sign when he calls after midnight.

"Are those all your dad?" Wyatt asks, because he can't mind his own business.

"Eyes on the road," I tell him and tip my head back against the headrest. "Fuuuuuck."

"How bad is he this time?"

I sigh and scroll through the texts, scan the voicemail transcripts. I hate how I can hear everything in his voice—his cadence that makes everything sound like an order, Tejano accent clipped by decades in the Navy.

"Could be worse," I finally say. "He wants to see me when I'm in Virginia Beach this week for my mom's engagement dinner. I had the temerity to tell him no when he first asked, and he's not taking it well."

As if I didn't have enough to worry about already. I've only met my mom's fiancé, Gerald, once, and only for a few minutes. He's a sweet, dorky naval engineer who's nothing like my father, and I *do not* want to fuck this up. My mom deserves better than me coming in and ruining another relationship. She was married to my father for thirty years; she deserves dozens of roses and moonlit carriage rides and standing on a balcony while being serenaded—all that shit. A new start without too much baggage.

She does *not* deserve me bringing my mess to her doorstep. Gerald seems like a nice, normal man, and I want him and my mom to have a nice, normal life.

"Fuck him," Wyatt says decisively. "You don't have to go at all. If you're not up to it, then you can always—"

"I don't need you to be my therapist."

"Someone's gotta do it."

"Not you."

Instantly, I feel like an asshole.

"Sorry. I mean, you've got stolen trash in the back of

your pickup truck," I say. "I'm not sure you should be an authority on anything."

Wyatt makes a face, then a different face. "Sorry," he finally says. "I swear I know better."

"You know better than to steal trash or know better than to tell me how to live?"

Wyatt rolls his eyes and slows down to turn off the highway. "One apology's not enough? You need an itemized list?"

"I wouldn't mind it."

"Fuck off," he says, but he's grinning. "You know what? I changed my mind. Go have lunch with your dad. Have lunch with your dad every day, and don't complain about it to me."

"Then what would I talk to you about?" I ask, and he snorts. "I want to see my mom and Bastien and make a good impression on Gerald, and I promised Castillo I'd have lunch with her."

Wyatt raises one eyebrow at that, and I sigh.

"Who are you, my mom? No, dude."

"I can't make facial expressions now?"

"Wyatt," I say slowly. "Do you *really* want to get into making facial expressions about hanging out with female friends?"

He doesn't answer for just long enough that I worry I've pissed him off.

"You packed yet?" he asks instead.

"Sort of."

That gets me a look across the cab of the truck.

"I made a list," I say, and Wyatt sighs.

"Sure you did," he says.

# FIVE

## MADELINE

I'M STANDING ABOUT three feet from the table, arms folded over my chest while I consider the flower arrangements, when the smoke alarm starts shrieking.

I wince, shove my fingers into my ears, and look up at the smoke detector, like that'll make it stop. It doesn't. It does announce "Fire. Fire." in a worryingly robotic monotone, though.

"Sorry!" my dad shouts from the kitchen. "Last week when I made that peach pie, some of it bubbled over onto the stove element, and I forgot it was there. It'll burn off." I hear the faint hum of the fan over the stove, which won't really help, but it's a nice thought.

"Open the window!" I shout back, because I have to say something.

A moment later, my aunt Susan comes bustling out of the kitchen and hands me a laminated placemat with a map of America on one side and a map of the world on the other. She nods at the windows on the far side of the room.

I open all three of them and assume the standard position: fanning as much fresh air as I can toward the smoke detector. On the other side of the dining table, Susan is doing the same in front of the sliding-glass door while occasionally casting rueful glances toward the kitchen, from where my dad might be calling out updates on the Burnt Peach Stuff in the Oven situation. I don't know—I can't really hear him. At least it's a nice evening for late August in coastal Virginia. I can even smell the sea air—sort of, maybe, if I use a little imagination—and it feels pleasantly cool and not too humid, or at least not like I'm stifling myself in a hot, wet towel.

This part of Virginia was built on swampland, but for once I'm not being reminded of that fact.

After another thirty seconds or so, the smoke alarm stops shrieking. Though neither Susan nor I were born yesterday, so we don't stop fanning. We know better.

"I think it's gone!" my dad shouts from the kitchen. "Sorry about that, I did mean to clean it off, but..."

"Did the salmon survive?" Susan asks, trying to look stern while still waving a placemat. I think hers has the alphabet printed on it; besides these two, my dad still has one with animals and one with vehicles. They are, I believe, used almost exclusively for Smoke Detector Events. Nothing else works quite as well.

"All good," he says. "Thank you for your ready willingness."

"As always," she says with a slight eye roll. "Are you planning any other surprises, or can we put these away?"

"Best not," I tell her. "You never know."

"I heard that!" my dad calls.

"Good," says Susan as I take both placemats and stash them just inside the kitchen, where they won't ruin the ambience but will still be within easy reach. Then I turn back to the table and resume what I was doing: judging its aesthetics.

It's nothing particularly fancy. I wouldn't call it, like, a tablescape, but my dad is hosting a dinner party for his bride-to-be and her son, so I figured I'd make it look nice with two small vases of those little round vine flowers Dad's got growing in the back and a bigger vase with crepe myrtle blooms in the center. If I'd thought of it, I'd have stopped somewhere for flowers on the way over, but *Dagger Legacy III: The Fortress of Night* is shipping in two months, so it's a miracle I managed to leave work by five.

"Wait," I ask, still looking at the table. "Who's the sixth person?"

"You," calls my dad.

"Is Mom coming?" I ask. "She didn't mention it."

My parents, who've been divorced for nearly twenty-six years, have been good friends for most of that time. I was too young when they split to really remember what they were like when they were together, but they've independently assured me that they made a truly terrible couple. It made for an odd time growing up. My parents had the most stable, functional relationship of any adults I knew, but teachers and guidance counselors liked to worry over me coming from a *broken home*.

"Paloma's bringing her sons," Susan says. "Your father didn't tell you? GERALD, YOU FORGOT TO TELL HER!"

"I told you!" he shouts. He didn't, but I'm not going to die on this hill.

"I thought it was just Bastien," I say, walking into the kitchen. Dad's at the stove, stirring something, wearing his prized *Kiss the Cook* apron. I'm pretty sure that thing is older than me.

"The older one's visiting this week," he says. "That's why we're having this shindig in the first place, so he can meet the family."

I grab a fork from the drying rack and snag a green bean from the stove. My dad swats at me half-heartedly but misses. I blow on it over the sink.

"The one who was in rehab?"

"He's in school for graphic design and lives somewhere south of Roanoke in one of those charming mountain towns," my dad says, giving me a look. "Apparently he's also an artist who's working on some kind of sculpture series that Paloma doesn't quite understand. No idea what *that's* like."

I ignore that last bit. My naval engineer dad is perfectly capable of understanding video games and simply chooses not to. It would take him, like, a day or two to get the hang of them, which I keep *telling* him, and he keeps interrupting me to extol the virtues of the slide rule or whatever.

"Does Charming Mountain-Town Artist Whose Past I Will Not Bring Up have a name?"

"Javier," my dad says. My head involuntarily jerks up, but he's still talking, his back to me. "And her daughter's name is Thalia, just in case you want to score brownie points by remembering that."

It takes a second for my mild panic to subside, and I'm glad he's not looking at me because he'd notice and then he'd ask me what was wrong and I'd have to make something up. I'm not the best liar, especially to my parents. Growing up, I was a good kid and they were pretty chill, so I never got into the habit, and now it's probably too late.

But the panic only lasts a moment because it's obviously not *that* Javier. If it were *that* Javier, there's no way I wouldn't know because I'm pretty sure the awkwardness would have ripped a hole in the time-space continuum by now. Or something.

Besides, I've met Paloma a whole bunch of times. She's a lovely, polite woman, and there's a zero percent chance that mister *I like your pretty little clit* is related to her. Which is good because I still use that night as masturbation fodder all the time and having my future stepmom involved would be kind of a boner-killer.

"Javier, Thalia, Bastien," I say. "Got it."

"Not that you need brownie points, of course," my dad says.

"I like having them."

"I know," he says, and then the doorbell rings.

"Shit," I say around my last bite of green bean. "They are *prompt*."

"You know Paloma."

"Mmph," I say, chewing, then stealing the towel on my dad's shoulder to wipe my mouth. He frowns but doesn't stop me. "I'll go get it."

"Thanks."

I don't, though, because I take two seconds at the mirror in the hallway to fix my hair and make sure my mascara isn't smudged, so when I get to the entryway, Susan is already opening the door and everyone is making their *Hello, Welcome to the Dinner Party* noises. I hang back a bit, smoothing my skirt, giving them a little room for hugs and cheek kisses.

Paloma's on the short side, and I think she's in her fifties but her wavy, shoulder-length hair has already gone steel gray, setting off her deep brown eyes and warm amber skin. She always manages to look put together, her earrings matching her necklace—that kind of thing. I always wonder how long it takes her to get ready because I swear I have to stand in front of a mirror for hours to get the same effect. Is it practice? Maybe it's just practice.

"Madeline," she says, "so good to see you again. How are you?"

Paloma's a hugger, so my head is somewhere over her shoulder as I answer that I'm fine, I'm glad she could come, it's always nice—

I'm halfway through some platitude when I finally see the man standing in the doorway. Everyone else is hugging and making their polite *hello* noises, and it's a very good thing because madeline.exe chooses that moment to fail catastrophically.

He's got his hands in his pockets, and he's staring back. His hair's a little longer than the last time I saw him, I think. He's more dressed up. He's a little heavier, his face a bit more filled out and his shoulders wider. He's still got those sharp cheekbones and those pretty lips, and god, he still looks good.

And he's staring right at me, not moving. Like that'll make him invisible.

Because of course, *of fucking course*, Paloma's older son is *that* Javier.

# SIX

## JAVIER

YOU KNOW what word never made much sense? *Thunderstruck.* Because thunder isn't what strikes you, unless it's very loud and there's a shockwave or something, but that's pretty unlikely and it's not really a strike anyway. And I guess it could damage your hearing, but could it really knock you over? There was that one incident in Cuba, maybe.

Anyway, it should clearly be *lightningstruck* because that's what would make you feel brain-fried and electrified and like every hair on your body is standing on end and your blood has suddenly reversed direction. Like you can't breathe or maybe you're breathing too much, reality is tilting, and yes, right—

When I walk through the doorway of Gerald's house, Madeline's standing there.

Her hair's different now, an electric turquoise that's got blue highlights and green undertones like she's the sea in an advertisement for the Caribbean. She's wearing a knee-length dark dress with a leaves-and-mushrooms pattern and a V-neck that doesn't show any cleavage but does show a gold necklace of a molecule. I think it's a molecule. Maybe it's a beehive or something—fuck, I'm not a scientist, and it's not like I'm focusing on the necklace because Madeline is *right there* and she's still as captivating as she was when I saw her from across that dive bar.

Maybe more. I swear she's even hotter than I remember. I'm staring. Her face is bright red. People are talking. To me. They're talking to me. *Fuck.*

"—my older son, Javier," my mom is saying, and for once social graces take over and I smile and shake Susan's hand. She says something pleasant, and hopefully I say something back.

And then I'm shaking Madeline's hand and smiling a totally normal smile and very, very carefully making my brain blank. I've thought about this a hundred times. None of them were like this.

"Hi. I don't think we've met—ever," she says, looking up at me. Her eyes are oddly wide, like she's trying to beam something into my brain. "Right?"

I smile a little bigger and squeeze her hand a little more.

"No, never," I confirm. "It's really nice to finally meet you for the very first time."

This is a perfect deception.

"Madeline, you said?" I ask. We are still shaking hands. It's a normal amount of time to be shaking hands.

"Yes."

"Javier," I say, and she nods, and at the same time we both realize that we are *still shaking hands* and release each other. I shove my hands into my pockets, and she twists her fingers together in front of herself. We look at each other some more. I'm desperately trying to remember how human beings stand when they're acting casual and also frantically trying not to think about how the last time I saw her, I told

tell me," he says. "You're the one acting like she's radioactive."

"She's not—" No *shit* she's not radioactive, shut *up*. "I thought you two got along."

"Did she say something to you?"

Yeah, she said *Tell me how you want me,* and then I lied about being on vacation. "No."

"She's a little standoffish," he says, shrugging. "Wouldn't really look at me. I got bad vibes from her tonight."

"She's not like that," I say, the words coming out before I can think about them. "Bad vibes? What the fuck? Did she say something to you?"

"No! No," Bastien says, and now he looks bewildered. "Sorry—no, I just thought..."

My little brother stares at me with a stare I really don't like.

"Wait," he hisses, suddenly whispering. "Is this part of your mating ritual?"

I am going to die, and I'm going to drag him to hell with me.

"No," I say. I know I'm beet red.

"It is! This is a straight people thing!" he whispers, glee-ful. "Where you're so embarrassed you think she's hot that you have to hide! It *is* weird that you're into our stepsister," he adds seriously.

"She's not our stepsister yet, and I'm not into her," I lie.

"You totally want to bang our stepsister."

"Stop it."

"There are movies about this, you know."

"I hate you."

"Like, a *lot* of movies. If the internet's taught me one thing, it's that banging your stepsister is very normal."

"She's not," I start, but that's a pointless sentence, so I give up and try something else. "She's cute, okay? It's not weird that I think an unrelated, adult woman is attractive, and I figured that you two already knew each other. That's all."

"I say you go for it. The wedding's not until February, so you've got, like, six months to bang her before it's incest."

"Bastien," I say through my teeth, even though twenty-three years of experience with this asshole have taught me that nothing I say is going to help. "There's no banging and no incest, and it wouldn't be incest even if—" Unhelpful. "I think a woman is cute. Can I fucking live? And can you please not mention this to—"

"Hey," says Gerald's voice behind me, and I jump. He's leaning around the doorway, peering in. Please, God, let him not have heard any of our conversation. "We're about to get a game of Apples to Apples going. You guys in? Leave the rest—you've already done too much."

"I love Apples to Apples!" Bastien says, pushing himself off the counter. "Yeah, for sure."

"Great," Gerald says and gives us one of his goofy smiles before disappearing. *Now*, of course, I can see the echo of it in Madeline's face, and my stomach lurches.

"We're not done here," Bastien says and points at me on the way to the door.

"We're absolutely done here," I tell him.

"We're not."

"We *are*."

He very quietly singsongs something that sounds like "*You want to bang our stepsister*," so I flick him in the back of the ear, and he smacks my hand, and that's why two grown men are slap fighting as we enter the living room.

# SEVEN

## MADELINE

BEFORE TONIGHT, I knew three things about Paloma's older son, Javier:

One, he did a stint in the Marines;

Two, he went to rehab a couple times for Oxy (and heroin, maybe—that part is unclear); and

Three, he lives in some tiny town west of here, in the mountains.

After tonight, I know several more, including what he looks like naked, that he's a lying liar, and that he's very bad at Apples to Apples. My aunt Susan has to explain the rules to him, like, three times, and he still puts down *Driving Off a Cliff* when the prompt is *Squeaky Clean*. That doesn't even begin to make sense.

Javier gets zero points, but his mom wipes the floor with the rest of us.

"Who wants dessert?" my dad asks after we put it away, slapping both hands on his khaki-clad knees. "I made a special run to Tidewater Creamery and got their world-famous butter pecan."

Technically, he says this to everyone, but he's directing it at Paloma.

"You didn't. That's an hour out of your way," she says.

My dad shrugs, his hands still on his knees. Besides the khakis, he's wearing his most tasteful Hawaiian shirt. He's *so* lucky that Paloma likes his personality.

"I wanted to go for a drive," he says. "I just got the remastered *Automatic for the People* and the car's the best place to listen, so I figured I'd take a ride out there. Plus, they pack it in dry ice for the ride home."

It would be gross if it weren't so cute, and I go put the game back in the closet before I can hear the rest of the conversation about how my dad made a two-hour round trip to get Paloma her favorite ice cream and is now trying to act like it's nothing. Of course, it's not nothing. He's got a lot going on between work (naval engineer) and hobbies (tennis and record collecting) and volunteering (he tutors math for free every Wednesday at our library), and if I know him, he used historic traffic data to find the most efficient time to make the drive to the Tidewater Creamery. All because Paloma really likes this ice cream place—which is very romantic, and I'm not in the mood.

Particularly since I had sex with her liar of a son under somewhat false pretenses. Which he invented so he'd never have to see me again. Which is the opposite of romantic. I'm not even mad that he didn't want to call the next day. I'm mad that, somehow, I come off as so clingy and needy that he had to lie to get rid of me.

He could have just said *That was fun, but it was a one-time thing—have a nice life.* I'm an adult! It would have been fine! It's been fine several times in the past!

"Eurgh," I say aloud to the game closet. Specifically, I say it to the copy of *Star Trek* Monopoly that we've played once but cannot get rid of. I bet James T. Kirk would sympathize with me right now. He probably banged Spock's mom, and they managed to have their healthy situationship anyway.

Then there are footsteps, and I stop thinking about the deal with Kirk and Spock because my own not-a-situationship appears around the corner as I shut the closet door.

"There you are," he says and pulls a hand through his hair.

For some reason, I do jazz hands and follow that up with "Ta-da!" Maybe to show how totally chill and not at all upset I am.

Javier doesn't crack, just looks mildly concerned. "Can we talk?" he asks. "We should talk. Privately."

No *shit* it should be privately, but I manage not to say that out loud.

"Yeah," I say, and fiddle with my necklace for a moment, thinking. It's got the caffeine molecule on it. "Can you be enthusiastic about really big goldfish?"

"The animal or the cracker?" he asks. "Actually, never mind. Yes to both."

"The animal," I say, though now I kind of want a giant goldfish cracker. Do they make those?

Javier nods soberly, so I forge ahead.

"Okay," I say and glance over my shoulder, just in case. "Here's the plan."

· · · · ★ ★ ★ ★ · · · ·

AS WE WALK across my dad's backyard with our bowls of ice cream, it occurs to me that I could have, possibly, acted normal about this. A quick *Hey, Javier, would you like to see the koi pond?* would have sufficed rather than the one-act play the two of us just put on in the kitchen regarding fish enthusiasm.

"So," Javier says, the two of us standing on the edge of the koi pond, determinedly looking into the water and not at each other. "If you get a goldfish from the pet store and plunk it into a pond, this is what happens?"

Below the surface, an orange fish with white-and-black splotches swims past.

"Maybe. I'm not sure," I admit, eyes glued to the fish. Javier's about a foot and a half away, but we're both perfectly still, like we might accidentally touch if we move. "Someone once told me koi and goldfish were the same species, but now that I think about it, that sounds wrong."

There's a long beat while we both stare hopefully at the fish, like maybe it'll magically pop out of the water and guide us through this awkward conversation.

It doesn't. May as well fucking get this over with, I guess.

"I should—"

"So when you—"

We both stop mid-sentence and look at each other. Javier swallows. "You first."

I've got a white-knuckled grip on my quickly melting bowl of ice cream, the condensation dripping off my fingers and onto the flagstone path below. Now that I'm here, I have no idea what to say.

"Did you ever actually live in New York?" is the thing that comes out first, and Javier's already shaking his head by the time I finish the question.

"Shit," he says, and rubs the back of his hand across his forehead. "No. I didn't. I wasn't on vacation, I just—wanted to make it easy." Like I would've made it hard otherwise.

"You lived here then, right?"

"I did. With my mom," he goes on, and it's mostly dark

outside next to the koi pond, and Javier's voice is deep and quiet and intense, and he's looking at me like he's never paid attention to anything else. "And—"

"And instead of just telling me you didn't want to see me again, you made up some story about a bachelor party," I ask, as quiet and controlled as I can be. I'm not mad or anything, not really. Just—he didn't have to *lie*, like I was going to beg for his phone number.

"It was stupid. I'm sorry," he says. "It seemed easier... that way."

I take a deep breath, look down at my quickly melting ice cream, and try to get a handle on whatever my feelings are about this. As lies go it's not that bad. Not really. It's not like it changed anything. It's probably not worth being mad about.

"We were looking for the exact same thing," I say. "If you'd asked for my number, I probably would have said no. I wasn't going to demand you become my boyfriend just because we fucked once."

Everyone knows that's not how it works anyway. I've never seen dating advice that says *To snag yourself a good man, fuck him before you know his last name.* In fact, virtually all dating advice says the opposite—that no straight man is going to respect or want to date someone who puts out immediately.

So, like, *obviously* I had no expectations beyond some orgasms. Which were excellent.

"I didn't think about it," he says. "It was the first stupid thing that came to mind. I shouldn't have lied."

"You didn't need to spare feelings I wasn't going to have."

"Yes. Clearly," he says, and now he rolls his eyes. "I'm *sorry*. It was stupid. Lo siento. Désolé. If you give me a minute, I can maybe remember Arabic, too—will *that* help?"

I glare at him and sigh and then look away because he does have a point. Which is annoying, because I kind of want to stay mad for another minute.

"No," I grumble. "Is that all you lied about?"

"It's not like we did much talking," Javier says, and I give him a look. He shrugs. "I was really at that bar with a friend I was deployed with, if that helps. I was also really taking graphic design classes. Did I tell you anything else?"

I clear my throat, because he told me plenty that night but not much about himself. "I don't think so."

Javier goes quiet, this tall, solid *presence* out here, looking down at the koi fish like they're gonna help.

"I'd been out of rehab for six weeks," he tells the fish. "It was my third stint, and I really, really wanted it to stick. But there I was, at a *bar*, watching people drink, and I couldn't stop staring at you, and I didn't quite feel in control and didn't want to admit any of that, so I made something up."

I take a deep breath, roll my shoulders, and then release it, because I know when it's time to give up being mad and move on. It's not like he can travel back in time and undo it, and he can't apologize much more, so I can be over it.

"Okay. Thanks," I say, and he looks at me, eating a spoonful of ice cream. I do not watch his mouth.

"That's it? We're good?"

"Gracias. S'il vous plaît," I say, a little sarcastic.

"That's *please*."

"Look, we can't all know French."

"You don't know *merci*?"

Oh. Right. "Merci. *Kwa-sawnt*."

"Wow, you're practically fluent."

I take a long, slow bite of mostly melted ice cream and

watch Javier's face for a minute. "You lied to get into my pants," I point out. "You don't get to make fun of me."

"It was a skirt, and you just spent the last five minutes telling me I didn't have to."

"That's completely beside the point."

Javier's smiling now, and he's relaxed a little. Still in his nice slacks and nice button-down shirt with the sleeves rolled up, his hair back because it's humid as balls. It's not hard to remember why I took him home so fast.

"Fine," he says, his spoon scraping the bottom of the bowl. "Should we talk about how we're about to be related?"

"*By marriage,*" I point out, even though he knows, because I really feel like that part can't be emphasized enough.

Javier just rolls his eyes. "Yes. By marriage. Anyway, I think I'd rather swim naked with piranhas than tell my mom that we've met before. You?"

"We could just say we've met and leave out exactly how," I point out.

"Yeah, but I'm pretty sure the second you saw me you shouted, 'WOW, I'VE NEVER MET YOU BEFORE,' so that might be a little suspicious."

I snort. "You're the one who was all 'WHAT AN EXCELLENT FIRST MEETING!' as soon as you came through the door." I eat the last of my goopy-but-delicious ice cream. "But I take your point. And honestly, I would also rather swim naked with some horrible animal than tell my dad we slept together."

We're both quiet for a moment. A fish makes a small splash. At least, I hope it's a fish. God knows what strange interests my dad could have that he hasn't told me about.

"I actually wasn't going to tell anyone," I say carefully. A handful of close friends heard about the hookup soon after it happened, two years ago. But I don't think they're going to connect the dots. "Were you?"

"Bastien knows I think you're cute, but I don't think he suspects the...extent of it," Javier admits, and I absolutely do not feel any kind of way about Javier admitting he thinks I'm cute. "He's going to be annoying about it, and he's going to tell our sister, and she's also going to be annoying about it. But I don't think they'll guess the whole truth. I probably should've beaten them up more as kids. I was too nice."

I raise one eyebrow, because I may more or less be an only child—I've got half siblings from my mom's second marriage, but they're over a decade younger—but would that have actually helped?

"I don't think they'll say anything to you, but let me know if they start," Javier goes on, misinterpreting the eyebrow. "I'm pretty sure I can still blackmail them both into silence."

"With *what*?" I ask. Blackmailing one of my little brothers has never occurred to me.

"When Bastien was eleven he broke the window in my mom's car with a baseball, and I told my parents we didn't know what happened," he says. "I think I can use that."

Fascinating. "When it happened, did you say that so you could use it as blackmail later?" I ask, because if so, Javier is out here playing four-dimensional sibling chess, and I didn't even know such a thing existed.

He laughs, a sudden burst of sound with his head tossed back, and god, he's striking like this. "God, no. At the time I was just afraid our dad would—"

The back door slides open, and Javier startles and stops talking, like we've been caught. Even though we're just talking and, I guess, contemplating the fish.

"Hey. There's coffee and tea," Bastien calls, walking

toward us. "And mom is making up leftover plates if you want to grab one. Are those the fish?"

"No, they're gorillas," Javier says, and Bastien flips him off without looking.

"Hey, bud," Bastien goes on, crouching next to the pond. "*Pspspsps.*"

"They're not *cats*," Javier says, and Bastien scoffs, and before they can get going, I seize the chance at an out and wave my spoon in the air as a farewell gesture.

"I'm gonna go claim leftovers!" I call, turn tail, and head back into the house at a speed that is not, technically, running away.

# EIGHT

## JAVIER

TWO DAYS LATER, I'm sitting at the kitchen table in my mom's house. It's late afternoon, and in theory, I'm going over the syllabi for the two classes I'm taking this semester and putting everything in my calendar because if I don't do it now, it'll never get done and then school will be the same near-disaster it was for the first thirteen years I tried it.

In reality, I'm embroiled in a group-chat discussion of what tie my friend Silas should wear to his work gala this weekend. He's in favor of the one with hot pink and neon orange stripes. I'm seeing if I can talk him into a bow tie, just for fun. Wyatt is spamming the chat with pictures of ties with cats on them, while Gideon is very responsibly pointing out that Silas works for a fairly conservative, Southern law firm and there's nothing wrong with a solid color.

Judging by the tone of the conversation, Gideon's winning when my mom's doorbell rings. I get up, still typing.

**Me:** Bow ties are distinguished
**Wyatt:** [kitteninspace.jpg]

**Gideon:** What color is the suit?

**Silas:** Navy blue

**Me:** You'd be the only man there in a bow tie, probably. You'd stand out. Your boss would love it.

**Wyatt:** how do you feel about dogs? [Dachsunddance.jpg]

**Gideon:** So wear a tie that's a different shade of blue. Pink and orange would look like a nightmare.

**Silas:** But that's so boring.

**Gideon:** Your law firm is boring. Your boss is boring. This gala will be boring. Wear the blue tie.

**Wyatt:** [threewolftie.jpg]

**Silas:** I hate that you're right.

**Gideon:** Take Kat somewhere fancy and wear the pink tie.

**Me:** OR A BOW TIE.

I'm only halfway to the door when the doorbell rings again. My mom said something about a package getting delivered, so I didn't think anyone was waiting, but now I shout "Sorry! Coming!" and practically fling the door open.

My father is standing on the other side of the screen door, his hands in his pockets but otherwise at attention. He's wearing a T-shirt for some 5k tucked into his jeans, along with some startlingly white tennis shoes, and I had no idea he was coming.

I stare at him, too surprised to say anything.

"Can I come in?" he asks with a clear undertone of *You're being impolite*, and isn't that some fucking irony.

"What are you doing here?"

"Visiting my son," he says and opens the screen door himself, stepping through and letting it slam behind him. He looks around the living room like he's cataloguing every change that's taken place in the last two and a half years, probably noting down every picture frame that's not perfectly level with the ceiling.

"I didn't know you were coming."

"I thought a surprise would be best."

Of course he did. Why ask for anyone else's input, ever, for any reason?

"I'm busy right now."

"I'll wait until you're done. Mind if I get a drink?"

My father doesn't wait for an answer, just walks past me and into the kitchen. The fridge is in the same place and the glasses are in the same place, and as he pours himself a glass of iced tea and drinks half of it while standing at the sink, everything looks exactly like it used to.

I don't want him here. I thought I was pretty fucking clear about where our relationship stands and how I feel about it, but I guess not. What, did I think he'd listen? Admiral Lopez doesn't listen. Listening might involve considering what someone else wants.

"What classes are you taking?" he asks, still standing at the sink while I shove papers together into an unruly stack. I'll organize them later. Probably. Or not.

"Art History II and Advanced Graphic Design Tools." I almost make up something he'd think is even more useless, like basket weaving or interpretive dance.

I don't have to look to feel the disapproval. "Any business classes? Math? Science? Computers?"

Yes, actually. I took an accounting class last semester because I needed a credit and it seemed practical. But telling him that would be giving in.

"No."

He clears his throat. "What are you going to do with those?"

"I was thinking I'd change my name to Gentle Rainbow,

join a commune, and sketch drawings of peoples' feelings for money. Maybe host a drum circle in my spare time." I close my laptop and put it on top of my paper stack, then shove it all off to one side.

My father walks over, pulls out a chair, puts himself in it. Puts the iced tea on a coaster. "Sit," he says.

"I'm good."

"I don't like you hovering over me. Sit, so I can look you in the eye." He pauses. "Please."

I step back so I can lean against the counter, arms folded over my chest. There, I'm not hovering; yes, I'm being childish.

His jaw moves, and I can *see* him forcing himself to not bark an order. The back of my neck prickles because I'm goddamn thirty and disobeying my father still makes my stomach twist.

Christ.

He fits one fist inside the other on top of the table, back ramrod straight. His temples are grayer than they were the last time I saw him, months ago. His haircut is the exact same shape it's been all my life.

"You're wasting your life and your potential," he starts. "All this is a hobby, Javier. When I was your age I had a mortgage, a wife, two kids—"

"How'd all that work out?"

His jaw flexes. "Don't interrupt," he grits out. "You need responsibility and stability, and you've got a good head on your shoulders if you'd only apply yourself. We all know you're perfectly capable. I know someone on the admissions team at Arlington College. Classes start next week."

In the past couple years, I have been to an absolute *fuckton* of therapy. Some of it was awful and useless—I have, in fact, spoken aloud to my "inner child" and no, it didn't help—but some of it was, honest to god, very useful and profoundly healing. If I'd listened to my dad, I'd never have done any of it.

Anyway, I can't resist the emotional tug of his bullshit (*a good head on your shoulders*, he said), but at least I can see it for what it is: an order masquerading as an offer. I've spent quite a lot of time hammering out a plan for scenarios like this one.

"I'm happy with the way things are," I tell him.

My father is completely stone faced. "Javier," he says, already disappointed.

"I'm content," I go on, trying to recall bullet points I wrote down once. "I'm in a good place. I have a support network. I do activities that I enjoy and find meaning in."

His lips are getting thinner by the moment. "You're working two dead-end jobs out in the bumfuck backwoods and living in a—I don't even know what," he says. "That's not a life. That's an existence. An embarrassing one."

My father has never visited my apartment in Sprucevale, the bumfuck backwoods town where I live. He's never met any of my friends. He's never seen my artwork, that I'm aware of.

But he's right that I have two jobs—three, if you count freelance work; guess he doesn't know that either—and live in a tiny mountain town, and it makes the rest of what he's saying feel right, too.

"I have a cat," I say, because I think Zorro was on that bullet-pointed list I wrote.

"Keep the cat, fine," he says. "If next week is too short of a notice, you can also start in January. Stay with me until you can find a suitable place. My townhouse is too big for one person anyway."

"No."

His mouth is a near-perfect line. "Think about it."

"I don't need to."

He stands. "Do yourself a favor for once, Javier," he says, radiating disapproval. "I'd appreciate an answer within a week."

I cross my arms over my chest and then immediately uncross them because that's a sign of weakness and uncertainty. Guess who taught me that. "I don't want your favors."

"You haven't given it any consideration."

He says it likes it's free, not an offer that's got so many strings attached it's a fringe. I can tell that making it an offer, and not an order, is costing him; I'm thirty years old and he hates that I don't call him *sir* any more. I've spent enough time trying to please someone who I'm fundamentally ill-suited to pleasing—someone who came in here, told me my happiness is trash, and then tried to order me around.

Everything his bullshit has put us through, and he *still* thinks he knows best. My father has spent my life watching me do what he wants, only to fail. As far as he's concerned, it's because I never did it right in the first place. Small wonder I gave up trying.

Except there's a squirming, writhing, desperate-to-please part of me that wants to say yes and try again because maybe this time I'll get it right and he'll be pleased with me.

"I'll think about it," I lie, and hate myself for it.

"You do that," he says. "This is a good chance, Javier. It'd be a shame if you wasted another one."

God, I want to tell him off. I want to spend an hour shouting at him, starting with *You don't understand me* and hopefully finishing with *And now get out*.

I don't do that, though. I just think about it while we stare at each other for what feels like an eternity, then gesture at the papers on the table. "I need to finish what I was doing."

"Of course. Well. It was good to see you."

I want to say, *Was it?* But I manage to say, "You, too," and then we watch each other for another moment because this is where many family members would hug each other. Neither of us moves.

Instead, the front door opens, and we both turn to the kitchen doorway.

A moment later, my mom enters through it and then stops short, her gaze flicking from me to my dad. Oh, fuck.

"Raul," she says, voice aggressively neutral.

"He was just leaving," I say.

"Paloma. Good to see you."

"How was the drive?"

"Too much traffic. I thought I'd be here an hour earlier."

"Still construction on sixty-four? That's been going on for years."

"As soon as they finish it, they start all over again, seems like."

I feel like I'm watching round seventeen of a boxing prize fight, where both contenders are circling each other, exhausted, bruised, and hurting, but they know if they turn their back, they'll take another hit. That, plus the weird way my mom keeps glancing at me, feels like—

"Did you know he was coming?" I ask her.

"He's a grown man. He goes where he wants."

So, yes. "And you didn't warn me?"

"What, you need warning now?" She gets the iced tea out of the fridge and pours herself a glass without looking at me.

"About him? Yes!" I say, flinging an arm in his direction.

"Or did you forget what happened the last time we were in this house together?"

"That was a long time ago, and you're fine now," he says, this man who drove three hours one way to so he could tell me everything I'm doing wrong. *Fine now.* My brain is going to implode.

"If I'm *fine now,* it's not because of you," I finally manage.

"What was I supposed to do? Sit back and watch you get coddled while you ruined your life?"

"*Raul,*" my mom says, and she sounds fucking dangerous.

"Someone had to make you take responsibility for your actions," he says. "And it worked, didn't it? You've stayed clean this time, you're working, the rest of your life is salvageable..."

He trails off, like even he knows he fucked up.

"I almost fucking *died,* and you're telling me it worked?"

"Get out." My mom's so quiet and controlled that it's terrifying.

"It's not my fault that's what it took to make you—"

"GET OUT!"

My father's bright red, his jaw set, and he's never been violent with his family but I've watched him break things before. Outdoor trash bins. Lawn furniture. Never people, but I know what's under the surface.

"This was your idea!" my mom shouts.

"*You invited him?*"

She whirls on me, and even though she's well shorter than me, I take a step back. "Yes. You two need to put this behind you because he is your *father*—"

"That's the problem!" I shout. "If he were some asshole off the street, none of this would be happening!"

"Don't call your father an asshole."

"Paloma," he says, and now she turns on him.

"Why are you still here?"

"Because you told me to come talk to him!"

"I told you—"

I leave. I can't do it fast enough, hurtling through the doorway and up the stairs into the guest bedroom that was mine once upon a time. I manage to shut the door without slamming it, as much as I want to, but their voices still come through loud and clear.

Fuck. Fuck this. Fuck *me* for letting this happen. I should have known he was up to something the minute he called me at one in the morning. I shouldn't have come to Virginia Beach in the first place because I know it's never good for me, being here, sleeping in my old bed. I used to keep pills in a cardboard box underneath it, and even after I'd gone to rehab and then relapsed that first time, no one thought to check the world's most obvious hiding spot. After that it was the desk drawers, inside the mattress, taped behind a dresser drawer, behind books on the bookshelf—

I sit on the bed, but that feels too dignified, so I slide to the floor next to it. They're still shouting, the same old argument. I catalogue all the hiding spaces I ever used, think about rifling through drawers, looking under loose floorboards. My old desk has hollow metal legs, and I've got a sudden, hazy memory of opening one up. Did I ever clear that spot? Probably.

Downstairs, a door slams. A car door opens and shuts, an engine roars, a car leaves. Good. I take some breaths and wonder if meditating would help or if I'd just fantasize about setting fire to a field of wildflowers or whatever. My mom's talking again, and I tune it out.

He's right. They're both right, or at least they're not

wrong. Getting a four-year degree and going to work for some defense contractor he knows is a strong, solid life plan, and so what if the thought of living with my father and following his playbook feels like red-hot worms wriggling under my skin? He raised me, he sacrificed for me, he worked hard to put food on the table, and here I am, an ungrateful asshole because he didn't do it exactly to my liking.

Before I can spiral much more, my phone buzzes in my pocket. I pull it out to see that Bastien's texted the sibling chat.

**Bastien:** Mom just called me and told me to try and talk to you but she wouldn't tell me what happened

I shut my eyes and lean my head back against the mattress. I love my mom, but she has a tendency to escalate a situation.

**Me:** Jesus Christ
**Bastien:** Not sure the lord can help you now
**Me:** She invited Dad over to give me a talk about everything I'm doing wrong
**Thalia:** Oh what the FUCK
**Thalia:** Why is she like this?
**Bastien:** She INVITED Dad?!
**Me:** Yup. Then we all got in a fight, I went upstairs, and he left.
**Me:** Did you know it's thanks to him and only him I've been sober for two and a half years?
**Bastien:** Holy shit, he didn't
**Thalia:** She's calling me now.
**Thalia:** HE SAID THAT?

**Me:** More or less.

**Bastien:** You want me to come over? I can be there in an hour probably

**Me:** No, it's fine

**Bastien:** Doesn't sound fine

**Me:** I don't think you being here will make it more fine

**Bastien:** Just let me know

**Thalia:** Okay, she's telling me that you're very upset when all she did was ask you to hear Dad out and wants me to talk to you so you'll see reason. I need a drink.

**Javier:** Just tell her you will

**Thalia:** I did

**Javier:** Thanks

**Thalia:** For the record I think the fact that you didn't start throwing things at him makes you extremely reasonable

**Bastien:** Agreed

"Javier," my mom calls up the stairs. Footsteps, and then the floor outside my door creaks. "Can we talk?"

# NINE

## MADELINE

PALOMA'S HOUSE has the exact same doorbell as my dad's and the same *DING-dong* when I ring it. The same awning over the front porch too—that striped aluminum that looks like my childhood and makes me think of carports and wood-paneled dens in cozy postwar houses. She's got a wind chime hanging from the end of the awning, one of those shiny ones with a hummingbird cutout in the middle. I focus very hard on that so that I don't think about whether Javier is here right now or not.

Probably not, right? If he's only in town for a week or so, he's probably out seeing old friends or going to the beach or—

The inner door swings open so hard it rattles the screen door in its frame, and then Javier's standing there. His face goes from glowering to surprised in a split second, and I take a quick step back.

"Oh," he says. "Hi."

"Hi. Sorry. Is this a bad time?" Great, I'm already flustered. I hold up the jacket in my hand as explanation. "Your brother left his jacket at my dad's house the other night, and

I told your mom I'd bring it by after work? So here I am. With the jacket. If you want I can just—"

But he's already shaking his head and holding the screen door open, so I stop making my offer to leave the jacket on the porch and run away, or whatever I was about to say. I'm not even sure at this point.

"I thought you were going to be someone else," he says as I step past him, his arm still extended as he holds the door. "My mom didn't mention you were coming."

"Just a quick errand," I say, and then we're standing together in the entryway.

"Right," he says, and he seems off-balance somehow. There's a flush on his high cheekbones, a certain set to his mouth, and his hair's held back with a pencil stabbed through a messy bun, strands sticking out everywhere. "I think she's in the living room. Let me take you—"

"Is that Madeline?" Paloma calls and bustles through the doorway. She's got the same color in her cheeks and the same look on her face and doesn't even glance at Javier. He goes stiff and silent beside me.

I am *definitely* returning a jacket in the middle of a fight.

"Bastien left this," I explain again, holding up the jacket like it'll ward off awkwardness. "My dad figured you'd see him again before we did, probably, and you're more or less on my way home from work."

"Thank you *so* much," she says, and takes it. "Actually, while you're here, did you want to take a look at that lamp? Your father said you liked this sort of thing, and it was a gift from my former sister-in-law..."

My self-preservation instincts are telling me to throw the jacket and run, but they're overruled by my politeness instincts. I go with Paloma, throwing one last glance at Javier as I follow her into the dining room. He's making a face like a thunderstorm on the horizon.

Then I briefly forget about whatever their problem is because the lamp is *great*. It's clearly old, the shade long-lost, and it's ugly and spectacular all at once. The pedestal is faded and carved like a wave, out of which emerges a topless mermaid, arms raised, long hair tastefully covering her nipples. I fall in love immediately, which makes Paloma offer me several more household items. I decline, not being in the market for decorative plates.

When I finally leave, Paloma sees me to the door with a hug, then tells me to drive safe. The whole time she studiously ignores the fact that Javier's loading a suitcase into the trunk of a car that's parked on the street right in front of mine. It's easily one of the top ten most awkward interactions I've ever had, and while I've seen Paloma and Bastien bicker and I've heard her complain about her daughter, I didn't know she could deploy this level of cold shoulder.

Javier looks up when I get close, one hand on the lip of the raised trunk. He's wearing a white V-neck undershirt, shorts, and flip-flops, and with his arm in the air I can see a strip of skin above his waistband. I grip the lamp a little harder, and he slams the trunk down.

Then the trunk pops back open, and Javier swears and slams it down again, a little harder, and gives it a tug that makes the whole car bounce on its suspension.

"Sorry," he says. "Sometimes you really gotta force it."

"Trunks are weird," I agree, nodding, even though that's not at all what he said. Close enough. My heart's beating a little too fast, and with the heat and humidity and being dressed for an office, I'm already sweating. "Hey, sorry if I interrupted...anything. I texted your mom earlier today, but I think she forgot."

He scrubs both hands over his face, fingers drifting into his hair, and it makes even more short pieces fluff out until he looks like he just ran through the woods or something. Unfortunately, it looks good on him.

"It's not your fault," he says, then turns and leans against his car, propping both hands on the edge of the trunk. "I should have known better than to think I could stay here a whole week."

"You're leaving?"

"Yeah. You took the lamp?"

I hold it up and let him change the topic because I'm nice like that. "Isn't it great?"

"I thought you'd like it." He did?

"It's naked *and* a mermaid. Great combination."

"Sure. The chocolate and peanut butter of interior decorating."

"Not peanut butter and jelly?" I ask, trying not to laugh, and now Javier's grinning. He still looks tired, the corners of his eyes pinched, but he's smiling.

"Peanut butter and jelly is utilitarian. That's, like, throw pillows and couches. Nudity and mermaids together is a *treat*."

I really can't argue with that.

"Where are you gonna put it?" he asks, and at the reminder that Javier's been to my place, I glance nervously at his mother's house. As if this tiny admission, that she can't even hear, will make her fly out of the front door and, I don't know, call me a harlot and then break things off with my dad.

Obviously, nothing happens.

"One of the side tables by the couch, I think. But it needs a shade first."

"Opposite the mushroom lamp?"

"Yeah, on the other side of the couch." I've been staring at the lamp in my hand this whole time, and I finally make myself look at Javier again. "You have a good memory."

Javier doesn't answer right away, but he presses his lips together like he's literally biting his tongue, glances away, and then says, "For some things."

I clear my throat, fiddle with the lamp, and make some weird agreement-type noise because I also have a good memory sometimes, for some things. I'm pretty sure we're currently remembering the same things. Things which, for the sake of everyone involved, it would be better not to remember.

"I rearranged," is how I change the subject. "I put the couch against the other wall and used the bookshelf with the plants to block off the living room space a little bit? There's some annoying glare on the TV now, but it's not like I use it much during the day. I'm usually at work."

"You still got the lion tamer?"

"She's a cheetah tamer, and yes, of course," I say. The artwork in question is a poster of an illustrated retro-looking white woman in a circus, brandishing a whip at a cheetah. It's eye-catching. "Do you want me to go over the exact changes I made so you can tell me if you approve, or...?"

"Or what? You gonna put it back if I don't like it?"

"I could lie and say I did. If it would make you feel better."

Instead of laughing, Javier makes a face and looks away, then runs a hand through his hair. It gets tangled, and his scowl deepens as he pulls the pencil out. For a moment it's loose around his shoulders, and I can't help but remember how it felt in my hands.

Then it's back in a bun, smooth and black and shiny, and Javier's still scowling. I don't think it's at me, though. "Tell me I'm not that bad."

"No, you're not," I agree, and it's sunset and he's leaning against a car that's seen better days, and he's in this T-shirt with his hair back, and if he had a leather jacket and some cigarettes, he'd be every bad boy that's graced the silver screen since James Dean. Jesus Christ, he's even *brooding*.

I shouldn't find any of this hot, especially after he lied to get out of seeing me again, and my palms shouldn't be sweating, and I should mind my own business.

Except, like—we're going to have to see each other again, so maybe we can embark on a normal stepsibling relationship. Right?

"Are you okay, though?" I ask, after a long silence.

"I'm not gonna go on a multistate crime spree, if that's what you mean," he says. "Or do anything that lands me back in rehab."

"You're storming out of your mom's house so you can drive through the night," I point out.

He broods directly at me, pushing wisps of hair off his face, and I don't find it appealing. At all. "I wouldn't say I *stormed*."

"Flounced, then. Is that better?" I say, and he snorts.

"I didn't *flounce*," he mutters. "My dad came over without telling me, and we don't get along." He swallows hard, his throat working, then props the bottom of one foot on the bumper of his car. "Felt like time to make myself scarce."

I've heard enough about Javier's dad—I think his name is Raul—to dislike him. His divorce from Paloma sounds like it was ugly at times, and it can't have been easy for their kids. And I wasn't particularly nice to Javier last night, and shouldn't I let bygones be bygones? If I say my feelings aren't hurt, I don't get to act like my feelings are hurt.

"If you want to talk, I don't mind," I'm saying, and wow, that's not selling it. "I mean—do you want to go grab dinner or something? You can wait for rush hour to die down while you eat."

Javier looks at me for a minute, a few strands of black floating around his face as he breathes, his chest expanding against the white T-shirt he's wearing. The thumb and fingers of one hand tap a rhythm against the trunk of his car.

"Yeah," he finally says, and now his voice is low and so quiet it's a little hard to hear over the noise of a city at rush hour. Even though it's eighty-five degrees and humid, a shiver works its way down my spine. "I could do dinner."

# TEN

## MADELINE

"HOW CAN I HELP?" he asks, thirty minutes later, in my kitchen.

I really meant to go out to dinner somewhere. *Anywhere* besides here, really; it could have been Chipotle or McDonald's or Sad Sam's Suspicious Seafood Shack—it didn't matter. But we decided to drive to my apartment first, since it was nearby, and take one car from there. And then we couldn't decide on a place, and then I casually said *I was going to make dinner anyway*. And now we're here and I have to pretend like it wasn't in the back of my mind the whole time.

"Stay out of the way and keep me company," I say.

· · · ★ ★ ★ ★ ★ · · ·

"SO *THEN*," he says, slicing a carrot with a bit too much force, "she called both my siblings and wanted them to talk sense into me."

"She called them about a fight the two of you were having?" I ask, and Javier just sighs. "Is that...normal?"

My parents were divorced by the time I started preschool, so I've never really experienced the allegedly standard two-parents-and-their-children nuclear family. I can't say I think I missed out.

"I have no idea," he admits. "According to my cousins, her sisters also do it, so I guess it's normal for us. Why? Gerald doesn't rope all your family members into each conflict?"

"He does not," I confirm, swiping a strand of spaghetti from the pot. Javier laughs. "I can't believe your mom did any of that."

I slurp the noodle into my mouth—it needs about *one* more minute—and fight the urge to offer advice, like *Talk to her!* or *Make sure you firmly establish boundaries before you visit the next time!* He doesn't want my advice; he just wants to complain.

"I shouldn't have been surprised," he admits, scraping the carrot slices off the cutting board and into the salad I had him make since he was too fidgety to stand still. "She's been telling me that I should at least listen to what he's got to say. If there's anything surprising, it's that she ever divorced him in the first place."

"I thought she was pretty Catholic," I admit.

"She is. It took a lot for her to leave him and then to make it legal. It was because of me actually."

"I doubt that," I say before I can stop myself. I'm not exactly a relationship expert, but I've got twenty-odd years of *it wasn't your fault* therapy under my belt.

There's silence while I pour spaghetti through a strainer, and when I look up, he's staring right at me.

"You know I used to be a junkie, right?" he says, like it's a challenge. "Am still a junkie, will always be a junkie, whatever."

I put the empty pot back on the stove, look into it for a moment, and wipe my sweaty palms on my pants. Is this fucker testing me?

"I'm almost positive that's not the preferred terminology," I say after a moment.

"For some reason, saying it nicely has never made me feel better."

"You could always try it," I suggest, even though I'm not giving advice. "But yeah, I knew. You mentioned rehab last time we talked."

"Right. Well. My dad's pretty old school. His parents were farm workers who came here from Mexico before he was born. He barely talks about his childhood, but when he does, he makes it sound like it was the eighteen hundreds. He shipped off to basic training the day after he graduated high school. And he's pretty sure that getting addicted to Oxy is a moral failing—and needing to go to rehab for it is even worse."

I nod because that's too much to unpack right now.

"So he thought rehab was stupid the first time. And then when I relapsed and went *back* to rehab, he was really not on board," Javier goes on. "And then I came back and I was living at home when I relapsed *again*, so he waited until my mom was gone one day and kicked me out of the house."

That's—I try to imagine it, but it's not really computing.

"What do you mean?" I ask, slowly.

"I mean he told me I had ten minutes to pack anything I wanted to take with me, then drove me to a cheap motel by the train yard in Norfolk, took my house keys, and dropped me off. He paid for three nights and told me that if I used that time to detox, I could come back home at the end."

I've never met Javier's dad and Paloma's made oblique references to something pretty bad that happened, but I didn't know exactly what until now. I know I'm staring at Javier in silence, but I can't quite wrap my head around it.

"And your mom...let him?"

Javier shrugs and looks away. "He wouldn't tell her where he'd taken me at first, and by the time he did, I'd already gotten kicked out of the motel and I was...staying with a friend," he says. "And it's not like he knew any of the people I hung out with, and I wasn't going to beg to come back home, so I drifted around for a few months." He swallows, still not looking at me. "Eventually I wound up in Richmond, overdosed, the hospital notified my mom, and I went back to rehab. And she still thinks that I owe him respect or affection or *something* just because we're related."

"Oh," I say, otherwise at a loss for words. I knew some of the story—that he overdosed and went to rehab—but not the whole thing.

"They got divorced after that," he goes on and shrugs. "And then my mom met Gerald, and now everything is perfect, only my dad doesn't understand why I need some space. Salad's done."

"Thanks," I say, and have no idea what *else* to say because that deserves something and I don't know what. "I mean, I'd need space, too."

"I know it's a lot," he says and then smiles over at me, like that'll erase everything. It doesn't quite reach his eyes. "I usually am. Are we doing plates or bowls?"

· · · · · ★ ★ ★ ★ · · · ·

WE SPEND dinner talking about koi and goldfish—goldfish are small koi, it turns out, not the other way around—about weird plates we've inherited from family members, about how we both have a T-shirt for the same 5k that neither of us ran. By the end, our dishes are pushed aside and we're still talking, Javier sprawling in his chair and tracing designs on the table with one finger. It's callused, one knuckle ink-stained. Under the table, our ankles are touching, and neither of us is drawing back.

"I should probably hit the road," he says, low and slow. He taps the side of his thumb against the table. There's a scar on it, diagonal, between the nail and the knuckle. It's slightly raised, and I wonder if I could feel it with my tongue if I put it in my mouth.

"What happened here?" I ask, like he didn't just say he was leaving. I lean forward and trace the tip of one finger along the scar.

Javier stills and flattens his hand on the table. "You know, I don't remember," he says after a moment. "Looks like I got in the way of a blade, maybe? Happens more than I'd like to admit."

"Right," I say, and I'm still tracing it. I'm blushing, and now I feel like an idiot, all *Ooh, tell me about your scars* when he's just trying to leave. Which, obviously, I also want him to do. Dinner is finished, he's gotta leave and go home, and *we are stepsiblings for fuck's sake—*

"This one was Zorro," he says, and he flips his hand over, palm up under mine. Two pale, raised lines slice down his wrist. I put my fingertips on them, and now his thumb is brushing the side of my wrist. Deliberately, back and forth, the callus a little scratchy. "My cat. He was still a kitten. I wanted to pick him up, and he disagreed. *Everyone* was very concerned for weeks after."

"What a dick," I say, his skin hot under my fingertips, and Javier laughs softly.

"Yeah." I can hear him pause, then inhale. I finally find

the nerve to look up at him. "I forgot to tell you—I like your hair. I liked it when it was pink, too."

"I change it up sometimes." I'm leaning farther forward despite myself. This is stupid, I probably look desperate right now, and I wish I were wearing something lower-cut and, I don't know, seductive. "Keep it interesting."

"That's not why you're interesting," he says. "Is it as soft as it looks?"

Fuck. Fuck. No. Do *not*. "You want to find out?"

He goes still again. His callused thumb presses into the side of my wrist. If I were malleable, he'd leave a thumbprint. It's too bad I'm not because right now he's looking at me all sharp and leonine, the held-breath stillness of a predator waiting to strike. I should do something to cut this off, like make a joke or get up and put the dishes in the dishwasher or just—leave.

Instead, I bite my lip. His eyes flick to my mouth, and his fingers curl around my wrist, warm and strong. Not a hold, but a question that expects the answer *yes*.

"C'mere," he says, low and soft and gentle.

There's a split second where I wonder what he'd do if I slid out of my chair and crawled to him. Whether he'd take it in stride or run screaming or maybe just tell me to get up. But I'm not sure I want to be on my knees, so I stand, and so does he, his chair scraping back over the tile. His hand doesn't leave my wrist, but he lifts his other hand and his blunt fingers slide into my hair, then over my scalp.

I don't moan, even though someone else playing with your hair is one of the top five best feelings in the world. My eyelids flutter, though, when I fight the urge to close them as his fingers move.

"This okay?" He sounds calm and collected, but he's

wild-eyed, pupils blown, cheeks flushed, the hollow of his throat moving with every breath.

"It's good," I say, and I swear his flush deepens.

Then his other hand is in my hair, too, stroking through. There's a cold spot on my wrist where his fingers were. I have to fight to keep my eyes open.

"Still good?"

"Still good."

He stills again, both hands in my hair. I look up at him, and I probably look wild, too—I can tell my face is hot and I'm breathing hard, my heart pounding.

"Our secret, right?" he says softly, dead serious. Both hands are still in my hair.

I have to fight the urge to laugh, and it must show on my face because his nose scrunches a little. "Obviously," I say.

"Just this once?"

I swallow, hard. "Just this once."

He nods once, decisive, and his eyes flick to my lips. "Do you still like..." He doesn't finish the sentence, just tightens both hands in my hair until I can feel it. Not pain, just—presence. I let him tilt my head back a few degrees, and he pulls a little harder. His breath catches, and this time my eyelids do flutter shut. My spine feels liquid.

Then his mouth is on mine, sweet and soft and gentle, delicate little kisses at odds with the grip he's got on my hair. I catch his bottom lip between my teeth, and he pulls back, laughing.

"Fuck, Madeline," he says, rubbing the tip of his nose along the bridge of mine, still holding me still. "Teeth."

"You forget I bite?"

"Not for a second." Then we're kissing again, harder but still slow, his tongue curling into my mouth. Somehow I've got both hands fisted in his T-shirt, twisted so my knuckles are against the soft skin of his belly.

Finally, he pulls back. Lets my hair go. Rests his thumb right below my lower lip. It's casual and possessive all at once, and I try not to think about it. I try not to think about anything. Thoughts aren't what I need right now.

"What?" I finally say because he's watching me, studying my face like he's looking for brushstrokes.

"Nothing," he says and then smiles this devilish little half smile, strokes his other hand to my lower back. "Just thinking. C'mon."

# ELEVEN

## JAVIER

THEN I'M on the couch, blue velvet and kitten-soft, and Madeline's climbing on top of me, anchoring her hands on my shoulders. Her hair's mussed where I grabbed it, and her knees are on either side of my hips. She leans in.

"Kiss me," I say, and she does. She's soft and warm, and even as I lick into her mouth it feels like she's holding back, her hands tentative on my shoulders, her weight held off my thighs. If this is the last time—and it *is*—then I don't want that. I want her mindless and slutty and wrung out by the time we're finished. If we're going to make stupid decisions, we're going to make them worthwhile.

I put my hand in her hair again. There's only one light on in here, a floor lamp on the other side of the room, so her face is shadowed, but it's easy enough to see the way her lips part. I pull her mouth to mine again. Close my hand—not pulling her hair, not *really*—and this time she makes a noise and her body sinks against mine.

Some deep, buried part of my brain hisses with pleasure, so I tighten my fingers—barely, god, it's so gentle—and she sighs.

Madeline lets me move her with the hand in her hair, tilting and pressing in, deepening the kiss until it's filthy with tongues and teeth. When I pull her back, she's flushed, her lips parted, pink, slick with spit, her whole body tense as she balances on her knees.

"Relax," I murmur, pressing one thigh down with my other hand, and she does. I take her weight, her hands resting on my chest, her breathing quick. She's wearing a red tank top tucked into dark blue jeans, and every time she inhales, I can see the faint line where her bra cuts across the top of her breasts. I can't fucking think.

So I don't. I keep one hand in her hair and take her face with the other, trace her bottom lip with my thumb and stop in the middle. For moment Madeline doesn't move. Then there's the soft, wet tip of her tongue against the pad of my thumb. I hear myself whisper "Oh," and then her lips close and her teeth are against my first knuckle. Her eyes close, her tongue stroking the underside of my thumb.

It takes me several seconds before my brain is anything but white noise.

"Do you like this?" I ask. It comes out a raspy whisper, and I clear my throat. Madeline hums around my thumb, the vibration a tiny shockwave. I pull it out, rest it on her lower lip.

"Yes," she says, and flicks her tongue against it again. *Fuck.*

"Will you take your clothes off?" I ask. "Please?"

I let her go, and Madeline scoots back to stand. She's off to one side because there's no space between my knees and the coffee table, and I lean forward, elbows on knees, to watch.

"You, too." She pulls at the hem of her tank top.

"Not yet."

She pauses at that, but it's just for a moment, and then the shirt's off, over her head, placed neatly on the coffee table. Then pants: she unbuttons, unzips, slides them off. Steps out. She's got on black underwear and a tan bra, her hips a little wider than her shoulders, belly a gentle hill, thighs muscular and soft all at once. She could probably suffocate someone with them. They'd be the luckiest motherfucker in the world.

Madeline keeps stripping, and it's not exactly showy but she's going slow. She skims her hands over her skin like it's for my benefit, then finally places the bra and panties on the coffee table and walks back to me, tossing her hair and waiting.

"Thank you," I say and run a hand up her outer thigh, stroking her from knee to hip and back again. "C'mere."

She settles in my lap again, gloriously naked, all that bare skin against fabric. I let her lean in and kiss me, deep and hard. Madeline moans softly when her nipples touch my shirt, her hands on my chest for balance, her hips rocking against me. I'm hard, my skin practically buzzing with this buried need suddenly awake and desperate. She rolls her hips again, and this time I groan into her mouth. Instead of grinding up into her like I want to, I take her wrists in my hands.

Gently, slowly enough that she doesn't lose her balance, I put them behind her back. At the same time I lean forward and plant a messy, open-mouthed kiss right between her breasts. Madeline's breathing goes ragged, and I move my mouth, inch by inch, until I'm flicking soft little licks over the flat of her nipple, and she's moaning.

It's so easy to lose myself in seeing what she likes, what noises she can make. After a minute I let her hands go so I can grip her thighs and stroke that smooth, velvety skin on the inside, which gets me a shaky inhale and one hand anchored in my hair.

Gently, I put her hand behind her back again. Then it happens again, her hand in my hair, when I bite a nipple and she swears, so I take both her wrists in one hand and pull back.

"Will you do something for me?" I ask her, looking up into her face. Madeline nods, swallows, then manages to get out a yes. "Do you think you can stay like this?"

She's breathing hard, the skin on her chest bright pink where my stubble's scraped against it, a few darker red spots where I couldn't help myself.

"For how long?" she asks.

I stroke my thumb along the inside of one wrist, taut tendons under soft skin. "You got somewhere else to be?"

That gets a laugh, huffed out between breaths. "Maybe," she says, but she pulls her wrists out of my hands and then laces her fingers together behind her back.

I'm dizzy for a second, running my fingers over her joined hands, but then I grab her hips and lick a long stripe over one nipple. Madeline moans. She moans, but she doesn't move her hands. They stay clasped behind her back for god knows how long while I get my mouth on every inch of her skin I can reach. Every so often I check again, running my hands over her fingers, but she never lets go. Not even when her nipples are bitten and sucked red and puffy and I'm stroking her entrance with my fingers, wet and slick and touching everything but her clit.

I want to memorize this. Take a picture—though I can't, obviously—but the way she looks right now is worth the keepsake: chest heaving, hair messy, shoulders back and arms behind her, eyes heavy-lidded with pleasure. Thighs bared and spread over me, my erection clothed and obvious.

I haven't touched myself. I'm a little afraid that I'll come as soon as I do.

"Look at you," I murmur without really meaning to. "Do you like this? When I do what I want, and you stay still and take it?"

Madeline snorts, then tosses her hair out of her face and rolls her eyes, but she doesn't move her hands. "Of course I do." The tilt of her head is defiant and coquettish, and I have to dig my fingers into her hip so I can keep control. "I'm here, aren't I?"

I run my fingernails up the inside of one thigh, and she inhales. "I'm just making sure."

"I know how to say *stop*, and you know how to listen."

I sit forward and put a hand in her hair again, bring her in, kiss her. She can't move too much without going off-balance, so I push my tongue into her mouth greedily, taking what I want. She gives it.

"I want you to lie down on the couch for me," I say.

"Can I move my arms?" she says, and I can hear the smirk so I bite her bottom lip.

"If you have to."

A minute later she's stretched out on the couch, a throw pillow under her head, one hand on her stomach and the other over her head. Her blue hair is fanned out around her, the tiger tattoo on her right thigh just as bright as it was two years ago. There's a stylized starburst on her left shoulder that I think might be new.

I'm staring. I'm standing here, staring at her like an idiot, wearing old shorts and an undershirt because my plan for today was to hang out at my mom's house and hammer out my schedule for next semester. And now I'm here with an absolutely ludicrous erection watching Madeline stretch out on her fancy couch because I told her to. She's breathing hard and stroking the skin on her stomach with one hand, nipples pink and puffy. There's stubble burn on her chest, and I did that.

She's watching me like she's waiting for further instruction, and it's indescribably hot that I could just—*say* something and it would happen. It's unnerving, too; this is uncharted territory, and I think I'm supposed to have a plan.

I don't have a plan. I have a lizard brain that likes it when she squirms and swears but holds still anyway because I asked her to.

"This is really fucking hot," I hear myself say. "Jesus Christ. *You're* really fucking hot. What the hell?"

That gets a surprised snort-laugh, and the hand on her stomach stops moving.

"What do you mean, what the hell?" she asks, still laughing. "Are you mad about it?"

"God, no."

"Are you just going to watch, or...?"

I swallow hard. "I could. I bet I could sit in that chair and tell you to touch yourself, and you would."

Her breathing picks up, her eyes wide. "Like this?" she asks, swirling her hand over her stomach.

"Come on, Madeline," I tease, and now I'm leaning over her, one hand braced on the back of the couch, our faces nearly touching. "I could tell you to rub your clit until you were close but not come, and I think you would. I think you'd do it until I told you to stop."

I lean in and kiss her, and she works a hand into my hair, snagging a little because I think it's still in a pencil bun.

"Is that what you want?" she murmurs, her other hand snaking down her body.

I catch her wrist lightly. Yes, I want that. I want at least a dozen things, and I know I can't have most of them. "No. I want you to spread your legs. More. *More.*"

"There's a wall in the way." She's too breathy to sound bratty.

I hook one hand behind her knee and sink onto the couch between her legs, pushing her thigh up so I can lean in and kiss her again. It's too frantic to be gentle. There are teeth in it, and when I pull back, her mouth is wet and bitten pink.

"Thank you," I say, as sweetly as I can manage, and kiss her on the cheek. Then I move down, plant a foot on the floor, and put my mouth on her clit.

Madeline's whole body jerks and she swears, the muscles in her thighs flexing under my hands, but I keep them spread as wide as I can.

I take my time. I explore. I don't spend too much time on her clit, even though I can tell she wants me to. She gets her hands into my hair, finally knocking the pencil out, and I have to stop, take her by the wrists, and sit up.

Gently, I put her hands on the armrest of the couch, interlacing our fingers.

"Can you keep those there for me?" I say, my face half-covered with her wetness.

"Can you ask nicely?"

I lean in, bracing my forearms on the arm of the couch, and manage to bite an earlobe. She squirms. "Please?"

I can feel the tendons in her wrists flex as she clenches her fists, and Madeline gets out a shaky "Maybe."

I put my hair back with the stupid pencil again and get back to it. She keeps her hands where I put them, even as she gasps and squirms and does her best to shove her clit into my mouth while I keep ignoring it.

I've thought about this all the time. I tried not to. I tried to think about other women or porn or that poster I had hidden under my bed when I was fourteen or the Montreal strip club I went to for my buddy's bachelor party. I've got an active imagination and an internet full of naked women, but I still had to force myself not to think about Madeline. It only worked sometimes. My brain is unruly at best.

It's not long before I have to touch myself. I moan when I press the heel of my palm against my dick, have to take a moment to shove my face into her thigh to recover. I can't help but bite it, which makes Madeline gasp, which makes my dick twitch against my hand, which makes me bite down harder—

"Condoms are in the same place?" I ask, half sitting up. I slide my thumb over her slick entrance, then plant it on her clit and press down without moving. Madeline tries rolling her hips, but I don't budge.

"Bedside drawer," she says.

"And lube?"

"Yeah."

"Any toys?"

"All my sex shit is in one place, okay?"

I laugh, bend down, and kiss her on the stomach. She squeaks.

"Thank you. Stay right there," I tell her and go look for her sex shit.

# TWELVE

## MADELINE

WHEN JAVIER HEADS into my bedroom, I take the opportunity to roll out my shoulders and wiggle my toes. I could sit up. I could stand. I could go into the kitchen and start making us tea, and I wonder what he'd do if I did.

I can hear him knocking things around in my drawer, and—he told me to stay right here, and I'm good at following rules. I like the way he looks at me when I do.

I start rubbing my clit anyway, though, one foot on the floor, the other slung over the back of the couch. I've already made a terrible decision by having sex with Javier again; why not really slut it up? *Stepsiblings* is a classic porn setup, after all.

A minute later, he comes back, big hands full of stuff. I spy a handful of condoms and a bottle of lube, along with at least two vibrators and I can't tell what else. God, what did he find in there? Do I own sex toys I've forgotten about?

"I don't think I said you could move your hands," he says, dumping it all onto my glass coffee table. I try very hard not to get even more turned on and fail, so I slide two fingers inside myself. Javier watches.

"The instructions were unclear," I say, fucking myself a little. His eyes don't move, but he finally takes off his shirt, then tosses it on top of the sex toys on the coffee table.

"Trust me, Madeline." He pops the button on his shorts and slides the zipper down. "If I wanted you to touch yourself, I'd say so."

With that, he slides his shorts and boxers off with one shove, steps over to me, and grabs my wrist. Gently. Mostly gently. I've still got two fingers sunk deep inside, but Javier pulls them out, then sucks them into his mouth.

"Oh," I say, and then he scrapes his teeth along the length, and my brain might fucking melt.

Javier gently puts my hand back on the arm of my sofa, then squeezes my wrist.

"Hold on to this and don't let go."

"What happens if I do?"

Javier grins and kneels between my legs, his cock bobbing in front of him. There's already a trail of precum leaking down the underside, and I want to lick it so badly I have to swallow.

"I guess we'll find out together. I'm sure I can come up with something. God, I love your tits. Did I say that yet?"

"More or le—oh *fuck*." There's suction and tongue and *teeth*, and my nipple was already a little raw from earlier. I swear I can feel every tastebud.

"Too much?"

He's rutting against my hip, hard and hot and already slippery. For a moment I'm annoyed that he got distracted by my tits, but then he bites my nipple again.

"No, but would you please just..." I start, and trail off.

"Please what?"

"Would you please just fuck me already?"

He groans, and I think he says *Fucking hell, Madeline,*

but his mouth is busy so it's hard to tell. But then he's moving down my body, nipping at the inside of one thigh, and he's sitting back and opening lube and sliding his fingers into me with a noise that's fucking obscene. Javier bites his lips as he crooks them, twisting until he finds the spot that makes me practically levitate off the couch.

He keeps going, stroking and adjusting, the squelch of the lube audible over my breathing, and he keeps up a running, murmured commentary of *There it is, That's right, Look at you, Does that feel good?* His thumb keeps brushing my clit but there's no intent and no pressure behind it, and I am going to lose my fucking mind in a very real way pretty soon.

"Up," he says, suddenly, and pulls his fingers out.

I obey mindlessly, and he shoves another throw pillow under my hips. It occurs to me that I'm going to have to get a new pillow after this, probably. It also occurs to me that I don't fucking care. "Thank you. *Fuck.*"

He slides a thumb over my lips before settling back onto his heels. I watch him as he rolls a condom on. He strokes lube onto himself while he looks at me, spread out on this couch with my arms up and my legs wide, lube and precum smeared on me. It must look ridiculous, but he's looking at me like he wants to eat me alive, so I squirm a little and bite my lip and his eyes light up.

"You can suck me off next time," he says, softly, his hand sliding down his dick as he fucks into it. "I still think about your mouth at least once a week."

"Is that all?"

He leans over me, one hand next to my head, his hair falling over his face. "*Is that all,*" he teases, rubbing at my entrance. "You greedy thing."

Javier slides in with one quick, hard thrust that makes us

both groan. He grinds into me when he bottoms out, and the pressure on my clit is pure relief. I try to grab the arm of the couch behind my head and rut into him, chasing my pleasure, but he kisses the side of my neck and pulls back. I'm about to protest and say *No, do that first thing again*, but then he's fucking me in hard, short strokes with one of my legs over his shoulder and the other around his hips, and instead of making requests I just moan.

Javier doesn't shut up, though. He starts off quiet, whispering something between panted breaths, and then he looks up at me, flushed and wrecked, hair everywhere and lips parted.

"What?" I manage. He swallows.

"Just asking if you liked that," he pants. "You sound like you like that. You sound like you love lying back and getting fucked, just—" He moves slightly and sits up a little, presses our bodies flush with his hands on my thighs. I swear and grind my hips against him again, desperate for that pressure on my clit.

"Jesus Christ, look at you take me," he murmurs, fucking me slower now. Looking down. Watching. Fuck, I wish I could see. "Your perfect pussy and your fat little clit, just begging for attention."

Oh, so he knows?

"Well, come on, then." It almost sounds normal.

"Is this not enough?" he croons, still fucking slowly. "It's pretty good from here. Hot and wet and practically begging for it."

He shifts again, and this time he slides one thumb up one side of my clit, barely brushing it. "How about this?"

"Close," I pant. "Try just—a little to the side—"

He slides his thumb down the other side of my clit, brushing the other side of it, and god*damn* it. "Was that it?"

"No! What the hell?" This is the first time in my life I've ever moaned that phrase. I'm squirming, trying to grapple him with my legs, and it's not working. "Would you please just—fucking touch my clit already—"

Instead, Javier hoists my other ankle onto his shoulders, and now he's leaning over, practically bending me in half, eyes frantic, and he goes deeper and harder, and it's good—it's really good—it's just not quite what I need and I honestly think I might cry.

Finally, he plants a thumb on my clit and he doesn't move it, but there's just enough friction that I'm getting close—come on, *please*—and then he pulls out.

"Can I come on you?"

I nod, frantically, and try to say *yeah* but my voice isn't working great. Javier strips off the condom, and then he's over me again, pumping himself with his hand and then letting out a punched-out groan as he comes in stripes over my chest and belly.

"Fuck," he whispers, and then he's on me, our bodies not quite touching, kissing me while my brain catches up. Because, uh, does he think I came? I snake my hand off the armrest and press my fingers against my clit, rubbing softly, and sigh into his mouth. He nips at my bottom lip, then sits up and grabs my wrist, pulling my hand off.

"I didn't come," I point out, somewhat bitchily.

"Oh, you didn't?"

"*No.*" I flex my wrist. He doesn't let go. "So could I please just—"

I stop because he's *grinning* at me, flushed and sweaty and devilish as anything.

"Oops," he cheerfully lies to my face. "My mistake. Think you can be a little more patient?"

"No," I mutter.

"Please? Three more minutes."

I didn't think I could get hornier than when I was actively getting well-fucked, but here we are. I can wait three minutes. I can do that.

"Three," I grit out, and he kisses the inside of my wrist, puts it over my head again, and stands up.

"Try not to move," he says, looking at the mess on me. "You've got a nice couch. I don't want anything to drip and ruin it."

He walks off. Fucking *walks off*. Water runs in the bathroom. I stare at the ceiling and try to, like, think peaceful thoughts or something. It doesn't work. I mostly think about how well I can feel every inch of my skin and how exposed I am, how vulnerable. I try not to squirm. In a minute, he's back with his hair suddenly neat, his boxer-briefs back on and a washcloth in his hand, and he—he fucking puts it on the coffee table, then contemplates everything else on it.

"Seriously?" I ask, and he glances up at me. "Come on. It's hell getting things out of velvet."

"You've managed to keep it clean so far."

"No thanks to you."

"At least give me some credit for my aim. You're a much prettier mess than the couch would be." He picks up a vibrator from the small pile on the coffee table. "I can put this one inside you, right?"

It's silicone with a slightly curved bulb at one end, one I don't use that often, and there's still semen on me as Javier asks whether he can fuck me with a toy. I could easily grab the washcloth myself or just use my hands, but that's not the point, is it?

"Are you asking for permission or about product safety?"

He leans back on the couch, back against my knees, and

turns it on, then up. "It was a product-safety question, but if you're revoking permission..."

"You can."

"God, you're eager for it," he says, and I forget whatever I was going to say as he turns it on low and circles my clit with it, then quickly grabs my hip when I try to move. "Careful. Your couch."

"Fuck the couch," I say, but I hold still.

"*Such* a pretty mess." He slides it into me, still buzzing. I jerk involuntarily, and he smooths a hand over my hip. "C'mon, you can do better than that."

I can't, I think, but I close my eyes and I fucking try. Javier turns the vibrator all the way up and quickly finds a short, fast rhythm at exactly the right angle, and holy *shit* I didn't know this vibrator could feel this good. Is this what it's supposed to do? Is it the angle?

"I think you could come like this, maybe," Javier's saying. I'm biting my lip so hard that it's probably going to bruise or bleed or something. "If I made you wait long enough for it. You think you could handle hours? I'd lie you down, eat your pussy until you were close, then tell you not to touch yourself and wander off."

Now he's circling my clit with his other thumb, brushing up against it, and I whimper, which I'll probably be embarrassed about later.

"How's this?" he murmurs and presses his thumb to my clit, then rubs it slowly. "Is this enough?"

It is. I come so hard my ears ring and my toes literally curl as I try not to move too much because, after all, it's a nice couch. When it's over I feel empty-headed, like my brain's made of cotton, and I have to nudge Javier with my toes to get him to stop.

I'm still breathing through it when there's something

cold and wet on my stomach, and I jerk away before I realize what it is.

"Sorry, sorry." He makes a face as he wipes carefully. "It used to be warm."

"No, no, you're fine." I shut my legs and cross them at the ankles because I'm suddenly aware that I'm extremely naked and he is wiping semen off me. "Thanks."

"Of course," he says, folding over the washcloth and giving me one last wipe. "I'll be right back, I'm just gonna—" He makes a gesture toward the bathroom that I assume encompasses *perform all manner of post-sex cleanup*, and I nod, then flop my head back onto the throw pillow as he walks away.

Sooner or later, I'm going to have to reckon with the fact that I've now had maybe-kinky sex with my future step-brother and also with the fact that it was extremely enjoyable. There was a part of me that was low-key hoping that either he'd say no or that this time would be terrible, but that part of me also plays the lotto sometimes because she's too optimistic.

Anyway, that was great and it can't ever happen again, because I clearly cannot keep having casual sex with my stepbrother.

· · · ★ ★ ★ ★ ★ · · ·

ONCE WE'RE both cleaned up and dressed again, I realize it's 10:15. Javier's clearing off the kitchen table. He sees me looking at the clock, follows my gaze, and swears.

"I thought it was, like, seven. I should go. Do you have a dishwasher?"

I do, but other people aren't allowed to load it. "Leave the plates in the sink."

I watch him, in my kitchen, carefully putting some plates and a fork into the sink. His hair is unruly again. There's something about him that makes him seem too big for this room, and it's not just because he's tall. He's got some loose, wild energy, like he's hard to contain, and he doesn't belong at all in my small, neat kitchen, but it suits him anyway.

"Sorry to...run." I'd bet money he was going to say *fuck and run* but chickened out. "But thanks."

I look again at the clock, but it wasn't lying before. Now it's 10:17, and I know it's three hours to Charlottesville and he lives a couple hours south of that, and...shit.

"You should stay." I don't make eye contact. "It's late—just leave first thing in the morning."

"It's only ten. I'll be fine. I can grab coffee," he says, still in my kitchen.

"You're gonna get home at three in the morning."

"That's not that late."

"That's late to be driving."

"I'm usually up then anyway. I'm a night owl, I swear."

I hate how desperate I sound for him to stay, and I also hate how desperate he sounds to get out of here. It's not like I want him to *stay*—not like that; we've been pretty clear about what this is—but come on. He can't start a six-hour drive at 10:00 p.m.

"Did you know it's just as dangerous to drive while sleep-deprived as it is to drive drunk?"

"Madeline. I'm not sleep-deprived. I woke up at nine this morning; I've been awake for thirteen hours." Now he's got his arms crossed, hip leaning against my counter.

"It's equivalent to a point-zero-eight blood-alcohol level, which will get you a DUI," I say. "I *know* you wouldn't drive drunk."

"Now you're being unfair."

"You mean I'm being right? It'll be dark, and those roads are probably very twisty, and you're sitting still and staring ahead." We glare at each other. "And *imagine* if you hit another car and hurt someone else."

I am not above using guilt to get my way.

"Just call whoever you need to call and tell them...you're not there yet," I say, because I don't have a good idea for how to finish that sentence.

"Oh, you mean lie." Now he's smirking.

"You could tell people part of the truth," I argue, even though I can feel my face turning red. "We had dinner and chatted, and now it's late and I made you stay over so you didn't die. I've got an air mattress."

We look at each other.

"Or lie," I finally agree.

"No one's expecting me back until Sunday. It's fine," he says. "Zorro and Barry look like they're getting along—he won't mind staying there until then."

Barry—the Baroness von Whiskers—is Zorro's sister and belongs to Javier's friend Wyatt, who has been faithfully texting pictures of them napping together in sunbeams. He showed me some over dinner.

"You're sleeping here, then? Great," I say, and Javier rubs both hands over his face.

I take it as agreement.

# THIRTEEN
## JAVIER

MADELINE, it turns out, has a whole guest setup that she rolls out for me. It's not just the air mattress—which is a really nice one, actually—but a whole set of sheets specifically for the air mattress, two pillows, extra blankets, and a phone charger with three different plug options. She's more prepared for the remote possibility of her stepbrother needing to stay over than I've ever been for anything.

No one acknowledges that she has a bed with enough room in it for a second person. I know for a fact that she has a bed, because I fucked her in it two years ago and then practically sprinted out the door. It's not that I'm expecting her to offer or anything, but like—sleeping is more casual than fucking, right? Did I do something wrong that I don't know about? It sure seemed like Madeline had a good time.

But no. It's like a door slammed shut the second she put her clothes back on, and I'm obviously not going to argue about where I sleep. Not when she's forcing her hospitality on me.

"I have the coffee maker set to turn on at eight, which is when I usually get back from my workout. If you want it before then, it's this button," she's saying, as if I've never seen a coffee maker before. "I've got cereal, milk, eggs, toast. I think there's an avocado in here if you're an avocado toast fan. You just have to mash it up and slap it on there."

"Thanks—I can probably figure it out."

"Right. Sorry." She makes a face that I think is supposed to be a smile. "Um, if there's anything else, you know where to find me. I'll just be. In there."

There's a tiny flash of what *anything else* could mean—she's got several toys I haven't tried out yet—but it's just my imagination because Madeline nods once and then walks quickly to her bedroom. She closes the door behind her.

It's very, very clear where we stand.

· · * * ★ ★ ★ * * · ·

I SLEEP LIKE SHIT. I finally doze off around two, only to wake up with a start at least once an hour. I've got the awful, crawling sensation that I shouldn't be here. I wish I hadn't let Madeline talk me into staying, but I also know she could probably talk me into shaving my head and rolling around on pinecones. Every time I wake up, I pace around the living room for a few minutes, thinking that I should leave Madeline a note and drive away.

But the coffee maker comes on at eight, she said, and it's the thought of Madeline sleepy and warm in the morning that makes me get back on that stupid air mattress and close my eyes again.

· · * * ★ ★ ★ * * · ·

WHEN THE BEDROOM door opens and then closes, sometime around dawn, I'm finally asleep and dreaming that

I lost important paperwork. I'm still half-panicked about it when I open my eyes and Madeline is tiptoeing out, a gym bag over her shoulder. She grimaces when I go up on one elbow.

"Sorry. Go back to sleep," she whispers.

*Don't go,* I want to say.

"Have a good workout," I tell her, groggy and rough, hardly human and barely awake.

"Thanks," she says, and then the door shuts and I'm alone in Madeline's apartment. On her guest air mattress, using her guest sheets and her guest pillow and her guest phone charger. There's no way I'm falling back asleep, and, what, am I supposed to stay here and pace the floor until she comes back? Am I supposed to be sitting at her kitchen table when she comes back? Drinking her coffee? Taking up her space?

I shouldn't have even spent the night. I should have left before dawn. My welcome was overstayed hours ago.

I deflate the air mattress, fold the sheets, stack it all on her pretty blue couch, throw on some clean clothes, and I'm gone.

· · · · · ★ ★ ★ ★ ★ · · · · ·

CASTILLO TEXTS me at exactly 8:30. I'm sitting in my car outside the North Carolina welcome center, drinking gas station coffee and looking at a map, when I get it.

**Castillo:** We're still on for lunch at 11:30, correct?

"Fuck," I whisper, because of course I'd forgotten, but Castillo is as routine as I'm chaotic, and thank god for that.

All the same, I nearly cancel. I have *Sorry, something*

*came up* all typed in, the car heating up in the morning sun, the bad coffee going lukewarm, but—well, I can't cancel on *Castillo.* She'd be disappointed, and she wouldn't respond *No worries, hope everything is okay!* she'd respond *That's too bad, I was really looking forward to getting to see you,* in that blunt, honest way she has, and I'd feel awful.

And where the fuck am I going, anyway? What am I doing in North Carolina? I didn't mean to cross the state line, I just got into my car and drove for thirty minutes.

**Castillo:** We can go to my favorite falafel place.
**Me:** Of course, wouldn't miss it!
**Castillo:** Do you need directions?

Castillo, despite being the same age as me, loves to ask if I need directions. I have never said yes.

**Me:** No, I'll be there.

She sends back the thumbs-up emoji, signaling the conversation's end, and I lean back in my seat, crack the window, and keep drinking coffee.

Three hours. Three hours, then I'll have seen Castillo and I can leave.

· · · · ★ ★ ★ ★ · · · ·

AN HOUR before I meet Castillo I'm in Walmart, staring at the clearance towels and wondering if I need anything. I'm not here for a reason; I'm here because I suddenly had a few hours to kill and no plan for how to spend that time. Even though I thought of at least five things I *should* be doing right now, I didn't do any of them, and then I passed this Walmart.

As I stand there, mind both utterly blank and over-whelmed by home goods, I realize that possibly—*possibly*—my current psychological state is related to the fact that I forgot to refill my ADHD meds before I left Sprucevale. They won't prescribe me the good ones—no stimulants for addicts, just Strattera and Wellbutrin—but wow, they sure are better than nothing.

· · ★ ★ ★ ★ ★ ★ ★ · · ·

I GET it together enough to be five minutes early to the hole-in-the-wall falafel place, but Castillo's already waiting on the sidewalk outside, her hands in the pockets of her slacks, looking like she's trying not to stand at attention. If I've ever been earlier to an event than Amy Castillo, I don't remember it.

"Hey!" she says, smiling, and then she frowns. "You look like shit."

I look down at myself: I'm wearing perfectly respectable shorts and a T-shirt—it's August in the South; long pants can go fuck themselves—and neither has *any* holes.

"No, I mean your face," she says, in a tone that suggests she thinks she's helping.

"Hi, Castillo." Now I'm trying not to laugh. "It's *so* good to see you."

She wrinkles her nose but then opens her arms, so I bend down and give her a proper hug. "Hi, how are you, lovely weather we're having, how about that football team," she says all in one breath.

"Football season hasn't started yet."

"Preseason has," she says, and I let it go because she

knows better than me. "Appalachia treating you right? Long time no see, et cetera."

We pull apart, and she's still frowning, her eyes narrowed, like she thinks I'm hiding something from her. Which, in fairness, I am.

"You do look like shit, though." At least she sounds apologetic about it. "Come eat falafel and tell me why."

· · · · * ★ ★ ★ * · · · ·

CASTILLO'S the only person I've ever known to have a "usual" at a restaurant. As in, she walks to the counter and the guy behind it smiles and asks "The usual?" and she says yes.

"It's not drugs, is it?" she asks me once we've got our food, drizzling tahini onto her chicken shawarma before she answers her own question. "No. If it were drugs again, you'd have flaked on me. Also, you're kind of thriving."

"Wow, thank you." I don't tell her that I thought about flaking, then didn't. Personal growth or whatever.

"Your hair is *very* shiny today."

"Thanks, I condition," I say, and we both take bites of our respective wraps. God, this is good. The only place you can get falafel in Sprucevale is this one diner that's near downtown, and it's not worth it.

"But you do look a little rough. Which I say out of loving concern."

"Next time I'm in town, we're getting lunch on my first day, not my last day," I say. "I always look like shit after a couple days with my family."

"I thought you were leaving Saturday."

"Change of plans." I take another bite. Castillo watches me expectantly, with this look of distaste. I'm ninety-five percent sure the distaste is at the thought of changing plans. "I'm heading back after lunch because I got into a fight with my dad and then a fight with my mom *about* the fight with my dad and then—"

I stop mid-sentence because: should I tell her? Wasn't it about twelve hours ago that we agreed to secrecy? Except it's *Castillo*, who's seen me do way worse things and still puts up with me and who also doesn't know any of these people. Who's she gonna tell?

"—do you remember about two years ago, not long after I got out of rehab, I went to a bar and hooked up with someone?"

"Sure. The highlight of your social calendar that year, I believe."

"My social calendar was great, thanks." It was not. "I saw her again."

"Do you mean you literally saw her or you had sex with her?" she asks.

"Sex," I say around a mouthful of falafel.

Castillo, also chewing, gives me a thumbs-up. "Fun again?" she asks after she swallows.

"Fun again."

"There are worse ways to blow off steam." She shrugs. "Unless that's why you're running back to the boondocks earlier than you'd planned? I know you..."

She stops, wrap held in front of her, and looks like she's trying to figure out the next move in a game of chess. Castillo is one of my favorite people on the planet, but nuance is not necessarily her strong suit.

I raise one eyebrow because I'm not helping her out of this one.

"...had a thing for her," she finishes, and I'm already shaking my head *no.*

"She's cool," I say, which is true. "And we had a good time together, but there's nothing else there." I look Castillo dead in the eye because I'm telling her the truth and that's what you do when you're telling the truth and you want someone to know that you're telling the truth.

Castillo just nods. "What was the fight with your dad about?"

Ten minutes later, we're both finished eating, I've just gotten through *and then she called both my siblings*, and Castillo is making a face.

"I don't blame you for leaving early," she says, and then, "You living with your dad would be a terrible idea. One of you would murder the other. And if you did the murdering, you'd go to jail."

I just look at her.

"He'd probably be court-martialed and disciplined but not given a jail sentence," she explains. "Come on. Admiral Lopez is going to do a better cover-up job than you would, and I'm sure he's got plenty of favors to call in, not to mention friends in high places."

I consider arguing, but I don't really want to talk about getting murdered by my own father, so instead I ask, "How are you?"

"I'm well," she says, accepting the subject change.

"You look great," I add belatedly, but it's true: Castillo is always polished and put-together in a way I couldn't even dream of. Obviously one of us made a better Marine than the other.

"My collection got a pub date, and I think I'm dating someone." A hint of a smile tugs at one corner of her mouth.

"Mmph!" Baklava flakes shower onto my plate. Castillo looks unimpressed. "When? Can I preorder it?"

"Not yet. I'll tell you when you can," she says,

preempting my next question. "And it's May of next year. Now they're trying to set up a reading at East Side Stories for the release, but I'm pushing back."

"*Why?*"

Castillo looks at me like I just asked why rain is wet. "Because I don't want to read poetry to strangers? What if someone I work with comes? What if there's *video* and they share it on *social media*?"

"It's poetry collection, not the Anarchist's Cookbook," I point out, but I only get a pitying stare in return. "I'm just saying! It's awesome that they want you to do a reading. I think you should."

"Maybe," she allows, straightening a napkin. Castillo's poetry is probably the reason we're still close friends instead of buddies who used to serve together; when we met, we were both Mexican kids who joined up for questionable reasons, but then it turned out we got along because she was quiet and awkward while I was too much and too loud, and eventually she showed me her poetry and I showed her my drawings.

Also, after I left the Marines with an honorable discharge and an Oxy problem, she's the only one who kept calling me. Castillo's been around through all of it, and, inexplicably, she still wants to hang out.

"Wait, and you *think* you're dating someone?"

"We've been out a couple times and slept together, but we haven't talked about labels or exclusivity yet." She shrugs. "We're going birdwatching this weekend."

"I think if you go on dates with someone you're dating," I say. I've got a straw wrapper in my hand, and I'm mindlessly twisting it around my fingers.

"Probably."

"Is birdwatching a big date thing?" I've never considered

going on a birdwatching date, but then again, dating has... not been a priority lately.

"No, but he likes it, and I'm curious about his hobbies," she says. "Besides, I've never been birdwatching. Could be fun to learn a new skill."

To me, birdwatching sounds like a mandatory activity in one of the circles of Hell—you have to stay still *and* quiet *and* vigilant?—but Castillo's cheeks have gone faintly pink, and I think I'm witnessing the friendship equivalent of the double-beaked vermillion featherback or some extremely rare bird: she's *blushing*.

"You're *into* this one." I grin at her. She wrinkles her nose like feelings are gross. I get it.

"Yeah," she admits. "I think I am."

"He does anything wrong, you let me know and I'll kick his ass," I offer. It's probably unnecessary—Castillo has either four or five brothers—but I like to try.

"Lopez," she says patiently, "if he fucks up, I'll kick his ass myself, and probably do a better job than you would."

"Harsh."

She shrugs, smiling.

· · * * ★ ★ ★ * * · ·

WE HUG goodbye in the parking lot, and then Castillo heads back to her civilian job in Naval logistics or something, and I get into my car and debate going back to North Carolina.

I feel better. Not better enough to stick around here, but better enough that driving until the road dead ends into a swamp doesn't seem like the best option any more. I'm still restless and twitchy, and I need to be away from *here*, right *now*. I needed to be away from here hours ago, but I don't feel like I might scratch my own skin off any more.

When I left Madeline's place early this morning, before she got back from her workout class, I had the vague idea that I'd get on the interstate and drive until I figured out where to go because at least I'd be away from Virginia Beach. It's easier to fall back into familiar patterns when you're in the place where those patterns got familiar. It took years for me to feel like leaving was a helpful problem-solving tool instead of an admission that I couldn't handle being around my old life.

It's why I moved to Sprucevale in the first place: a guy I barely knew offered me a lifeline, and I took it. That was nearly two years ago, and it's probably the best thing I've done for myself since...ever.

If I were smart, I'd go straight home, tell both of my jobs I'm back early, and then work on the freelance design project I've got a deadline for next week. Actually, no. If I were smart, yesterday I'd have had a calm, rational conversation with my—

"Not helpful," I say out loud to my windshield. It doesn't respond, which is rude of it.

· · · ★ ★ ★ ★ ★ · · ·

IN THE END, I decide to drive toward home and see if I get a better idea on the way there.

# FOURTEEN

## MADELINE

FRIDAY AFTERNOON, I'm at work, at my desk, wondering if I can somehow get out of my four o'clock meeting when my dad calls. *Calls.* During work hours, without texting first.

I answer on the second ring.

"Sorry to call you at work," he says, the moment I say hello. "I won't be a minute."

"What happened?" I ask, my voice about an octave too high.

"Did Javier say anything to you when you ran into him at Paloma's house the other day?" he asks, and sighs.

Oh my god, he knows. Shit. Fuck. This is one of those trick questions parents ask you when they already know the answer and they just want to see if you're going to lie to them. And then when you do, they make that disappointed face that's ten times worse than the angry face, and then you feel guilty for weeks afterward just because you didn't trust them enough to tell the truth.

Maybe I should just admit what we did. What's the worst that could happen, really? He'd be mildly scandalized and a little worried and maybe request that we all go together to couples' counseling? Except Javier and I are *not* a couple, so it would be one-couple-and-two-people-who-fucked counseling, and I would have to *say that out loud* to both my dad and Paloma, and he'd want to work through it. And I think Paloma might be grossed out and disappointed, and maybe they'd even call the wedding off or something until I worked through my issues, and fuck, *fuck*, I can't do that—every time my dad looks at Paloma it's like little hearts circle his head, and he would be *crushed*—

"Mads?" my dad asks, and I stop spiraling.

"Nope. Not really. We chatted a little—he said he was going back home," I manage. None of it is technically a lie: we did chat. He did say he was going back. I'm totally not lying to my dad.

"Thanks. That's what I figured." He sounds slightly put-upon. "He won't answer Paloma's calls, and she said you two ran into each other, so she asked me to call and grill you for information. Apparently Thalia and Bastien have formed a united front and are refusing to call him on her behalf."

I come very, very close to saying *Oh, yeah, he mentioned his mom's habit of involving entire branches of the family tree in their fights* but don't. Then I feel bad about not saying it, and I very seriously consider giving up a little more information and then don't do that, either. If I told my dad that Javier came over to talk and wound up sleeping on the air mattress, there's no way he wouldn't read between the lines and figure out what happened. And then it's counseling, horror, wedding off, lives ruined, et cetera.

I also don't really know Javier all that well. Mostly his dick—oh my god, what is my *life*? But I think if his mom texted him and said *I know you spent the night with Made-*

*line*, he'd probably be pissed at his mom. And *also* pissed at me, which wouldn't help matters at all.

I clear my throat, slightly worried that my thoughts are so loud my dad can hear them. "He did mention a disagreement," I say as blandly as I can. "He probably just needs some space to cool down."

"That's what I told her, but you know Paloma. She hasn't taken the time to cool down, either. Honestly, it sounds like they could both use a break right now."

"For sure," I agree.

"Anyway, I'll let you get back to work. Thanks for humoring me."

"I'm just glad no one is dead," I say. "You didn't even text first."

"Where *are* my manners?"

After we hang up, I stare at my phone for a moment and wonder if I should text Javier a quick *Hey, is everything ok?* text. But I've got a pretty good idea of how he feels about his mom's habit of involving everyone and their dog in arguments, so I don't.

Not to mention that we're casual acquaintances at best: we fucked twice, he slept on the floor, then left without saying goodbye. Which is fine! Completely fine, obviously. There were never any strings attached.

All the same, I glance quickly around the office, then slide one hand under my desk, find the spot on my inner thigh where he bit me hard enough to bruise, and press down until it hurts.

· · · · · ★ ★ ★ · · · · ·

MIDDAY SATURDAY, my dad texts me to cancel our dinner plans that night because they still haven't found

Javier. I just got home with groceries, and I'm sitting in my car that's getting hotter by the second, staring at my phone.

"What?" I say out loud, and call my dad.

When he answers, I can hear Paloma talking in the background.

"He's *missing?*" I squeak.

"Hey, kiddo." He sounds tired and worried, and my anxiety shoots through the roof. "Yeah. No one has heard from him since he left Paloma's on Wednesday."

I stare through the windshield of my car, and panic prickles along my skin.

"They haven't?" I ask, my voice about an octave too high.

"No. Paloma's been in contact with his friends from Sprucevale, and no one has talked to him since Wednesday. He's not at his house. Paloma's worried. You know. Given his...history."

"Right," I hear myself say.

Sometimes, when I'm in the mood, I'll binge-watch *Law & Order* or *CSI*, and one of the tried-and-true red herring stereotypes on those shows is the Suspect Who Lies the First Time. You know, the detective asks where she was on the night of the murder, and the suspect says *Out with friends—I didn't even see the victim*, and it turns out she was lying, so the suspect gets hauled into the police station a second time, and this time tearfully admits that yeah, okay, she saw the victim that night and didn't tell the cops because they illegally downloaded the new Batman movie and she didn't want to get into trouble, but she swears he was alive when she left? I always thought the Suspect Who Lies the First Time was an idiot.

Suddenly I understand where they're coming from. Because in *Law & Order*, knowing that the victim illegally downloaded a movie doesn't help solve the crime, and half the time she's hauled off in handcuffs for piracy anyway.

I have no worthwhile information, is what I'm saying. Javier left early Thursday without saying goodbye. Not even a note. It's fine. I, like everyone, assumed he was going back to Sprucevale.

So, like the Suspect Who Lies, my options are: one, tell everyone that he spent the night. Since I already lied about that they'll all figure out what really happened, and everything will be awful for the rest of time, and it still won't help find him. Or two, keep lying.

"You're sure he didn't say anything at all to you?" my dad asks. "He didn't mention a friend? Maybe someone he's seeing? Something he wanted to do?"

"Nothing at all," I say and willfully ignore the fact that the Suspect Who Lies always gets caught.

· · · · ★ ★ ★ ★ ★ · · · ·

**Me:** Hey, my dad said no one can find you? Is everything okay?

**Me:** I'm sure this is the 500th text you've gotten, but, you know.

**Me:** Anyway, everyone's looking, so if you see this you might want to call your mom sooner rather than later? Sorry, I know you hate when she gets other people involved.

· · · · ★ ★ ★ ★ ★ · · · ·

"IS this a tea visit or a whiskey visit?" Ben asks as he lets me in.

"It's three in the afternoon," I point out.

"Five o'clock somewhere."

"Not here."

He's already walking into the kitchen, talking over his shoulder. "Shoes off. I've still got that weird stuff you like."

"Green tea isn't weird. Everyone likes green tea. Literally millions of people all over the world drink and enjoy green tea. I'm not interrupting anything, am I?"

"What? No." He gives me a weird look as he pulls tea bags from a drawer that seems to also contain plastic wrap, tin foil, a stick of deodorant, and a travel-size chess board. Ben has two roommates, also surgical residents at Chesapeake University Hospital, and for an apartment with three dudes it's actually pretty okay.

"Thanks for letting me come over," I say, and he gives me the weird look again.

"Since when do I 'let' you? You text me and say *I'll be there in fifteen*, and it's my job to make sure I've got pants on."

"You might have been busy!"

"That has *never* stopped you before."

It has, actually; he's just never noticed. The thing is that Ben, who's been my best friend since before either of us could talk, sometimes has a girlfriend. Sometimes the girlfriends are weird about me, his female bestie. I have zero romantic interest in Ben, but I have also grown up in a society that tells us women should fight over available men, so I get it. I hate it, but I get it.

Anyway, Ben has now been on three dates with this girl he's really into and who seems really cool, so I don't want her to be suspicious of me or anything before we even meet.

"Be nice—I came here with a crisis," I say, only half kidding.

It wipes the smirk off his face, almost literally. "Shit. Sorry," he says. "Your stepbrother's missing? You want me to try calling hospitals to see if they'll give me any info or something?"

Oh, god, I hadn't even thought of that. Maybe Javier got into a car crash and he's in an ER somewhere, or he's dead, and they couldn't identify him—

"They're not supposed to tell me anything because of HIPAA, but sometimes people slip in these kinds of situations."

"It's not that. Not yet...at least? Fuck. Okay. I am going to *swear* you to secrecy."

Ben raises one eyebrow and makes an X over his heart.

"Everyone is panicking because no one has heard from him since Wednesday afternoon," I start. "Except. I did see him. He seemed like he was having a rough day, since he'd just fought with his parents, so he came back to my place to vent and have dinner. And then it got late, and it's a long drive, so he slept over. On the air mattress. And then he left first thing Thursday morning."

"Okay," Ben says. We both pause for a moment. The water on the stove steams but isn't boiling yet. "And you didn't tell anyone this."

I rub my hands over my face. "No."

Another long pause. "Did something...happen?"

I sigh into my hands, my face going hotter than asphalt at noon in August.

"Kind of," I mumble.

When I finally look up, Ben's staring at me, wide-eyed and alarmed. "Okay, so, I meant *did something happen*, like, did you get into an argument and you shoved him and he fell and hit his head—"

"You think if that happened, I'd lie about it and hide the body?!"

"No! I was really surprised!"

119

"I wouldn't come to you if I had to hide a body! I'd—I don't know, deal with it myself. I wouldn't want to get anyone else involved." The water's boiling, so I grab the pot off the stove and pour it into waiting mugs. I should've gotten him and his roommates a kettle as a housewarming gift.

"Thanks, I guess," he says. "Though I thought we were friends."

"That's why I wouldn't drag you down with me," I explain, because I've watched enough *Law & Order* that I've thought about this. "*Anyway*. My dad called me yesterday and told me that Javi wasn't answering his phone, had he said anything to me, et cetera. And it sounded like Javier was just mad at his mom because they got into a fight, not like he was a *missing person*, so I said I hadn't seen him."

I finish pouring and put the rest of the hot water back on the stove.

"Meaning that now if I go back and tell the truth, everyone will know exactly why I lied, and we still won't have any idea where he is."

Ben grabs a saucer for tea bags, and we walk to his living room and sit on a sectional that's way too big for the space, but one of his roommates got it for free from their grandparents or something.

"Just to make sure I'm super crystal clear on this—you and your stepbrother hooked up, right? That's what you're trying to insinuate to me?"

"You cannot tell *anyone*," I say, pointing at him. "Seriously, Ben."

He makes a second X over his heart.

"Not your brother, not your sister-in-law, not your parents' dog. *Not your mom*."

He gives me an excruciatingly patient look.

"When," he says, "have I *ever*."

"I know, I know," I say, because he's right. Ben has been keeping my secrets, and vice versa, basically since birth, when we came home from the hospital fourteen days apart. Our moms have been best friends since before we were born, and I'm pretty sure that when my parents got divorced, my mom's decision to only move two blocks away had more to do with Rachel Goldstein than me or my dad.

"Did I fuck up? Should I go back and tell my dad? I don't *know* anything." Both hands are now in my hair. God, why doesn't Ben have anything to look at in here besides this ugly sofa and a big TV? Even one *Live, Laugh, Love* sign would be something. "What would it help? He left the Virginia Beach area twelve hours later than his mom thinks, but I still don't know where he *went*. He didn't say anything to me."

"Maybe it would help because he has some sort of secret post-sex ritual," Ben muses. "In med school I had this one classmate who would always buy a hat after she hooked up with someone new."

"We should be looking for Javier at hat stores?" I ask. "Wait, how do you know that about her?"

"We hooked up a couple times."

"What kind of hat did she get afterward?"

"We're not talking about that. We're talking about your problems."

"Was it a beret?"

"No."

"A fedora?"

"*No.*"

"A...pork pie?"

"Is that a hat?"

I blow on my tea and then take a sip. "I think so?"

"It was sort of...big and floppy. A sun hat?"

I nod and consider this information, which is fitting somehow. "I approve."

Ben rolls his eyes. "Great. Thank you."

"I don't think Javier is a hat guy," I say. "And it went, you know. Pretty well. It wasn't bad."

He's making an absolutely tragic *do not tell me details* face, so I drink more tea.

"Except you're related," Ben points out.

"We're not *related*."

"You're almost related."

"It doesn't count if you meet when you're adults. Then you're just people with common...interests."

"You mean common family members?"

"*It doesn't count.*"

Ben says nothing, but he hums the theme from *Deliverance.* I flip him off.

"My point *is*, I would like you to tell me I'm not a bad person if I don't tell the entire world that he and I hooked up, because he's probably just treating himself to a spa weekend and he'll show up tomorrow, and if our secret's out he might murder me," I say. "It was a dumb, spur-of-the-moment thing that I shouldn't have done, and it's not going to happen again, and if our families find out it'll..."

Ben sips some tea and waits for the rest of that sentence.

"It will create problems. Besides, it was no big deal. We were just casually blowing off some steam like adults, and it's not going to affect anything going forward. Obviously."

"Obviously," he says, though I don't approve of his tone. He considers for a moment. "And I don't think you're a bad person for trying to balance your respect for his privacy with your concern over his whereabouts. His parents don't sound like they'd be very chill about this, honestly."

"I like Paloma a lot, and I think she's really good for my dad," I say. "But I think she'd freak the fuck out."

"I think I'm being pretty chill."

He has a point. "You're being very chill. Thank you."

"If he doesn't show up, when are you gonna tell them?" he asks, giving me a pointed look. "Not to be gross, but I'm assuming his DNA is all over your place—"

"It's not *all over*," I mutter. It's not on my couch, for example.

"—and you know that if you try to clean it up it'll only look more suspicious."

"I don't know. Tomorrow?" I try to ignore the awfulness of *what if something happened*. Not to sweet, messy, chaotic Javier who loves his cat and puts towels down on nice couches. "I texted some with his brother, and apparently sometimes he goes off for a few days and forgets to tell anyone what he's doing? So—tomorrow."

"Tomorrow," Ben agrees, and I drink my tea and wonder if I'm an awful person.

# FIFTEEN

## JAVIER

I MISJUDGE THE LAST ROCK, and my foot slips off and into the creek, the water up to my mid-calf.

"Dammit," I mutter to myself, readjusting my pack that just jostled out of place.

Then I consider for a moment, put my other foot in the creek, and walk to the other side. Honestly, the water's kind of nice. It's maybe an hour past sunrise and hot already, and only getting hotter, and besides, I'll probably be home by noon. It's not like I have to hope my boots will dry overnight so I can walk in them more tomorrow.

Nature, it turns out, is soothing as fuck. In the past two years, I've discovered that being outdoors is an extremely healing balm to my troubled soul. It makes me feel whole and grounded and centered and all that shit, which causes me no end of irritation. Everything else I've tried being—a Navy brat, a city kid, a Marine, an addict—and it turns out I'm one of those 'hiking is my therapy' assholes? The sanctimonious outdoorsy types were *right*?

Thanks, I hate it. It's almost as bad as how much better

getting enough sleep, eating properly, and exercising regularly make me feel.

But the fact remains that hiking is therapeutic as hell, and all the white people who talk about going into the woods to find themselves are right. The last time I went to rehab—the one that's stuck, so far—the place was on the edge of a forest, in the rolling hills, in the middle of nowhere. On a former dairy farm. There were even horses and shit.

I rode a horse *once*. My blood did not sing of any vaquero ancestry or the freedom of the wide plains under open skies—whatever it is people are supposed to feel when they get on horseback. I mostly felt like my ass hurt.

I walk in the creek for a while, since it's easy and there are fewer spiderwebs, then check the GPS when I climb onto the other bank. I've been trekking cross-country for some of yesterday and all of this morning, since the Hickory Notch Homestead isn't on any trails, but as long as I head downhill I'll hit Split Oak Road, so it's not too dangerous. Also, I brought the GPS this time because I got shouted at last time. I don't need Gideon to use his Oldest Brother voice on me again.

Anyway, I've got about a quarter mile to the road, and then it's an easy half mile to Hollow Ridge Trail, which intersects the old logging road that runs right by Wildwood. Like I said, I'll be home by noon.

· · · · · ★ ★ ★ ★ · · · · ·

I'M WALKING along the side of Split Oak Road, minding my own business and wondering what I can scrounge together for lunch in my kitchen, when the first car I've seen all day drives past.

It slams to a stop about fifty feet in front of me, pauses,

and reverses. I check for oncoming traffic in a panic because you can't just *back up in the middle of a road, Jesus Christ*, but then the car stops again and the driver's-side window rolls down.

It's Josie, my friend who helped me look for cameras at the Lost Mountain Motor Lodge, and she looks like she might have a heart attack. My mouth goes dry and my chest constricts because I suddenly have the awful, sickly feeling that I fucked up and I'm about to find out how.

"Javi?" she shouts. "Are you okay?"

I glance down at myself. I'm not bleeding or anything.

"I'm fine," I shout back, but she's already pulling over to the shoulder, leaving her car half-on and half-off the road and then *leaving the keys in the ignition*. Who does that? "Did something happen?" And was it my fault?

"Javi," she says, jogging across the empty asphalt. "Holy shit. What happened? Are you all right?"

Oh, *fuck*. I know exactly how I fucked up.

I got home Thursday with every intention of using my free weekend to get ahead on homework and clean my house. But then I woke up Friday with a better idea: a two-night solo backpacking trip to check out an abandoned homestead that's not too far from the cabins in Wildwood. I found a local legend about a particularly weird cryptid that's supposed to live in a cave nearby, and when was I ever going to get a better chance to check the place out?

I may have, technically, forgotten to tell anyone where I was going.

"I'm fine," I tell her.

"Do you know what year it is? Who's the president?"

"I don't have a head injury. I went for a hike," I tell her, though I can already tell it's not nearly enough explanation.

Josie takes a deep breath and pushes the heels of her

hands into her eyes, then rubs them and drags her hands down her face.

"You idiot," she says, not unkindly. "*Everyone* is looking for you."

· · * * ★ ★ ★ * * · · ·

"WHAT IF I just drove back to my place without talking to anyone here?" I ask Josie when we pull into Wildwood's tiny parking area. Really, it's a glorified dead-end that's partly gravel and mostly dirt, and she's blocking in three cars, including mine.

"Javi," she says, very seriously, and puts a hand on my shoulder. "If I let you do that, *I* would get yelled at, and I don't love you enough to face that firing squad."

I bounce my head off the headrest of her car and mutter "Fuck, fuck, fuck," in time with it. It's pretty much the only thing I've said since I got into her car thirty minutes ago.

"Will you go warm them up?"

"I will not," she says, cheerfully.

"Will you go tell them not to shout?"

"Do you think that would work?"

Unbelievably, I've actually done something similar before: last summer, on a whim, I decided to go check out the partial eclipse from Bloodroot Meadow because I'd heard it made the sheer rock wall on one side of it look like a face. I didn't think to tell anyone where I was going or that I'd be gone, and when I came back, no one was happy with me.

I think I was gone longer this time. Thursday afternoon to Sunday morning is what, three days? Though—oh, god, do they know where I was Thursday morning? Did Madeline tell them? Did anyone talk to Castillo?

Shit. There's going to be *screaming*. I can't even think about that right now.

"Probably not," I say to Josie and consider simply sprinting into the woods to avoid this. I don't think it would work for long.

"Out of the car," she orders, and as much as I don't want to, I follow her through the tiny parking area and through the gap in the trees to Camp Wildwood.

It's not really a camp. Or it used to be, but now it's a clearing in the woods, deep in the Cumberland National Forest, with four cabins and a fire pit in the middle. I built one of the cabins, and Silas, Gideon, and Wyatt built the others because Silas got some sort of lease deal on it or something. I actually don't know the logistics. Do I ever?

The camp—cabin collective, whatever—is still and pretty in the early morning, a fire smoldering in the fire pit, dew still on the grass. Something clanks in a cabin, and I can smell coffee, and then I spot Wyatt in a chair by the fire pit, staring into the coals. He's a mess.

I think I might throw up from the guilt.

Then Josie shouts, "HEY! I FOUND HIM!" and it stops being quiet.

· · · ★ ★ ★ ★ ★ · · · ·

"YOU CALLED *SEARCH AND RESCUE*?!" I'm shouting. "What the fuck?"

"You were gone for three days. What the fuck were we supposed to do?" Gideon's not shouting, but he can be very loud when he wants to be and right now he apparently wants the whole damn forest awake.

"Not call my mom!" I shout, making some wild gesture with both hands. "Not call my *father*! Now half the Navy is probably going around Norfolk and Virginia Beach, hanging up *Have you seen this unfortunate young man?* posters!"

"We didn't call your father," Silas calls from across the clearing, practically falling out of his cabin door. He's still pulling his shirt on and looks like he was asleep ten seconds ago.

"Someone fucking did!" I call back, because apparently my father's been texting for updates. "You called the cops? You called *Search and Rescue?*"

"Your car was here and you weren't." That's Gideon again, sounding even more pissed off. "Tell me, what were we supposed to think?"

I don't have a good answer because the real answer is too stupid. I can't say *I had a good idea for a hike and forgot to tell anyone* because then they'll start wondering if I'm too dumb to have a driver's license. Maybe I could if this were the first impulsive, irresponsible thing I'd done in the past two years. Maybe if it were the fifth.

I should have texted someone—anyone!—about my plans, but I didn't, and now here I am, acting like I've got some secret when the secret is I forgot something—again.

Jesus *Christ*, though, they had to tell my dad? They had to call Search and Rescue?

There's a small voice in the back of my mind whispering that I'm being an asshole right now, but I'm too pissed off to listen.

I shove the door to my cabin open, and it bounces off the wall, shuddering. Every time I open it, I half expect the whole structure to fall down. It hasn't, yet.

I built this. I had plenty of help, but I built it: I scavenged the plywood for the walls, the old barn doors for the floor, the corrugated metal for the roof. I even scavenged the windows and the skylight, though scavenging the skylight might have been the wrong call because it leaks when it rains too hard. Right now, there's an orange five-gallon bucket under the spot where it drips. The only thing I actually bought was the insulation for the walls because apparently you're not really supposed to scavenge that.

I can hear people talking behind me. I know they're probably talking about me because I've fucked up very badly in an exciting new way. I need to *think*. I need to contain this somehow—convince my mom I'm okay and keep my dad from having me kidnapped and sent to military school. I'm not sure they do that for thirty-year-olds, but if it's possible, I'm sure Admiral Lopez will find a way.

Fuck. *Fuck*.

All my pencils on the table are lined up. They're squared with the sketchpad that's also on the table, and both things are squared to the edge of the table, and I know I did not leave it that way. I don't know how I left it, but I've met myself before. I turn around, still in the doorway, and everyone stops talking.

"Did you go through my shit?" I ask.

"We were hoping you'd left a note."

That's Silas, who's standing there with his arms crossed over his chest and his feet bare, looking tired and relieved and pissed off, and fuck him. I know exactly why they went through my shit, and for a moment I'm so fucking worn out and tired, and I can't believe that two years of toeing the goddamn line doesn't get me three days of privacy.

"You find anything?" I ask, trying not to shout. I think I'm failing. "Anything at all? Some pills? A beer bottle? Did you find a fucking S*nickers*?"

This is—I—fuck. I think my voice is shaking, my pulse is hammering, and I've got that awful feeling that things are really going to shit, like a train careening off the tracks.

"No," says Silas, who's finally raising his voice. "We also didn't find a *single fucking clue* of where you'd gone for three days without telling anyone."

I shove a hand through my hair. I feel like I'm derailing in slow motion. I can't think of a lie to save my life. I can't say *I fucked my stepsister and then went looking for monsters*, and I can't say *I forgot, that's all*. That's fucking ludicrous.

"I don't owe you knowledge of my every movement." I cross my arms over my chest. "You don't have to keep an eye on me."

"Where the fuck were you, then?" That's Gideon, who's still very loud and still not shouting.

I swallow hard and press my lips together because somehow there's nothing worse than the truth.

"It's none of your business." I manage to keep my voice steady.

"Javi—"

"Maybe next time you could put a tracker on me," I suggest. "Save yourselves the frustration."

"We're not putting a fucking tracker on you."

Silas steps forward. He's frowning, and his eyes dart between my own, right to left, right to left. I thought I couldn't feel worse, but I do.

"Are you checking to see if I'm high right now?"

"No," he lies, and I almost scream. I want to tell him that he should be, that it's the first thing anyone with half a brain would have checked, that if any of them were smart we wouldn't be standing here having this conversation, we'd be halfway to rehab number four already. I disappeared for three days; I know what I'd put money on.

"I don't tell you guys everything," I hear myself say.

"There. Happy? Do I still get to keep some things to myself?"

Gideon's closer to shouting with every word. "Jesus fucking Christ, Javi, there's keeping things to yourself and then there's disappearing for—"

I'm so busy being a dick to my friends that I don't even see Wyatt coming toward me until he practically knocks me over, as he smashes my arms against my sides and my face against his hair. I struggle for half a second because what the *fuck*, but he just squeezes harder, and I give up.

"I'm sorry," he says, somewhere near my ear, and no. *This* is the worst I can feel, a brand new emotional low: Wyatt apologizing to me because I'm being the world's biggest asshole. Jesus. What's wrong with me?

I shut my eyes and swallow hard, wrap my arms back around him, and pretend there aren't tears leaking out.

"Fuck," I mutter. "Me, too."

We stand there, hugging and crying, like a couple of idiots. A couple seconds later, my other side is engulfed as either Silas or Gideon joins us. Or maybe both—they're blocking out the sunlight and I can't see.

None of them says anything. I've got my face buried in Wyatt's unshowered orange hair, clenching my jaw so hard my teeth might crack, trying and failing not to cry because they shouldn't be doing this. They should be furious and shouting and probably packing their shit and ending our friendship. I don't understand why they stick around, why they'd want a friend who's always two steps from disaster. Maybe they're all masochists or something.

"We were scared," Wyatt says softly. His hair smells like smoke.

"I'm fine. I swear," I tell him, and I really hope it's true.

# SIXTEEN

## MADELINE

SUNDAY MORNING, I'm sitting at my kitchen table with my laptop and my phone, a *Star Trek: The Next Generation* episode on in the background. In theory, I'm menu planning for the next two weeks while the crew keeps me company. In reality, I'm trying really hard to think about sandwiches but actually spiraling about Javier, and I find Picard very soothing.

I'm just saying, he'd know what to do right now. He'd give me orders in his commanding-but-surprisingly-gentle voice, and then I'd be sure I was doing the correct thing: waiting until 10:00 a.m. to call my dad and tell him more of the truth. Also, this would probably happen while the *Enterprise* was being tracked by Romulans and forced into a wormhole or something, so my problems would feel minor in comparison.

I'm still staring vacantly at my television, wondering what moral lesson *Star Trek* would impart about my dilemma, when my phone buzzes in my hand and I startle so hard I drop it on the floor.

**Javier:** Hey, sorry, I'm alive. I went for a hike and forgot to tell anyone

I have to take a deep breath and rest my forehead on the table. Between the relief that he's okay and the disbelief that he did something that dumb, I'm too overwhelmed to respond. Also, thank god I don't have to tell my dad where Javier slept on Wednesday night, because I'm a really bad liar and he would want to know why I didn't say something sooner, and I still haven't thought of a good reason. I'd probably either say I forgot, in which case my dad would want my brain checked out, or I'd come up with something like *Javier was going to throw a surprise party for his cat, and he didn't want anyone to know where he was so he could get cat party supplies in secret.*

I finally lift up my head, stare at my phone for several seconds, and gather my wits.

**Me:** Glad you're okay! That's a long hike.
**Javier:** Yeah, it was overnight
**Javier:** I gotta go but I'll talk to you later?
**Javier:** By the way
**Javier:** shit I'm in a car with someone nosy
**Javier:** How long do people think I've been gone?
**Me:** Since Wednesday afternoon
**Javier:** Perfect, thanks
**Me:** No problem

Okay. Great. Great, right? He's fine, my decision to wait another twenty-four hours before letting everyone know we fucked was the right one, and now everything is normal and no one needs to panic.

I stand up, pace through my apartment for a bit, sit back

down, text my dad to double-check that Javier's actually turned up and that wasn't some creepy weirdo who murdered him and took his phone, and then I get back to figuring out what to do with the eight pounds of beluga lentils I bought by accident.

· · · · ★ ★ ★ ★ · · · ·

"BACK HERE!" Emily shouts when I open her front door, and I say a silent prayer of thanks that I got the right house. She and her fiancé live in the far-flung suburbs, and all the houses look just similar enough that it makes me uncertain.

When I walk into the back room, at least six heads turn toward me, all attached to women who are sitting on the floor. The room looks like there's been a craft-and-glitter explosion.

"Madeline!" Emily yelps, throwing both her hands in the air. "Hi! We just got started! You look so cute! Hold on!" She pushes herself off the floor, grabs a wineglass that's mostly full of what I think is a mimosa, and comes over to me. "You remember everyone?"

"Mostly!" I say, trying to match her energy. *Everyone* is Emily's college friends, all of whom were in her sorority and all of whom have manicures and hairstyles and "natural" makeup that makes them look like they woke up with flawless skin and well-shaped eyebrows. Even though I wore mascara *and* blush *and* did my eyebrows, I still feel like a swamp witch right now. I have an old, ugly suspicion that all the other girls got a pamphlet titled *How to Do Femininity Right and Not Be a Total Weirdo* one day in eighth grade while I was out sick.

"We're still waiting on Sarah and Katie," she says,

gesturing at everyone with her drink. "Let's go get you a mimosa. Does anyone else need anything?"

There's a chorus of "No!" and Emily leads me into her bright kitchen.

"Thanks for coming," she says as she grabs a glass and the champagne. "I know crafting for a bridal shower isn't really your *thing*."

"It's not *not* my thing," I say, chipper and cheerful. "Make it mostly orange juice—I gotta drive in a few hours."

She obliges. "You know what I mean. All this, like, *woo, wedding!* stuff. You never seemed that into it."

There's a part of me that wants to say something disparaging about weddings and flowers and girly excitement, but it's not worth listening to.

"I promise that I like drinking and throwing glitter around as much as the next gal," I tell her and immediately wonder why I said *gal*.

Emily pours orange juice and gives me a skeptical look.

I sigh. "Just because I don't have a vision board for engagement rings doesn't mean I don't like doing wedding stuff with you! This is fun, and I like seeing your other friends. Last time we hung out, Katie told me about boob tape."

"You didn't know about boob tape?" She sounds scandalized. "Boob tape is *important*."

Sure. It was in that manual I never got, probably.

"This is why I need crafting and glitter and shit."

"All right," she says. "Cheers to that."

She hands me my glass of mostly orange juice, and we clink them together.

· · · · · ★ ★ ★ ★ · · · ·

"YOUR HAIR IS *SO PRETTY*," Katie is saying to me, both of us sitting on the floor trying to make flower crowns. "Do you have to bleach it first?"

"Yeah, it's a whole thing." I carefully tape a daffodil to a flower crown. I've decided this one is "springtime sunrise" themed. "I have to get it bleached and then re-dye every few weeks, and I do a lot of hair masks and deep conditioning. It's a lot of upkeep, and sometimes I dye my bathroom by accident."

"Ooh, I bet that stuff stains," offers Piper, who's sitting on my other side.

"I've ruined a lot of towels," I admit. "And pillowcases."

"You should do a whole rainbow," Katie says. She's had a few mimosas. Possibly even several. "Like—your head could be a rainbow. You could have a rainbow head."

That would be a logistical nightmare, and I'm about to explain why when my phone starts ringing in my pocket. With a *voice call*. My anxiety levels rise, and when I pull out my phone to see that it's Javier, they spike.

I make some excuses, head outside to the backyard, take a deep breath, and answer as casually as I can.

"Hey, sorry," he says immediately. "For everything, I didn't mean to...put you on the spot like that."

"It's okay," I say automatically, then have to backtrack. "I mean. You're fine, right? You didn't get mugged and kidnapped and left for dead on the side of the road? Or in a car crash? Or abducted by aliens?"

There's the briefest of silences, just long enough for me to regret the aliens thing, but then he makes a noise that might be a laugh. "No," he says. "No kidnapping, no aliens."

"Well, I hadn't told anyone yet." I stare pointedly into Emily's nice backyard. "So it's a moot point."

"Thank you."

I snort. "You're welcome. It's my skin, too, you know."

"Your dad would probably take it better than my mom," he says. "She'd probably renounce her earthly possessions and become a nun or something, after everything I've put her through, and I couldn't blame her."

"I think it would be equally awful in a different way," I say without elaborating, and Javier laughs. "Did you at least have a nice hike?"

"It was great until this morning when I got back to my cabin and realized I'd sent everyone I know into a panicked tailspin." He sounds resigned. "I just needed a little time to, you know. Clear my head. After everything."

Ah, yes. *Everything.*

"Did it work?"

"Sort of," he says and huffs out a laugh. "I feel better about my dad. And I talked to my mom this morning. I apologized, and then she apologized, and then I apologized again. I'll probably get at least a one-month reprieve from her suggesting I call my dad."

"There's gotta be a way to distract her. Get her to renovate her kitchen or something."

"I think something would have to break catastrophically for that to happen."

"How catastrophically?"

Javier laughs, throaty with a slight rasp, like he's had a rough day. "Bad enough that she'd have to rip it up anyway," he says. "A flood? Something falling through the ceiling?"

"I know someone who once had a raccoon fall into her bathtub," I offer. "It wasn't very happy. Neither was she, actually."

He laughs again, all warm and lovely and relaxed. "What do you think the worst animal would be to fall through your ceiling?"

"Specifically into the bathroom, or any room?"

"Let's stick to the bathroom."

I lean against the warm siding of Emily's house and wiggle my toes in the grass. They're painted bright, glittery purple today. "I think any apex predator would be pretty bad. Like, a bear or a wolf or something. I wouldn't want a tiger in my bathroom."

"True, but you could just close the door on a tiger."

"For what, sixty seconds? A tiger wants to get out of the bathroom, a tiger's getting out of the bathroom."

"I think something that could hide would be worse."

"Worse than a tiger? In your bathroom?"

"Okay, think about it," he says, and there's a slight squeak on the other end of the line, like springs compressing, followed by a *mrrrrprowr!* "Yes, I know you're also upset with me," Javier says and is answered by another cat complaint. "Imagine going into your bathroom and there's a hole in the ceiling above your bathtub, but instead of a tiger or a bear, there's nothing but tiny footprints."

"Is that Zorro?"

"Yeah, he's telling me how horrible I was to leave and how he suffered with Wyatt and Barry. Did you suffer *so much?*" he asks, presumably to the cat. There's another meow.

"What kind of footprints?"

"Little ones. Ooh, or snakeprints. Little slithery squiggles in your bathtub that disappear after two feet."

A chill runs down my spine because I do, in fact, really hate this idea.

"I'm not convinced this is worse than a tiger," I point out. "Tigers are the size of a small car or something, and you *know* cats don't give a fuck."

Meanwhile, I can hear purring.

"If a tiger fell through your roof, you'd know it right away and deal with the problem within, like, hours," Javier points out. "If all you had was a hole and snakeprints, it would torture you for days. You'd shower for a week wondering whether there was something lurking in there. Every time you went to the bathroom, you'd be on edge. After a while, you'd start thinking maybe you were crazy and it was just the ceiling, there was no snake. Then you'd tear the place apart trying to find it. But by then it would have moved on into the walls of your bedroom. It would be like that movie where the guy thinks there's surveillance equipment in his apartment, so he destroys everything and the last shot is him playing his saxophone in his ruined living room."

I have to process that for several seconds.

"I don't play the saxophone," I finally point out.

"There would be slight differences."

"I would also call an exterminator or animal control as soon as I saw snake prints and a caved-in ceiling, rather than continuing to shower in there."

Javier just sighs. "Where's your sense of adventure, Madeline?"

"Not in my bathroom."

"I guess that's fair," he admits. "Why were we talking about this?"

"To get your mom to renovate her kitchen so she stops bugging you about your dad."

"A tiger's probably a bad idea, then. I could probably cause a flood, but she'd get suspicious if it happened while I was visiting."

"How hard is it to cause a flood?" I ask. I've got my eyes closed and my face in the sun, and it's nice, even though I'm getting a little sweaty.

"Not hard at all."

"Well, let me know if she starts bringing it up," I say. "I bet I could help you out."

There are several seconds of near-silence, with nothing but the low rumble of a cat purr coming down the line.

"Thanks, Madeline," he says, and his voice is quiet and thoughtful and somehow he sounds *closer*, like he's saying it right into my ear instead of into a phone a hundred miles away. I ball my other hand into a fist.

"Yeah, of course," I say, like I didn't just get all fluttery over two words. "We gotta stick together, right? Since we're..." I nearly say *family* but holy shit, what a minefield. "Co-conspirators!"

"Yup," he agrees, and then makes a surprised noise. "Shit, sorry—you're in the middle of something. I'll let you go."

I want to tell him I don't mind. That I like talking about animals in bathrooms while I'm standing in the sun with my toes in the grass, imagining him and his enormous cat lounging on a couch, one foot up and one on the floor, his head back and his throat exposed, stubble on his chin—but yeah, going down that path does nobody any good.

"Talk to you later," I say instead, and we hang up.

· · · · · ★ ★ ★ · · · · ·

THEY'RE all talking about something when I quietly come back in and attempt to make my way back to my cushion as inconspicuously as possible.

It does not work.

"Madeline!" Emily says, slightly pink and a little too loud. Her wineglass is empty. "Who *was* that? You're smiling!"

"I smile all the time," I say without looking her in the eye.

"No, you're, like. Silly smiling," she says, raising her glass to her lips, then making a face when she realizes it's empty.

"My dad's fiancée's son," which I know isn't enough explanation. But I also don't want to get into *we slept together and then he disappeared from the face of the earth* for three days, so I need some lie that—

Oh, fuck me running. Emily was there the first time I met Javier.

"We were talking about candles earlier this week, so he called to say that, uh, he found some good beeswax alternatives."

Emily blinks at me, looking mildly suspicious. I do my best to forget that I once literally sat on Javier's dick while on the phone with her, even if she laughed about it when I finally confessed.

"So, your stepbrother?" someone else asks.

"Not yet."

"Your *future* stepbrother."

"I guess, technically," I say, trying to get as interested as possible in this flower crown. There was a vision I was trying to execute, but I don't remember it now.

"Ooooooh," she says and wiggles her eyebrows salaciously.

"I think I read that romance novel," says the same person who supplied the word *stepbrother*. I'm ninety percent sure she's Jess.

"Isn't that the plot of *Emma*?" Katie says. "Or whichever one *Clueless* was based on."

I try, and fail, to remember the plot of *Emma*.

"Did she get with Paul Rudd in the book?" Emily asks.

"I don't think so."

Jess looks up and narrows her eyes. "Did you just ask if the heroine of a Jane Austen novel got with—"

"She knew what I meant!"

"I did," Katie confirms.

"Could you marry stepsiblings back then?" Emily asks, still cross-legged on her giant floor cushion. "I know they were into marrying their cousins, and stepsiblings are less weird."

"Well, that depends on the stepsibling," Jess points out, then looks at me. "Is yours hot?"

Jesus Christ, yes. "He's okay, I guess," I shrug.

"What's his naaaaaaame?" Emily prods. "Hey, he could be your date to the wedding!"

I freeze because Emily *has met Javier*. Maybe. Sort of. They were in the same place at the same time at the very least. Though Emily was drunk and I'd had the one and a half drinks required to make me bold enough to talk to an extremely hot stranger.

I have no idea if they ever spoke. Did I introduce them or just stick my tongue down his throat? Did they chat when I went to the bathroom? Afterward, did I ever tell her his name?

She definitely saw him, at the very least, but that's not the problem right now. The problem is that I am in a room with the only people who might be able to figure out that *my one-night stand* and *my stepbrother* are the same person. And one of them just asked me a question. And now I have to lie.

"I don't know." It is the worst possible response.

"You don't know your stepbrother's name?"

I'm the dumbest person alive. "Uh," I start, hoping genius will strike. "Well, his family all calls him...Bob...

143

because it's some inside joke? So that's kind of his name, but it's a nickname, but it might be a family only nickname? Which is why I know it."

"Oh. Weird," Emily says, then apparently decides that this discussion is over and holds up her current flower crown. "Does this need more ribbons?"

· · * * ★ ★ ★ * * · ·

LATER, when I'm trying to fall asleep, I think about texting him. It's kind of funny, what happened today, and I could send a friendly little *haha my friends who were there when we first hooked up asked about you but I told them your name was Bob* text.

I get as far as typing half of it into my phone, then delete it because it's late and a text that essentially says *Hey, don't forget we had sex!* has definite *overtones*, especially at this time of night. And one, we are in agreement about the nature of our relationship, and two, it's pretty clear that Javier is only here for a good time, not a serious time.

Which is fine, *obviously*—that's also all I want, but that means I have to be strong and hold the line and respect everyone's boundaries and oh my god, it's so hard to be a person sometimes.

I stare at the ceiling for another ten minutes, then get up, take my phone off my bedroom charger and go put it in the kitchen charger so I don't have any more good ideas.

# SEVENTEEN

## JAVIER

**September**

"I STILL DON'T KNOW why we can't just email these," Madeline is saying, her voice a little distorted by speakerphone. "That's perfectly good etiquette."

"It's not *done*," I say, mimicking my mom.

"It absolutely is."

"Not according to her."

"The only other person I know who sent snail mail save the dates also had a cotillion, and her wedding got featured in *Southern Bride*," Madeline says. "All the other commoners send email."

"I didn't know you mingled with high society."

"I'm pretty fancy. Couldn't you tell?"

"I thought it was just your couch," I say without thinking as I adjust a font size for the zillionth time and then freeze because why am I bringing up her fancy couch? What the hell?

Over the past few weeks, we've managed to exchange

texts and a few phone calls about our parents' wedding without ever mentioning...anything else.

"Couches take on the characteristics of their owners. Like pets," she says, breezing right past it, and I exhale.

"Okay. *Please save the date for the wedding of Paloma Rivera to Gerald Williams, Saturday, February Seventeenth, in Virginia Beach, Virginia, invitation to follow.* That's all we need, right?"

I hear typing over the phone, followed by a moment of silence. "I think so," she says. "That's what all the save the dates on Google have."

"I thought you were a fancy wedding expert."

"Just fancy," she says, laughing. "Though I was sort of my mom's maid of honor when she got remarried, but it was at city hall, so it wasn't the whole shebang. She didn't even have flowers for me to hold."

I snap a picture of my computer screen, because I'm lazy, and send it to her. Since I'm the one getting a degree in graphic design, I got nominated to graphically design all the invitation stuff, and Madeline volunteered to figure out the printing logistics.

It means we talk on the phone sometimes or text back and forth, and I ask her inane questions like which of two near-identical fonts she likes better. I tell myself that it's all because I'm a helpful son who's helping my mom. If I spend a significant amount of mental energy on *not* thinking about Madeline, well, that's my business.

"Looks good to me," she says after a moment. "Not that I'm an expert or anything, but I like it. Once your mom gives the go-ahead, I'll get them printed and sent."

"Great," I say.

"Great," she says, and then it's quiet for a moment. "So..."

There's a brief pause, and the only thing I can think is: *Not yet.*

"When do we need invitations by?" I blurt out, even though I know it's not for a while.

"Good question. Um, that giant crazy checklist I found says the wording and graphics need to be finalized eight weeks in advance and then printed at least seven weeks in advance so the bride has time to hand-address them all, and-slash-or get them to the calligrapher? Please tell me she's letting us use mail merge."

"I'll ask," I say. "What size are invitations supposed to be? Does your crazy list say that?"

"Google is free," she says, but she's laughing.

It's another hour before we hang up.

· · ★ ★ ★ ★ ★ ★ · ·

WE START FOLLOWING each other on Instagram, and I'm completely normal about it. I make myself use my laptop to scroll all the way back to the beginning of her account—harder to accidentally like a five-year-old picture that way—and I have a rule that I have to wait at least an hour before I view any of her stories because I *cannot* be a weird stalker who views all of them the moment they go up, no matter how much I want to.

She doesn't post that often—once, maybe twice a week—but it's a record of her life over the past ten years: friends, family, vacations, selfies with every color of hair. There's a phase where she posted mostly pictures of birds in the wild and then pictures of ice cream cones. She went to Japan in her early twenties with a small group—two men and another woman—and I spend way too long trying to figure out if one of them was her boyfriend.

It doesn't matter; I'm just curious.

As far as I can tell—and I'm not counting or anything, just casually getting to know the woman who's going to be a family member of mine soon—there are three ex-boyfriends in her Instagram feed. The most recent picture with the most recent boyfriend is from a little over two and a half years ago. Madeline isn't really the type to be over-the-top on social media—there's no *happy birthday baby I love you so much you're the number one man in the world* type stuff, but if you're looking for it, you can tell.

The boyfriends—the probable boyfriends—all are a pretty similar type, not that I've noticed. All three are white, clean-shaven with medium-brown hair, no beards, and have the general look of someone who knows about sailboats. Preppy, I guess. And in the few-and-far-between pictures of them, every single one of these men looks fucking *besotted* with Madeline.

And then there's Ben.

Ben is always around. Ben is tall and wide and dark-haired and *handsome* in an obnoxiously obvious way. Like whoever drew him did it as a joke to show what someone with *too* strong a jawline would look like and then forgot to fix it later. Her captions about Ben are about twice as ebullient as the captions about any boyfriend, all about how much fun they had birdwatching or paddleboarding or roller-skating. She congratulates Ben on graduating college (sure, fine) and also medical school (ugh) and also on getting selected for a neurosurgery residency in Virginia Beach (are you fucking kidding me).

Ben's Instagram is private, and if I had a little less self-control, I would absolutely make a fake profile with someone else's picture and pretend we went to college together so I could see it. The fact that I put down my phone and go for a walk instead is, honestly, a huge improvement in my impulsivity.

The pictures with Ben drive me up a wall. They don't look like the years-old pictures of her with ex-boyfriends, but only because she looks happier. She's pretty in every single picture she posts, but when she smiles like that, her nose scrunched and her too-sharp eyeteeth showing, she's...fuck, I don't know. Radiant. Magnetic. Glowing. And what's so special about this guy that he gets to make her that happy?

I'm not jealous. There's no point in being *jealous* because Madeline and I now have a relationship with very well-defined boundaries, and that's fine. It's ideal, really. The best way that this situation could possibly have gone.

And that's fine. Most of the time, it's great. It's enough. It's only once a week or so that I find myself opening Instagram after midnight, scrolling through her feed, and wishing I could make her smile like that.

· · * * ★ ★ ★ * * · ·

## October

**Madeline:** I bet Sprucevale has a good Halloween, it seems like a spooky small town
**Javier:** Did I tell you I'm leading ghost tours this year?
**Madeline:** No!
**Javier:** Well, they're just Spooky Stuff tours around downtown. A couple church graveyards, the legend about the highwaymen, all the monsters
**Madeline:** Highwaymen? All the monsters?
**Javier:** It's Appalachia!
**Madeline:** You can't just say "all the monsters" and not elaborate.

**Javier:** Google is free, Madeline
**Madeline:** [middle finger emoji]
**Javier:** If you ever come visit I'll give you the tour, how's that?
**Madeline:** Now I have to drive six hours to get a couple of spooky stories?
**Javier:** They're really good stories
**Javier:** Want to see my costume?
**Madeline:** Is it good?
**Javier:** I can't believe you're even asking

I TOSS my phone onto the bed and busy myself with leaning a mirror against a wall so that I can maybe forget that I just *invited Madeline to Sprucevale*, which is definitely not the behavior of casual stepsiblings with a normal stepsibling relationship. Or maybe it is? Blood-related siblings visit each other; why wouldn't the step version? It's fine, it's normal.

I finally get the angle right on the mirror and snap several pictures of myself.

Then I decide the lighting is atrocious so I set it up again somewhere else because I want to look good in this picture for reasons not worth thinking about. I spend a few minutes picking my favorite and then editing it a little, because why not?

But then once I send it, she leaves me on read for a good five minutes.

**Madeline:** Are you an old-timey dia de los muertos skeleton?
**Javier:** Close enough
**Javier:** Dia de los muertos bootlegger. This is moonshine country, baby

**Madeline:** Is that a thing? I've seen Coco.

**Javier:** It is now

**Madeline:** I like it

**Madeline:** Does your family do the altar with the marigolds and stuff?

**Madeline:** Again, my main frame of reference is a Pixar movie, sorry if I'm asking dumb questions

**Javier:** They don't, it's just me. I started a year or two ago.

**Javier:** I tried to make sugar skulls this year but they're pretty hard and I burned the shit out of my finger

**Madeline:** Oh no!

**Javier:** You got Halloween plans?

**Madeline:** Ben's got Saturday night off and him and his roommates are throwing a pirate-themed party so I'm Madeline the Marauder, Terror of the Chesapeake

**Javier:** If I were a merchant vessel I'd give up all my wares immediately

**Madeline:** Thanks

Then she sends a picture of herself in her costume, and I almost fucking die. Of *course* Madeline in a pirate costume is insanely hot: she's wearing tight pants and Captain Hook boots that go *over the knee*, Jesus Christ. There's a red sash belted around her waist, a men's lace-down shirt with billowy sleeves, and an eyepatch. She's got one foot up on a chair and one hand casually on the hilt of the plastic cutlass tucked into her belt, and she's looking at the camera like— like—I have to throw my phone onto the bed and pace my apartment for several minutes while my brain helpfully offers up several scenarios.

The one where she uses the cutlass to back me against a wall and tells me to walk the plank wins almost immediately. I don't even know what *walk the plank* means in this context—like, no shit it's innuendo, but for what?—but that absolutely doesn't matter, it's in my brain forever now.

"Was walking the plank even real?" I ask Zorro, who doesn't answer but continues to watch me. Judgment radiates off his fur.

"She's going to *Ben's*," I continue, and saying it out loud only makes the unpleasant sensation in my stomach get worse. "She's wearing *that* to go to *Ben's*."

Is Ben straight? He has straight vibes—whatever that means—in her Instagram pictures with him. Straight and tall and handsome and an *apprentice surgeon* or whatever it's called. Of course he's going to want her the moment he sees her tonight. How could he not? How could *anyone* not?

**Javier:** Shiver me timbers!
**Madeline:** Thanks, I think
**Javier:** I should probably head out, gotta tell the nice people about spooky shit and then the roller derby team is having a party
**Madeline:** Have fun
**Javier:** You too!

I very carefully save three separate copies of the photo to three separate places on my phone, then email it to myself for good measure. I have a very strict *no masturbating while thinking about Madeline* rule that I only break once or twice a week, so it's not for *those* purposes, it's just...in case. Of anything.

· · · · · ★ ★ ★ · · · · ·

HOURS LATER, I've mostly recovered my wits and I'm at the derby girls' party, drinking my fourth club soda with lime. Gideon's little brother Reid and I are talking about transferring community college credits—that's right, I party hard—when I get a text.

It's just a picture, no caption, no context: Madeline, still in costume, at a party, leaning into some man's side with her elbow propped on his shoulder. His face isn't in the picture, but I think it's Ben, and she's grinning saucily at the camera, tipping a pirate hat with the point of her plastic cutlass, and the lace-up shirt is unlaced far enough that I can see she's wearing some sort of corset situation that makes her tits look so incredible it shouldn't be legal.

"Cool hair," Reid says, craning his neck a little over the top of my phone because everyone I know is nosy. "Who is that?"

Was this picture even meant for me? Not that it's explicit or anything, but—Jesus Christ, my whole body goes hot and my mouth goes dry. It's the look on her face. I've seen it before. Up close.

"Uh," I say, belatedly realizing I've been asked a question. "She's my mom's fiancé's daughter?"

Reid narrows his eyes. "So, your stepsister?"

Now even the back of my neck is hot. "Yeah, my stepsister," I say, then put my phone back into my pocket and change the subject.

· · · · · ★ ★ ★ ★ · · · · ·

BEFORE I GO TO BED, I email the second picture to myself as well. In a stunning show of restraint and impulse control, I don't even jerk off about it until the next morning.

# EIGHTEEN

## MADELINE

THE MORNING after Ben's Halloween party, I wake up in my own bed, which is a good start. Not that there was much chance of me waking up in someone else's bed, but a couch or the floor would've been undignified.

But no, I remember calling a rideshare, paying about a million dollars, and trying not to think of any other rideshares I'd been in while the driver drove me to my house and Javier didn't text me back.

I do, however, wake up in most of my Halloween costume. The boots are off, the shirt fully unlaced, and the corset undone but still on because clearly I freed my feet and tits and then I fell asleep.

"Shit," I tell the ceiling, sit up, and regret it.

Half an hour later, I've put on comfy clothes, drunk water, taken aspirin, and ordered iced coffee for delivery because I'm just that wretched right now. I can't even *make coffee*, a task I perform every day. It's embarrassing. I'm embarrassing, and I haven't even looked at my phone yet because I'm afraid that the picture I remember sending

Javier isn't the last thing I sent him. I can't face total mortification while I'm this hungover.

If it's just a picture of my tits or something, I'll live. Not great, but—well, we've been down that road. But there was definitely a point last night where I'd had a few drinks and I was pretty buzzed, and I was talking to Ben's girlfriend, Amy, about birds and books, and then we got onto how Shakespeare actually *invented* a bunch of words we still use because he was a literary genius, and Ben came over and just...kissed her on the top of the head because he's a billion feet tall and she's, like, five foot two.

It was cute and sweet and tender, and I had one thought blaring through my head while I watched it happen: *I wish Javi were here.*

Obviously it was the booze making me all maudlin and shit, so I downed the rest of my beer and proceeded to get considerably drunker so that maybe I wouldn't have that thought again.

My point being, there's a non-zero chance that in addition to a picture where my (clothed) tits look pretty good, I also texted him some clingy shit like *I love forehead kisses* or *I wish you were here,* and I cannot yet face that possibility.

So instead of finding out, I watch several episodes of *Bob's Burgers* and only get off the couch when I need to pee. I'm in the middle of another episode when my phone buzzes, so I swear a lot, take a deep breath, swear again, and it's just Ben.

**Ben:** how you feeling
**Madeline:** like ass
**Madeline:** microwaved ass
**Ben:** yeah you went kinda hard last night
**Ben:** btw you can turn your location sharing off, I made you

turn it on with me last night so I could see you got home in case you decided not to answer your phone
**Madeline:** I wasn't that drunk, I remember that
**Ben:** Sure.
**Madeline:** Thank you.

I take another deep breath, debate whether I want to know the answer to this question, and then decide that I may as well hear bad news from Ben if I'm gonna hear it from anyone.

**Madeline:** Did I...do anything embarrassing last night?
**Ben:** You wouldn't stop telling Becca how pretty her costume was
**Madeline:** that's not embarrassing, it was really pretty
**Ben:** You sword fought Mike in my living room
**Madeline:** Yeah, and I won
**Ben:** Also you told Amy what a good hugger I was for like twenty minutes straight
**Madeline:** She probably already knows that, huh
**Ben:** I like to think so
**Madeline:** Did I do anything besides embarrass myself to your girlfriend?
**Ben:** You also made Aaron walk the plank

The good news is one, I remember everything, and two, no one heard or saw me sending Javier any more pictures or leaving some sort of "I think about your dick and also your eyes all the time" voicemails, so I make myself be brave enough to open our text chain.

Thank *fuck*—the last thing is the mildly thirst-trappy picture of me, which he read at 11:49 p.m. and did not respond to. I sigh in relief and flop back onto the couch.

It's not great, but it could be so, *so* much worse. I can feasibly play this off as *Sorry—I was drunk and wanted to send you another picture of my cool costume*, not *My tits looked great, and I thought you should know.*

"This is completely fine and normal," I say aloud to my empty living room and then spend the next three hours watching *Bob's Burgers* and playing *Stardew Valley* until I feel somewhat human again.

· · · ★ ★ ★ ★ · · ·

## November

"THEY'RE IN THE MAIL," I tell Javier when he answers his phone Saturday afternoon.

"The save the dates?"

"Yup."

He says something just out of phone range, gets a response, and then I hear a door shut.

"Shit, sorry—are you at work?"

"It's time for my break anyway. Plus it's a little slow right now—past the Halloween rush, no Thanksgiving rush yet."

"There's a Halloween rush for flowers?" It's a nice day in Virginia Beach, cool but sunny, and I'm walking back to my apartment from the post office. I could've just as easily texted Javi about the save the dates being mailed, but this is the kind of thing that warrants a call, right? This way he can confirm that I put them in the right slot, check it off his list, ask any follow-up questions he has about the process. All things I'm sure will actually happen.

"Floral arrangements add elegance and class to any event, Madeline," he says, and I grin at the empty sidewalk in front of me. "If someone wants to pay hundreds of dollars for black-rose bouquets for their Halloween party, who am I to stop them?"

"There are black roses?"

"There are every kind of rose if you've got money."

"What do black ones mean?"

"Mean?" he echoes, and I can hear something being shuffled around in the background. "I think these meant *welcome to my spooky party*."

"There's a whole language of flowers," I tell Javier, who works part-time at a florist and should honestly know these things. "Like, roses are for romantic love, and yellow carnations mean *I don't like you*, and daffodils mean, like, *I think we should just be friends* or something." Turns out I know the meaning of exactly two flowers.

"Maybe black roses are *I love you to death*. Which is a little creepy."

"I think the whole idea is Victorian, and they were into that sort of thing," I admit. "They also thought people looked really hot when they had tuberculosis, so you can't trust all their opinions."

"Tuberculosis?" he echoes. "The one where you cough up blood? That was hot?"

"Have you even *seen Moulin Rouge*?"

Javier scoffs loud enough for me to hear. "Of course I've seen *Moulin Rouge*. Bastien and I watched it in secret like once a week after I stole the DVD from the public library. When my dad found it, Thalia claimed it was hers, so none of us got into trouble."

"It was okay that *she* stole it?"

"I think she said she'd lost it or something, which was why it was in Bastien's room. But he thought it was Bastien's at first, and that was..." Javier clears his throat. "Bad."

I don't consider myself a violent person, but then again, I've never met Raul Lopez in the flesh.

"Why are we talking about how tuberculosis was hot?" he asks after a beat.

I grin down at my feet as I navigate a spot in the sidewalk where tree roots have fucked it up. "Flowers, I think."

"Right."

"Anyway," I say, because it's so easy to get sidetracked by Javier, so easy to talk to him for so long his break runs out and he doesn't get to enjoy any of it. "The save the dates are done."

"Thanks," he says, and now I can hear a chair scraping along the floor. "Are we supposed to be doing anything else?"

"I have no idea. I've never gotten married." And then, on a sudden whim: "Have you?"

"Me?" he says, like there's anyone else I could be asking right now. "No. Do I seem like I've been *married*?"

"I know a lot of people in the service get married young for benefits and living together and shit," I protest. "And feelings."

"For all my mistakes, getting married young wasn't one of them," he says, and oddly, I realize I know what he means. That Javier at twenty was a mess, not fit for lifetime companionship. "Why—have you?"

I snort, which is not a pretty sound. "Nah," I say. "I'm not—um."

"Not what?" he asks after a moment.

*Not the kind of girl you marry* is what I almost said, something a man I was dating once told me after a few drinks. He'd followed that up with *No offense, but like...* and then waved his hand at me and my hair and my tattoos and hadn't had to explain any more because I just laughed.

I'd laughed and then rolled my eyes and acted like anyone who'd take offense at that was too dumb and fragile and needy to be worth bothering with, and after the drinks I'd still slept with him, like I had something to prove. Like I needed him to know that I was cooler and better than all the girls who'd mind him saying something like that.

I used to carry that shit around like a badge: the weird, quirky, cool girl who was up for a good time and wouldn't be mad if you never called again.

Back then, I hadn't quite realized that there are polite, respectful ways to tell someone you're not interested in a serious relationship. That you can have casual sex with someone and still treat them like they're a whole person. That it's not lame to want to actually date someone.

Anyway, therapy is great.

"Not a divorcée," I tell him.

"Do people still use that word?"

"I just did."

"It's very classy, like your couch." His voice goes a little lower, like he's tilting his head back or something, and I can picture it: little back room, folding chair, Javier sprawled over it in all four directions at once, looking up at the ceiling. "Like you should be flitting around Paris on a Vespa, with a scarf over your head and a cigarette in a holder."

I'm not opposed to it, honestly. "Who says I'm not? You don't know my Thanksgiving plans."

"Bonjour, mademoiselle," Javier says. "Which means *hello, miss*."

"I knew *that*."

"Did you?" he asks, and I laugh and keep walking.

# NINETEEN

## JAVIER

**December**

"I FIGURED OUT THE ANSWER," my mom says. It's not late yet, but it's dark, and I'm walking back to my car from class on the Cumberland Community College campus. I'm half listening to her and half trying to iron out a list in my head of everything I need to do: I need to go home and eat dinner and check the florist schedule for tomorrow and see whether that extra shift I volunteered for this weekend is happening, and I think Zorro needs more cat litter and shit, I've gotta refill the ADHD meds that they'll only give me for a month at a time because it's not like they're *effective* effective, but it's finals and god help me if I don't have them.

"Yeah?" I ask, not really listening.

"We're going to come there for Christmas."

"Where?"

"*There*. Sprucevale."

"Oh," I say, fishing my keys from my pocket. I point my key at the car and hit the button, because everyone knows the door won't unlock if you don't point the key. It's science. "Wait. What?"

"We'll come to Sprucevale for Christmas," she says patiently.

"For Christmas?"

"Honey, are you all right?"

"Um," I say, and the answer is *not really* because it's dark and cold and I'm tired and my brain feels like several wind-up toys at once, all clanging their cymbals and marching in different directions. "Where...in Sprucevale?"

"Well, I was thinking your house, since you're my son who lives in Sprucevale," she says, and okay, I deserve that. "But if we're not welcome—"

"Of course you're welcome," I blurt automatically, starting my car and turning on the heat. "I was just surprised."

"That way you don't have to worry about taking off work for the travel time," she says. "Thalia and Caleb can see both families, and Gerald has never been to Sprucevale. I told him that you'd be happy to show him and Madeline around all the interesting graveyards."

I take a deep breath and flex my fingers on the steering wheel. "Madeline's coming?"

"She's interested, and she has that whole week off of work," my mom says. "Don't you think it'll be nice to spend Christmas together as a family?"

"Yeah, definitely," I say, *as a family* ringing in my head. "Really nice." Family!

"Now, I know cooking for a group at a holiday isn't necessarily your strong suit, so I think we'll drive up the twenty-third and we can spend Christmas Eve cooking so you're not too stressed. Oh, or if we come the twenty-second, you and your brother and sister could help me make tamales, though I don't know if you've got the right kitchen setup..."

I zone out and start thinking about my apartment. Madeline's seen it a little bit on FaceTime, but she's never *been* there, and it's not nearly as nice as her place. There are still car parts in one corner, and a half-finished mosaic that I'm slowly making from broken thrift store plates, and my couches don't match and the table is questionable at best, and I've still got that stolen Lost Mountain Motor Lodge sign leaning against one wall. I thought it was cool when I acquired it, but it's probably kind of gross, right? She's going to take one look and wonder why I stole something weird from the trash—

"...if that's all right with you," my mom is saying, and I make an agreeing noise. What did I agree to? I have no idea, but it probably pales in comparison to the fact that Madeline is going to be *in* my *apartment*. "I'll let you go—I'm sure you've got something important to do. We'll plan more soon."

"Yeah," I manage to say, and we hang up, and I spend a while blinking at the building in front of me.

· · · · · ★ ★ ★ · · · · ·

**Javier:** Guys I gotta postpone tonight
**Wyatt:** Disagree
**Gideon:** Why?
**Javier:** This final project is due Thursday and I have to work all day tomorrow and it's not done yet and I'm freaking out
**Wyatt:** Dude, you have to eat
**Javier:** I'm not sure that's true

**Wyatt:** Your body actually needs more than coffee to continue working properly

**Javier:** Yes, no shit, thank you for your medical expertise.

"Humans cannot survive on coffee alone," groundbreaking

I PUT my phone face down on the table and stalk into the kitchen, open the fridge, and stare into it. I've got eggs, a container of spaghetti sauce, some green onions, and about fifteen jars of things. Lettuce, cheese, and the fancy-pants coconut creamer I like in my coffee. Nothing very inspiring, and all of it too hard to make into actual food. So I dig through my pantry until I find a jar of peanut butter and eat a spoonful.

When I come back to my phone, everyone has left me on read. Shit. It rings before I can feel bad about being a dick to Wyatt.

"Javi," Silas says, and it sounds like he's driving. "What have you consumed today *besides* coffee?"

"I literally just had a snack," I say self-righteously.

"Was it a can of expired black olives?"

"Those were *barely* expired," I say, and regret ever admitting my snack habits to my friends.

Silas makes his *I'm not going to argue this* noise, and I roll my eyes at my empty apartment. "How many cups of coffee have you had today?"

"I don't see why this matters."

"Have you had more or less cups of coffee than expired olives?"

"I haven't had any olives, expired or otherwise, thank you very much. And they were fine, for the record. Usually canned food is still good for a while after the expiration date. Companies just want to avoid lawsuits."

"I..." Silas starts, and I can practically hear him deciding not to engage. "Okay. Anyway, I already made chili and Gideon already made chickpea pilaf and Wyatt already made the Rice Krispie treats he won't shut up about, so we're coming over because you have to eat."

He's right and how dare he. But now that the peanut butter is entering my system, or whatever food does when you eat it that makes you feel better, I'm realizing I've been kind of an asshole.

"Thanks," I manage to say. "My place is kind of a mess —sorry."

· · · · · ★ ★ ★ ★ · · · ·

GIDEON AND WYATT ARRIVE TOGETHER, and when they come through the door, Gideon hands me a bag of trail mix.

"Here, it'll help." He walks through my apartment to put chickpea pilaf on my kitchen counter. Then he takes another bag of trail mix out and puts it into my pantry, and I kind of want to protest that I don't need his trail mix charity, but I'm too busy practically unhinging my jaw so I can pour the first one into my mouth.

"Have you eaten anything today besides peanut butter with a spoon?" Wyatt asks, also in the kitchen, and I swallow a mouthful of peanuts, M&Ms, and raisins.

"It's efficient," I tell them, and he sighs.

· · · · · ★ ★ ★ ★ · · · ·

"BRING them to Clara's for Christmas Eve," Silas says when I take a break from talking to shove a third Rice Krispie treat into my mouth. Wyatt followed some "elevated" recipe, which would sound ridiculous except that they're fucking delicious and I want to eat ten more.

"You can't just invite random people to someone else's house," I say.

"It's not *someone's* house, it's Clara's house, and it's a free-for-all anyway," he says. "Besides, your sister's coming, right?"

"She's not even your mom."

"Close enough. She's put me in time out before."

"Kinky," mutters Wyatt, and Silas throws a velvet throw pillow at him. "Ow! You could have killed me."

"We were ten—gross," he says.

"What did you do to deserve time out from someone else's mom?" Gideon asks calmly, as if no one is throwing pillows.

Silas sighs. "It wasn't that bad," he says. Wyatt throws the pillow back at him, and Silas catches it. "Levi and I...lost track of some frogs. Inside the house." He clears his throat. "Again."

"*Some frogs*," I say, just Gideon raises one eyebrow and says, "*Again.*"

"Did you ever find the frogs?" asks Wyatt.

"Technically, no," Silas says. "Two we let go in the back-yard, and the third probably found its own way out. And then Levi and I had to sit quietly on the couch and not go anywhere or do anything or even speak to each other until my mom came to pick me up. And *then* she told my mom what had happened, and I got into more trouble because my mom assumed I'd talked Levi into it."

"Had you?"

"Yes."

"So, for Christmas Eve, you're inviting me to invade someone else's home where there may or may not be a thirty-year-old frog skeleton waiting to be discovered," I summarize.

"There are probably also other skeletons," Silas offers, picking up another Rice Krispie treat. "I'm about ninety percent sure Seth and Caleb smuggled a snake in once. You should ask Caleb when you see him."

"Is this what people do for fun in the country?" I ask. I grew up a lot of different places, but I don't think any of the houses we lived in had unfettered access to frogs and/or snakes. "You bring wild animals into your home and let them loose? Did none of you have video games?"

"I didn't let them loose," Gideon says. "Don't lump us all in with Silas."

"I didn't bring wild animals home," Wyatt offers. "Though I did once find a bird skeleton, so I took the skull and put it over one of Georgia's Barbies' heads while she was asleep and then posed it on her bedside table. She screamed really loud."

I have never in my life felt so civilized.

"I brought home a rabbit with a broken leg once, but I got in a lot of trouble and then my father took it away," Gideon adds.

"My point *is*, if Clara Loveless can put me in time out, I can invite you to her Christmas Eve open house, which is pretty much an open invitation anyway," Silas says. "Bring the whole family. Is your stepsister coming? I forget her name."

"Madeline," I say. Then I clear my throat because I feel like all three of them just went from casually looking at me to staring with the intensity of a thousand suns, even though that's ridiculous. "Yeah, I think she's coming. She said something about wanting to see Sprucevale? And she had Thanksgiving with her mom and her mom's family, and she said she's excited to see mountains besides Mount Trash-more. That's the old city dump in Virginia Beach," I over-explain. I manage to keep myself from also offering the information that her favorite Christmas cookies are rasp-berry jam thumbprint cookies and she's one of those people who actually likes Christmas carols, which is generally unforgivable but cute on her, that she loves *Elf* and hates *It's a Wonderful Life* and never believed in Santa because Ben—yeah, *that* Ben—was her next-door neighbor and he's Jewish so he knew the truth all along and told her.

Next-door neighbors, all the way until they graduated high school. The Hallmark movie just writes itself, doesn't it?

"Sounds fun," Wyatt says, and then he and Silas start comparing the weird shit they found in the woods as children.

# TWENTY

## MADELINE

"BUT THEN, Hendricks ended up having to sell that land for some ridiculous price after his scheme to rig the duck race got blown up," the man in front of me says. His name is Eli, and he's spent the last twenty minutes telling me fascinating small-town gossip. "Which he was doing in the first place to try and pay off his gambling debts, which no one knew about."

"And that's also why they renamed Hendricks Road to Lookaway Road," I say, trying to keep up. "Because it was named after his family and he brought shame on them? With a duck race."

"You got it."

I take a long sip of my beer, a delicious wintry stout that's got notes of, I don't know, winter. It tastes like a cinnamon-dusted pine tree, but in a good way? Who cares—my dad's driving.

"So is this duck race like the Kentucky Derby, but for ducks?" I ask. "Please say yes. Please tell me people wear exciting hats and drink mint juleps and the ducks have names like *Menace to Society the Fourth*."

"That would be incredible," he says, very seriously. "I should suggest that. But no, it's rubber ducks on a river. You buy one, and a bunch of businesses offer prizes, and if you have the fastest rubber duck you win. And also get to be a Sprucevale celebrity."

Before I can ask what that entails, a woman with light brown hair walks up and rests one elbow on his shoulder, leaning in.

"Eli, did you teach the children how to sharpen candy canes?" she asks, taking a long swig from a beer bottle.

He grins at her. "Of course not."

"So you've got nothing to do with the fact that Daniel is currently running triage in the downstairs bathroom for candy cane wounds?"

"Okay, *first* of all, when he was seven he jammed one of those little round lollipops up my nose and my dad had to use Vaseline to get it back out, so he knows all about using candy as a weapon," Eli says. "And second, I told them *not* to stab each other. This is Madeline, by the way."

"Hi, I'm Violet," she says, and we clink beer bottles together. "Sorry about him."

"Don't apologize for me—I'm perfect."

She rolls her eyes and doesn't otherwise acknowledge that. "Are you new in town?"

I'm currently at an event that I can only call a *shindig*. Maybe a *hootenanny*. A barn burner, though there's no barn and the only fire is in the fireplace, so maybe not. Whatever it's called, I'm pretty sure that most of Sprucevale is here in the middle of nowhere, packed into an old farmhouse that I'm afraid might literally burst apart at the seams any minute now.

It's Christmas Eve, I'm three beers in, and I'm talking to Thalia's boyfriend's older brother about small-town scandals and desperately trying to ignore Javier's presence, even though he's wearing a plaid flannel button-down with the sleeves rolled up and his hair pulled back and, like, *leaning* on things. It's obscene, the leaning.

"She's Caleb and Javier's people," Eli explains, and I guess that's a good enough explanation because Violet makes an *oh!* noise and grabs his shoulder.

"Wait, is Javi here?" she asks. "He completely saved my ass last week with flowers for our fundraising event. I gotta go thank him."

I, unfortunately, know exactly where Javier is—leaning against a wall near the Christmas tree, laughing at something, can of seltzer in hand—so I point him out.

"Ah, perfect." She turns to Eli. Their faces are only a few inches apart, hers tilted up and his tilted down, and even though they're pretty much just standing there, it feels sweet and intimate and, I don't know, *nice* in a way that makes it feel like something deep inside is clawing to escape. "Please stop teaching kids to make weapons. People keep coming up and telling *me* about it, like I could possibly stop you, and it's really cramping my style."

"Don't they know anything?" he asks. I realize he's got a hand on the small of her back. I scrunch my toes in my shoes.

"Clearly not about you, if they think I can intervene. Stop creating problems," she says, and then kisses him on the cheek. "Great meeting you! I love your hair, by the way," she tells me, and I call out "Thanks!" as she walks over to Javier and starts talking.

"So, right," Eli says, and I tear my eyes off of Javier and try to remember what we were talking about. "Brian Hendricks thought he could stand downriver with a fishing line attached to his duck, pull it along, and no one would get suspicious."

· · · ★ ★ ★ ★ ★ · · ·

BY LATER THAT AFTERNOON, it's started snowing. It looks like it's snowing kind of a lot, actually, though it's not like I'm a snow expert. Virginia Beach gets snow sometimes, yes, but we don't really get major snow. We get *stay home for thirty-six hours until it goes away again* snow, which usually got me out of school, but it wasn't *big deal* snow.

But this is like...a lot of snow? It's all over the ground and everything, including the driveway, which seems like something someone should worry about.

No one does, as far as I can tell, but then I hear small footsteps thumping up the attic stairs and I scoot under the desk where I'm hiding, making myself as small as possible.

"Is anyone in heeeeeeere?" Thomas shouts, because he's the kind of kid who likes to narrate his seeking loudly. Luckily it's adorable. The light's already on, so he barges in and stomps over to the wardrobe against the far wall. Besides that, the attic's got a bed and a desk and also an impressive collection of boxes, like someone could sleep up here if they wanted to, but it's probably a last resort. "In here? Noooo," the kid goes on. I think he's three, but I wouldn't swear to it. "In here? Noooooooo. *HMMM.*"

In a very cute lapse in spatial reasoning, he checks the drawers in the wardrobe. Next, he rips the blanket off the bed and looks under it, as if I could be perfectly flat.

Finally, he sighs to himself, loudly says "No one's here!" turns, sees me, and screams.

"Sorry!" I yelp and try to stand so fast I bang my head. "Ow."

"You scared me." This poor kid looks like he's about to cry. Shit.

"I know, I know—I'm sorry," I say, still sitting on the floor, and I half reach out to this kid I don't really know just in case a hug would be comforting. "I didn't mean to."

He frowns and his lip wobbles for another moment, but then he frowns, his eyes narrowing.

"You were under the desk?"

"Yeah. Good spot, huh?"

He nods, clearly bookmarking it for later use.

"Was I the last one? Should we go back down?"

"Yeah." He runs toward the stairs. "I already found my dad. He was behind the stairs, which was really easy. Caleb tried to hide behind a curtain but I found him right away, and that other guy was in a closet but that was *easy*, and Grandma's friend was…"

The kid goes around a corner and I can't really hear him anymore, which is too bad because I could use some hints on hiding places.

I'm apparently very slow because by the time I get downstairs, he's already counted up to twelve, face smushed into a corner of the couch while various adults chat nearby.

Am I a grown-up who could easily opt out of this game if I wanted to? Yes. But instead, do I panic a little and then scamper downstairs because we're *playing* a *game* and I need to win or at least make a respectable showing? Also yes.

At the bottom of the stairs, there's a door that turns out to have a coat closet behind it, and just as I pull it open Thomas shouts "READYORNOTHEREICOME!" and wow, I'm bad at this game.

"Shut the door," Javier's voice says from behind the coats. I jump a mile in the air but, to my credit, don't scream.

173

"Sorry," I hiss as tiny steps run toward the stairs. "Do you know where—"

"There's room in here. Just close the door, for the love of god," he hisses. So I lurch forward into a face-full of coats, close the door behind myself, and flail vaguely downward until Javier's hands find mine and guide me.

"It's really dark in here," I whisper, settling in and removing—a shoe?—from underneath me.

"Well," he says, and he has a point.

"Does anyone else ever get to do the seeking?" I ask in a whisper. "Or just Thomas?"

"When it's just him and adults, I think Thomas does all the seeking," he whispers back. "Hiding is a lot easier. You just sit here in the dark and wait while he expends energy."

"Good point," I say, still trying to fold my legs in a way that makes sense. There's floor space in here, just not a *lot*, and I think I'm sharing it with at least one vacuum cleaner and what might be some tennis racquets. My knee brushes Javier's, and I jerk it back on instinct.

"Sorry."

"You're fine."

"There's not much space and I can't see shit."

He snorts softly. "Madeline. Don't worry about it."

I squirm some more—there's a baseball bat and, I think, a fan—and end up briefly pressing my side against his, our faces too close in the dark. I can feel his hair on my cheek, and I've had a couple beers over the course of several hours and it's enough that I don't pull back immediately.

I do pull back, though, finally shoving the baseball bat to the side.

"There," I say, and my legs are angled awkwardly, but at least they're not touching his. "Perfect."

We sit in silence for a minute. I've got my head against the back wall of the closet, someone's coat in my face, my entire body is tense with the effort of absolutely, definitely not touching Javier at any point.

"How's your Christmas Eve been?" he asks after a bit, voice low but no longer whispering.

"Well, I've spent the last half hour in a bathtub, under a desk, or in a closet," I say.

"Is that better or worse than Charlie's dad asking you whether you are part Smurf?"

"I got asked that by two separate people tonight." I can feel him laugh in the dark. "I've never even heard that one before."

"Silas's dad calls me his long-haired hippie friend," Javier says. "I think it's a compliment, though? Like he thinks I'm a kindred spirit?"

I blow a coat sleeve out of my face. Or try to, anyway. "Is he the tractor enthusiast guy?"

"No, he's the hot sauce guy."

"Oh, *him*," I say. "I saw him put hot sauce on pie, and then he told me everything about the Scoville scale and hot pepper cross-pollination. Did you know you can die from eating hot peppers?"

"What kind of pie?"

"I think it was blackberry."

There's a brief, considering pause, and then: "That actually sounds like it might be good."

"What the *fuck*, Javi," I mutter, and I can feel him laugh in the dark.

* * * * ★ ★ ★ * * * *

175

AFTER A FEW MINUTES I get a charley horse from sitting in such a weird position and try to scoot around so I can straighten my leg out, but all I do is knock a coat down and kick the vacuum and make a ruckus. *Then* Javier is whispering at me that we're going to lose to a three-year-old *again* and he can't believe I'm causing him to bring shame on his sister like that, and we're both giggling like idiots, flailing and groping in the dark.

Only Thomas never shows up to throw open the closet door and shout *Found you!* and when we're done rearranging ourselves, we're shoulder to shoulder and the edge of my right knee is touching his left thigh, and it doesn't have to be, technically. Technically there is enough space in here to not touch. Technically we could leave this closet and lose this round of hide and seek. But I'm tipsy enough to be stupid and Javier's always been a little too sweet, a little too accommodating of graceless, awkward me, so we don't.

Then he rests his hand on my knee and apologizes but doesn't move it, and I have to lean my head back against the wall and take a deep, silent breath because I'm always ready to read too much into a casual gesture.

"I heard," he says, low and slow, in a voice I swear I can feel through the floor, "there might be dead frogs in here."

I have to blink into the dark about that one for a minute. "What?"

"Also, possibly, a snake."

"Does *here* mean *here*, in this closet, or does *here* mean, like, Sprucevale."

"The house," he says, like it's a normal thing to say. "Apparently out in the country, children bring live animals into the house for fun."

"Like, as pets?"

"I think as entertainment."

"They don't have video games out here?" I ask, and Javier starts laughing, silently, his thigh shaking under my knee and his fingers tightening on my leg, and I grin at the vague outline of his face.

"You know, that's exactly what I said, and they acted like I was the weird one."

"Well, if the shoe fits."

"I'm completely normal."

"You disappeared for two days so you could investigate whether an abandoned homestead in the mountains was haunted."

Javier sighs a long-suffering sigh. "I didn't think it was haunted, I'd heard stories that Frog-Mouth Hobbler had taken up residence either there or in a nearby abandoned mine, so I wanted to check out it. Get a feel for where a Hobbler would live."

He told me that the last time we talked, or maybe the time before last—a phone call that was ostensibly about travel logistics but ended with him telling me where he'd gone after the last time we saw each other, what he'd been looking for. The call lasted two hours. It sounded like a secret. I don't know if it was, but I haven't told anyone.

"Did it feel monster-y?"

"At night."

"Everything here feels monster-y at night," I tell him, and it comes out like a compliment. "That's probably why you like it."

"There are lots of reasons—" Javier starts, the closet door opens, and someone yelps, which makes me also yelp, and Javier's hand tightens on my knee.

"Who's—" Thalia's voice says, and then she's shoving

coats apart and the hall light floods into the closet, so bright I have to shield my eyes. "What the hell? Why are you guys in the closet?"

"Hide and seek," Javier says. "Thanks for blowing our cover." He doesn't move his hand and I don't move my knee, and even with an arm over my eyes, I can see Thalia notice.

"Thomas is the seeker," I explain. "Sometimes it takes him a while."

"Thomas left, like, twenty minutes ago," Thalia says, and suddenly I realize that it's quiet behind her, in the rest of the house. The general cacophony that I got used to all afternoon has dimmed in favor the clink of a few dishes, footsteps on the stairs. "Uh, pretty much everybody left, actually? It's snowing like hell."

That gets us out of the closet. Javier goes first, favoring his left ankle and right shoulder before he reaches down and pulls me up, hand warm and strong. I can tell my face is flushed, and I tell myself it's because the closet had gotten too warm.

"You guys are still here?" Caleb asks when we get into the living room and Thalia hands him a coat. He glances outside, and—*shit*, that's snow, that's for real snow that's covering the ground and everything. I've had too many beers to drive a bumper car down at the pier, let alone a real car in actual snow.

"Hide and seek," I explain, and I'm pretty sure Caleb and Thalia exchange some sort of look, but I decide I don't see it.

"He's a dictator, huh," Caleb says of his nephew with a fond little smile that says *and he deserves to be*. "Which car's yours?"

Javier sighs and scrubs his hands over his face. "The red Ford Focus."

Caleb strides to the front door, opens it, and very judgily scans the parking area at the top of his mom's driveway. Apparently he doesn't like what he sees because he comes back inside, nods once, and announces, "We'll drive you home, and you can come get your car later."

# TWENTY-ONE

## JAVIER

"JUST BE NORMAL," I beg, arms folded over my chest. "How hard can it be? Just act normal for, like, eight hours. *Please.*"

I get no response whatsoever.

"I'm sorry I vacuumed," I tell Zorro, who's atop the bookshelf-wall structure that separates my bedroom from the rest of my apartment. I even put up a proper curtain across the entryway so no one can look in and realize that the only reason my place is so clean right now is because I shoved everything in there. "I know you think it's unnecessary, and now you're mad because you have to jump up here to escape and you consider that undignified."

The tip of his tail twitches, and he looks away, pretending that he's tracking a bug or something. That's the best response I'm going to get, so I shrug and put the vacuum back in the old industrial cabinet-thing that I use as a closet, since my place features zero *actual* closets.

Then I go put on the nice slacks and the button-down shirt that I actually *ironed*, thank you, even if I had to go over to Silas's place and borrow his, and figure I'm as ready as I'll ever be for my family to descend.

· · * * ★ ★ ★ * * · ·

"FELIZ NAVIDAD, BABY!" Bastien shouts. I swear and fall over, because I was crouching on my kitchen floor, trying to remember if I stuck some extra mugs behind the pots and pans or just had a weird dream that I did.

I swear, but I do it quietly because if Bastien's here, that means everyone is here and I cannot start my first Christmas hosting gig off by swearing in front of my mom.

Everyone streams in, already talking. Bastien is saying something about my apartment, and my mom is already giving me cooking instructions, and Thalia is telling Caleb where to put things down, and I still haven't found the last two mugs yet. It's probably too late now.

It's so chaotic that I don't even realize Madeline has come in until Bastien shouts "JAVI, DID YOU MAKE THE COAT RACK?" at me like it's at least the third time he's asked. I've got a spoon in one hand and a potholder in the other—I own potholders?—look over to answer him, and she's over there, hanging her coat on it.

"YEAH," I shout back, the only currently viable volume. In another moment, I'm out of my kitchen, the spoon and potholder lost, walking toward where Madeline and Gerald are still hanging hats and coats.

"Yeah, he made it," Bastien is telling them, head turned away from me. "JAVI—oh, shit, you're right there. Did you make the hooks, too?"

"No, those are from...around," I say, because Madeline's *here*, in my apartment, and she's on her tiptoes looking at this one coat hook that's wrought iron, I think, and shaped like a mermaid, her tail curving out. I got it before I knew she liked mermaids, but I did hope she'd like it. "That one's from that weird thrift store in Norfolk that the SPCA runs. Near Ocean View."

"Wait, the one on Bayview? I love that place—it's so weird. I almost bought, like, a five-foot-long painting of some thoughtful-looking seagulls perched on a wreck once. But then I didn't, and when I changed my mind and went back it was gone."

She's wearing an emerald-green sweater dress over black tights, her hair down around her shoulders, a big chunky gold necklace with red stones around her neck, and she looks so good it's hard to think.

"Yeah, you gotta move fast on that stuff," I agree and realize that Bastien and Gerald have both moved on. "You know, thrift stores, it's not like they've got more in the back. That's my favorite coat hook, too. I'm glad you like it." I'm rambling. "Do you want to come in? There's coffee, though I couldn't find all my mugs. It's fine—Bastien can drink it out of his hands."

Now she's laughing, and her cheeks are pink, and my hands are jammed into my pockets, and I feel like there's a spotlight on me as well as a neon sign above my head that's got an arrow and says *THIS MAN WANTS TO BANG HIS STEPSISTER. AGAIN.* But no one's looking right now, so I get away with it for a few more minutes.

"Thanks for hosting, even if it was at gunpoint," she says, and then my sister shouts something at me, and chaos reigns again.

* * * * ★ ★ ★ * * * *

WHATEVER I WAS afraid would happen doesn't. My family all manages to keep it together, and Gerald and Madeline are polite and low-key as ever. Bastien, Thalia, and I only get into one fight where we pelt each other with balled-up wrapping paper from our Secret Santa exchange, which my mom watches with outright exasperation and which Madeline and Gerald watch with curious bafflement.

Caleb, Thalia's boyfriend, has, like, sixteen older brothers or something, so he can practically meditate while this shit happens.

("Four," Thalia says to me later, rolling her eyes after I mention this fun fact to Madeline while we're setting the table. "He has *four* older brothers.")

"You've only got one, and you're not handling it well," I tell her, and she throws a napkin at me and then immediately asks for it back, which I think proves my point.)

I do see Gerald grab my mom's butt when he thinks nobody's looking, and I leave the room so fast I walk into a wall. I believe that my mom deserves an active and healthy love life, or whatever, but I also might die if I think about the specifics.

· · · · · ★ ★ ★ ★ · · · ·

"HEY, JAVI," Madeline calls later, when I've taken a break from the nonsense to hang out with Zorro in a corner. "Is this real?"

She's over at the corner near my bedroom, where the Lost Mountain Motor Lodge sign is propped crookedly against the wall, a pile of other things propped against it.

I put Zorro down and walk over to her, and he follows me, complaining.

"I mean, did you make it for an installation or something? I could see you doing a 'Bigfoot the Motel Manager' art experience."

"I should write that down."

"First one's free."

"No, I didn't make it," I finally say and glance over my shoulder at the rest of the apartment. Gerald and Caleb are doing the dishes and probably bonding over how weird my family is. My mom and Thalia are on a couch having some intense-looking discussion, and Bastien's in my favorite chair, scrolling on his phone.

"I stole it," I finally say, and her eyes go wide.

"From *where*?" she whispers, looking from me to the sign and back.

"From the Motor Lodge," I say, pointing at the name. "Where else?"

"How did you steal a motel's entire sign?" she asks, all skeptical, her eyes narrowed. "Are you fucking with me?"

"It was already condemned," I admit. "I did have to break in and haul it out of a bathtub, but it was like three days before they leveled the place. It was stealing, but not *stealing* stealing."

She tilts her head, considering for a moment, and reaches out one finger to touch the bubbling, peeling paint, then slides it along the underside of the *O* in *Mountain*. There's a tight feeling between my shoulder blades, and I look away before I have to face the fact that I'm jealous of a motel sign.

"Why was it in a bathtub?"

"Everyone asks me that, and I have no idea," I say. "It was tricky getting it out of there—must've been tricky getting it in."

"Were they anticipating a nuclear bomb or something?"

she asks. I stare, and Madeline frowns back for a moment. "Wait, no, that's fridges. Tornados?"

"Not a lot of mountain tornados."

"Why'd they tear it down?"

I know I read the answer at some point, but I don't remember it now. That doesn't stop the urge I have to make up some answer so she keeps asking more questions and I get to keep answering them.

"It's just what happens to old motels," I say. "For a while you're a fun, trendy destination for fun, trendy honeymoons, but the time comes when your heart-shaped Jacuzzis and pink shag carpeting just aren't as much of a draw as they used to be."

"Tell me it had both those things," she says. "Wait, do you have pictures?"

"If you're the cops, you have to tell me right now."

"No, I don't." She's grinning. "Take your chances, Javier. You think I'm the abandoned-motel police? Maybe this whole thing has been a long con."

I come so close to saying *If you fucked me to get a confession it was worth it,* but I bite it back at the last second because there are other people around, even if I wish there weren't. It's been so long since I slept on her air mattress that I've nearly forgotten how it felt to wake up, desperate to leave. All that replaced by the sound of her voice over the phone.

I shouldn't forget. I know better than that; I know remembering the air mattress is my best defense against the way she fucking—sparkles when she laughs, the way she touches shitty old scrap metal like it's fascinating. Suddenly I feel like I might fidget out of my skin.

"Want to take a walk?" I ask, and if she's thrown by the change in topic, she doesn't act like it.

"Sure," she says and looks around at the rest of our families. "Should we—"

"No. Just us."

She looks up at me, right in the eyes, and tucks a strand of blue hair behind one ear. Takes a slow, measured breath, her necklace catching the light as it shifts.

"Is that a good idea?" she asks.

"Just a walk," I tell her. "Up to you. But there's something I think you might like."

"More than the motel sign?"

"You like the motel sign?"

"Of course." She takes a step back and looks it over, eyes flicking up and down. "It's so..." She gestures, and I know what she means.

"Come find out," I tell her, and that gets a smile.

# TWENTY-TWO

## MADELINE

JAVIER'S A LYING LIAR, because this isn't a short walk. After twenty minutes, we're still "almost there" and "just a few more blocks," and I'm gladder than ever that I wore my rarely used snow boots for this.

He wasn't, however, lying about this only being a walk. I didn't really think he'd pull me into the hall and ravish me in a broom closet or anything, but it...crossed my mind.

"You're a liar," I tell him, my breath fogging as we trudge up this hill. I'm wearing snow boots, tights, a dress, and my nice winter coat, and I'm somehow cold and sweating at the same time.

"I didn't lie," he says.

"You said it was two more blocks three blocks ago."

"I said it was a *couple* more blocks."

"That means two!"

Javier huffs, his breath fogging in the air, and glances over at me. He's got on a Carhartt canvas winter coat, a black scarf, and his hair's down beneath a hunter-green knit hat, like he's a classy lumberjack or something. Though when I think *lumberjack*, I think of big white dudes, but

187

obviously there are other ethnicities of lumberjack, right? Mexico has trees.

"A couple is anywhere from two to nine," he says, which is factually incorrect, and I tell him so. We go from there to *how many is several*. Then he starts making some nonsense argument that *a dozen* is sometimes literal and sometimes an estimation, and I'm ready to lose my mind about that when he finally points at something up ahead.

"There," he says of a tall, spindly glowing thing another block away. I was expecting something Christmassy, but this isn't. It looks like some sort of tree monster had a nuclear accident and escaped from the lab.

"What *is* that?" I ask, arguments over numbers forgotten.

"That's Bartholomew," Javier says, like it explains anything.

There are no cars out and not many people have shoveled the sidewalk since it snowed like hell last night, so we're walking in the street, the quiet hush of winter all around us. I know it's Christmas and that means no one is out, but I'm not used to it: even here, right in the heart of Sprucevale, it's quiet as a church. I like it.

"It's a Christmas skeleton?" I say once we're close enough for me to make out the shape. "It's got a Santa hat."

"The hat was hard to find," Javier says, and I'm sure it was because Bartholomew the Skeleton is probably twelve feet tall, and I don't imagine they sell Santa hats for twelve-foot skeletons just anywhere.

"It's very festive," I agree. We crunch up onto the sidewalk—Bartholomew's owner has shoveled it, so that's one point for them—stand at the wrought iron fence, and stare. This is a really nice part of Sprucevale, all historic-looking houses with big yards and big trees and planned-out flowerbeds. Not at all where I'd expect to find a giant skeleton.

In addition to the hat, Bartholomew has white Christmas lights wrapped around his torso, head, and each limb. There are giant light-up candy canes stuck in the ground around him, one of those wicker sleds, and two light-up wicker reindeer. Dangling from the fingers of Bartholomew's right hand, extended toward the gate in the fence, is what I can only assume is light-up mistletoe.

My insides twist instantly and my heartrate spikes. Mistletoe? He brought me to a giant skeleton who's holding mistletoe? Is that an accident, the mistletoe, or is the mistletoe the point? And which of those things do I want it to be?

"We got a neon sign that says *Ho, Ho, Ho,* but we couldn't figure out a way to attach it to his head like a speech bubble without his skull falling off," Javier says. I make some sort of agreeing noise, still looking at the mistletoe and trying not to think about it. Javi glances over at me. "You okay?"

I want to say no, point at the mistletoe, and demand an explanation. Does he even know it's there? God, maybe he doesn't even realize it's there.

"Of *course* you had something to do with this," I finally say and make myself smile and look over at him. "I should have known from the second I saw it that the big, spooky sculpture was your doing."

"It actually wasn't—I just helped."

"Which Appalachian monster-god is this?" I ask.

He sighs and makes a face. "That sculpture series kinda...floundered," he admits. "I made the first three, but once I realized I was gonna have to come up with nine more monsters to match Olympian gods, my enthusiasm waned. I didn't even realize I told you about it."

"It was on your Instagram." I keep my eyes on the non-mistletoe parts of Bartholomew, the Christmas lights searing themselves into my retinas because I'm slightly afraid that otherwise Javier's going to read my mind or something. Following someone—a family member—on their social media is an extremely normal thing to do, so it's not like he's going to assume that I immediately went Instagram Sleuth about it and examined every picture and caption for clues about Javier like it was a treasure map to pirate gold or something.

It's mostly his art—big sculptures, made from whatever he can get his hands on, it seems—plus a few shots of him and friends, some pretty sunsets. Nothing revelatory. Not that I was looking for a revelation about his love life or anything else.

"This could be your death god," I say, tilting my head. "Bart, ferryman to the afterlife."

"Bart, collector of souls," he says.

"Bart, bringer of doom."

"The Bart reaper."

We go quiet for a moment, because I don't have a good riposte to *The Bart Reaper*, and I shift my feet on the sidewalk. Our shoulders bump, and I move away but then move back. This is—normal, right? We can be normal together. With this giant skeleton, ablaze with Christmas lights, in the middle of this otherwise staid, conservative neighborhood.

God, I think I love Bart.

"If he showed up at my front door, I'd let him drag me to hell, no questions asked," I say.

"I can't fight a twelve-foot skeleton."

"He wouldn't even have to drag. I'd probably go willingly."

Javier looks over at me, grinning. "I'll have to remember that."

My insides smoosh, then riot. "What does *that* mean?"

"It means...if I ever want you to go somewhere, I just have to bring Bart with me? I don't know, Madeline, just enjoy it."

"Why do you want to drag me to hell?"

"That's not—I did not even remotely say that." He's trying to act all offended but smiling too much to be believable. I have to look away from him and his ridiculous face. I look at Bart, at the stupid mistletoe, at the orange glow of the old sodium-vapor streetlights, at the other decorated houses on the street all done up like gingerbread houses or Santa's workshop.

I try not to think about Javier showing up at my front door one night, with a giant skeleton in tow, and saying, *Come away with me.* It's an act of nonsense I don't even want.

"You kinda did," I say, and I get to watch him roll his eyes. "Why'd you bring me here, then?"

It's not to kiss me under the mistletoe—I know that much. Even if it's there, just beyond the gate, taunting me. Even though there's no one else out here to see us. It's a stupid, silly thought, and I try not to think it as Javi goes quiet and swallows.

"I thought you'd like it," he says after a beat and shrugs. "It seemed like—a big weird skeleton lit up like radioactive terror Santa Claus would be right up your alley."

He's dead fucking right, of course. Javi probably clocked my love of outlandish, weird shit the moment we met, and when I took the mermaid lamp, and it only makes me squirm a little bit that he can tell so easily. It's not like he's going to find my notebook doodles I made during history class and make fun of me for the rest of the year or find *one* magazine cutout and tell everyone I want to fuck cartoons. Javi's not even acknowledging the existence of this mistletoe, and if he's not bringing it up, I'm *definitely* not bringing it up.

"Of course I like it," I finally say. "Who wouldn't?"

"Oh, everyone," he says, grinning like we've got a secret. "The tourism board. The chamber of commerce. Wells's HOA. This is his house, by the way. His next-door neighbor over there"—he tilts his head—"especially hates it. Wells actually put Bart up to spite him."

"And it worked?"

"Like a dream." Javier looks over at me, smiling and softly lit, and I wish it didn't make me want stupid things.

· · · · ★ ★ ★ ★ · · · ·

LATER THAT NIGHT, after we've all said goodbye to everyone, said it again, and then one more time for good measure while trying to leave, I spot my scarf across the back of a chair. Javier's in the kitchen, fully visible from where we are, and his collar's unbuttoned and his sleeves are rolled up his forearms as he unloads the dishwasher, his hair pulled back off his face.

All I've had to drink is virgin eggnog—we've never talked about it, but people seem to mostly avoid drinking around Javier—but it's been an odd two days after an odd couple of months, and I've spent so long not thinking about the things I want that I give in, just for a moment. Because he looks fucking *good* like this, casual and relaxed, putting plates away and laughing with his brother and his sister. He looked good yesterday in that closet and he looked good earlier tonight staring up at a giant skeleton, and I've come to the conclusion that I might think Javier looks good all the time.

I wonder, for half a second, if he's been *looking good* for anyone else lately, which isn't my business and which I don't care about, but—I wonder. Lately I've been running down a lot of batteries *wondering*, trying to fuck myself with my vibrator at the same angle he managed, but my arms aren't long enough so I come face down on my pillow with one knee hitched up and I'm still not quite satisfied.

"You ready, Mads?" my dad asks, and I instantly stop thinking about vibrators.

"Yeah, are *you*?" I give my scarf one last glance as we head for the door.

# TWENTY-THREE

## JAVIER

THE NEXT MORNING, I wake up the usual way: to Zorro headbutting me directly in the face. We go back and forth for about fifteen minutes because in a post-Christmas miracle, I don't have to work at either Calhoun Insurance or Blooming Blossoms today—he headbutts me, I pet him, he's not pacified—and I finally roll over and throw the sheets off when he escalates to biting my hand. *Literally* biting the hand that feeds him, because for all their majesty and snootiness, cats are dumb as rocks.

"Okay, okay," I tell him, sit up, and he prances out of the bedroom like he's really taught me a lesson.

One of my small victories in life is charging my phone in the kitchen instead of next to my bed. Yeah, it's next to the coffee maker, so it's the third thing I look at in the morning instead of the first, but I take what I can get. That means I've got my elbows on the counter, wearing a flannel robe that's seen better days, listening to Zorro crunch on kibble, when I see Madeline's text.

**Madeline:** Hey, I think I left my scarf over there last night. Can I swing by this morning and get it?

**Madeline (thirty minutes later):** no worries if not, I can also grab it when we see you this weekend.

I have to read it at least three times, glancing at the clock on the microwave to double-check the time and then comparing that to the clock on my phone to corroborate before remembering that I could look at that clock in the first place.

*Swing by this morning.* I don't read into it. I will not read into it. A scarf is a scarf is a scarf, even if she was kind of flirty last night, maybe, and we took a nice walk to a giant skeleton. A giant skeleton that was practically *waving* mistletoe at us, which I swear wasn't there the last time I visited. Hopefully she didn't notice and think that I took her there solely for mistletoe purposes, which I didn't.

**Me:** Sorry, just woke up. Sure, come by whenever.

**Madeline:** Thank you so much! Be there in twenty.

She doesn't even say if she's coming alone. Is she coming alone? Fuck.

· · * * ★ ★ ★ * * · ·

I GULP A CUP OF COFFEE, get dressed, brush my hair, brush my teeth, change my outfit into something less embarrassing but still casual, brush my hair and teeth again, gargle some mouthwash, frantically collect all the cat fur that accumulated in the corners since last night, and brush my teeth again just in case I have coffee breath.

I've barely started looking for the scarf when there's a

knock on the door, and my heart leaps into my throat. I open the door.

She's alone.

"I haven't actually found your scarf yet," is what I choose to lead with.

"Oh," she says. Her winter coat is on but unzipped, her hands in its pockets. Her cheeks and her nose are pink. "Maybe I didn't leave it here? I could have dropped it on the way to the—"

"I'm still looking," I blurt, because it sounds a little like she's about to offer to leave. "If you want to come in and also look?"

"Thanks," she says and walks into the room. Her eyes track up the walls to the ceiling. "You have such good light in here. I didn't get a good look yesterday, with the chaos."

"It's the windows," I say and immediately wish I hadn't because *no shit* it's the eight-foot windows. "Do you know where you might have left it?"

Madeline clears her throat, like she's nervous, still looking out one of the massive, beautiful windows. Through them there's a parking lot and then a tangle of trees and, somewhere beyond them, the river. Though it's late in the year, there are still a few orange-and-brown leaves left, twisting in the breeze on their branches.

"Could be anywhere, really," she says, with this funny little half smile. "Guess we'll just have to...look?"

That's accompanied by a single eyebrow raise, and—god, she's here, alone, "looking" for her "scarf" and raising one eyebrow at me, and I'm not oblivious. But I *am* someone who remembers the last time we were alone together and the finality of that air mattress.

"Madeline," I say, and even though we're alone my voice

is pitched only for her, low and quiet. "What, exactly, do you mean by *look?*"

She takes a deep breath and glances out the window before she faces me again.

"They're not married *yet.*" She looks me dead in the eyes.

Madeline is standing about three feet away from me, the cold still coming off her, cheeks and nose bright. Her hair's still blue threaded with green, like she's a mermaid. More appropriately, a siren. I give her a long, hard look: winter coat, wide-necked soft-looking shirt, leggings.

"No," I agree. "They're not."

"We're going to that folk art exhibit today, and my dad wants to leave by ten, so I should be back at the rental before then," she says. "If I leave by nine thirty, I should be there in plenty of time. Which gives us half an hour."

She trails off. I'm staring at her mouth, the way it shapes around her schedules and *shoulds*. It's all suggestions and hints. I want her to *say* it.

"Half an hour to do what?" I ask, settling myself against the back of a couch.

*Now* she rolls her eyes. "What do you *think?*"

"Watch an episode of *Schitt's Creek?* Make some avocado toast? Play a round of *Settlers of Catan?*"

"*Settlers* takes way more than thirty minutes."

"Then I have no idea what you want," I say and swallow. "Unless you tell me."

Madeline's eyes lock onto mine, and it feels like something snaps into focus. Her lips part and she scrapes her teeth along the lower one. She shifts her weight and her hips. My whole body feels like a compressed spring.

"I want to have sex." Her face turns bright red. "Again."

It's hard to breathe, hard to stay in one piece. "I thought we decided not to."

"We did," she says lightly. "But what's one more time going to hurt?"

I know exactly what it'll hurt, but her hair's a little messy, like she hasn't been awake long, and there's a tiny freckle by the edge of her right eye, just where her eyelashes sweep over it.

"Nothing much," I say, and I finally *look* at her the way I want to, slow and open and hungry, and she tilts her chin up as if to say *go ahead*.

"C'mere," I tell her, and now, suddenly, I understand what I'm doing.

In two steps she's between my legs where I'm leaning against the couch from behind it, her fingers twisting in the T-shirt I put on ten minutes ago.

"I really shouldn't be late." Her voice is low and urgent. "I'm glad you didn't sleep in today."

"Better make it efficient, then," I tell her and slide a hand around her waist, inside her coat. She's so warm. "What now?"

Madeline pushes at my shirt. I raise one eyebrow and don't help her.

"Take this *off*," she says as she steps backward and finally shoves her coat from her shoulders. I do it, then slouch a little harder, leaning on my hands.

"What now?" I ask her, and Madeline looks uncertain, like she thought I was going to do this part. I can tell she's squirming. "Whatever you want."

She sucks in a tiny breath and closes the distance between us again, her hands on my thighs, and presses a kiss into my neck, right at my pulse point.

"Stay right there." She nips my throat and palms my dick.

I gasp, because she just *bit* me, but she kisses the spot and circles her palm around the head of my dick, so I forgive her.

"I like these pants," she tells me between neck kisses. "They look good on you."

"You just like that they don't hide much," I tell her, already raspier than I'd like.

"You knew what you were wearing when you opened the door," she says, planting a kiss on my collarbone. Her other hand cups my balls through the thin material, and I groan low in my chest. "Dressing up like a slut to help me find my scarf."

My dick twitches in her hand.

"How dare you," I gasp. "I'm a nice boy."

Madeline grazes one nipple with her teeth, then flicks her tongue over it. "Of course you are," she says, and does the same to the other one. "The *nicest* boy."

And then she's on her knees, and she's looking up at me, and there's a small but very obvious wet dot right at the tip of my still-clothed dick. Madeline mouths at it, her hands back on my inner thighs, and it's warm and soft and *dry*, dick still constrained, and she looks up at me when she does it. I have to close my eyes and take a deep breath.

Then her hands are tugging at my waistband, and I know what *that* means, too, but that's not the game today.

"Ask for it," I tell her.

"Take your slutty pants off," she says, rocking back a little on her heels. "Please."

I shove them off and kick them away. My dick is at attention, precum already beading at the tip. I take it in my hand and stroke it once, just to see her watch me.

"Tell me," I say, and she glares up at me, blushing hard again. On her knees, still completely dressed. "How am I supposed to know what you want otherwise?"

"Iwanttoputyourdickinmymouth," she says in a rush without making eye contact, her face scarlet. Then she looks up at me again, glaring some more. "Or are you going to tell me to say *please*?"

"Would you?" I ask, and I grip my dick at the base, then hold it out to her in offering. I don't think I want *please* out of her mouth; I want—whatever this is.

She flattens her tongue and gives a broad lick to the underside of the head, and then her eyes shut as she closes her mouth around me and her lips meet my hand.

"Holy *fuck*," I choke out. I move my hand, and her lips slide down, her eyes still closed. I keep my knees from buckling through sheer willpower and deep, calming breaths.

For all her talk of only having half an hour, Madeline takes her time. It's slow and lazy, her hands gripping my inner thighs, her mouth hot and wet. The noises are *obscene*. When she pushes her mouth down as far as she can and swallows, I swear everything goes white and I have to slide a hand into her hair so I can keep a grip on reality.

She pulls off with a wet *pop*—holy Christ—and looks up at me, blinking hard.

"Go ahead," she says and sucks me down again. I'm not exactly sure what she means, but she's too busy to talk and I can guess, so when she does it again, I tighten my fingers in her hair until I can feel the tiniest pull of tension, exert the smallest amount of force I can for a split second.

Madeline *moans* around my dick, and I gasp and swear and hit the back of the couch with my other hand. I don't want to come after approximately three seconds, but I'm pretty close to completely losing my shit. She pulls off again, and this time she looks up at me with the tip of my dick on her tongue, and I would swear I've never had a thought in my life.

"Let me hear you." She licks me again.

"What," I say. Words? Ha. "Like. You want me to make noise?"

"Sure," she says, and then her mouth is busy again.

"Or you want me to talk?" I go on, and now I've got both hands in her hair, and I'm not hurting her and I'm not holding her, not really, but if I do—just a little, just for a second—she makes that noise again. "I can talk," I say, which is technically true. "I can tell you how pretty you are right now, but I think you know. I think when you get on your knees like this you know exactly what it does to me. Holy shit. Jesus Christ. How am I supposed to—"

She swallows around the head of my dick again, and this time I hold her there, fingers tangled in her hair, for half a second longer. When she pulls off, we're both panting. Her eyes are shining.

"Are you—"

"Do that again," she says. "And don't come."

"Fuck, you're bossy."

"You said I had to tell you what I wanted." She takes one hand off my thigh and slides it between her legs, rubbing the heel of it against herself. "And I want you to do that a few more times, and then I want you to fuck me."

She doesn't wait for a response, just slides her mouth onto my dick, and I oblige her request, both hands in her hair, and I babble on and there's lots of swearing, of taking the Lord's name extremely in vain, of the words *so pretty* and *so good.*

Per her instructions, I don't come, but finally I have to pull her off and hold her there, head tilted backward.

"I can't," I say. Her eyes are glassy and her lips are pink, and she grins at me like she's the cat who got the cream. I run a thumb along her lower lip because I can't stop myself, and she licks it.

"You're gonna fuck me, right?" she asks, my thumb still on her lip, and I have to take a breath. I think about a world where we have all day for this. Where I can come in her and on her. Make a mess. Where I can spend an hour with my face between her thighs and see what she likes best.

A world where we go on wintertime walks together and hold hands and sometimes, for no reason at all, she leans into me and I can put my arm around her, kiss her if—

But that's asking for too much, so instead I nod dumbly and point at my bedroom, partitioned off behind a bookshelf and a curtain. Madeline rocks to her feet, then kisses the top of my head—confusingly sweet but also hot, like it's a promise, and Jesus Christ am I going to get horny about head kisses for the rest of my life now?—and walks through the curtain.

I take a moment because, holy hell, I need one, and then I follow her.

Madeline's sprawled on my bed. It's unmade, but thank god I changed the sheets three days ago, before people came over. All the shit I moved out of the rest of my place is stacked around it, but it's too late to worry about that.

I lean against the bookcase, curtain swishing shut behind me, fold my arms over my chest, and try to look as casual as I can with the world's hardest, leaking-est dick, her spit still drying on it.

"I already told you what I wanted," she says, going up on her elbows. Her shirt is long-sleeved and loose, and I can see where the waist of her leggings cuts into the soft curve of her belly.

"And yet there you are, fully dressed," I say. "Seems like you missed some steps."

"Come over here and take my clothes off."

I cross the room and kneel between her spread legs, pushing them wider. The leggings are bright purple, and I run my hands up her inner thighs until my thumbs meet in the middle, somewhere near her clit. The fabric is slightly damp, and I have to suck in a breath.

"What?" She sounds little defensive.

"I guess we both like it when you're on your knees."

"Are you going to undress me, or do I have to do it myself?"

Madeline in full-on horny-brat mode is a sight. I reach behind her, manage to unhook her bra, and then push that and her shirt over her head to her wrists, leaning over. Watching her and the way her lips part and her pupils swell and her cheeks go pinker, all the way down to her chest, her arms over her head. There's a pink line around her ribs where her bra band was, and it gives me an idea.

"Hold still," I tell her, then gather the fabric between her wrists, her hands still trapped in the arms of the shirt, and twist. It brings her wrists together and lets me hold them both at once in the world's softest, least-effective handcuffs. I barely catch the soft noise that comes out of her mouth.

"Does that hurt?" I ask, and she shakes her head. I squeeze the fabric a little more, get it tighter around her wrists, but it's T-shirt material, not rope or something. "Do you like it?"

She nods, ribs expanding under her skin.

"Hm?"

Madeline rolls her eyes. "*Yes*," she says. "Colloquially, a nod usually denotes—"

I duck my head and lick a nipple, which has the desired

effect: she gasps and squirms and stops telling me what a nod means. It stiffens under my tongue, which is maybe the second or third most gratifying sensation I've ever felt.

I stop and wait, blowing on it lightly. It doesn't take her long.

"Do that again," she says. "Use your teeth."

She doesn't have to ask twice. I'm a little rougher than last time, and beneath me, Madeline squirms and clenches her hands, but she doesn't actually try to free herself, just whimpers and groans and swears quietly. I lose myself in it a little because Madeline has incredible tits—plush and full and soft—a shade paler than the rest of her. I suck hard enough of the underside of one to leave a bruise, and she moans when I do it.

"You want anything else?" I ask after a bit, once the bite is turning bright red and both nipples are bright pink and stiff, her skin red where my stubble scraped it.

"Will you..." she starts and squirms a little bit, raising her head enough to look down. "Oh. Take my pants off?"

I let her hands go, and she squirms out of her shirt the rest of the way as I peel her leggings off. It's not the most sensual clothing removal ever—she nearly kicks me in the face and then apologizes—but it's effective because she's finally naked, leaning on one elbow, reaching for my nightstand as I stare at her.

"Drawer?" she asks, even as she opens it. "Ah."

Madeline tosses me a condom, and I roll it on as she pulls out the lube and half the stack of McDonald's napkins I've got in there because I'm classy.

"Tell me how you want me," I say, snapping open the lube and spreading some on. She watches my hand greedily but doesn't say anything, so I keep talking. A specialty of mine. "I could put you on your back with your legs over my shoulders," I say. "It'd be hard and fast, and you wouldn't have to do much. You could sit on my dick again and give me a great show, or sit on it backward and give me a different great show." Fuck, how many sex positions are there? "You could get on your hands and knees, and I'd fuck you into the mattress. You could stand up and bend over the—"

"Here." She rolls over onto her hands and knees. My breath catches.

"You wanna get fucked into the mattress?" I ask, stroking down the back of one thigh. I sound ten times steadier than I feel.

She arches her back in obvious offering and glances over her shoulder. "If you don't mind." Her voice is still husky from my dick hitting the back of her throat, and her hair's mussed, and she's pink and panting. I palm her ass and she presses back against my hand, so I dig my thumb into the crease right between her hip and her thigh and listen to the choked-off noise she makes.

"Javier." It sounds like her teeth are gritted. "Come *on*, I want you to—"

I line myself up and slide in all the way to the hilt in one smooth thrust. My eyes roll back in my head. She's hot and slippery, and I can feel her yield to me, letting me in as her words turn into a groan.

I lean over her back and plant an open-mouthed kiss on her spine, a little because I like drawing this out and mostly because I really need a minute.

"Like this?" I ask, doing my best to sound like a person and not the panting, desperate mess I am. "Is it good, Madeline?"

She sighs, and the slight sound feels like it rolls through her body. She bends her knees and points her toes and arches her back. I bite into the muscle over one shoulder blade—not hard, not *too* hard—but Madeline makes a broken, throaty noise and ruts back against me, pushing me even deeper, so I bite down harder and try not to lose my mind.

It gets messy after that. Messy and blurry, a tangle of tight slippery heat and soft skin. Madeline starts out noisy and only gets louder when I put a hand between her shoulder blades and push her down, her hips still in the air and her shoulders on the mattress. *My* mattress, in *my* bed. When she moans, she moans into *my* pillow, and she turns her head and manages to glance back at me for a moment, eyes hazy and mouth open, one hand clenching the sheets.

"Look at you." I'm babbling, half out of my mind. "This is what you wanted when you showed up at my door? You wanted me to hold you down and fuck you just like this?"

"God, yes," she manages and squirms her right arm underneath her.

"You're so much more agreeable with my cock in you." I can feel the tips of her fingers against my shaft as she rubs her clit, and I fuck her with short, hard, deep thrusts because it's what she seems to like. "And you're so fucking pretty like this. Like you can't help yourself, all splayed out and slutty for me. Does that feel good? Feels fucking good to me."

"'Sgood," she mumbles, face half in the pillow. I'm gripping her hips so hard I can barely feel my fingers, pulling her back as hard as I can.

"You can come if you want," I hear myself say, ten times steadier than I feel. "I won't make you wait. You look like you want to. You're a fucking sight, Madeline. I wish you could see the way your pretty cunt is stretched around—"

Madeline convulses, swearing. She turns her face into the pillow and shoves back against me, grinding and rutting as she shudders and her toes curl. My vision goes white as she clenches around me and I dig my fingers into her hips and somehow don't come.

After she finishes, gasping into my pillow, I pull out and she raises her head with a questioning noise.

"Over," I tell her, and Madeline obeys—of course she does, Jesus—and then she's on her back, putting her ankles on my shoulders, fucked-out and post-orgasmic, and I line myself up and slide in so goddamn deep.

We both moan, and she's got one arm over her head and the other—the other's between her legs, again, rubbing her clit, sliding her fingers around my cock where it's sunk inside her.

"I just like feeling you," she says, still hazy and sex-drunk. "More, I mean. God, you feel so good." I hear a noise like a sob, then realize it's me, pleasure coiled tight and hot in the base of my spine. "Fuck, I'm gonna feel this all day," she whispers, and I come so hard there are black spots in my vision.

"Wait," Madeline says before I can pull out, and I glance up at the desperation in her voice, too sex-stupid to do anything but stare. "Stay," she says, voice soft and strangled. "Just—please."

It takes me several more seconds to realize that she's still working her clit, fingers rubbing and circling as she bites her lower lip and stares up at me while I start to go soft inside. I don't think and barely breathe because if I do it might be too much, the way I can feel her muscles twitching around my exquisitely sensitive dick until suddenly she clenches again, her head going back. It's just this side of painful, but I stay in her because she asked me to.

When it's over, she takes a deep breath, moves her hand, and looks up at me.

"Thank you," she says, and I make sure I grab the base of the condom before I pull out.

· · · ★ ★ ★ ★ ★ · · ·

AFTERWARD, there's a minute. Sixty whole seconds where we lie together, in my bed, on my pillows, and don't say anything. Madeline's on her back, still breathing hard, her face pink and her blue hair sticking to her forehead.

And she's grinning at me. Laughing, almost, one arm draped over her head, lazy and carefree. The winter sunlight through the blinds is bright, but she's brighter, like I'm staring at the sun. It hurts to look at her. Breathing feels alien.

Finally she levers herself up on one elbow, still in all her naked glory, looks at my bedside clock, and collapses back into the sheets.

"I should go," she says. "I'm already late."

"We can't do this again," I tell her, and she grimaces a little, looks down at the sheets.

"I know," she huffs. "I'm sorry. This was such stupid timing—"

"At all, I mean." That gets her attention. She goes still, waiting. I sit up so I don't have to look at her. "I don't want to do this anymore. It's too hard."

I swing my feet over the edge of my bed, run my hands through my hair so it's not too wild, and stand. She hasn't made a noise, and I think, she knows now, and that should be good enough to scare her off. Madeline never wanted *more* from me, so that admission ought to be enough.

"Oh," she finally says. "Right. Yeah, I mean, yeah. Good point. It's—yeah. Too much, all this." She clears her throat. "Do you mind if I use your bathroom?"

"No, of course. Yeah. It's right through there," I tell her, giving directions even though she was here for most of the day yesterday. While she's in there, Zorro pushes past the curtain that serves as my bedroom door, sits, and sniffs the air haughtily.

"You can just *ask* if we fucked again. You don't have to be a dick about it," I say, and he *mrrps* in response. I pull on boxers, then sit on my bed. Water is running in the bathroom. "I made a good choice. You proud of me?"

And as much as cats are assholes all the time, as much as I'm pretty sure Zorro would snack on my body within hours if I died, he comes over and rubs his face against my leg. He's purring like an engine.

"Thanks, bud," I murmur, and then Madeline comes out of the bathroom and says "Bathroom's free!" as cheerfully as I've ever heard her speak, so we swap and I close the door behind me.

When I come out, she's left. I know it doesn't matter because I'm going to see her again—and again and again, for another whole fucking *week*, but—I wish she'd said something. I wish a lot of things.

Zorro's sitting by the windows, majestic and green-eyed in the sunlight, so I go sit by him and stroke his back for a while. He lets me.

"I'm working on it, buddy," I say, just to use my voice. "I'm working on it."

# TWENTY-FOUR

## MADELINE

I'M IN THE CAR—MY dad's Subaru—and backing out of my parking spot before I realize I still don't have my scarf. You know, the scarf I deliberately left last night so I could go back over to Javier's this morning and get fucked like I've been thinking about for months?

It's still in his apartment. So, now I get to head back to the vacation rental where my dad, Paloma, and Bastien are waiting for me. I've got no explanation for the forty minutes I've been gone, I probably smell like sex, and I don't even have my scarf.

For half a second I contemplate going back in, but I think I prefer the alternatives. Freezing slowly to death, for example, or getting so cold that I jump into a lake of boiling lava, or accidentally stabbing all my fingers off trying to knit a new scarf because there is absolutely no *fucking* way I'm going back in unless it's at gunpoint.

*Too hard.* I take a deep breath and grit my teeth and shift into Drive, ease the car out of the building's parking lot. How could it be easier than me showing up, getting on my knees, and then leaving without a fuss? That has to be the lowest-maintenance form of sex that isn't masturbation, and if that's too much—if that's somehow *still* too much...

At the exit of the parking lot, I take a deep breath, crack a window, and press my cold fingers against my eyes because I can't look like anything's wrong when I get back. It's fine. I'm fine. I don't even know why I'm freaking out like this—it was fun, but it was never anything more.

And if I ever had any brief moments of stupidity when I thought otherwise, well, that's my problem.

· · · ★ ★ ★ ★ ★ · · ·

"WE'RE BEING PAID OFF, RIGHT?" Bastien says from the passenger seat of my dad's car. "My mom and Gerald wanted to have some *alone time*, and so we're being sent off to go bowling?"

"Errgh," Thalia and I both say, pretty much in unison.

"Sorry." We're all silent for a moment: Bastien and me in the front, Thalia in the back. "They did have the fireplace going, though."

"I'm *sure* it's so they can play Monopoly," I say. "Or Uno. Or Clue!"

"Think they've landed on Park Place yet?"

"I wanted *one* nice outing with my siblings," Thalia says from the back seat. "One. I wanted to go out, see my brothers, bond with my future stepsister, escape the chaos maelstrom of Clara's house. But no."

It's a few days after Christmas, and my dad and Paloma handed Bastien and me a hundred bucks and told us to do something fun with Thalia and Javier. They're staying in the vacation rental they rented for the four of us for the week, a faux-rustic cabin outside town that's got three bedrooms, two hot tubs, and an enormous stone fireplace. My dad was already uncorking a bottle of wine as we left.

"I think this is very nice," Bastien says.

"It was nicer before you made sex jokes about Park Place," I tell him, and Bastien turns to me, both eyebrows raised.

"If you interpreted that as a sex joke—"

"No!" Thalia says, and suddenly her face is there, between us. "Don't you even. Madeline, you're correct—that was an uncalled-for sex joke."

"Wow, so you're both perverts," Bastien says.

"Is this sibling bonding?" I ask, and saying *sibling* feels considerably more normal when Javier's not here. "I don't really have any. Is this how you bond? You call each other sex perverts?"

"No, most siblings are *normal*," Thalia says pointedly at Bastien. "Caleb and his brothers are a loving, supportive sibling group with strong and appropriate emotional bonds, for example."

I turn onto the four-lane road that runs into the middle of Sprucevale and think for a moment.

"Didn't one of them catapult another one's shoe into the woods? Like, last week?" I ask. I'm pretty sure I heard this story at Christmas Eve.

Bastien starts laughing. "I've never catapulted one of your shoes," he points out.

"You've never had a catapult," Thalia says.

"Why does Caleb have a catapult?"

"Caleb catapulted the shoe?" I ask.

"No, Seth catapulted Eli's shoe and Caleb got involved because..." Thalia makes a gesture that clearly means *who fucking knows*.

"They have strong and appropriate emotional bonds?" Bastien asks, and now Thalia laughs. I would like them to stop saying that phrase, but I'd also rather jump out of this moving vehicle than tell them why.

"I'm just saying, I've never heard them call each other sex perverts," she says.

"They probably behave around you, since you're the girlfriend," Bastien says. "Meanwhile, you can never get rid of me."

"I know where there's a catapult," she points out, and then we turn into the parking lot of the Blue Ridge Bowl-o-Rama, which is cheesy and worn down in all the right ways.

"Can we please go bowling first?" I ask.

"Ooh, look who's getting the hang of it," Bastien says, and I shoot him a questioning look. "The bossy older sibling thing."

"I'm not being bossy. I just want to go bowling before catapults!"

"I didn't know we invited the fun police," Thalia says.

My headlights sweep over Javier's car as I park, and my stomach tightens. Shit, are these two going to realize how weird we're acting? I shouldn't have come. I should have read a book in my room with my noise-canceling head-phones cranked all the way up.

"You're not gonna tell my mom if I have too much candy, right?" Bastien asks, grinning.

"Get out of my car," I say, and both of them cackle.

· · * * * ★ ★ * * * · ·

WHEN I AGREED to go bowling, I didn't remember that it was Friday night, and I also didn't realize I was agreeing to *cosmic* bowling, which is apparently the hot date-night activity for every teenager in the Blue Ridge region.

It's dark. There are black lights. There are disco balls. There's loud music and occasional sirens and a fun little light show if you get a strike. The four of us share a lane, sandwiched between two groups of teens. Bastien asks for bumpers, and the girl running the shoe rentals has never been less amused by anything in her life.

If Bastien and Thalia notice that Javier and I hardly speak and barely make eye contact, they don't say anything. Which I think means they don't notice. I've yet to see them not give one another shit for something, so we must be doing a pretty good job of acting like stepsiblings who've never had sex.

"How am I supposed to do *that*?" Bastien's asking toward the end of the second game. He gestures at the two bowling pins left, one on either side of the lane, indignantly.

"You don't. Hurry up," says Thalia, sprawled in an uncomfortable plastic seat.

"Did you watch the demonstration?" Javier asks. "The turkey can do it."

Bastien marches back to where we're standing and stares up at the screen over the lane, where a cartoon turkey has just finished knocking two pins down with one ball.

"That turkey's a good bowler," I offer. "I'm really impressed."

"It's a cartoon," Bastien huffs.

"Still. Incredible athleticism."

"Can you not bowl as well as a turkey?" Javier asks.

"Right now, the rankings are one, turkey, two, Madeline, and then alllll the way at the bottom, Bastien," Thalia says from her seat. "You have to scroll pretty far."

"Hahaha," says Bastien, who rolls his eyes unconvincingly. "Yeah, I get it—I'm not that good of a bowler."

"If you practice, maybe you can beat the turkey someday," Javier says as Bastien plucks a ball from the rack, then whirls around to face us.

"It's an animation!" He points up at the screen. "It's got —cartoon physics! That's cheating!"

"No rules against cartoon physics," Thalia calls, and Bastien flips her off, then turns to the bowling lane. Behind his back, Thalia and Javier fist bump, and then Thalia holds her fist out to me.

I bump it, too, even though I'm not totally sure what we're celebrating. Annoying a younger sibling? Is it really that hard?

Then I glance up at Javier, who's standing next to me, colored lights playing over his face, and I offer him my fist because why the hell not. If this is the relationship we're going to have, may as well have it and enjoy it, right?

"Oh." He blinks at my hand. "Yeah, sure."

Javier goes to fist bump me and *misses*, which makes his knuckles graze my boob, which causes me to make a funny squeaking sound, which makes Javier say "Shit, sorry!" in a very alarmed way, and now both his siblings are looking at us. I'm desperately glad for cosmic bowling and its attendant darkness because I think my entire body is tomato red right now.

Very carefully, we redo the fist bump. Properly this time.

"Thanks," I say once it's accomplished, which is a very normal thing to say after a fist bump.

"Yeah, nice," Javier says in response. We nod at each other.

Over on the uncomfortable chairs, Thalia's giving us some kind of look, but I can't really see it so it doesn't count.

· · · · · ★ ★ ★ ★ · · · ·

LATER, after two more rounds of bowling, some terrible nachos, beers for Bastien, Thalia, and me, and an intense air hockey tournament in the arcade, we've said our totally normal goodbyes and I'm getting into the car when Javi jogs over, waving something.

"I found it," he says and holds out my scarf.

"Oh." I can't meet his eyes, so I stare intently at the scarf while I take it back. "Thanks."

"I didn't think you'd actually left it, but then the other day I saw something green dangling off Zorro's cat tower and —right, anyway, there you go."

"That...rascal," I say. "Scarf thief."

"You know, it's probably got cat fur on it. If you want, I think I've got one of those lint rollers in my car—"

"It's fine," I cut him off. "I think I've got one."

"It's no problem."

"I'm good, really," I say and awkwardly stick my hand into the car and toss the scarf over my headrest and onto the back seat. "Thanks for finding it."

Then we stare at each other, and I've suddenly forgotten how to gracefully exit a conversation. Can I just, like, point some finger guns, get into the car, and drive off? Is that better or worse than *this is too hard*?

He shoves his hands into his pockets, and it's unfair that he's pretty like this, his hair loose and his coat open, under the ugly parking lot lights. I think, briefly, of Bart and the mistletoe and all the signals that I apparently misread.

Behind me, Bastien clears his throat, and oh *fuck*, they're both standing next to the car, watching us like we're a mildly interesting weather report.

"Right. That's all. See you around, I guess?" Javi says,

and then he turns and walks away. His siblings are both watching me across the roof of the car, wearing the exact same expression, and I choose to ignore it.

"They're probably done with Monopoly by now, right?" I ask, and both of them sigh.

# TWENTY-FIVE

## JAVIER

THE EVENING AFTER COSMIC BOWLING, I'm over at Silas's because he told us to come over, eat leftover Christmas cookies, and hang out.

I *wanted* to head up to my cabin in Wildwood after my shift at the florist tonight because I've got the day off tomorrow. But since I'm a responsible adult who doesn't disappear for no reason, I told Wyatt what I was planning and he pointed out that there'd been a huge snowstorm two days ago, there was no way the road to Wildwood was clear yet, and we *literally* knew someone who was stuck in a cabin in the mountains because of the snow. Thank god for Wyatt because I'd replayed the Worst Fist Bump in the History of Celebratory Gestures so many times that I kind of forgot that Gideon was still up there, counting birds and rescuing damsels in distress.

Or...something. All I know is he rescued a woman who was chained to a tree and now he's being real fuckin' cagey about it.

"So," Lainey's voice says behind me as I'm staring into Silas's fridge, looking for a soda behind the beers. Would anyone notice if I just grabbed one? This is exactly the kind of situation where people drink and then feel better, I'm pretty sure. And it's not like booze was *really* the problem.

"So." I finally spot a cherry soda way in the back. I'm not in the mood for everyone to *look* at me tonight. Also, I only just convinced them that they were allowed to drink casually around me, and like hell I'm gonna go back to square one.

"You want to talk about it?"

I twist off the cap, open Silas's trash—it's in a drawer because he's fancy—and take a long swig before I answer her.

"Talk about what?"

"Ah." She nods. "You're gonna be like that. Cool."

"I'm not being like anything."

Lainey scrunches her face in an *are you sure about that?* kind of way and takes a sip of what I'm pretty sure is red wine in a whiskey tumbler.

"Shit," I mutter.

"Wyatt mentioned that he basically had to tackle you and pin you to the floor to keep you from driving up a mountain in the snow today," she says. "Though I'm glad you told him you were gonna go. Good progress."

"One, I don't need 'good progress' from *you*," I grump, and Lainey laughs at me. "Two, he wishes he could pin me down and keep me from doing anything."

"Was it family stuff?" she asks, grinning like I didn't just tell her off a little bit. "That's always a mind fuck at the holidays. One year my dad's older sister insulted my mom's potatoes and my dad was pretty much ready to fight for her honor. Words were *had*. We were nearly asked to leave."

I've met Lainey's parents once, briefly, and her dad is a very amiable older Black man who wears glasses and has a moustache. I can't quite imagine him throwing down over a side dish.

"What kind of potatoes?" I ask.

"Mashed," she says. "My mom tried a new recipe that deviated from the one passed down by my grandmother, which was practically Scripture, so people got mad. Mainly my aunt." She looks over her shoulder, toward the door to the living room where everyone else is doing whatever they're doing, and leans in toward me. "She *baked* them first, instead of boiling."

"Heresy," I agree. "Were they good?"

"They were mashed potatoes, so, yes," Lainey says. "Point being, every family is crazy once you dig a little, so don't worry about it."

I think about it for a moment. Lainey is literally a therapist—she works mostly with teenagers, I think, but still—and she would probably not judge me for banging my stepsister. And she would probably not tell Wyatt. And it's tempting, *so* tempting, to just tell someone the truth after all these months. Even Castillo only knows half of it.

I don't, though.

"They're a lot," I say, which is completely true. "And, you know, my mom's really been through it in the past few years, and she's getting remarried, and that's an adjustment and all. And even though I don't live at home or anything, it's going to be a little weird to have a stepdad and a stepsister."

"Do you get along?"

She has no idea. "They're great," I say, which is an understatement. "It's just weird, not to mention I don't think my father is taking it very well." He texted me a few times: *Merry Christmas*, which I also sent back, and then *Have you thought about your college options?*

I didn't respond to that last one, and I feel shitty about it, too. Not as shitty as I feel about other things, but shitty because it is, technically, a nice offer he's making.

"Divorce is hard, even for adult children," she says, nodding. "Even though it's not quite as destabilizing as it might be if you were younger, it's still a big change in the family unit. It's okay if it takes time to settle into a new normal."

I stare at her for a long moment. She's right, obviously, but come *on*.

"Did you just *therapize* me?"

"You needed it," she says, primly, cupping both hands around her wine in a whiskey glass.

"I did not."

"*All* y'all need therapy, for starters." She gestures with the glass in a way I assume means *everyone currently under this roof*. "And *some* of you need a friendly professional to tell you that feelings are normal, you're allowed to have them, and having them isn't gonna send you running for the nearest pill bottle."

"I do *not* have feelings."

"This is exactly my point."

There's a part of me that wants to tell her off, not least because ever since I've known Wyatt, he's been looking at Lainey with the world's most obvious giant sad-puppy heart eyes, and she keeps leading him on and never reciprocating. It's not like she owes him anything, obviously—I'm not an *actual* caveman, even if I was raised by one—but at some point it would be nice if she stopped stomping on his heart all the time.

I'd probably dislike her on principle, except she's also awesome. So I settle for just wishing Wyatt could move on.

Case in point, she then says: "It's been three years, right? The nineteenth?"

"Wyatt told you?"

"It's on the calendar in his kitchen," she says. "*Javi*, next to a sparkly gold star. I figured that was you. Did you celebrate?"

"Not as much as I probably should have," I admit and can't quite make eye contact with her. It's easy for people to say *You should celebrate not fucking up for three years!* and harder to accept that three years of the bare minimum is something to celebrate. "We went over to Gideon's and ate the Christmas cookies that Reid made."

I'd also meant to go to a meeting that week, but they're not that frequent, and the closest one is kind of a long drive, and they've never really...felt like my thing. For a long time I went anyway, but after I met Silas and moved to Sprucevale, skipping them didn't feel quite so bad.

"Were they good cookies?"

"Of course."

"Three years is a lot, and anyone who says it isn't doesn't know what they're talking about." Suddenly Lainey's all intense, staring me down, both hands holding the glass in front of her. I'm literally a foot taller than she is, and it's still intimidating. It's probably the same look she gives to all the Amazons on the derby track right before she whips past them. "That *includes* you."

"I'm positive I just told you not to therapize me."

"I'm positive you haven't told me what's really going on." She finishes off her wine, puts the glass in the sink, and then comes over to put a hand on my shoulder. "Not that you have to. But consider that you've got friends who like you a lot. Like, I'm pretty sure Wyatt would help you hide a body."

"I swear I haven't killed anyone, Lainey."

"Speaking of which," she says and points at me like she's just had an idea. "One of his redneck cousins has recently come into possession of a haunted-ass abandoned barn full of haunted-ass abandoned tractors, and I know you love that shit."

She does, in fact, have my number.

"Thanks, Lainey," I say, and she walks out of the kitchen.

# TWENTY-SIX

## JAVIER

"I'LL BE THERE IN TEN," I say, not bothering with *hello*. I'm already late to dinner and Family Game Night at my mom and Gerald's rental, so it's not really a mystery why she's calling.

"What? Where? Do you know where she is?"

"Who? Thalia?"

My mom loves to lead with a rhetorical question when she's calling to complain to me about a sibling.

"Madeline!"

My heart gives an involuntary kick.

"No, where is she?" I ask as I pull my shitty, paint-stained shirt off and paw through a drawer for something more presentable. Vaguely, I wonder where Madeline could be that my mom's calling to complain about it. A Satanic ritual sacrifice, maybe?

"I don't know! That's why I called to ask you. To see if you know where Madeline is," my mom says.

I swallow and hope she can't hear it, one hand on my phone and the other tight around a black T-shirt. "No, I don't." My voice sounds calmer than I feel. "Why? Is everything okay?"

"She was supposed to be back an hour ago," my mom says. "The other day Gerald and I went to dinner and Gerald fell in love with—I don't know, some red wine, but everywhere in town is out of stock and I wanted to surprise him, so Madeline volunteered to drive out to the winery…"

My mom keeps talking, and I turn to look out the windows. It's completely dark outside because it's—shit—nearly six. I'd only meant to work on some papier-mâché experiments for a possible art project until four or four thirty, but now I'm late and Madeline is…also late.

Madeline is late and my mom thinks I might know where she is, and that combination has my lungs in a vise.

"I'm sure she hit traffic somewhere," I say.

"She would call."

"Maybe she's out of cell range?"

"How would she be in traffic for this long? What traffic?"

I pull my shirt over my head and run a hand through my hair. My heart's pounding. "Wyatt's got a long story about being stuck in a traffic jam behind a rogue cow once when he was in high school," I say. "Maybe there's a cow?"

"He says maybe there's a cow." My mom's voice is a little distant, like she's pulled the phone away from her face. I rub my knuckles across my forehead because that's not what I said, *Mom*, I was trying to give an example of why she might be perfectly fine, but I don't start that argument now.

"A cow?" Gerald is saying, and yeah, he sounds pretty bad.

"Mom, I'm coming over." I grab a sweater off a pile on my bedroom floor. "Don't do anything before I get there, okay?"

225

"—supposed to go down into the twenties tonight—"

"Okay, see you soon," my mom says. Before she hangs up, I hear, "Gerald, stop *pacing*. Javi is coming over, and he's familiar with—"

I put on shoes, a coat, and practically run out the door, but as I start my car I wonder if this is the first time my mom has ever sounded relieved about my participation.

· · ★ ★ ★ **★** ★ ★ ★ · ·

"THAT'S NOT A PROBLEM," I'm saying for, I think, the fifth or sixth time. "I'm borrowing a vehicle with four-wheel drive."

"But what if *you* get stuck?" Gerald asks, pacing back and forth in front of the kitchen island. "Or what if it's worse? What if she stumbled across some sort of—illegal activity or she was carjacked or she's been carjacked by the gun-running drug gangs—"

"Gerald," my mom says gently. It's a little odd, watching her be the calm one. "I think we're getting ahead of ourselves. Chances are she drove into a ditch and we'll hear from her any minute now."

"Sorry. I know." He tries to smile at her. There's a noise outside, the rustling of tree branches near a window, and Gerald practically jumps. It's spooky. I get it. "Javier, you said you'd done research into the rum-running routes through the mountains?"

It wasn't research so much as it was an after-midnight rabbit hole I fell down. I probably shouldn't have mentioned it.

"I think we should focus on real roads first," I say, and he just nods, still pacing. "My friend with the truck will be here in a few minutes, and we'll drive the route between here and the winery. She'll probably call you to say she's fine before we're five minutes down the road."

Sometimes I feel like I have all the wrong emotions. By rights, I should probably be more anxious that we don't know where Madeline is. After all, I've probably got the best idea out of all of us of all the terrible things that could happen. Steep hills, iced-over hairpin turns, mountain lions, bears, rednecks. And of course I'm worried—the thought of her hurt makes my spine turn to ice—but there's something about emergencies that transforms me from Javier, General Disaster, to Javier, Natural Born Leader.

"Should we call the police?" he asks.

"They're already keeping an eye out," my mom answers. To put it mildly, the Burnley County Sherriff's Department wasn't yet concerned about an adult woman being late to dinner, even if her father swore she was never late.

The room goes quiet for a few moments, and then we all startle when there's a knock on the door. Wyatt comes in, and Gerald practically sags with relief.

"You're the young man with the truck? Good," he says, then goes on before Wyatt can even respond, pulling out a road map of the county. "I've marked our current location in red and her destination in green. Now, as you can see, there are several different routes available, but I think this is the most likely, based on the directions Google Maps gives."

Wyatt is nodding along, very serious. I've already heard this at least twice in the fifteen minutes I've been here.

"Now, Madeline is—sometimes she likes to take a scenic route, even if it's inefficient," Gerald says. "And, you know, if there's the world's largest ball of yarn or something down one of these roads, then go there first because she could never resist—"

Gerald's phone rings, and he jumps so hard it flies off the counter.

"Is it—" he starts, but Bastien's already grabbed it off the floor, and Gerald looks at the screen in horror, then stabs it twice before it connects.

"Sweetheart," he says in a rush. "Are you all right? Where are you? Is everything okay?"

# TWENTY-SEVEN

## MADELINE

THE VERY NICE on-call doctor is trying to keep me from seeing the needle, but it's not working. It's sharp, shiny, curved, and *right there*.

"I'm never using Google Maps again," I say. "I promise."

"It doesn't usually steer people quite this wrong." I'm pretty sure the doctor, an older Black woman, is laughing at me behind her mask. "I think this is the first time I've had to give someone stitches because of bad directions."

"A little common sense does go a long way, kiddo." My dad squeezes my hand. There's still blood under my fingernails and in my cuticles, which is gross, but he clearly doesn't care.

"Dirt roads are very normal around here," I say as the doctor prods my forehead with her fingertips. I don't feel anything. "It didn't seem weird that it was telling me to drive on one."

"The county should probably contact Google and see if they'll take it off," the doctor says. "All right. Close your eyes and take a deep breath—you may feel a pinch."

I do, and my dad squeezes my hand again. Then I feel

what I can only describe as a hard tug on my skin, and I'm *very* glad I can't see what's happening.

"Wow," my dad says.

"Don't watch," I beg.

"It's kind of fascinating, actually," he says, and then, to the doctor: "You're very good at this."

"I've stitched up a whole lotta people," she says. "Plenty of them much worse than this. You're a cakewalk."

"You hear that? I'm a cakewalk," I tell my dad and then flinch when the needle hits some skin the novocaine didn't reach.

"Sorry," she murmurs. "Three more."

Getting five stitches in my forehead is, actually, not how I was expecting my day to end. My dad, Paloma, and Bastien were starting to drive me a little crazy in the cabin, and Paloma was making noises about some wine that my dad liked, so I volunteered to drive to a winery to buy some. It was ten percent out of the goodness of my heart and ninety percent to get out of the house and be alone for a while. Maybe play some sad loud music and shout along because I'm still stuck here for a few more days, constantly seeing a man who thinks that hooking up sometimes is *too hard*.

Which just means he doesn't like me, right? I'm pretty sure it's that simple.

Anyway, Google Maps is a filthy lying liar that directed me down a dirt "road" through the forest, where I promptly swerved to avoid a giant pothole and slid into a ditch. Then, when I got out of the car to see if I could fix it, I slipped on some ice and sliced my forehead open on a rock. Luckily while I was standing there bleeding, a handful of Starbucks napkins pressed to my head, some teenagers in an ancient Ford Explorer came along. I think they were planning to park somewhere and fool around, but they were nice enough to take me to the emergency room instead.

All around, a *wonderful* day to cap off a wonderful week.

"Do I look like Frankenstein?" I ask when she's done and snapping off her gloves.

"Of course not." My dad leans over, peering at me. "But you do look like Frankenstein's *monster*."

I narrow my eyes at him for a moment, which is weird because I can't feel about half my forehead. I'm pretty sure the doctor is trying not to laugh.

"Your only child is in the *emergency room* getting *stitches*," I say. "And you're being pedantic about literature?"

My dad sighs, then smiles. Then starts laughing.

Then he doesn't *stop* laughing, and he's taking his glasses off and wiping his eyes with one hand because he's still holding mine with the other. There's a slight hysterical edge to the laughter, which I guess is only fair.

"I'm so glad you're all right," he says. "I was so worried."

· · · ✦ ★ ★ ★ ✦ · · ·

WHEN I WALK into the waiting room forty-five minutes later, I've got a giant bandage on my forehead, dried blood in my hair, and on my shirt and pants. I've also got a hefty printout about wound care and another hefty printout about concussion protocol even though they said I "most likely" don't have one. My dad is carrying my winter coat, which also has some blood on it.

Naturally, Javier is there.

He stands back as Paloma wraps me in a big hug, pulls me into the light so she can see better, and then frowns over my injury.

"Another victim of Google Maps," my dad says, which obviously doesn't explain anything to anyone.

As we walk out and into the parking lot, Javier falls in next to me. He looks the same as the last time I saw him—coat open, hands in pockets—but I can feel him studying my face as we walk.

"I know—I look like Frankenstein's monster," I say, because all the adrenaline wore off long ago and my dad's car is still in a ditch on a dirt road somewhere and I'm exhausted. I'll have feelings tomorrow. Right now all I feel is a little hollow, like an indentation waiting to be filled. "That's my Halloween costume next year sorted, I guess."

He clears his throat and looks forward again. "Right," he says. "That's a good one."

"I'm a believer in using what you have," I say, and *then* I remember last Halloween. When we traded pictures. And I sent him a mildly slutty one that he never responded to. God, I've never taken a hint in my *life*. "And I'll have a cool scar along with a new respect for dirt roads."

He laughs softly, and we walk in silence after that. It's cold and windy when we leave the hospital through its sliding glass doors, and inanely, I wish I'd worn my scarf today.

"Hey," he says suddenly, and when I glance over, he's—intense. All dark eyes and sharp cheekbones. Did he look tired like this the last time I saw him? Did he have stubble? "I'm glad you're okay."

He stops walking, and so do I. We're next to a bench and a flowerbed full of dead plants. Our parents are up ahead, leaning into each other as they head for the car.

"I was worried." He takes a half step closer. "I don't know what—"

He cuts himself off, looks away, and I'm tired and bloody

and he broke up with me a couple days ago, so I say nothing. Just let him talk.

"I would hate it if something happened to you." His voice so low it's almost a whisper. "I don't want that."

Javi's got this intense look in his eyes, his hair blowing over his face and his coat collar up like a Victorian vampire or some shit. But we're in the parking lot of a hospital, fluorescent lights buzzing above us, and whatever Javier thinks he's saying to me right now, I'm out. I'm tired and hurt and gross and I'm just—out.

"Yeah, that would've sucked," I say, turn, and follow our parents to the car.

# TWENTY-EIGHT

## JAVIER

NO ONE at the rental cabin is awake when I drop off
Gerald's car in the morning, so I put the keys under the door
mat and get back into Wyatt's waiting truck. I probably owe
both him and Silas a fruit basket or a spa retreat or something for getting up before dawn to help me pull Gerald's
car out of a ditch. I can't do much to make Madeline feel
better, and God knows I can't make her like me back, but I
know people with trucks.

"Back to yours?" he asks, already reversing.

"Yeah," I say. "Thanks for helping me out."

"All I did was follow Silas's instructions. Exactly how
many cars has he driven into ditches?"

"There are questions I don't ask."

"I heard some story about him and a football," Wyatt
says.

There's a long, long silence.

"I don't know where I was going with that. I think he ran
off the road because of a football? When he was in high
school?"

"Sounds right," I say and lapse into silence. The sun is

just barely cresting over the trees. I'm tired because I got up before dawn, but I drank three cups of coffee so I'm also way too awake. It's a rough combination.

We're quiet all the way to my apartment, but before I can open the door Wyatt suddenly clears his throat.

"Hey. Listen, you know you can talk to me, right? About anything?"

It's way too early for a conversation about feelings or fucking up or anything else, but Wyatt's one of those *morning people*.

"Thanks, but I'm fine," I say, and hope it sounds convincing.

"I'm not saying you're not fine," he goes on, and this sounds a little like...he's practiced? "I'm saying that I'm— part of your support system, and I want to support you."

We look at each other, and I think: *aw, fuck.*

"I haven't even had a sip of beer in months," I tell him, my voice coming out more tired and ragged than I feel. "I promise, there are plenty of people I can talk to. I still go to meetings sometimes. I've got plenty of resources..."

"That's not what I'm worried about."

"Then it probably should be." It's out of my mouth before I can stop it, but fuck it, I'm right. No one ever says *Yeah, you'll probably relapse again* out loud, but I can feel it lurking behind every careful conversation I have. The worst part is that everyone is right to worry about it. I worry about it. How could I not?

"Can I decide that?"

I almost say no, but I swallow it instead. "Sorry."

"No, you're fine. It's just—" He takes his hands off the wheel and scrubs them over his face, and now I feel bad for snapping at him. "That was a weird way for me to say that we're friends and if you want to talk to me about how your

235

family is driving you up the fucking wall, you can." He gives me a tired but jaunty little half smile. "That's all I meant."

I blow out an exhale and tilt my head against the headrest because he's half-right, actually. Maybe three-quarters. And thank god he essentially said *Your family is nuts* and not *Have you been fucking your stepsister? You seem like you've been fucking your stepsister.*

"They can be a lot," I say.

"You have tells," he agrees, and then I complain about my family for the next five minutes while he nods.

· · * * ★ ★ ★ * * · ·

NINE HOURS LATER, I'm back at the vacation rental with a thousand-piece puzzle, a box of Abuelita, a box of candy canes, and some cookies that Wyatt's mom brought by my receptionist job and informed me I was taking to my poor stepsister who trusted her GPS, bless her heart.

"Those are *not* for you," I tell Bastien when he reaches for the third one.

"You just said they're for everyone."

"Yeah, so let everyone have a chance!"

"There are..." He starts counting. "Still twenty-three left, and I bet you've already had a couple—"

He reaches for another one, and this time I smack his hand.

"Ow! What the fuck?"

"*Bastien.* Language," my mom says from across the kitchen, and he rolls his eyes at me.

"Javi hit me!"

"Javier, don't hit your brother."

"He's eating Madeline's cookies!" I shout, and Bastien's eyebrows fly up his forehead. "Not like that," I grumble.

"*Madeline's* cookies," he says, sotto voce, just to me.

"They're from Wyatt's mom," I say because surely, that will help. "She heard that Madeline was in the ER, so, cookies."

"There're cookies?" says Madeline's voice, and I turn. She's coming down the stairs in flannel pajama pants and a blue hoodie, with a bandage on her forehead and another on her right hand. She looks like she just woke up.

"It's really chivalrous that you're defending her cookies," Bastien mutters, just loud enough that no one but me can hear it.

"Shut *up*," I hiss.

"Javier told me to shut up!" he calls over his shoulder, and my mom turns toward us.

"You're grown men!" she says, exasperated. "Work it out!"

"Am I interrupting something?" Madeline asks, coming up to stand catty-corner from me at the kitchen island.

"Not at *all*." Bastien smiles dickishly. "Here, Javi saved these for you."

"Wyatt's mom heard you got injured, so she came by my work and gave me cookies to give to you," I explain while I also try to kill Bastien with my mind. "They're chocolate chip."

"Wow, news travels fast," she says, taking one. She stands ramrod straight and considers the cookie for a moment before taking a bite.

"It's a small town," I say, shrugging. Now doesn't seem like the time to mention that, actually, *the blue-haired girl who followed GPS instructions instead of common sense drove into a ditch and had to get stitches* is the biggest story in Sprucevale at the moment.

"So everyone knows I'm the dumbass who drove off a

road?" She covers her face with her hands. "Sorry. I'm just..."

Bastien reaches out and claps her on the shoulder. "We've got, like, two more days here," he says. "Buck up."

"You can say that because you don't look like a horror icon."

"You're more *Bride of Frankenstein* than *Frankenstein's Monster*, though, and Javi used to think she was a total smokeshow."

"When have I *ever* said that?" I ask, and Bastien grins, probably because I'm blushing now. I redouble my attempts at mind-murder.

"Every time it came on TV at Halloween? I think you were especially into her unusual hair."

Madeline is no longer making eye contact with anyone but the kitchen counter, and I would personally love to fall through a trapdoor and into the basement, ideally taking my brother with me.

"How are they?" I ask Madeline instead, because I'll make any kind of boring conversation to make Bastien stop acting like I'm a high school kid with a crush.

"They're good," she answers and gives us both an attempted smile. One hand is resting on the counter, bandaged, where I guess she scraped it on the gravel when she also hit her head.

"Great." I nearly say *They're from Wyatt's mom* again, because I'm very good at conversations. She finishes it off.

"I'm gonna go attempt a shower so I can finally get the blood out of my hair and be one percent less horrifying." She tries to make it sound like a joke but doesn't quite succeed. "I'll be back in, like, two hours."

"Take a cookie with you!" Bastien shoves the plate at

her. Madeline grabs another one, holds it up, attempts another smile, and leaves.

As soon as she's gone, I turn to Bastien, both hands flat on the countertop, and lean in as aggressively as I can.

"What the fuck?" I hiss, and my asshole brother just snorts.

"Your thing for her is cute."

"There is no *thing*," I lie, and he has the nerve to burst out laughing.

"You can't think I believe that!" he crows. "What the hell, dude. I have *eyes*—"

"Would you just shut the fuck up about it?" I say, hoping my mom can't hear. "It's not a big deal, okay—just *stop*."

We stare at each other for a minute, which is just long enough for my mom to come over and grab a cookie.

"Are you two fighting?" she asks around a mouthful of chocolate chip. "Does one of you need a time out?"

"No," we say in unison, and my mom shrugs.

# TWENTY-NINE

## MADELINE

I'M WALKING QUIETLY DOWN the stairs, carrying what might be the entire Band-Aid selection from the nearest drugstore, when Javi walks past on the floor below. I stop so fast it's probably comical, one foot suspended in the air and everything. I quietly hope he doesn't notice me and goes on with his usual evening plans for hassling Bastien or doing a puzzle or whatever his deal is.

Obviously, I then drop a box of fingertip Band-Aids (why, Dad?), and it bounces down the stairs because sometimes my life is a screwball comedy.

Javi turns, and then we're staring at each other for what feels like the fiftieth time in five days. Him in a black T-shirt and jeans ripped at one knee, hair down, looking unfairly hot. Me in pajamas and a hoodie, cradling an unreasonable number of Band-Aid boxes, looking like I just woke up from a nap. Which I did.

"Oh. Hey." He bends to pick up the Band-Aids I dropped. "These are great," he says, looking at the box.

"Yeah, they're pretty good," I agree, coming down the stairs until we're face-to-face, both looking at a box of fingertip Band-Aids like it's the Rosetta Stone. "I got some a couple months ago when I sliced my finger pretty hard cutting up bell peppers. Really kept my wound covered while it healed."

There's a brief silence, probably because this is a terrible conversation.

"I'm not really sure why my dad got them? My fingertips are, like, the one part of my body that's fine right now, actually. It's everything else that hurts. I'm just taking them all downstairs so I've got the widest possible selection."

He nods once. "Here," he says and then takes all the Band-Aid boxes from my arms before I can fight him about it. One of them falls, and I manage to pick that one up, at least. "Where are we going?" he asks, looking at the assortment in his hands. "And why's there a knee brace?"

"I can get those myself," I say, and I'm not quite too out of it to be annoyed.

"I know."

I have this brief flash of this morning, when I walked into the kitchen around nine, groggy and out of it, to find my dad extolling Javier's car-rescuing virtues to my mom. I had to leave without coffee and tiptoe back later because I couldn't handle hearing all that about this stupid, sweet man who can pull cars out of ditches at dawn but not sneak around a little.

Maybe I had him clocked all wrong. Maybe he found religion or something and decided that he's too good and virtuous to keep lying to his family about me.

"Thanks," I finally say, because if he wants to carry Band-Aids for me, *fine*. "I was heading this way."

· · · ★ ★ ★ ★ · · ·

"YOU HAVE TO DO IT FAST," he's telling me. "There's a whole saying about this."

"Stop telling me what to do," I grumble. "Some of it's on my hair, okay? I don't want to yank my hair out with it—"

He reaches over and grabs a hair clip off the counter. "Can I?" he asks, holding it up.

I'm sitting on the counter of the vanity in this house's downstairs bathroom. The bathroom is huge and fancy, with a glass-enclosed shower, a huge jacuzzi tub, a towel warmer, and the kind of fancy lighting I might kill for in my own bathroom. If I got ready in this bathroom, I'd probably wear blush and highlighter because they'd *never* come out looking weird. It's that nice.

I want Javier to leave this bathroom so I can suffer alone and not have to deal with him being a fundamentally nice person even if we're not sleeping together, but slightly more than that, I want him to stay. I sigh and take my hands off the huge bandage on my forehead. "Yeah," I say.

He puts the clip between his teeth before I close my eyes, and I sit very, very still as he runs his fingers through my hair, then clips it back off my face. I'm a mess right now because I didn't even shower last night, just crawled into bed and slept for twelve hours. The side of my face below the stitches is scraped up and a little bruised, I think there's dried blood in my eyebrow, and there's *definitely* dried blood in my hair.

"It's not too bad, only a little," he says, and I can feel him tugging at the edges of the bandage. "I'll try not to pull your hair out."

"Thanks," I say, and we lapse into silence again. I keep my eyes closed, but his hips are touching my knees and I can feel him leaning in. He's got careful, steady fingers as he pulls my hair free of the Band-Aid, and I wonder if this is what he's like when he's making something. Last year—not that I stalk him on the internet or anything—he had this series of bird sculptures at a gallery, all made from charred pieces of trees that had been struck by lightning. They were spooky and beautiful, and I wonder if he was this quiet and painstaking and intense when he was making them. I wonder if they turned his hands black.

"I think I got it all," he says and smooths a hand over my hair like he's petting me. I don't hate it. "Ready?" I hold my breath. "One, two—"

"Fuck, ow!" I say and clap a hand over my forehead. "Shit. Fuck. *Ow*. Dammit."

"It's over," he says, tossing the bandage into the trash. "See?"

I take my hand off my forehead, and as soon as I do, something drips down my face and onto my hoodie, and I've barely realized it's blood when Javi is leaning away and then has a wad of something to hold against my forehead.

"Sorry," he says. "I think some of the sticky part was stuck to the cut."

I pull the wad away a bit, turn, and look at myself in the (beautifully lit) mirror behind me. Blood starts trickling again, so I clap it back on.

"Is this toilet paper?"

"It was the first thing in reach," he says with one of those half smiles. We make eye contact in the mirror, and I tear off a little piece off to wipe the rest of the blood off my face. "Sorry," he murmurs.

"No, sorry for being gross," I say and turn back. "I'm fine. You can—"

"I've seen *much* worse." He's rifling through the drawers under the counter.

It takes me a second to remember that, right, he was in the Marines. What a thing for me to forget.

"I once watched someone fall off a balcony and break his leg so bad it came through the skin," he says, finally straightening up, washcloth in hand.

"Wow, Jesus."

"It was bad," he agrees, then glances at my face. "That's not a war story. He was high. Here, swap me."

I take the washcloth and put it on my forehead, tossing the wadded-up toilet paper into the trash. Javi looks like he's trying to decide whether or not to say something, and then: "I was also high, actually. Just lucky enough not to fall off a balcony. Or jump."

"And here I thought you were putting your medic training to work or something."

"Sorry to disappoint you," he says, like he's holding back a smile. "My ability to deal with a very small amount of blood and put a Band-Aid on a minor wound probably stems from having two younger siblings, not from being in the military. In the military I mostly dug latrines and tried to avoid getting shouted at." He cocks a hip against the counter and looks at me conspiratorially. "I wasn't a very good Marine."

"You don't really seem like the type," I admit, which— are people allowed to say that? Am I?

"Great, an insult to my patriotism *and* my masculinity."

"Okay, you *just* said—" But he's grinning, of course, so I use my non-washcloth hand to flip him off, and he laughs.

"There were good parts," he says. "But I also shattered my ankle, discovered Oxy, and never *did* get my father to respect me, so I may as well have gone to art school instead. Is that still bleeding?"

I pull the washcloth away, gently, and Javi seems satisfied.

"But then you'd probably have student loans," I point out.

"I *did* escape those."

Now he's holding up various Band-Aids to my forehead —judging their size against the gash, I think. I close my eyes again.

"I rushed a sorority my freshman year of college," I admit. He stills, and I open my eyes. "I got rejected. Same thing, right? If we're talking about things we probably shouldn't have done?"

He's so close, looking down at me from six inches away, maybe, and I realize that he's got dark circles under his eyes and a spot of stubble that he must have missed shaving.

"A *sorority*?" he asks. "Was it the art sorority or something?"

"It was Tau Zeta Phi, which was the hardest one to get into because it's the one all the popular, cool, pretty girls joined," I say. "I have no idea why I thought they'd take me."

"Well," he says, so softly I might have imagined it.

"I had a whole plan," I tell him. "It was written down and everything. Bullet pointed. *How to be cool and popular in college.*"

"Is that the kind of thing cool, popular people do?"

"I don't think so, but I was uncool and unpopular in high school, so it was worth a shot."

"Here," he says and steps even closer. At some point I moved my knees so he could step between them, and he's nerve-rackingly, breathtakingly close. I close my eyes and feel like my heartbeat must be echoing through the space between us, a constant refrain of *why this, why this*. "Hold still."

I'm a statue. A rock. I barely breathe while he presses the bandage over my wound, inhaling through my teeth when his fingers brush the gash itself through the Band-Aid.

"Sorry, sorry," he murmurs, fingertips light on my forehead, then barely skimming down my cheek. "There you go. Good as new."

"Javi."

"Better than ten minutes ago?"

"Thank you."

He doesn't move away, though, and I don't dare open my eyes. After a second, I realize that his hand is on my thigh, just above my knee, his heat soaking through my soft pajama pants. And I know, down to my bones, that if I do anything, I'll shatter the moment.

So I don't. I want to open my eyes and say *Isn't this harder?* But I don't. It's not like telling someone *I think you should feel the way about me that I feel about you* has ever changed their feelings.

"I'm glad you settled on this version of yourself," he says, his voice low and quiet. His thumb strokes across my thigh, once, then stops, like he was doing it without thinking. A shiver rolls down my spine. "It suits you."

I take a deep breath, then put my hand on his. If I leaned forward, I could kiss him probably, and it would feel like taking off a Band-Aid for days. I think about it anyway.

"I kind of wish you'd gone to art school," I say, and it breaks the tension because he snorts and gives my knee a friendly squeeze and then he steps back, tension shattered.

"Me, too, sometimes," he says and gives me a hand as I hop off the counter.

# THIRTY

## JAVIER

I COME by the next night, too, because Mom and Bastien are leaving soon, and it's good to spend time with your family while they're in town. Also, it's not like my place is a very good hangout spot for everyone. If I spend a while doing the puzzle with Madeline and making her Mexican hot chocolate with a candy cane in it, well, I'm just being friendly.

"You didn't even offer to make me hot chocolate," Bastien says as I'm putting mugs into the sink. "And put those in the dishwasher."

"You didn't ask!"

"Okay, well, I'm asking now. Next time you're standing over the stove, stirring milk for ten minutes—"

"It doesn't take *ten minutes*."

"—half-ass some for your favorite brother, too."

"It's a lost cause—he doesn't want to stick his candy cane into your..."

Bastien and I both turn toward Thalia, who's appeared in the kitchen. She's bright red. We're all dead silent.

"Never mind," she finally says. "I didn't think the end of that sentence through when I started it."

"You're both embarrassing," Bastien declares. He nods at Thalia. "You're gross." Then at me. "And you want to bang our stepsister."

"No, I don't," I say, pinching the bridge of my nose. Thalia snorts. "Shut up," I tell her, maturely.

"You know it's not *actually* weird, right?" she asks, hopping up to sit on the counter. "You're both adults. It's barely even scandalous."

"Do you seriously think Mom would find it *barely scandalous*?" I ask before I can think better of it.

Bastien's eyebrows fly up his forehead, and Thalia wrinkles her nose.

"She'd come around," she says, shrugging. "Eventually."

"That wasn't a denial," Bastien says. "Hold on, you just—"

A door shuts, and then Mom's and Gerald's voices start coming toward us. Thalia, Bastien, and I all shut up automatically. Thalia hops off the counter, and she and Bastien look at each other.

Then, with no warning *whatsoever*, Bastien lunges forward and puts me into a headlock.

"*Shut up shut up shut up,*" he hisses as I whisper-yelp, "*The fuck are you doing?*" and Thalia's behind us, shoving Bastien and muttering, "*Go, go, okay, turn left—*"

"*That's the bathroom!*"

"*I know it's the bathroom, just go!*"

"*Get off me!*"

I'm unceremoniously shoved into the downstairs bathroom, and before I can turn around, there's the click of a lock and both my siblings are standing in front of the door like they're guarding it.

I wish I'd been an only child. Madeline seems well-adjusted, and no one is dragging her into bathrooms by her neck.

"What the hell?" I ask, because we've gotta start somewhere.

"This is an intervention," Thalia says. "You obviously have a thing for Madeline, and we're going to help."

"No, I don't, and no, you're not," I say, folding my arms over my chest. I wish it were just Bastien in front of the door, because I don't mind wrestling him. I'd feel bad doing that to my sister, though.

"You just *said* that the problem was Mom finding out—"

"That was an example of a possible problem."

"No, that was you finally admitting—"

"I'm not admitting anything!"

Bastien rubs his hands over his face. "Look, okay, I'm sorry for teasing you," he says, which I wasn't expecting. I relax a little. "But I can't keep waiting for you two to start making out on the couch, and it's starting to get awkward for us."

"Wow, sorry," I say.

"Thank you."

I take a deep breath. Maybe I can reason my way out of this bathroom? Does that work with siblings? "Look. I'm not into her as anything other than a completely platonic friend and stepsibling, and she *definitely* isn't into me as anything but that, so can you please let it go?"

"Wait," says Thalia, and now she's frowning. "Did Madeline say something to you?"

"I'll have words. I don't care if she's family," Bastien adds.

I look from one to the other, both in front of the bathroom door, their *I'll fight anyone* faces in full swing because

I insinuated that someone doesn't like me back. Shit. They've figured it out, right? I've probably lied to them enough for a lifetime, right?

"Okay, okay, fine," I say. "We hooked up a couple of times, but I called it off after— Why do you *look* like that?"

"You slept together!?"

"*A couple of times?*"

Shit. SHIT. The bathroom goes dead silent. The only sound is Mom and Gerald chatting in the kitchen. Is this what hell feels like? Am I dead right now?

"What did you drag me in here for?" I hiss-whisper.

"To talk about your huge, obvious crush on our stepsister!" Bastien hiss-whispers back.

"I was gonna tell you to ask her out!" Thalia adds. "To coffee! Or dinner! Or drinks! But you've already—" She waves her hands in a gesture that I guess means *had sexual relations*, and I cover my face in my hands. Jesus Christ, I want to rewind this conversation by about thirty seconds.

"Look," I say as calmly as I possibly can, though I might be shaking with adrenaline and I'm positive I'm bright red. "It's not some perverted taboo incest thing. We met a few years ago."

"*Met,*" Thalia says.

"And by *met* you mean—"

"Yes! Jesus, could you not—"

"I am *trying* to keep my *facts* straight, you secret-keeping sneaky bastard," Bastien sniffs.

"I was supposed to just *tell you?*"

"Yes! Also can I point out that I literally just suggested you ask her out on a date," Thalia says. "*Clearly* I'm not judging your penchant for keeping it in the family."

"At least she's not your calculus professor," Bastien adds, and now Thalia turns to him.

"That is *not* the issue at hand," she says. "Also, it worked out fine, okay?"

"Is there any sort of award for having the least scandalous sex life?" Bastien asks, addressing the ceiling or perhaps God himself. "Maybe it comes with a lifetime supply of vanilla?"

"What would you do with a lifetime supply of vanilla?" I ask. "Have you ever used vanilla?"

"I make cookies sometimes," he says, offended. "And sometimes I add it to a protein shake for a little extra—"

"*Anyway,* you're fucking our stepsister," Thalia interrupts.

"No, because we called it off after—uh, a few days ago, which I *already told you if you would listen.*"

They make more faces.

"A few days?"

"You didn't say a few days ago," Bastien agrees. "I thought you meant, like, months."

"Years," offers Thalia. "Where did you two sneak off to on Christmas?"

Bastien looks horrified. "Did you go—"

"No! No, I showed her Wells's giant skeleton," I say. "Come *on.*"

"I can't tell if that's a euphemism," my brother says to Thalia.

"No, the giant skeleton is real," she replies. "One of his weird friends has it in his front yard because of...the first amendment, or something."

"It's to annoy his asshole neighbor," I clarify.

"So, you stopped fucking and now you're just walking around making sad heart eyes at each other," Bastien says. "I feel like there's an obvious solution here."

"We're not making sad heart eyes," I protest, even

though I know it's pointless. Their pitying stares are identical.

I take a deep breath, rub my hands over my face, and wonder if there's some way I can escape through the bathtub drain. "She's not making heart eyes."

They look at each other. I don't like it.

"Madeline has been very clear that she wants to keep things casual." I am calm and quiet and totally in control of this situation. "Wanted. When there were things to keep casual. The things that have now concluded. *What,*" I say when Thalia literally raises her hand.

"You said she's been clear about keeping things casual?" she asks, because of course Thalia is going to question every step of this process like it's undergoing peer review.

"Yes."

"Clear how? Did she say that with words?"

"Yes," I say. Which is basically true.

"Recently? What exactly did she say when she broke things off at Christmas?"

This conversation is starting to feel less like an intervention and more like walking down a staircase that's crumbling behind me. I know what's happening, but I keep going.

"Technically, I broke things off at Christmas and she agreed."

I do not like the silence that follows.

"But she's told you, in those words, that she wants to keep it casual," Thalia presses on, because my stupid sister doesn't know when to quit.

Of course Madeline has literally told me she wants to keep it casual. She said so at—well, she didn't *say* that at Christmas, she just...agreed. And the thing with the air mattress earlier this year was clear as day, but technically it wasn't words.

My siblings look at each other again, which I wish they'd stop doing.

"Have *you* used *your* words?" Bastien asks, like Thalia's handed off the interrogation. "Like, does she know you're ready to go full *ballads under her window in the moonlight with a rose in your teeth* about her?"

"How am I singing a ballad if I've got a rose in my—"

"I take *one* poetic license—"

"So, no?" Thalia cuts in.

"Technically, no, and also I don't even want to sing ballads!" I say. I'd probably sing ballads. "But I don't need—"

"You're so dumb," Thalia says, then turns to our brother. "Bastien, he's so dumb."

"It doesn't matter!" I say, and sit on the edge of the jacuzzi tub behind me, my elbows on my knees, face in my hands. "Even if you're right, Mom would freak out, and our whole extended family would have some sort of collective gossip panic party and never shut up, and—I can't *do* that to her. I've pulled way too much shit in the past couple of years—"

"Be fair. Thalia's also pulled some shit," Bastien offers.

"I can't ruin this for her," I say. "Mom deserves a good husband like Gerald and a normal wedding and to not have to deal with my shit for once."

"So tell her after the wedding," Thalia says, like it's an obvious, practical solution that's just that easy. "Telling her might make the wedding weird, but she's not gonna divorce Gerald just because you're fucking his daughter."

"I'm *not* telling her we're fucking."

Thalia rolls her eyes so hard it practically makes a sound. "Obviously. Tell her you're *dating*. She's still hoping that Bastien gets his first kiss someday."

"She's not *that* bad," says Bastien.

"I also hope Bastien meets a nice boy and finally gets his first kiss," I offer.

"We're rooting for you," Thalia adds.

"Okay, fuck you *both*. I've had sex before. I just choose appropriate partners, and no one has to go DEFCON Five over it!"

"Five's the lowest," I tell him. He flips me off.

"But when are you going to bring someone home to Mom? She'd love grandchildren," Thalia says and makes a face. Bastien groans, tilting his head back against the door.

"Did you know she sends me *every* gay marriage article she comes across? The last one was about some artist who does custom cake toppers so you can get two grooms," he says.

"You're the one who wanted a prize for having the least scandalous sex life," I point out. "Congrats."

"Great. So, you're going to use your words and stop making the rest of us suffer?" Thalia says, like she's summarizing this sibling fight.

I glare at them. It has no effect whatsoever, but neither did telling them that I know what happened, okay, and would they please stay out of my business?

"Sure," I say, because I'm under duress.

We get into another whisper-fight over leaving the bathroom. Mom eyes us suspiciously but doesn't seem interested in asking questions. Which is for the best because between the three of us, I'm pretty sure we'd accidentally tell her everything.

· · · · · ★ ★ ★ ★ · · · ·

THAT NIGHT, I lay in bed, staring at the ceiling in my apartment. It doesn't have the best insulation, given its former life as a lumber warehouse or something, but I've got three blankets, a space heater, and Zorro in his spot, tucked up against my side. Every time I try to get more comfortable, he grumbles at me.

It's cozy. It's warm. The space heater even makes some nice white noise, but I still can't sleep.

"It's easy for *them*," I finally tell the cat. "They weren't there. 'Oh, Javi, just use your words. It's so simple!'" I say in a very bad imitation of my sister.

Zorro doesn't react. I don't think he even wakes up. I scratch the top of his head and try not to think, but of course I do. I think about her grumbling about ripping off Band-Aids, apologizing about blood, saying I don't seem like the military type. Like I'm—fragile or delicate. Like I need to be handled with care or I'll break. I should hate it, probably; an old, almost-buried part of me knows that.

But it's not that small or that simple, is it? Everyone I've ever known is fragile sometimes; the people who wind up breaking are the ones who won't admit it. I don't think I can name the last time someone treated me like I was too precious to break.

After a minute, Zorro lifts his head and offers his neck for gentle scritches. I oblige him.

"Shit," I whisper to my cat, who cracks his green eyes open at me. "Did I fall for the first person who was nice to me?"

He doesn't dignify that with an answer.

# THIRTY-ONE

## MADELINE

MY DAD IS, somehow, having a New Year's Eve party. He seems baffled by this fact—I don't think he set out to have a New Year's Eve party—but at this point, it's unquestionably true. There is a New Year's Eve party happening, and my dad is hosting.

"I didn't think this many people would be here," he tells me for at least the third time as he opens another bottle of sparkling cider. "I would have gotten more snacks."

"It's fine. People are bringing snacks," I point out as I go through the cabinets. Which is true: there's a random assortment on the kitchen island, including a plastic veggie tray and homemade bean dip.

"Wish I'd had this kind of social pull in college," he says. "Every time I threw a kegger, no one came."

I momentarily give up on trying to find a big enough bowl for tortilla chips and close a cabinet to look at him.

"Dad. You never threw a kegger." I've seen pictures of my dad when he was in college. There was always a pocket protector.

"I threw parties," he says. "Cool parties."

"Was there a keg?"

"Technically, no," he says. "But one year we did steal dry ice from one of the chemistry labs. We used it to carbonate grapes."

"Wow," I say as I try another cabinet.

"It also kept vodka shots really cold," he says. "And then there was the party where Dave took all the leftover beer and distilled it into whiskey on the dorm stove." My dad sighs wistfully. "We had to borrow the equipment from the chem lab. It was awful. Tasted like pants. We drank it all, of course."

"Who wouldn't want to party with you guys?" I tease, finally pulling a big enough bowl out. "Here, does this work?"

"Sure does," he says, pouring in chips. "I'm good in here. Go hang out with your friends."

"You sure?" By *my friends*, he means my future stepsiblings, Thalia's boyfriend Caleb, two of Caleb's brothers and their wives, one of Javi's friends and his girlfriend Kat, who I talked to about *Game of Thrones* for an hour at Christmas Eve, and at least two more people I don't know. Maybe they know Bastien? Does Bastien know people out here? It's a mystery.

"Go before I start asking you about *your* college parties," my dad teases, and since I don't want to tell him about the time I took shrooms (never again) and talked to a garden gnome for an hour, I leave the kitchen.

· · * * ★ ★ ★ * * · · ·

"IT WAS JUST luck I didn't wind up in the ditch, honestly," Kat is saying. We're not *hiding* from the party, but we *are* in a corner and have been for at least thirty minutes.

257

"And then, when I made it back to civilization with a giant hole in my jeans and mud everywhere, everyone acted like I was supposed to just *know* when not to trust the GPS. What's the point of GPS if you can't trust it?"

"*Thank* you," I say. "If the GPS is unreliable, I may as well be using paper maps or something. Like a pirate."

"Did they use paper maps?"

"I don't know. They probably had star charts or something?"

We're both quiet for a moment, considering this.

"You don't think of pirates as navigating by starlight, do you," she goes on. "It's always *shiver me timbers* and *walk the plank*, never *watch for the Pleiades to your left*. I don't know anything about navigating by the stars."

"Wow, really?" I say, and she snorts. I think she's about to say something else when Paloma comes up to us and puts a hand on my shoulder.

"Five-minute warning," she says. "Refresh your drinks if you need to. Are you Kat? I think someone was looking for you. Tall? Very charming?"

"God, don't give him ideas," Kat deadpans.

"Hm?"

"Nothing. I'll go find him, thanks. Good talking to you," she says to me, and I lift my sparkling cider in a cheers as she leaves.

"You haven't seen Javier, have you?" Paloma asks me. "I don't know where he's gotten to."

"Javi? No," I say way too fast. "I mean, not for a while." Am I being suspicious? "I was talking to him and his friend with the hair for a bit, but then I went to get another drink and we haven't spoken since. I'm sure he's here somewhere."

"Oh, I'm not worried," Paloma says. "I just don't want him to miss out. Four minutes!"

She walks off with a smile and a shoulder pat. Once she's gone, I down the rest of my cider, put the glass on a side table—I'll grab it after the party—and pretend I'm going to the bathroom.

He's not in the hallway or the kitchen or the screened-in porch, but there's a little loft area upstairs, a weird corner with a big window and no foot traffic, and that's where he is. Staring out of the window at the dark forest, the glow of the porch light illuminating the trunks below.

He turns when I come in, then smiles when he sees it's me. It's what I tell myself, anyway.

"I think the countdown's about to start," I say.

"Ah. Thanks."

He's wearing a soft-looking casual sweater that's a deep rust color. It looks almost gray in the dark. He's got his hands in his pockets. He's watching me and not moving.

"You're not going down there?"

"I wasn't going to."

I glance over my shoulder, like someone might be there, think for a moment, and then join him by the window. It's a few degrees cooler next to the glass, and I shove my hands into my pockets, too.

"Who are we hiding from?" I ask.

# THIRTY-TWO

## JAVIER

I'M HIDING FROM HER, but it's not like I can tell her that. I'm hiding because everyone downstairs is a little tipsy and a lot happy, looking forward to the bright promise of another year, and I'm not ready yet. It's all *Out with the old and in with the new,* and I'm still working on *Out with the old.* I might always be working on that.

And most of all, I'm hiding up here because everyone is going to do that stupid thing where they kiss at midnight, and I am not in the mood to see it.

"Who says I'm hiding?" I ask.

"*Well,* you're lurking in the dark where no one can find you."

"You found me."

"My finding skills are exceptional." She shoves her hands deeper into her pockets and tightens her arms against her sides. She's wearing a black sweater with a pink lightning bolt down one side, the kind of thing you can see from across a room.

"Maybe I'll test them by actually hiding someday," I say, and she elbows me in the side. "What? If I were hiding, I'd at least be behind a couch. In a coat closet. Something."

Madeline sighs, then tilts her head to look up at me. "Like I can't find you in a coat closet? I didn't even look that hard. I saw you come upstairs earlier," she says. "And then you never came back down. I drew my own conclusions."

The thing about hope is that it hurts sometimes. It doesn't grow like a flower but like a snake, bursting out of its own skin and slithering new and raw across the dirt. Hope is tenderness and stupidity and your little sister saying *But did you use your words?*, and it sucks.

"Thanks for not dragging me back down," I say.

"I figured you had your reasons for being up here."

I don't tell her that the reasons just found me and I'm powerless to tell them to leave. Madeline shivers, drawing herself in tighter.

"You cold?"

"I'm fine."

"These windows aren't really built with insulation in mind." I glance around for a jacket or a blanket or something. The only thing is the sweater I'm wearing, and right now I don't think clothing removal sets the correct tone.

Neither does putting my arm around her and pulling her against my side, but I do it anyway. It takes Madeline a minute, but she relaxes into me.

"Better?"

"Yeah. Warmer," she says, and we both stare out the window for a moment. Downstairs, it's getting louder—not raucous, but excited. People love a shiny, new thing, and I can't blame them.

"Do you make resolutions?" I ask.

"Nah, they never work. There are studies about it," Madeline says, and I can't help but smile at the dark forest through the glass because she read the studies. What a dork. "No one changes themselves because they get champagne-drunk and swear they'll earn a million dollars or eat kale every day or finish their novel."

She pauses, for a moment, then glances up at me.

"Why—do you?"

"Of course I do," I say. "Every single year. I make one, and I really believe it for about twenty-four hours, that this is gonna be *my* year. And then by January second, I'm done with it."

"But you keep doing it?"

"I'm an optimist. It's easy to believe that January First Javier can do impossible things."

Someone downstairs calls out *One minute!* and the hubbub increases.

"What if you made one you could keep?" she asks. "Make one to pet your cat every day. Learn to bake cookies from scratch. Call your mom at least twice. Then a year from now, instead of thinking about what you didn't do, you can be happy that Zorro was well-loved."

Her arm is around my waist, her hand gently settled on my hip. I was listening to her so intently that I didn't notice at first, and now my brain's flooded with her touch.

"Isn't that against the spirit of the thing?"

Madeline snorts. "You're allowed to set yourself up for success. Trust me, I've been in therapy since I was, like, six."

I take a deep breath, nod, and think for a moment. I could pet Zorro every day. I could perfect my lasagna recipe. I could put gas in my car *before* the light comes on. Those are all solid, practical ideas that are eminently *doable*.

Then I look down at Madeline and pick the stupid, impossible promise anyway.

"All right, done," I say.

"What is it?"

"I can't tell you."

"It's a resolution, not a birthday wish."

"But I want it to come true."

"Javi," she says, and I can't help but like the way the nickname sounds in her mouth. "The whole point is that you *make* it come true."

*TEN!* they shout below.

"Doesn't mean I have to tell you."

*NINE!*

"What if I could help?"

*EIGHT!*

She's tucked against my side, deliriously warm, her sweater soft under my hand.

"Yeah, but what if you tried to sabotage me?"

*SEVEN!*

"Why would I do that?"

*SIX!*

Now she's looking up at me and her hand is in the small of my back, and she's all argumentative and annoyed and so pretty I forget how to talk for a second.

*FIVE!*

"I'll tell you if you guess by midnight."

"What?! That's—"

*FOUR!*

She's so close I can see every eyelash in the dark, the wide black pools of her pupils, the scratches down her cheek from where she fell. I swallow.

"Better hurry."

*THREE!*

"Shit, I don't know. You—"

*TWO!*

"—made a resolution to do more art?"

*ONE! HAPPY NEW YEAR!* everyone shouts, and the cacophony echoes through the cabin.

"Not even close," I say, and kiss her.

It's stupid and soft, and her fingers curl against the base of my spine, dragging the knit fabric of my sweater along with them. There's a faint sweetness on her mouth, and the very tip of her nose is cool when it brushes my cheek, and part of me knows that I should pull back and apologize, but then she's turning toward me and her fingertips are on my jaw, in my hair, and I'm a lost soul again.

It's the sweetest kiss we've ever shared. The slowest. It's the first time we've ever kissed that we weren't also trying to get each other's clothes off, and it's terrifying how much I like it.

I don't know how long it is before I pull back. My breathing's gone uneven, and I've got a hand buried in her hair, the other still around her waist. Madeline takes a deep breath. She bites her lip and runs a thumb along my cheekbone, and if I lean into it a little, no one else has to know.

"You're really fucking confusing," she says, but she says it the way she'd say *sweetheart*.

"I've never been any good at resisting temptation," I admit.

There's a long pause, then she swallows loud enough that I can hear it. "Is that why you broke up with me? So I'd do it for you?"

I feel like she jammed a stick into the spokes of my brain, because the whole thing crashes.

"You have to be dating to break up," I finally say.

"Right." She looks away, lifts her hand. "Instead of—"

I grab her hand and hold it to my face again, my heart beating so hard I can feel it pounding through my temple. My mouth is dry, and it's dark, and I feel like I'm standing on a knife edge, here, at midnight, in this space between one year and another. We're a minute into January first. I always have such high hopes for January first.

"I'm sorry I broke up with you," I tell her, and her hand flexes softly under mine.

"Oh," she says, and then there are footsteps on the stairs.

I don't know what to say to that—I never know what to *say*; I'm never good with words—so I lean in and kiss her again. It's rushed and exuberant, warm lips and her hand sliding into my hair.

"Madeline?" calls Gerald. "You up here?"

She pulls away too fast and runs a hand through her own hair. "I'm here," she says.

"You seen Javier?" Gerald's voice says, and at the last second, I lean against the back of a chair and hope it looks casual.

"Yeah, we're...looking at trees," she says, and I don't even have time to wince at the lie before Gerald comes around the corner

"Hey, you two," he says cheerfully. "Happy new year! Why's it dark?"

· · · · ★ ★ ★ ★ · · · ·

"I KISSED HER," I tell Zorro as I double-check the area around my space heater. The thing gives me anxiety—I *know* I'm messy—but the insulation in my apartment is truly atrocious, so I have to choose between definitely being cold and having a slight chance of a house fire. "I *only* kissed her. And then she said I broke up with her."

Zorro yawns from where he's sitting on my bed, then glares at me. He takes it as his sworn duty to answer the door whenever it opens, but he's clearly unhappy that I missed my curfew by several hours.

"I know," I say, just to keep the conversation going. "I thought that, too."

Cats can't really roll their eyes, but they can sure give that impression. Zorro radiates attitude as I turn the space heater on.

"Goodnight, Prince of Darkness," I tell him. I think it's his favorite nickname. Not that I can really tell, but he seems to tolerate it more than others? "Sweet dreams."

Once I'm under the covers, Zorro gets up, stretches, and assumes his usual spot directly next to my head. I have a really strange dream about a giant pineapple.

# THIRTY-THREE

## MADELINE

I AWAKEN, far too early, to gentle knocking on my door. Followed by my dad's face peeking in, haloed in light from the hallway.

"I'm awake," I say, instinctually. High school habits die hard, I guess.

"Forty-five-minute warning, sunshine." He's already chipper. He's also wearing a short-sleeved button-down tucked into slacks. It's what he wore on the five-hour drive down here, too. It's insane. This man is insane. A danger to society.

"Okay," I manage. It's still dark outside.

"I'd like to be past Roanoke before rush hour," he says. "If we manage that, we can get through Richmond before lunch and be home with time to spare before the sun goes down."

"Isn't it a holiday?"

"Still," he says. "Here, I'll get the lights."

I make a noise and bury my face in my pillow.

· · · · · ★ ★ ★ ★ · · · ·

"NO, you have to enter the code and *then* press the lock button," Bastien is saying to an increasingly frustrated Paloma, who is pushing too many buttons. "Here, do you want me to—"

"I am perfectly capable of *locking a door*, Bastien," she snaps, because I don't think anyone in Javi's family is good with mornings. We're not driving in the same car, so I have no idea why they're also leaving at the crack of dawn, but I'm too tired to ask questions.

"I'm just trying to help," he huffs like a sullen teenager.

"Text your brother and see where he is. He said he was going to see us off."

He did? He is? I straighten from where I'm leaning against my dad's car, looking at my phone while he talks to himself about routes, then try not to look too interested.

"He texted fifteen minutes ago and said he was—"

"I think that's him," my dad says. The driveway to the rental cabin is pretty long—it's the last building on this road, back in the trees—and we all turn to watch a ten-year-old sedan drive toward us.

"I told you," Bastien says, and Paloma doesn't reply.

"You were serious about leaving at seven?" is the first thing he says when he gets out of the car.

"*Yes*," his mom says, just as my dad says, "We're hoping to make it past Roanoke before rush hour."

Javi, who doesn't quite look awake, takes a moment.

"Isn't it a holiday?" he asks, pushing a hand through his hair. It looks unbrushed. I think there's a pillow line on his face. I wonder what it would feel like if I traced it with a fingertip.

"Why risk it?" my dad says, and then Javi's eyes finally land on me. His coat's open, and his breath is fogging in the air. The headlights of his car are still on, and his shoelaces are untied like he had to run out the door to get here on time. Paloma and Bastien are discussing whether *take the trash out* means "put the trash into the bins" or "take the bins down to the street," and Javi's not paying them any attention. We're just looking at each other. Fuck. *Fuck.*

Inspiration strikes. "Is the back door locked?" I ask, a little too loudly. "I'm not sure I locked it—let me go check."

"I think I got it, but it can't hurt…" my dad says, but I'm already pushing open the gate in the wooden fence. Behind me, Javi says something I don't catch, and then the gate swings open and shut again. I don't dare look back until I'm on the porch, by the back door. Javi's steps behind me.

"Is it—" he starts, but I grab the front of his jacket and kiss him.

He makes a surprised noise, and it's ugly for a moment there, teeth and lips sliding together. Then we both shift and everything locks into place. I probably taste like coffee and his face is sharp with stubble, but he's warm and solid as he backs me against the side of the house, then grabs the backs of my thighs and lifts.

I don't yelp as I wrap my legs around him, pinned against the wall, but I do bite him a little. It's mostly an accident.

"Ow," he says, but he's smiling. "Teeth, Madeline."

"You didn't warn me."

"I didn't know I was going to until I did," he says, and I tilt my head back against the wall, trying to catch my breath. How long does it take to check if a door is locked?

Javi takes it as an invitation because then there's lips and teeth on my neck, and I clench my teeth so I don't make a sound and squeeze his hips with my thighs for good measure.

"Don't—"

"I won't, I wouldn't," he promises. "Not now."

And god, that's his tongue, hot and wet and gentle.

"When's the wedding?" he says, warm lips against my cool skin.

"Seven weeks? Six?"

He sighs. I realize my hand is in his hair, and it tightens.

"We should get back out there," I say, squeezing him with my thighs again. "Before someone comes to check up on us."

Javi makes a low noise, almost like a growl, but he lets me go and we untangle. I get one more kiss—sweet, gentle, lingering—before we're straightening our clothes again and I'm checking my face in the reflection in the windows, hoping I don't look freshly ravaged.

We walk to the front together in the quiet, and right before he opens the gate, he looks at me and says, "Happy new year."

· · · · · ★ ★ ★ ★ · · · ·

AFTER WE GET HOME, my dad gets a message from the owners of the house that we left the back door unlocked.

"I thought you checked that," he says, bewildered, as I transfer my suitcase to my own car.

· · · · · ★ ★ ★ ★ · · · ·

THE NEXT EVENING, I'm standing in a classy wine bar, sipping a glass of classy white wine, wearing my classiest heels, and trying to chat to classy people about the incredible work being done at the Chesapeake University Hospital, where Ben is currently a neurosurgery resident. I don't actually know very much about the incredible work being done, but I get to tell the story of the bandage on my forehead about thirty times. Every single person makes the joke that at least I'm in the right place.

"I *think* they're the people who own that pomegranate juice company," Ben says, sotto voce, when the couple we've been chatting with drift away. "I didn't know pomegranate juice tycoons existed, did you?"

"The world is full of surprises," I say.

"Well, the hospital is naming a building after them." He slips a hand into his pocket and looks around. "So I guess pomegranates can get you *donate enough for your own building*–type money."

Ben all-caps texted me this morning HELP I NEED A PLUS-ONE TO A DONOR EVENT TONIGHT AND AMY CAN'T MAKE IT, and because I'm an incredible friend, and also like free wine, I agreed to come. I think these things make him kind of nervous, and he feels better if I'm there to talk to. My hair usually gets some looks from the fairly old, fairly conservative attendees, but Ben will have to deal with that.

"By the way, I'm supposed to ask what you're wearing to your dad's wedding," he says.

"A dress, probably."

"What *color* dress?" he huffs, as if this is the question he asked the first time. Which it isn't.

"I don't know. It's, like, six weeks away. Why—are you afraid I'm going to embarrass you by showing up in cutoffs and a tube top?"

"Why would that embarrass *me*?"

"Aren't you my date, sort of?" I point out.

"Oh, then I'd disavow you in a heartbeat," he says, grinning. "Everyone would be like 'Who's the lady with her whole tramp stamp showing?' and I would not *hesitate* before claiming not to know you."

"Fuck *you*, it's not a tramp stamp, it's in the middle of my back," I say, and Ben immediately straightens and sips his wine as two (classy-looking) people walk past. I turn my head away from them and pretend I didn't just swear at him about a tramp stamp.

"Why do I take you anywhere?" he mutters.

"Because I'm charming and cute," I say, and he rolls his eyes.

"*Anyway*. My mom has informed me that, as your sort-of date, my pocket square needs to match your outfit, so I need to know what color your outfit is."

"We're supposed to *match*? It's my dad's wedding, not prom."

"Have you not been to *one* formal event?"

"I've been to more formal events than you," I say, which may or may not be true; I have no idea. "Sorry I haven't memorized every rule about who wears what."

Ben sighs as if the weight of the world has settled on his shoulders and not the simple need to wait a few weeks to buy a pocket square. "Just tell me when you decide so my mom doesn't get on my case about the pictures," he says.

"Is there anything else I'm supposed to know about bringing a date?" I ask, because I guess, technically, I'm bringing a date to my dad's wedding, even if it's just Ben. I can bring a date and still hang out with other people, right? Like, on the dance floor, or possibly off the dance floor?

Is it poor wedding form to bring a date even if you're... involved...with another wedding guest? If we're involved? If we've figured it out by then?

"Why are *you* asking *me*?" Ben asks, as if personally affronted.

"You knew about the pocket square thing!"

"I only knew that because my mom asked, so trust me, that's all I know. Do I escort you? Are you in the wedding party?"

These are all excellent questions that I will definitely ask someone, any day now. "I don't think so," I tell him because, like, someone would have alerted me if I were a groomsman, right? Groomswoman? Groomsgal? Terrible, all of it. "But I think you get to sit in the front row during the ceremony."

"Sweet, those are the best seats."

"You took the day off, right?"

"Yes. Like three months ago already." Ben, as a surgical resident, has tried to explain his schedule to me multiple times. I've never managed to remember it.

"Thanks for coming," I say, because I really am glad he'll be there.

Ben snorts, then puts an empty wineglass on the bar we're standing next to. We're off to one side of this fancy event space, and I think some of the others have started to leave. "Are you kidding? I love weddings, and I'm glad your dad's happy, and I'm gonna have a great time watching you and your stepbrother avoid eye contact and pretend you're normal and not fucking," he says. "Or I'll have a really awkward time watching you eye-fuck on the dance floor during your parents' first dance."

"Oh my god," I mutter, closing my eyes.

"Speaking of which, how is boning your stepbrother going?" he asks with the world's most obnoxious grin.

"*Boning?*"

"I can come up with a worse word," he offers.

I nearly flip him off, then remember where we are and settle for a glare.

"It's fine," I say, and I can feel my face heat.

I debate not telling him anything or simply saying *The boning continued as expected* or something. But then Ben makes a stupid, interested little face and I tell him basically everything, even if it's short on the sex details and long on the complaints about GPS.

"He dumped you and then decided he wanted to bone again anyway?" is his unimpressed summary of my week.

"You *cannot* keep saying 'bone.'"

"Sorry—he dumped you and then changed his mind and wants to have carnal relations—"

"Oh *god.*"

"—again, or something."

"It's complicated," I explain. I didn't tell Ben *everything* everything, because even I am aware that *I'm sorry I broke up with you* doesn't sound like a romantic overture to most people. Even if I'm almost positive it was.

"So, you two are 'talking,'" he says. There are scare quotes.

"Sure."

Ben lifts one very judgmental eyebrow.

"I'm giving him some space," I say. "This is good, honestly. I just don't want to be clingy."

"Clingy," he mutters to himself, then sighs, rubs his face, and swears. "Shit, okay. Not to give you a mushy pep talk, but you know he's all the way across the state and you'd have to actively try for more space than that, right?"

I look away, my face burning.

"You deserve someone who'll text you all the time if that's what you want," Ben is saying. "You're, like, a *catch*, and you shouldn't settle for someone who *needs space* from across the state. Just because you've dated some dickheads doesn't mean you *have* to date dickheads."

"Javi's not a dickhead," I hiss. "Look, he's nice, I swear, okay? We just need to figure our thing out."

"Am I gonna have to defend your honor at the wedding? As your date?"

"Ben. Be serious. What honor?" I ask.

"You said it, not me." He shrugs, and I roll my eyes. "But listen, the offer stands. Even though I'd probably lose a fight to a Marine. Hey, you think Amy knows him? Maybe I can ask her about his deal."

"You can't just ask Marines if they know each other," I say, faux-offended, and Ben snorts up at my stupid joke. "Also there're a billion Marines, and he got out, like, seven or eight years ago."

"Okay, okay, I'm just saying—I'll lose a fight in your honor. And you *still* haven't told me what color dress you're wearing."

"Whatever, you called me a catch," I say, and Ben sighs.

# THIRTY-FOUR

## JAVIER

MY PHONE RINGS while I'm in the grocery store wondering what to make for dinner for the rest of my life, and when I see it's Madeline I accidentally throw it into some lemons.

"My dad put me in charge of the playlist for the wedding," she says, once I've retrieved my phone and said hello. "I need ideas."

"Can't go wrong with the chicken dance."

Dead silence.

"Yes, you can," she finally says. "I don't think they're looking for a chicken-dance vibe."

"Just put it on the playlist toward the end, when everyone's drunk."

"I already regret this phone call."

"I'm thinking, I'm thinking," I say, staring at some celery. It's like I've never heard of a song in my entire life. "Are you going for romantic or a party vibe or...?"

"A romantic party?" she says. "I guess that's what a wedding is, isn't it? I've got some suggestions from my dad and Paloma, but I could use more because they're..."

"You're telling me those two aren't coming up with *party vibe* songs?"

"I had to tell my dad that under absolutely no circumstances can their first dance be to that Dave Matthews song 'Crash Into Me.'"

I try to remember which one that is. I feel like I heard it a lot in grocery stores as a kid.

"Is it that bad?"

Madeline sighs. "It's about kinky bondage sex," she says. "I cannot watch our parents slow dance to a song about kinky bondage sex."

I make a mental note to revisit the Dave Matthews Band's oeuvre sometime.

"My mom got pretty into *Hamilton* when it was first out. Is that anything?"

I must circle the produce section for thirty minutes while we talk. It's about the playlist for a little bit—I try to remember what music my mom liked while I was growing up; Madeline shares that she had to limit her dad to two Weird Al songs—but after a while we wander off topic.

"Have you ever had a turnip?" I find myself asking. Mostly because I'm looking at them.

"Maybe?" she says after a moment. "I think kids in England carve them for Halloween? Or maybe that's New England. And maybe parsnips."

"Are parsnips and turnips different?"

"Yes?" she answers. "I think so. They have different names."

"So do eggplants and aubergines, but they're the same thing."

"*That's* what an aubergine is?" Madeline starts laughing. "I thought it was some kind of flower."

"So you thought that when British people made

aubergine Parmesan, they were eating flowers," I tease. Do British people make aubergine Parmesan? We watched a lot of cooking shows in rehab, but my memory's not *that* good.

"I never thought about it that much, to be honest," she says. "It was mostly in books, and they also eat meat pies and spotted dick—"

"Can't be healthy," I mutter, and she snorts.

"It's *cake*. I think."

"Sure."

"Well, it's some kind of—holy shit, it is really eight thirty?"

"I'm not the right person to ask about time."

"Sorry. I didn't mean to bother you for that long," she says. "Are you still at the grocery store?"

"You're not bothering me."

"You know what I mean," she says, laughing in that embarrassed, dismissive way she has sometimes, and I almost let it go, almost say *No, but I should get back to grocery shopping*. Someone's gotta be honest, though; someone has to take that first step while staring deeply into the eyes of the cartoon cow on the 2% milk.

"I like talking to you," I say. "It's not a hardship, Madeline."

"Oh," she says after a moment, and I can practically hear her swallow back an apology. "Okay, well—what are you making for dinner?"

· · · · ★ ★ ★ ★ ★ · · · ·

"IS BASTIEN GETTING A PLUS-ONE?" Madeline's asking about a week later. I'm sprawled on one of my couches. This one is from Wyatt's grandma's basement— she was getting rid of it, and I was happy to take it off her hands. A year and some YouTube-led DIY later, it could be worse.

"I thought nobody was getting a plus-one that wasn't a significant other," I say. Zorro's on the other couch, and I make wiggly fingers in his direction. He pretends not to see them.

"That's what I thought, but this list says *Bastien Lopez, plus one*. Is he seeing someone?"

"If he is, he didn't tell me." I put my phone on speaker and text my brother *Hey, are you bringing someone to the wedding?*

Then I chew on my lip for a moment and wonder if this is a good time to tell Madeline that I cracked. We're all going to see each other in a few weeks for a get-together that is Absolutely Not a Bridal Shower, so it's probably only fair to Madeline.

"They know, by the way," I confess.

There's a pause on the other end of the line.

"You have to be way more specific," she says, and, okay, I can see her point.

"Bastien and Thalia know we...hooked up," I say, choosing to stick with the facts.

"You told them?"

"I would say the information was taken under duress. They locked me in a bathroom because they said I was being 'all weird and stuff.'"

"There's no way that's normal," says Madeline, an only child. "They *locked* you? In a *bathroom*?"

"You're making it sound way worse than it was," I say. Bastien texts me back *Yeah, your mom*, which is the single dumbest thing I've ever read. "They weren't even holding me down or anything. I definitely could've called for help. Bastien's not bringing a date, by the way."

"Uh-huh," she says, after a moment. "Did they say anything? In the bathroom?"

"They made a lot of stepsibling jokes. So, it went as well as can be hoped for."

Earlier today, Thalia, Bastien, and I had a text exchange that began with me politely asking them to act normal the next time we see each other in front of our family. It ended with both of them suggesting they could now blackmail me whenever they want. I'm ninety-nine percent sure they won't.

"But they're not grossed out or anything," she says, and I snort.

"Thalia fucked her calculus professor when she was a senior in college," I point out. Madeline *gasps*. "Wait, did you not know?"

"*Her professor?* Thalia did?! Is she—what happened? Was it bad? Is she okay?"

"She swears it was her idea," I say. "I wasn't...around much, when it happened, but now they live together and they're talking about getting a dog, so it worked out. And honestly, he seems great."

"Wait," she says. I swear I can hear her sit up straighter. "No. *Wait.* She said they met in college! Caleb was her calculus professor? He was a *professor*?"

"I can't believe no one told you that my goody-two-shoes little sister had a sordid affair with her own professor. While she was taking his class and everything," I say. Zorro finally jumps up onto my chest, and I make an *oof* sound, then scritch him behind the ears while I contemplate saying this next part. He starts purring like a chainsaw.

"Hi, Zorro," Madeline calls, and he chirps a little. "Zorro, did *you* know all this?"

"Zorro wasn't born yet," I say. "The whole thing with

Thalia happened after my dad kicked me out, so I didn't know anything about it until I overdosed and went to rehab months later."

"The most recent time? With the horses?"

There's something soothing in the way she says it so matter-of-factly, like it's not a forbidden subject spoken of only in hushed tones. Madeline says it the way she'd say *That's the night you had spaghetti for dinner*, like it's morally neutral. "Right. We kinda put my mom through it that winter."

"Her *professor*," Madeline says again. "Okay, what other scandalous family shit have you been hiding from me?"

· · * * * ★ ★ ★ * * · ·

"WHY'D you wait until *today* to take this down?" I ask Wyatt as dry pine needles stab me in the face.

"Because it's potluck night," he says. "Higher."

I turn my face away and lift the very dead Christmas tree another inch so he can finally get the stand out from underneath it. On the other side, through the needles, I can see Barry sitting on the fireplace mantle, fluffy orange tail swishing.

"Don't you dare," I tell her.

"Barry would never," Wyatt says. "Would you?"

Barry gives me a look that says *I absolutely the fuck would.*

"Didn't Beast cause Christmas-tree problems at Silas's parents' house last year?" I say, still making eye contact with this cat. "Maybe it's genetic."

"Okay, I've mapped a course around the couch, past the table, and through the front door," Wyatt says, ignoring my cat concerns. "It's not the most direct route, but it avoids carpet, and *fuck* vacuuming pine needles out of carpet."

Ten minutes later, Wyatt's month-old Christmas tree is no longer a fire hazard, he's vacuuming pine needles from carpeting despite his best efforts, and I'm walking through his kitchen to the laundry room so I can toss the tree skirt into the washer.

On the way, I walk past a Fancy Chickens calendar, open to January, and I remember what Lainey said about a gold star on my three-years-sober anniversary. The one I didn't really celebrate. On a whim, I flip to next December, and that's how Wyatt finds me: standing in his kitchen with his calendar held open, a fancy chicken on the top and the December grid on the bottom, the tree skirt still in my hand.

On the nineteenth, there's a sparkly gold star, and beneath it, simply, *Javi, 4 yrs*.

"My sister got me that because she said the chicken on the front looked like me," Wyatt says, passing behind me.

"It doesn't have your charm," I say without really thinking, because there's this *star*, in *December*, with my name.

"More charm than a chicken. Got it."

"You don't think you're jumping the gun a little?" I ask. I haven't moved a muscle since he walked in here. Wyatt doesn't say anything, but I can feel him walk up and stand next to me. It feels like a long time that we stand here, like this, looking at a date eleven months from now.

"No," he finally says. "I don't think I am."

Then the door opens and it's Gideon, all bundled up and holding a Dutch oven, so I drop the calendar and put the tree skirt in the washing machine and grab the hummus platter that I put together earlier while I was on the phone with Madeline. Then Silas shows up with some fancy Brussels sprouts that he *swears* are actually going to be good, and Barry tries to steal the bacon out of them because she's a nightmare and I have to pick her up off the counter while she shouts about it, and it's all warm and chaotic. And on that calendar, eleven months in the future, there's a star.

· · * * * ★ ★ ★ * * · ·

"YOU'VE BEEN QUIET," Silas says as we're leaving Wyatt's house. "Everything okay?"

"I never said thank you," I tell him.

He stops and looks at me in the middle of Wyatt's asphalt driveway. From here, in the winter, you can see the road he lives on. A car goes by.

"For what?"

"For...this," I say, which I know is wildly unspecific. "For coming to meet Thalia's fuckup brother and talking some guy you didn't know into moving across the state."

The summer after I was out of rehab, I helped my sister move into a new apartment with her boyfriend. Her boyfriend's older brother also helped, and for reasons I'll never know, his best friend, Silas, came along, too.

"Yeah, that was a little reckless," he admits, but he's smiling. "Worked out, though."

I want to say *Did it?* or *Are you sure about that?* Or *Hahaha joke's on you—all you got out of the bargain was me,* but I don't. I'm not sure whether Silas has a calendar in his kitchen or not, but I'm starting to realize he's got a gold star in December anyway. I think, maybe, they all do.

I think, maybe, I'm the only one who doesn't. I think that maybe I've taken so many days one at a time by now that thinking in months feels dangerous, like it's tempting fate. But fate's not why I'm here right now, is it?

"Yeah," I say, and I'm nodding. I'm nodding too much? I'm nodding a weird amount? Shit. "It did. Work out."

"Hey," Silas says and puts his hand on my arm. "Hey, Javi, it's—"

I don't really know who hugs who, but there we are, in Wyatt's driveway, my hands clenched in Silas's puffy jacket. He's saying something soothing—"I've got you," over and over again, I think—and I should let go soon. I know I should, but I don't. Not for a while at least.

· · · · ★ ★ ★ ★ ★ · · ·

"I TOLD YOU THAT," Castillo says when I call her the next day to ask if she's got a gold star. She doesn't, but once I explain the whole thing, she agrees that she's fully expecting me to be four years sober next winter.

"You did *not*."

"I literally did," she says, all matter-of-fact, the way she usually is. "A month ago, when you were bitching about putting up with your mom being in town for a whole week, I told you that if you could get through rehab three times, your mom being nearby was nothing."

"I thought you weren't taking me seriously!"

Castillo sighs. "Well, you were being very dramatic," she admits. "But that's the point I was trying to make. You obviously know how to do hard things. Probably better than most people. And."

I wait a reasonable amount of time, which makes me nervous because if there's something *Castillo* isn't sure about saying to *me*, it might be very bad.

"And?"

"And the way you're so self-deprecating about it is probably bad for you. Like, psychologically," she finally continues. "Plus, it's pretty annoying. The more you think you're gonna fuck up, the more you fuck up."

I want to roll my eyes at the phone and point out that I've got a history of fucking up and history only ever repeats itself, but for once I listen to what she's saying. So I keep my mouth shut, even if I'm not sure I believe her.

"I wish you'd told me that before," I finally say, mostly teasing.

"Lopez," she says, very patiently. "I have been *trying*."

⋅ ⋅ ⋆ ⋆ ★ ★ ★ ⋆ ⋆ ⋅ ⋅

"BEN ALSO KNOWS, BY THE WAY," Madeline says. I've got her on speakerphone in my car while I eat a peanut butter sandwich in the parking lot of Blue Ridge Community College. Thursdays are long—I've got work at the insurance office, then the Composition 101 class I put off until this semester, followed an hour later by Computer Design II. The registrar strongly suggested I get the composition class out of the way my first semester, and I didn't listen.

"Ben?" I say, my mouth full of peanut butter and jam.

"He's basically my sibling, and he can keep his mouth shut," she says. "My mom still doesn't know what happened to all her tomato trellises that one year."

"What did happen?"

"That's on a need-to-know basis," Madeline says primly, and I laugh. "Shit, I still haven't figured out what I'm wearing to the wedding."

"You don't know?" I haven't gotten my suit yet—I will, I swear—but I know what I'm wearing.

"Women have a lot more sartorial choices than men," she says. "It's more complicated than deciding what color suit I'm going to wear. But Ben is locked into this idea that his pocket square needs to match my dress since he's technically my date."

I swallow another bite, and my jealousy, because I know it's got no basis in reality. She just said they were basically siblings, which—okay, maybe not the best criteria, given our relationship, but we're two completely different kinds of almost-siblings.

"Right, I forgot about that," I say in an extremely neutral way.

"I think it basically means we're sitting together at dinner," she says. "Maybe during the ceremony? I don't think they're taking the seating charts very seriously. It's a pretty small wedding. Hey, are you in the bridal party, and is there a bridal party?"

I shake my head, which is pointless, and swallow the last bite of my sandwich. "No, my mom was considering it, but then Bastien and Thalia disagreed over who should be the flower adult and she scrapped the whole thing."

"Obviously it would be me," she says.

"Take it up with them."

"I'd be a great flower adult."

"Maybe you should all be co–flower adults," I say in a spirit of conciliation. "You can each fling different flower petals."

"You don't fling them, you scatter them. Gracefully. This is why you'd be a bad flower adult."

"I'm the only one who hasn't made a bid for it," I point out. "I'm perfectly happy to sit in the audience and watch."

"We could find you something. How do you feel about ring-bearing?"

Class starts in ten minutes, and I should go, but the car's warm and the night is cold, and Computer Design II doesn't have Madeline on the other end of the line.

"Would you honestly trust me with an important ring?"

Madeline thinks for a minute. "An important one, sure. You can usually keep track of things when they matter."

"I can't tell you how many keys I've lost."

"Well, first, I wouldn't hand you anything else at the same time," she says, and I squirm a little because yes, she's found my weakness. "You might lose your own wedding ring, but you wouldn't lose your mom's."

"I like to think I wouldn't lose my own, either."

"Whose side are you on?" she asks, laughing. "Ten seconds ago you were ready to lose a whole jewelry store."

"Either way, there are no flower adults or ring bearers, so I don't even know why we're having this conversation."

"Because you started it."

I'm grinning helplessly in the car, in this parking lot, in the dark. "I gotta go, or I'll be late to class," I tell her.

"Break a leg," she says, then laughs. "Whatever I'm supposed to say. Learn a lot? I don't know."

"Thanks. You, too," I say, and right as I end the call, I could swear I hear her blow a kiss.

# THIRTY-FIVE

## MADELINE

"I HAVEN'T SEEN the first five," Amy is saying. "I won't have any idea what's going on."

"You don't need to know what's going on—it's a *Mission: Impossible* movie," Scott, Ben's roommate, argues. "Just go with the flow and enjoy it."

"How can I enjoy a movie if I don't know what's going on? Knowing the plot is the point of a movie," she protests. "And to know the plot of this movie, I'm fairly sure I need to see *Missions: Impossible* one through four or five or whatever."

"I do like calling them *Missions: Impossible*," Ben says.

"So, okay, Tom Cruise does a lot of cool stunts, and also everyone has rubber masks that make them look exactly like someone else, and they're always removed at a very dramatic moment," Scott explains.

"You can't possibly think that's an explanation."

"What about the Barbie movie?" I interject, because I'm pretty sure Scott is just trying to annoy Amy at this point, and I'm tired of it.

"We saw that already," says Ben. "I would watch *The Batman*."

"No," Amy and I say in perfect chorus. I hold up my hand, and she high-fives it from her spot next to me.

It's Saturday night, and I'm over at Ben's place for movie night, which also involves pizza, Twizzlers, popcorn, and baby carrots with hummus. The carrots and hummus are clearly an afterthought.

"There are too many movies about Batman," Amy says, which I secretly agree with.

"Blasphemy."

"Just the truth."

Turns out my nerves over Ben's new girlfriend were completely unfounded because she's awesome and I love her. We almost went and got pedicures together last weekend, until we finally both admitted we don't like it when people touch our feet, so we went to brunch instead.

After a few more rounds of bickering, we all manage to settle on *Fury Road*, which Ben hasn't seen because he lives under a rock.

"Blood donation is major plot point," Amy says, patting his thigh soothingly. "It's really unsanitary, you'll hate it."

"Wow, thanks," he says, and then the movie starts.

· · · · ★ ★ **★** ★ ★ · · · ·

THIRTY MINUTES LATER, my phone buzzes on the coffee table where I left it, because for once I'm not playing on it while also watching a movie.

"Ugh, rude," says Ben, as I roll my eyes and flip him off. "You're ruining the *immersion*."

"Your mom is ruining the..." I start, then see that it's Javi and forget where I was going with that sentence. Ben gives me a raised-eyebrows *oh really* type of look over Amy's head. I pretend I don't see it.

"I gotta take this," I say, already pushing the green button before I can second-guess myself, heart tripping over itself in my rib cage. "Don't pause it—I've seen it before! Hi."

"Hi. Am I interrupting something?"

"If you were, I wouldn't have answered."

The sound of an explosion tears through the surround-sound system—by *far* the nicest thing in this apartment—and I'm sure Javi can hear it.

"What are you watching?"

"*Fury Road.*"

"Oh, Wyatt loves that movie."

"It's a good movie," I say, walking into the kitchen and shutting the door behind me. "What's up?"

"Invitation questions," he says. "Since you're fancy, if the woman of a married couple is a doctor and her husband is just a mister, who do I put first on the invitation?"

I blink at cabinets for a moment.

"Weren't these supposed to be out last week?"

"Shhh."

That's not much turnaround, and tight deadlines make me kind of anxious, but not my circus, not my monkeys, et cetera.

"I don't know, I'm not *that* fancy," I tell him. "How formal is this anyway? Are people going to refuse to come to the wedding if we get the order of their titles wrong?"

"I think that depends on Doctor Jones's attitude," he says, and I laugh.

"Oh, she won't give a shit," I say. "Next question."

"Your grandmother's gentleman friend," he says. "Not her husband? Different last names?"

"Different last names," I confirm. I check that the counter behind me is clean, and then hop up onto it so I can go through a whole guest list with Javi and debate what to call people. On one hand, it's the twenty-first century and this is a low-key wedding; on the other hand, a lot of those guests are older Southern folks with thoughts on How Things Ought To Be Done.

"All right, that's it," Javier finally says. "Thanks."

"Isn't the bride supposed to do this?" I ask, since I don't want to get off the phone just yet.

"The bride has never done a mail merge in her life and isn't going to start now," he says. I can hear him walking through his apartment, then the creak of a couch as he sits. Half a second later, Zorro meows. "Nor is the bride at all interested in hand-addressing these, so here I am."

"I hope the bride is showing proper gratitude," I say.

He huffs out a laugh. "Well, she did keep me alive throughout my childhood. I probably owe her something," he says, and I can hear Zorro make a noise of protest in the background. "You need to get back to the movie?"

"I've seen it," I say quickly. "I'm over at Ben's place. They're still watching it. Probably don't even know I'm gone."

I'm sure I imagine the beat of silence that follows.

"Oh," Javier says. "Fun?"

"Just pizza and movie night. It's been a long week," I say, pointing my bare toes and kicking them back and forth, careful not to kick the cabinets. "What are you doing?"

"Mail merging invitations for my mom's wedding," he says. "Now I'm on the couch with a cat."

"Sounds cozy."

"It is." There's another pause. I can hear him shift, take a breath, and then: "I've got on those pants you like."

I stop kicking my feet. "Uh," I say.

"The slutty ones," he clarifies. "Just thought you should know."

"Okay," I say, now bright red in Ben's kitchen. I'm pretty sure I should say something besides *Okay*, but I'm not really sure what. "Thank you for that information."

"You're welcome," he says. "Would you like any more?"

I would like a *lot* of information, and I have no idea how to ask for any of it. I would like pictures and sound and possibly a full-length feature film of said information, but that seems unreasonable.

"Yes. Why are you wearing...those...pants?"

"They're comfortable. I didn't realize you were going to be at someone else's house, though, so maybe I shouldn't have said anything."

What I *should* do is get off the phone and go watch this movie, because the wedding is in a little under a month, and that's not that long. Really, it's not.

What I *actually* do is take a deep breath and say, "No, I think you should keep talking to me," and he laughs, deep and relaxed and throaty. I feel like it rolls down my spine.

"You'd like that, wouldn't you?" he says, and no *shit*, I just requested this—of course I'd like it. "Remember the time you fucked me while your friend was on the phone?"

My face goes instantly hotter, and I glance at the door as if the people on the other side can hear. "Of course I remember that. It was memorable," I say. "She forgave me, by the way."

"You told her?"

"Yeah, like a year later. I felt too guilty. She laughed and then gave me a high five."

"God, I remember how desperate you were for it," he says, and I have to shut my eyes in embarrassment or arousal or some mixture of the two. "Even though you'd already come once. Your friends all think you're nice, don't they?"

"I *am* nice." My voice is low, not quite whispering. "I'm a nice person, Javi."

"Do they know how *good* you are?"

I swallow, then clear my throat. "Of course," I say as evenly as I can.

"Like I do?"

Jesus, no one else knows *that*. "I don't know what you mean."

"Liar," he says, and I can tell he's grinning. "Do they know how well you follow instructions? I bet your couch is still spotless."

"My couch is fine."

"Are you thinking about getting fucked on it right now?"

I roll my eyes and glance at the door to the living room. Vague action movie noises are still coming from behind it. "Fuck you, I am *now*."

"Tell me."

It's vivid, suddenly. Down to the velvet on my bare skin and the low, moody light from my mermaid lamp. I lock my ankles together and squeeze my thighs, gripping the edge of the counter in one hand.

"I'm, like, ten feet away from Ben *and* his roommate *and*—"

"You said there was a door," he says, like that's reasonable. "They're watching this movie, they don't know. Come on. Are you on your back or your hands and knees?"

I take a deep breath and close my eyes because I'm not really *doing* anything and they can't hear, and if they come in here, I can just pretend I've been talking about wedding stuff this whole time, right?

"Hands and knees," I say. "With my elbows, like— braced against the arm. Of the couch."

There's a ragged inhale on the other end. "Are you still dressed?"

I look down at myself and nearly say *Yes, I'm in Ben's kitchen* but manage to stay in the spirit of things. "Yeah. I've got on...a skirt."

"What else?"

"A tank top," I say and pinch the bridge of my nose, because why is my imaginary sex outfit so boring?

"That's all?"

"That's all."

"*Fuck*," he whispers, and I can hear him swallow through the phone, so maybe my imaginary sex outfit isn't that boring. "If you're already there, your skirt's up around your waist and your shirt is pushed up over your tits the way you like it, yeah?"

*The way I like it.* Jesus Christ. "Yeah."

"I'd eat you out first," he says, and his voice is low and rough. "Just—slow. I'd take my time. Listen to you moan. Wait until your thighs were shaking before I made you come, and you'd be—"

There's a long, ragged breath on the other end, and I grip the counter even harder, my eyes squeezed shut as I imagine Javier, on his couch, head back and legs wide as he touches himself through the slutty pants.

"Begging?" I ask, voice horrifyingly loud in the empty kitchen.

"Demanding," he says. "I'd have to hold you still with both hands so you didn't suffocate me."

"You love it," I say.

"Yeah. After you came, you'd be all boneless and wet, and I'd slide in. No condom, just skin on skin—"

294

A thrill of alarm washes over me at that, and I hear myself say, "Right."

"I'm not gonna wrap it up for imaginary phone sex," he says, teasing. "This is as safe as it gets."

"Maybe for you, alone in your apartment with no one but a cat." I glance at the door.

"I think you like the danger, Madeline."

"I think you like that I'm still on the phone with you, Javier."

That gets a sound that's half laugh and half groan, and it makes my toes curl. "You have no idea. I'm leaking like a faucet over here, Jesus. I don't know which is better—the idea of you naked and demanding on the couch or the idea of you in someone else's apartment, fully clothed and wet and watching the door."

"So you'd fuck me?" I ask, nearly a whisper, because we're getting off topic. "Tell me how."

"Slow and deep, until you moaned," he says. "After a while you'd start rubbing your clit again when you wanted to come. Maybe I'd let you."

My real-life clit is throbbing, offended that the attention is imaginary, and I squeeze my thighs together. It does nothing.

"What do you mean, let me?"

"I mean, I like making you wait, too. Uh, can you come without touching your clit?"

"I don't think so. I mean, I haven't ever."

"Good. I'd keep it slow until you were—grinding back into me on every thrust, dripping with it, and you'd be desperate to come but you wouldn't touch yourself yet. God, I'd make you feel so good."

I shift slightly on the countertop so the gusset of my jeans jolts over my clit, and it feels something like relief but also something like shame. I do it again anyway, and maybe? Maybe if I move just right I can come like this—

"Would you bite me again?" I ask, and Javier makes a choked-off noise of surprise.

"God yes," he says, and he sounds strangled. "Did you— Last time, were there—"

It's suddenly a million degrees in here, hard to breathe, impossible to open my eyes. Javier sounds like he's dying, slick noises in the background, like he's on the edge of losing it. It makes me feel like I'm high.

"Were there teeth marks?" I answer, my voice low and throaty and surprisingly even. "Yeah. There was a ring of bruises right on my shoulder blade. I looked at them every day."

Javier makes a shaky, desperate noise.

"I was so disappointed when they faded," I say, and then I can hear him saying "Fuck, fuck, fuck," and his voice fading, suddenly far away. I have to bite my lip and close my eyes and breathe evenly, in and out, because I'm pretty sure I look like I'm having phone sex *while sitting on the counter in Ben's kitchen*, and that is not the look I want right now.

"Holy shit," he says, a minute later, his voice small and far away. "God, I'm—wait, um, there," he goes on, and suddenly I can hear him again. "Sorry. There we go. I dropped my phone. Christ, I made a mess."

"Did you," I say, my entire body hot, my skin too small for me. "I'm still in Ben's kitchen."

There's ragged, rough breathing on the other end. Finally he inhales. "What are you doing?"

"Sitting on the counter," I say. "Staring at the magnets on the fridge."

"Is that all?"

"I'm in someone else's kitchen, and he's right on the

other side of a door," I say, voice still low. "I guess I could start doing the dishes."

"Did you touch yourself?"

"*Kitchen*," I hiss, and his breath catches.

"Not even a little?" he murmurs. "Over your clothes, just for some relief?"

I decide that squirming against the seam of my jeans doesn't count. "Not even a little," I say. "Not the tiniest bit."

"But you wanted to," he says, and it's not a question. "You want to right now."

I lean my head back against the cabinets, close my eyes against the bright white of the overhead light, and wonder what the hell I'm doing with my life. "Yeah. I want to."

"You should go finish the movie," he says. "You've probably missed too much."

"I've seen it before," I say. "I've got a better idea: I go home right now and call you back—"

"Finish the movie, Madeline," he says, and I can hear the semi-feral grin in his voice. "Call me when you get home afterward."

"Fuck *that*," I say, my heartbeat picking up. "I'm supposed to just go out there and sit on the couch and watch *Fury Road* like everything is normal? There's at least another hour left."

"I'm sure it'll be a distraction."

I swallow and squeeze my thighs together again, which —again—does not help for shit, and I briefly wonder how I got from *normal person* to *playing sex games with my stepbrother in my friend's kitchen.*

"What if it's not?" I ask. "What if for the next hour, I have to sit there, watch car chases, and think about how I'd rather be on my hands and knees?"

"Then call me when you get home," he says. "Talk to you soon. But not that soon."

"I hope Zorro bites you."

Javier hangs up on a laugh, and I scowl at the door to the kitchen.

Then I turn my phone off, take a deep breath, go back into the living room, and sit on the couch.

"What'd I miss?" I ask.

# THIRTY-SIX

## JAVIER

SHE CALLS me back two hours later, the moment she walks through her front door. I'm already in bed, waiting, and I can hear her taking her clothes off as she walks through her apartment. Madeline's too impatient for it to be more complicated than narrated masturbation, and by the end I've come all over myself for the second time that night.

It's after that, after we say good night and I'm taking a shower, that the guilt really shows up in earnest. When she said *I'm at Ben's*, I should have said *Enjoy the movie*, not *What are you wearing*. I've gone to so much therapy and done so much work on myself, and for all that, I'm still a seething mess of jealousy and impulses, and I hate it.

I know she and Ben are just friends. I know she's been pretty clear on this fact, and I believe her, obviously. I just don't understand it. He's an attractive, stable doctor-in-training who's been her confidant for thirty years. He throws Halloween parties. He's physically present in Virginia Beach. Meanwhile, I'm a mess with no college degree, just over three years of sobriety, a cat who doesn't respect me, and I live five hours away in a two-horse mountain town.

Deep down, I think the only explanation is that she hasn't noticed all that yet. All it'll take is one simple pros-and-cons list, and she'll realize her mistake, right? Until then, I'm on borrowed time. Which is why when I found out she was at *his* house, my first stupid impulse was to do the one thing I know I can do for her: make her horny. A great skill, which I'm desperately pleased to have, but—well, insecurity isn't really a good look.

"Why am I like this?" I ask Zorro, who's patiently waiting on the rug outside the shower because he likes to lick the tile after I bathe. It's kind of gross, but I choose my battles.

He doesn't answer me anyway. I put some conditioner in my hair, wash my face, and turn the water off so I can trade places with my weird cat.

· · · ★ ★ ★ ★ ★ · · ·

THE NEXT TIME WE TALK, when she calls me to ask if I know what color the napkins at the reception are going to be and we talk for ninety minutes after that, we don't discuss the phone sex. We also don't discuss the fact that we're going to see each other in a week and a half. Maybe, if we're lucky, one won't affect the other.

· · · ★ ★ ★ ★ ★ · · ·

"WHAT IF THAT'S LINGERIE?" Thalia asks, nodding at a few wrapped gifts on a side table. "You think they'll make us watch her open it?"

There's a distressed noise, and it takes me a moment to realize that I made it.

"Who would want that?" I finally say. "Mom doesn't want that. Her sisters don't want that. We don't want that."

"It's traditional at a bridal shower," she points out. "You get wine-drunk and open all the embarrassing presents people get you in front of everyone while they make lots of wedding-night jokes."

"Is that real?" I ask. I've never been to a bridal shower, only seen it on bad reality TV shows. "Also, she's fifty-five years old. This isn't a bridal shower, she doesn't want a bridal shower, what would she need with a bridal shower?"

Thalia snorts at my impression of my mom. We've both been here since late morning—I left my apartment at five this morning and if that's not proof of filial love, I don't know what is—and now, in the early afternoon, we're standing in a corner and hoping no one gives us any more tasks. I *cannot* move another chair.

Technically the party started five minutes ago, so people have been trickling in—relatives, my mom's friends. Gerald is already here, but Madeline isn't. I know she's coming, and every time I hear the front door open, a thrill runs down my spine and I have to pretend I don't feel it.

"This could be so much worse," Thalia admits. "One of my friends went to a bridal shower where the bride made the attendees vote on which sex position she should inaugurate her marriage with." I choke on my Jamaica agua fresca, and Thalia smiles innocently at me. "Joke was on her because *piledriver* won."

I'm coughing and trying to pretend I'm not—if I make too much noise someone might notice my presence and want me to move another chair—and Thalia calmly takes another sip of her wine, smirking so hard she might hurt herself.

"I have a feeling they didn't take the suggestion," she

goes on. "I had to look up *piledriver* and it doesn't look very comfortable. Anyway, at least Mom and Gerald aren't asking us to do *that*."

"It could always be worse, is what you're saying?"

"Exactly. And besides, Mom isn't—"

I can hear the front door open, and my stomach knots. I take a drink and a deep breath to cover it up, try to focus on what Thalia's saying.

"It's not her," she says, rolling her eyes.

"Not who?"

"Javi, don't. I'll tell you when it is, okay?"

I give up on acting cool because it's clearly not working. "Thanks," I say and manage to get Thalia talking about her research.

· · · · ★ ★ ★ ★ ★ · · · ·

"—BEHAVIOR IN A CONTROL GROUP," Thalia's saying. If I'm being honest, my mind has wandered a bit, at least until she nods at the room behind me and says, "*That's* her. No, don't—"

I turn and there Madeline is, still closing the front door. She's wearing the same coat she wore at Christmas, and I swear her hair's even bluer, ten different shades of blue and green, like sunlight on a perfect Caribbean lagoon. I remind myself to breathe. Madeline's flushed from the cold, smiling, holding a gift bag in one hand. She takes off her coat and hugs my mom, then hands over the gift.

"*Javier*," my sister hisses. She finally grabs my elbow. "How many times do you think I said your name?"

I can tell I'm blushing, the rest of my skin prickling with awareness at her proximity. This room feels too big and too small at the same time.

"Jesus, I turned back around, okay?"

"I'm not the one trying not to get caught."

"I looked to see who came in when the door opened!"

"Look." She glances down into her drink. Thalia is... blushing? "You can't stare at her with your tongue out like a cartoon skunk if you want to keep whatever this is a secret."

"I wasn't—"

"Javi, I just *watched* you. It was gross. Kinda sweet, but gross." She takes another drink. "And maybe trust me on how to not get caught fucking someone you shouldn't?"

I've got about ten responses for that, but I end up going with, "I like how you told Madeline you and Caleb met in college."

Thalia grimaces. "It's technically true," she says. "We were in a college. *Don't.*"

"I wasn't!" I say, pretending like I wasn't going to turn around again.

"You have to give it at least thirty seconds, and you have to make a *normal face.*"

I maintain eye contact and flip my sister off as subtly as I can.

She snaps her fingers. "Pepé Le Pew!" she says. "That's the cartoon skunk's name."

"You're the worst sister in the world."

"I like her dress," Thalia says. "You think it's vintage? Maybe it's vintage. It's cute. Ooh, she's meeting the aunts. I think she just told Alma she likes her necklace. It does match her hair. Madeline's, not Alma's."

"I don't need a play-by-play."

"Now she's getting nice-to-meet-you *hugs*. What a lovely young woman this Madeline is."

"Are you done?"

"No. Now she's laughing politely at—"

I don't need my sister to tell me Madeline's laughing at something because I can hear it, the specific way it bubbles out of her and bursts through the room, rising above everything else.

"Thank you," I say and stack my empty cup into the empty cup in her hand and turn to go say hello like a completely normal person.

· · · · · ★ ★ ★ ★ · · · ·

THE SECOND I make eye contact with Madeline, she smiles, and I grin like an idiot. For half a second, I go to kiss her before suddenly remembering that the rest of the world still exists—for example, my aunts who are all *right there* and watching every second of this unfold—so instead of giving her a kiss I manage a whole-body twitch that I try to cover up by offering a handshake.

Only, as I do that, Madeline tries to go in for a hug, and then we both laugh, and she goes for the handshake and I go for the hug, and when we finally manage to do some sort of greeting that's half of each, we're both bright red and trying to play it off like it's nothing.

From the corner of my eye, I can see Bastien over by the wine, rubbing his temples.

# THIRTY-SEVEN

## MADELINE

IF JAVI and I don't manage to act completely normal when I get to the certainly-not-a-bridal-shower event, at least we act too awkward for anyone to think we're fucking. Or... fucking with benefits. Is that what you call it when you're fucking and also having frequent conversations that aren't about the fucking? I mean, in theory we're not fucking right now, except when we accidentally have phone sex while I'm at someone else's house, because we're waiting until after our parents get married to resume fucking, at which point I believe we'll also start dating. Which we obviously aren't doing yet—we're just fucking sometimes, talking a lot, not seeing anyone else, and sometimes, secretly, at least one of us is wondering whether our boss would care if we moved across the state even though that is putting the cart about ten miles before the horse.

I would like the record to show that this morning I fully planned on following through with our (renewed) *not until after the wedding* agreement. I even went to an eight o'clock yoga class to work out some energy and frustrations, and during the part at the end where you lie on the mat and think about your day, I even set the intention to only interact with Javi in a G-rated manner.

Unfortunately for my intention, it's been a month since I last saw him and today he's wearing slacks that fit him very well and a button-down shirt with the sleeves rolled up, and I'm not made of stone.

"Hey," is the brilliant, witty thing I manage to say when we finally disentangle from our far-too-polite hug, during which I didn't press my entire body against his the way I want to. "Haven't seen you in a minute."

God, who let me interact with attractive people? I've still got my hand on his wrist, and I can feel the tendons flexing. It sends a tingle down my spine, but I can't make myself let go.

"Yeah," he says. His hair's down, just past his shoulders, and he rakes it back with his other hand in a way that makes me blush even harder. "Not since New Year's, right?"

"Nope!" I say cheerfully, and then *thank god* someone taps me on the shoulder and tells me where to put my purse and my coat, and I finally break away.

· · · ★ ★ ★ ★ ★ · · ·

"IT'S ROSA, then Alma, then my mom, then Maria," Bastien is saying. "What, your dad didn't make you flashcards?"

"I'll suggest that for next time," I say. Bastien holds up two bottles of white wine, both dripping onto the counter from being in ice, and I hesitate long enough for Bastien to apparently read my mind.

"Javi's fine," he says. "He doesn't drink, but it's not a problem if other people do. Promise."

It's tempting because wine makes me both friendlier and

funnier, but it still feels...weird. "I don't think that'll do me any favors with remembering who's who," I say.

"Probably not," he says, pouring one for himself. "But it'll help you feel better when they start asking you nosy questions, which they will since you're family now."

"How nosy?"

Bastien grins, and it makes him look a *lot* like his brother. "Why—you worried they'll figure it out?"

Shit, is this—is this sibling stuff? Is this sibling-type harassment?

"Figure what out? I don't know what you mean."

"That's a good strategy." He nods approvingly. "Make *them* spell it out. Don't let them fish for information. Or don't give them any fish when they do."

"No fish. Got it."

"And if it makes you feel better, Alma didn't ask Caleb about his intentions toward Thalia until they'd been dating for three whole months."

"Wow, great," I say and glance out at the living room, where one of Paloma's sisters—either Rosa or Maria, it's hard to tell from here; sue me, they look alike—is talking to Javi, who's nodding intently and looking a little hunted.

· · * * ★ ★ ★ * * · ·

JAVI'S extended family are all kind, warm, welcoming, *talkative* people. They're delightful, but after an hour or so I'm full of pulled-pork tacos—apparently there was a debate about whether they should get tacos or barbecue for the party, so they got both—and need a break from, you know, people.

That's what I'm doing in the hallway that leads to the downstairs bathroom: taking a break. I'm not *hiding*, and I'm certainly not hiding from my aunt Susan and her wife, Kate, who want to discuss wedding-day transportation logistics, or Javi's cousin Luis, who has shown me at least fifty pictures of his kids. I just need a minute to breathe, and if I made prolonged eye contact with Javi before coming back here, well, isn't that interesting.

When I check my phone, I've got a bunch of notifications, including a million texts from Ben, who's never sent one message when fifty will do.

**Ben:** What are you doing tonight?

**Ben:** Scott's GF has the flu so they canceled on us and now I've got two tickets to go ice skating at the MacArthur Mall in Norfolk

**Ben:** It'll be fun, you can watch me fall over

**Ben:** Oh shit, are you at that thing with your stepfamily?

**Ben:** How late is that going?

**Ben:** If you want you can bring the stepbrother you're boning

**Ben:** Unless ice skating is too much of a DATE and you've got other, bonier plans

I'm wondering, briefly, what it'd be like to have subtle friends, when Javi rounds the corner. He leans against the wall opposite me. The hallway suddenly feels half the size it was a minute ago.

"Who are you hiding from?" he asks, and I stick my phone back into my pocket.

"Who says I'm hiding?"

"Just lurking, then." He moves one of his feet to tap against one of mine.

"You can tell I'm an ambush predator by the way my

eyes are on top of my head. Like an alligator, or Cookie Monster."

"And I've walked right into your trap," Javi says, putting both hands into his pockets, letting his fall head back. "Oh *no*."

"Grr," I say, fake-snarling, a totally normal thing to do. Javi just laughs, and I tap my foot against his, and I don't mind feeling a little predatory right now. "I was just taking a break. Not from you," I say quickly as he opens his mouth. "From people."

"Should I be insulted that I'm not people?" he asks, clearly feeling anything but insulted.

"No."

"Good. I wasn't planning on it," he says, and then there are footsteps around the corner. We both move our feet back as one of his cousins—Sandy?—appears.

"Is this the bathroom line?" she asks, and we both explain at once, over top of each other, that no, the bathroom is free—we're just standing here for other reasons having to do with the pictures on the walls (me) and something to do with the architecture of this interesting prewar house (Javi). Sandy just nods and goes into the bathroom. Javi and I look at each other. He clears his throat.

"If you go down to that end of the hallway, the wainscoting is still original," he says in what I have to assume is a Museum Tour Guide voice. "It's beautifully painted in an interesting example of post-classical art."

He nods toward the end of the hallway, which has no wainscoting, but which does have three doors that look like they lead to bedrooms.

"I *love* post-classical wainscoting," I say and follow his lead.

· · * * ★ ★ ★ * * · ·

JAVI PULLS ME INTO A BEDROOM, the floor crowded with two air mattresses and sleeping bags. He kicks one aside, then pushes me up against the closed door and kisses me.

I've been thinking about his mouth for a month, and this is somehow even better than I remembered: slow and warm and intense. One hand tilts my face up, the other spreads wide over my rib cage and presses me back.

It's nearly silent, except for the sounds of our lips together, and those seem so loud. I try to swallow the needy little noises I want to make, though I don't quite succeed because Javi pulls back after a bit, both of us breathing raggedly, and whispers, "Shh."

"You *shh*," I whisper back, but he's already got his teeth on my earlobe and I have to gasp through clenched teeth so I don't make a noise.

"God, Madeline." His voice is a little shaky. "I want to eat you alive."

His hand is still cupping my face, and I grab his wrist so I can suck his thumb into my mouth, run my tongue over it with the knuckle between my teeth. Javi braces himself with his forearm over my head, pulls back, and stares at me with something like awe.

The blinds are down and the lights aren't on, and with his back to the windows it's dark enough that I can't tell where the black of his pupil turns into the deep brown of his iris. But I can see that his hair's in disarray and hear that he's breathing like there's not enough oxygen in the air. He looks down to where I've got his thumb in my mouth, and I suck a little harder. Javi swallows, and his breathing hitches, and slowly, gently, he pushes it in.

I take it. I tilt my head back and let my eyelids lower, the slight taste of salt on my tongue. He stops when my teeth are at the second knuckle, just hard enough to *feel*, the pad of his thumb on my back of my tongue. I suck a little harder, move my tongue against it—listen to his ragged inhale—and swallow.

He groans. It's quiet, just a few notes from deep in his chest, more of a creak than a groan, but it's there. His eyelids flutter closed for half a second. I can feel my heart pounding through every part of my body—in my *bones*, I swear—so turned on my skin is heated. If he put his thigh between my legs right now, I think that friction alone might make me come.

Thankfully—his whole family is still on the other side of this door—he doesn't. Instead, he pulls his hand back slowly, the pad of his thumb pressing on my tongue, dragging softly over my bottom lip, and without breaking eye contact he puts his thumb into his own mouth and sucks it clean.

It shouldn't be hot. It is. We kiss one more time—so gentle it's almost tentative, which is good because I can't take much else—and then he steps back, kicks a sleeping bag aside, and sits in a desk chair. He scrubs his hands over his face.

I smooth my dress and my hair and go sit on the bed. Our knees are touching and nothing else, but each brush still feels electric. It's a secret, cozy silence, just us existing in the same room for once.

Finally Javi takes a deep breath and shifts in the chair, glancing around. "I don't think there's wainscoting in here," he says.

I laugh so suddenly that I snort and have to clap a hand over my mouth. "Wow," I finally manage. "Okay, wow, that's what we're talking about."

"What else would it be?" He grins, his knee knocking against mine.

"Is wainscoting when there's fancy stuff on the lower half of the wall or fancy carvings where the wall meets the ceiling?"

We both glance up at the same time. "I thought it was the lower half of the wall, but now I'm less sure," he admits.

"Well, this room doesn't have either. And I should probably let *post-classical* slide, huh."

He makes a face, twisting in the chair, our knees still touching. "I was horny and trying to remember words from my art history class last semester," he says. "Sorry if my mind wasn't entirely on architectural details."

I'm tempted to ask what his mind *was* on. I'm also tempted to point out that inventing architectural details was his idea to begin with.

"Was this your childhood bedroom?" I ask instead. My phone buzzes again in my pocket. It's probably Ben, and I ignore it because *ice skating* is such a...date thing, and we've never done date things.

"It was my bedroom for the three years of high school we lived here," Javi answers and shrugs. "And then I stayed in here on and off for a long time after that, whenever I needed a place. But it's really just a guest room now. My mom drove the last of my stuff out to me when she came for Christmas. I think she thinks it's a deterrent to me moving back in again."

He says it like it's a joke. But it's not, not all the way.

"Or she thinks you're out for good," I say.

"Maybe," he allows, and now he's looking around the room, eyes lingering on a lamp, then on a big, abstract art print on one wall. "At least she redecorated before I came back the last time. Rearranged the furniture and everything."

"And it helped?"

"It helped. Maybe that was the secret ingredient this time around." He's half smiling, half joking, like he thinks that if he makes light of it, it's not so bad.

"Is this where you slept after the first time we met?"

"It is, not that I slept very well," he says, and now he's leaning forward, one fingertip on my knee. I'm wearing tights, so the sensation is dulled, and I barely feel it when he nudges the hem of my dress an inch higher. "My mom woke up when I got home, wanting to know where I'd been, who I'd been with, what I'd been doing, the whole time trying to look at my pupils and smell if there was booze on my breath without me figuring out that's what was going on."

Now he grins, tracing a circle on my knee, and it finally reaches his eyes. I lean back on my hands, the comforter cool under my palms. "Joke was on her since I was dead sober but desperately trying to hide that I'd just been fucked within an inch of my life by a woman whose last name I didn't know."

Obviously, my face goes hot.

"Paloma wouldn't approve?"

"Not really, and especially not then."

"Do you want to go ice skating tonight?" It's been banging around my brain this whole time, and it finally gets out of my mouth. "You can say no. It's pretty last-minute; maybe you're doing—"

"Absolutely," he says before I can give him more reasons not to. Somehow it catches me off-guard.

"It's basically a double date with Ben and Amy," I warn. "Out in public, and I know we're off until after the wedding."

"It's just ice skating, Madeline," he says with a little smile and a little shrug. "Stepsiblings can hang out."

"Right," I say, because that is a very important fact that I somehow forgot: related people often spend time together, even if they're not also fucking. "We should probably head back out there before they send a search party."

Javi rubs his hands over his face again, then stretches, then finally stands. He offers me a hand up, and when I take it, he tugs a bit too hard and I stumble into him with a small "Oh!" noise as his arms go around me.

"That was on purpose," I accuse his shoulder, even though I'm pleased about it.

"Yeah," he says, and gives me a short, chaste kiss, his hand on the back of my neck. "But I've got something to look forward to now."

"You didn't before?" We didn't actually discuss it, but I'd been assuming I was going to get laid tonight.

Pleasingly, Javi goes a little pink. "Something else," he says, and I step over a sleeping bag and to the door.

# THIRTY-EIGHT

## JAVIER

I'VE BEEN ice skating once before in my entire life. We lived in Washington State for a year and a half when my dad was briefly stationed at Everett, and for half a second, I considered playing hockey instead of football. Still a violent, manly sport, so my father approved, and I thought it was a little more interesting.

But hockey's expensive, so it lasted for one public skating session, and that was it.

"Yes, I've been ice skating before," I'm telling Madeline as we stand outside the rink, drinking hot chocolate from a nearby coffee shop. We're here early—a novel experience for me, if I'm being honest—so we're waiting for Ben and Amy, who have our tickets. The rink is set up in an open, grassy spot between a mall, a road, and an apartment building, so Madeline and I are doing nothing next to a fountain that's been shut off for the winter.

It's the best time I've had all month.

"A lot?" she asks. It's cold out, and we're in hats and scarves and coats, standing close enough that our arms are touching.

"Technically once," I admit. "Though I've also been roller skating."

Madeline scrunches up her face and then exhales hard, breath fogging into the air. "We're fucked," she says succinctly.

"Well, with that attitude."

"With any attitude!" she says, laughing, nudging our shoulders together. Even through two winter coats, I swear it tingles. "The right attitude isn't going to make me suddenly have good balance, and I'm probably going to take you down with me."

"Is that a threat or a promise?" I ask. "You remember this was your idea, right? Is this all so you've got an excuse to knock me over?"

"This was *not* my idea, this was Ben's idea," she says. "And also, do I even need an excuse—oh! Hey!"

She waves with the hand that isn't holding hot chocolate, and fifty feet away, a man and a woman wave back. I stand a little bit taller and ignore the knot in my stomach, some combination of vague jealousy and the secret hope that her oldest friend will like me.

"We escaped the family event and got here early," she says as they get closer, finally coming into the light. They're both wearing hats and scarves, so it takes me a second before recognition dawns on me "Ben, Amy, this is Javier. Javi, this is my friend Ben and his girlfriend—"

"Castillo?" I interrupt, staring at Ben's baffled-looking girlfriend.

"*Lopez?*" she says. "You're...?"

"You're *that* Amy?" I say, looking from Madeline to Ben to Castillo. "Birdwatching boyfriend Ben is *this* Ben?"

"Wait," she says, and looks for a moment like she's doing equations in her head. "Is—Madeline—are you the one-night stand girl? *Madeline* is the girl I heard about on a biweekly basis for all those months?"

Next to me, Madeline has gone very still, and my face has gone very hot, and Castillo has suddenly gone very quiet. I clear my throat into the silence.

"Yeah, this is her," I offer.

"He's also her stepbrother," Ben says, in a possible attempt to make this less awkward.

"Not yet!" That's Madeline, and Ben rolls his eyes.

"They're T-minus two weeks from being stepsiblings," he says. "I'm going to their parents' wedding. It's going to be *so* interesting."

"I didn't know you were dating anyone—and definitely not your stepbrother," Castillo says with a sideways look at Ben. It's a little accusatory.

"It was a secret! I told you I could keep a secret," Ben says.

"We went to *brunch*," Castillo says this time to Madeline. "I thought brunch was a friendship event where we shared our personal lives! I told you about my reading!"

"Your reading is on the bookstore's website. That's not a secret," I tell her.

"It's a secret that I'm A. Y. Castillo."

"It's got your picture."

"I haven't told very many people about...this," Madeline says, making a vague gesture between the two of us. Fair. "Uh, pretty much, I told Ben."

Ben is currently giving me a long, thoughtful look. I return it with one of my own.

"Well, I guess I understand why," Castillo's saying. "Even if you're not technically related, it's still kind of taboo. Maybe that's part of the appeal?"

"I think we should ice-skate now," Ben says, and gestures us all toward the front kiosk.

· · * * ★ ★ ★ * * · ·

"I HATE CHILDREN."

"Wow."

"Look at them," Madeline says, gesturing one gloved hand at two kids zipping through the throng of ice-skaters like they were born with skates on their feet. "Why are they good at this? They learned to *walk*, like, three years ago."

The gesture throws her a little off-balance, and she wobbles before righting herself. I hover my hand over her arm, just in case, but it's more out of a desire to help than confidence that I actually could. At best, I'd heroically go down with her.

"Kids have a lower center of gravity and haven't learned to fear death yet," I say. "And their bones are rubber. And falling from two feet off the ground hurts less than falling from six feet off the ground."

"That's no excuse," she grumbles. "Ben couldn't have had tickets to a sleigh ride?"

"We're a mile from the beach. How many sleighs do you think there are here?"

"A winter-themed booze cruise?" she says, then glances over at me before wobbling again. "Or whale watching, or something where you sit down."

We're skating side by side, slow and careful, along the outer circumference of the rink. It's noisy, the speakers playing a combination of country music and mainstream hits from twenty years ago, and the rink is full of people on and off the ice. She's not wearing her hat anymore. On a whim, I lean over and kiss the crown of her head, warm blue hair under my lips.

Madeline looks up at me, and there's a moment where I think she's about to tell me I shouldn't have done that. Then she smiles, cheeks already pink from exertion, and I smile back helplessly because everything seems so *possible* right now. Like it's me and her, together, and nothing else— parents and family and distance and life—matters. Maybe it doesn't.

"I'm glad you came," she says, still looking up at me.

"You thought I might say no?"

"I thought there was a chance you'd want to just go to my place."

"But then I'd miss watching you swear at children," I say and carefully, *carefully* take her hand. I'm not wearing gloves, but she is, fuzzy and scratchy against my skin. "And I'm really enjoying that."

"They're too good at skating," she says, and she squeezes my hand in hers. My heart might explode. "It's unfair." She's silent a moment. "But I'm enjoying this, too."

There are dozens of people on this rink right now, but we're looking at each other again and it's like we're alone, the rest of the world an unimportant blur. I've got the dizzy impulse to open my mouth and tell her everything—*I think about you all the time, I love you, I think I've loved you since the moment I laid eyes on you*—but I stuff it down, and instead I lean in as she tilts her head up.

Then my foot hits hers, or hers hits mine, and Madeline yells "Shit!" and I grab the railing in a death grip and try to get my feet in the right place and fuck, fuck, *fuck,* don't fall on Madeline, but she sprawls on the ice and my feet slide out from under me.

"Are you okay?" I gasp, trying to haul myself up.

"Ow. *Fuck*," she says. "I'm fine."

"Sorry." I've managed to get one knee on the ice, and I'm doing my damnedest to get my feet under me. It's not going very well.

"I think that was me," she says. She kneels up, shaking out her hands. She gets one skate under her and slips. Meanwhile, I haul myself to standing.

"Here." I offer a hand.

"I'm just gonna pull you down again."

"You're not. I'm good," I tell her, so she grabs my hand and then we're both flailing until she lets go and sprawls back on the ice. This time she's sitting, leaning back on her hands with her skates in front of her. She laughs with her head thrown back.

"That almost worked," I lie as I get upright again. There's ice sparkling on her knees, quickly soaking through her tights. "Here, what if you—"

It takes a minute, but we work it out: Skates braced against the wall, I grip the rail like it's a lifeline, and finally she stands in front of me and we're both of us back on our feet. Her hair's wet where it touched the ice, and she's breathing hard, but she's smiling again.

"Romantic enough?" We hover near each other, almost touching.

"There's no one else I'd rather face-plant with while ice skating," she says. "You sure you're okay?"

My shoulder has felt better and my ankle might need some ice later, but I'll live. "I'm positive," I tell her. Other skaters go past. On the other side of the rink, Ben and Amy are lazily skating hand in hand. Someone races past us going backward. It's all peripheral, the hum of life around us, bright and cold and alive as anything.

"I really want to kiss you, but I don't think I should risk it," I say. "I'm too far from the ground."

"You can owe me," she says, eyes sparkling, and then someone in a uniform comes by and tells us to keep moving, so we set off again, wobbling and laughing, and I can't remember the last time I was this happy.

· · * * * ★ ★ ★ * * · ·

"THERE GO MY OLYMPIC DREAMS," says Madeline, clomping toward a bench, still in her ice skates. The only thing harder than ice skating is walking in ice skates. We both look like drunks trying to pass a field-sobriety test. "Shot to hell."

"Come on, I believe in you," I say.

"You're sweet when you're delusional."

Someone walks right in front of me, and I windmill to a stop.

"I thought I was sweet all the time."

"You're sweet most of the—shit!" Madeline's skate slips on something or other, and she flails sideways into me. The following ten seconds are dicey, but at the end of it we're both upright, clinging to each other and panting.

"You okay?"

"Sorry—I nearly took you down with me again," she says. "I'm telling you, no Olympics."

We get the last few feet to the bench where Ben and Castillo—Amy? I have no idea what to call her now—are already sitting and looking down at their feet, like maybe the ice skates will magically remove themselves. I manage to deposit Madeline, then turn and carefully flop backward. Nothing breaks.

"I used muscles I didn't know I had," says Ben, still staring at his feet.

"Didn't you graduate med school?" I ask.

"I'm not a muscle doctor," he says, like that explains anything. I don't push.

"My bones feel like mud. Is that something that can happen?" I wonder.

"There's a sentence I've never heard before," says Madeline.

"Thanks. I try to keep things interesting."

"I think that condition is called...*muddius bonius*," Ben offers.

"Babe, you didn't even try," chides Castillo.

"And who can blame me?"

Castillo, sitting on the other side of Ben, takes this opportunity to lean forward and look over at Madeline and me. "Also, a lot of elite distance runners are in their thirties. You could still have a shot at the Olympics."

"I really don't think I could," says Madeline. "For starters, I think I'd have to like running."

"That's a problem," muses Castillo, and we all stare down at our skates for a moment. "Okay," she finally says and cracks a few knuckles. "We're doing this. Skates off."

· · · ★ ★ ★ ★ ★ · · ·

SINCE WE'RE GENTLEMEN, Ben and I wind up returning the rental skates to the counter. Madeline and Amy wait on the bench and debate which Olympic sports they'd be best at. Amy has claimed that she could probably manage the biathlon, where you shoot while skiing. Madeline is wondering how hard bobsled can be, really.

"There's gotta be an obscure one I could train really

hard for," Ben is saying while we stand in the line, waiting to give these skates back. "Racewalking, maybe?"

"I think Madeline was onto something with bobsled," I say. "Luge? I bet I could do luge. You just have to lie down."

There's a brief silence, and when I look over at Ben, he's studying me with a slight frown. I have a brief, unpleasant memory of my father waiting in the living room for Thalia's prom date.

"Be good to her," he says, and I stand a little taller. Just in case.

"Of course I will," I say. "You're not going to try and give me the *hurt her and I'll kick your ass* talk, are you?" I've observed that talk, and I've gotten that talk, and it annoyed the shit out of me every single time.

Ben snorts. "What? No, I'm not prepared to kick anyone's ass, are you kidding?"

Shit. "Sorry," I say. "I've been with my family all day. It's easy to forget that some people are normal."

"Technically you're still with your family," he says and nods toward where Madeline and Castillo are sitting.

"Wow, clever."

"If Madeline's gonna get with her stepbrother, I'm gonna give her shit about it." Now he's grinning. "Sorry."

"Are you?"

"Not really," he says and then looks thoughtful for a second. "Well, maybe a little. I didn't realize—"

He breaks off, his eyes over my shoulder, and I glance back to see what he's looking at. It's Madeline and Castillo, of course, still on the bench in their winter gear, talking.

"Realize what?" I ask, and I try not to sound as desperately curious as I feel.

Ben shrugs, unhelpfully. "I didn't realize... She acts like herself around you," he says like he's thinking aloud. "I'm pretty sure this is the first time she's acted like herself around someone she's dating, and I didn't realize that she wasn't until tonight."

I want to say *How does she act* and *Who else has she dated* and *I hope they didn't hurt her*, but I don't because it's not my business.

"Who wouldn't want that?" is what I eventually say, because I'm not sure what else there is. "She's great."

*Great.* There are probably a hundred better words to describe Madeline, but that's the one that comes out while I talk to her oldest, closest friend.

"Yeah, she is," he agrees. "Just, you know, treat her well, okay? She means a lot to me, and I like it when she's happy."

It's such a one-eighty from the *hurt her and I'll kill you* talk I was half expecting two minutes ago that I can't think of what to say. I'm just suddenly so, so glad that Madeline has him in her life.

"Me, too," I finally say and sneak a look back at her.

# THIRTY-NINE

## MADELINE

"DO YOU NEED TO LEAVE?" I ask, putting my glass in the sink.

"Eventually." Javi reaches around me to do the same, boxing me in against my kitchen counter as he does. "If I'm not at my mom's house in the morning, there'll be questions."

He's got on the same sweater he did at New Year's, something soft and lightweight that feels nice when his arms rub against mine from behind. He changed out of his button-down and slacks to go ice skating, and I wonder if this sweater is his Nice But Not Too Nice outfit. Date Nice. The thought gives me butterflies.

"You don't have a curfew?" I tease, and now his body is pressing against mine, his hands on the counter next to my hips.

"Not these days. Why—you want me to break rules for you?" He presses against me harder, the points of my hips against the countertop, the line of his erection grinding against my ass. I'm still wearing the dress and tights I had on earlier, at the Not a Bridal Shower, and my whole body's gone hot.

I flatten my hands on the counter and arch just enough to push back against him. "Of course I don't," I say. "I'm only here for an above-board, fully approved liaison with the t's dotted and the i's crossed."

"It's important to always dot your t's." He gathers my hair in one hand and tilts my head. He's gentle but he's got a grip like iron, and a horny little sigh escapes me. My eyes seem to have closed at some point.

"Shit," I say, and his teeth scrape down my neck.

"Hard to think straight?"

"I'm thinking great." I mean to say *right now*, but he bites my earlobe and the words turn into a moan.

"'Course you are," he says. His tongue traces the shell of my ear. "Bed?"

My bed is, like, a whole room away.

"Your mud bones aren't up for bending me over the counter and having your way?"

That gets his face buried in my hair and a sound that's half laugh and half moan.

"That what you want, you—you vixen-minx?"

"I wouldn't say no." I can feel his smile against my neck. Now is the coyness part of the game. Saying demure shit like that while shamelessly grinding back against his cock through all our clothes, practically begging for it.

"I think you'd like it." Now his other hand is around my hip, squeezing, like he can hold me still. "Some morning, maybe. You're in here wearing nothing but my shirt, at the counter, making coffee. Standing just like this when I come in." Now his lips are in my hair, his hand splayed over my stomach. Fuck, he has nice hands. "I wouldn't even say anything, just push our clothes out of the way and fuck you like this. You'd love that, wouldn't you?"

My breathing sounds like it's through a megaphone, I swear. "God, probably," I rasp out.

"I think you get off on letting me use your body like that," he goes on. "On me being so fucking sure of what you want. I think you like seeing what you can take, Madeline, and I think it turns you on *so* much to know that what you can take makes me feel good."

"Would it?" My voice comes out scratchy and strangled. I swallow. "If first thing in the morning, you found me making coffee in your shirt and nothing else?"

"Jesus, yes. I'd fuck you without saying a word. Just slide in and fill you up, but don't worry, I'd go slow." He presses a gentle kiss to my ear. "I'd be so gentle. Savor the feeling of you giving it up inch by inch, all tight and warm, first thing in the morning. Even if you begged for it harder, I'd be so soft, so sweet. As gently as I could."

"No bruises? No bite marks? Not even *one*?" It comes out pleading.

"Why would I torture you like that, you delicate thing?"

This from the man who came when I told him he left teeth marks. He knows what he's doing, and maybe he can do this forever. I'm going to lose my mind, so I wriggle my hands under my dress, then squirm my tights off and leave them in a pile on the floor. Javi steps back a bit to let me complete the (unsexy) process, and then he's pressing me in again, one hand on my lower back, the other locked around my upper thigh.

Slowly, he strokes the edge of the lace with one thumb.

"Did you wear these for me?" he asks, and I'm not too horny to roll my eyes at the cabinets.

"No, I wore them in case the aliens landed tonight and

wanted to do some probing," I say, and he pinches the soft skin on my inner thigh just hard enough to make me gasp.

They're Fuck Me Panties, all see-through lace that shows off most of my ass with strings over my hips. I wouldn't call them comfortable, exactly, but judging by Javi's reaction, they're effective.

"They match my bra," I offer. "Unzip me if you want to check."

Javi fumbles with the zipper and swears at the hook-and-eye closure at the top, and God help me, it's hot. By the time he pushes the dress down over my shoulders I'm practically wriggling against the counter. He leans in and bites the muscle where my neck meets my shoulder.

I make a shaky, desperate noise, and he lets go, kissing the spot softly.

"I could leave marks all over your pretty neck," he says. "Let everyone know where you've been and what you like."

I shove my dress up over my arms and manage to push Javi back enough to get it all the way off, then turn around, still leaning against my kitchen counter.

He stares, which he goddamn ought to because one, my bra and panties match, and two, my tits look great right now.

"Hi," I say after several long moments with zero eye contact.

Javi still doesn't look at my face—which is fine; I didn't wear this so he could look me in the eye—just skims both hands over my very-pushed-up breasts, then down my sides, until he hooks two fingers in the waistband of my panties and pulls until it cuts into my skin.

"Were you wearing this all day?" he asks, sounding bewildered. "Was this under your dress the whole time?"

I put my elbows on the counter and lean back a little,

pushing my hips into his hand. "That's the first thing you ask? You want an outfit report?"

"When I asked if you wore it for me, you got all sarcastic," he teases, then hooks two fingers under the center front of my bra and tugs. "Fine. I like the outfit you wore just for me, Madeline. Your tits are fucking *spectacular*."

"You can touch them if you want," I say. "Or keep looking. I like that, too."

"Fuck," he whispers and finally makes eye contact. "I'd bend you over right here, but I don't think my ankle's gonna take it after ice skating."

I laugh, and he rolls his eyes a little. But he's smirking about it, so I pull him in and give him the filthiest kiss I can, our bodies pressed together—him clothed, me nearly naked —rubbing myself against him. I moan into it, and he bites my lip, grinding against my hip, and finally I pull back.

"Come to bed. I'll take care of you," I say.

Thirty seconds later, he's sprawled on top of the covers, grinning up at me as I stand next to the bed.

"Off," I say, waving at his clothes.

He sits up and takes his shirt off deliberately, shakes out his hair, then tosses it into a corner. He takes his pants off more slowly, with considerably more dick-touching and groaning than strictly necessary. By the time he's fully nude I'm twitching with impatience.

"At your service," he says, grinning, one hand on his cock with the thumb sliding over the slippery head.

I crawl on top of him, pushing down on his sternum with one hand, and give him a long, slow, dirty kiss while he fingers the edge of the lace between my legs, just barely dipping underneath it.

Then I slide a hand into his hair, knee-walk forward, and sit on his face.

"Oh *fuck*," he manages to say before his eyes close and his arms wrap around my thighs, tugging me down. I've still got the panties on, and I can feel his warmth soaking through them, his tongue and lips at the edges of the fabric, his teeth dulled. It's all I can do not to grind against his face. I press my forehead against the headboard of my bed, gasping and swearing.

"Madeline," he says after I don't know how long.

"Sorry," I pant. "Are you—"

"Fuck my face. I can take it."

It takes me a second to process, but then I swallow hard and move my thumb to stroke his cheekbone. He's staring up at me, his hair fanned around his head, face in the V of my thighs.

"You sure?" I ask. "I don't want to get too rough with your pretty face."

His eyes go wider and his breath catches, hands even tighter where he's holding on to my thighs.

"Yeah, I'm sure," he rasps out.

The look on his face makes me feel drunk or high or something, and I slide my fingers over my lace-covered clit, right in front of his face.

"You want these off?"

He looks up at me, a smile playing around his lips.

"Yes, please," he says.

There's definitely a market for panties that can be removed without having to get off your lover's face, because nearly kneeing Javi in the temple isn't my sexiest move. I don't think it matters, though, because when I sit on his face again, he moans loud enough that my neighbors can probably hear.

I forget about trying not to suffocate him. I forget about pretty much everything that isn't my clit in his mouth or his hands still wrapped around my thighs. I've got one arm against the headboard and one in his hair, grinding against his face, swearing and moaning.

I come fast and hard and loud, my whole body jolting with every stroke of his tongue, and Javi keeps going until I pull his hair harder and gasp "Stop, stop, too much," and he lets me push back enough to sit on his chest. He looks me in the eye and licks his lips.

"You okay?"

"Are you kidding? I'm *great*," he says, sliding his hands up my thighs and stroking over my hips. "You wanna go again?"

I shake my head and reach behind myself, groping for his dick. I wonder if I could put a condom on him like—

"Don't," he says and grabs my forearm. I freeze. "I, uh, need a minute."

Then he *blushes*, and I'm going to die.

"You almost came?" I ask, because my brain is still a little orgasm-foggy. "Because I sat on your face?"

He blushes harder. I am *transfixed*.

"Did you hear yourself?" he says a little helplessly. "The noises you made. Jesus."

I scoot back a bit further and lean down, our mouths nearly together.

"Is this gonna make you come?" I ask, teasing.

"One way to find out," he says and kisses me. I can taste myself, and he makes a little noise, and it gets harder and dirtier from there.

"You good now?" I ask when I pull back, still leaning over him. Javi grins and lightly smacks my ass in answer. I grab a condom and a vibrator from my drawer, and then he pushes me off and we lie side by side. At some point, my bra came off. Javi tries to roll me onto my back, but instead I shove him back and straddle his hips.

"Your ankle," I say, like that's an explanation, line myself up, and slide onto his cock. His head goes back, his eyes close on a low groan. His hands grip my thighs so hard it might bruise. Fuck, I hope it bruises.

"God, fuck, okay," he bites out, chest heaving. I grind against him, slowly, and have to bite my lip. His eyes come open. "I forgot how good you look like that."

"Like what?" I ask. I want to hear it. Javi grins and grips my hips, the muscles in his arms flexing.

"Sitting on my cock," he says. "Does it feel as good as it looks?"

"Better, probably."

"You do like getting fucked after you've already come once," he says, rocking up into me. I push back, my hands on his chest. A small moan escapes me. He moves a hand up to pinch one nipple, and now I bite my lip, close my eyes, roll my hips against him. He's still fully seated inside me, and I can feel every millimeter he moves. "You beautiful, greedy thing."

"*Greedy*," I say, and I sound all throaty and breathless. "Just because I want more?"

"I didn't say it was a bad thing."

I'm still grinding on him, slowly. I half want to keep doing this forever, staying on this maddening plateau that feels good but isn't going to make me come. I wonder how long I could do this, whether I'd eventually lose my mind.

But I also remember going back out into Ben's living room and trying to watch *Fury Road* like I wasn't squirming at the memory of Javi's voice in my ear.

"I can be greedy," I say and grab the vibrator I pulled out. It's pretty no-frills—basically a vibrating silicone cylinder—and I turn it on low. I brace myself against Javi's chest, put it against my clit, and hold as still as I can.

It doesn't take me long at all to come again. I force my eyes open so I can look him. I don't say anything, just breathe and gasp and moan.

"Jesus, I felt that," Javi says, his hands spanning my thighs, fingers digging in, his blunt nails white-hot pinpricks that send a thrill up my spine. "Is it good, Madeline?"

"Yeah," I get out and squirm a little, then clench down. Javi's mouth opens and a broken groan comes out. "But it was only two."

"You want more?" He tries to tilt his hips up into me. I push down on his sternum a little harder, his heartbeat wild under my palm.

"Hold still, I'm busy." I turn the vibrator up a notch and put it back on my clit with a gasp. Javi takes his hands off my thighs and goes up onto his elbows to watch, his face flushed, his gaze practically tangible. His hair's stuck to his forehead and there's sweat beading on his chest.

"Come on, come on, come on." He's murmuring filthy nonsense. "God, you love this—fucking *hell*, Jesus, fuck, Madeline."

This time, I don't take the vibe off my clit; I just turn it up and hope it's got fresh batteries. By the time I come again there's a bead of sweat rolling down his sternum and Javi looks drunk, his breathing harsh and uneven. He's up on one elbow, his other hand on my thigh again, murmuring a stream off sweet-sounding filth.

Finally his eyes close and his head tilts back, the lines of his neck stark and beautiful.

"Please," he gasps and pushes himself up to his hands. We're nearly face-to-face. "Madeline, please."

I take his face between my hands and kiss him, dropping

the vibrator somewhere into the sheets. "I can't take much more," he mumbles into my mouth. "You're using your cunt as a torture device."

I'm unsteady, even shaking a little. Or maybe that's him. Fuck, I can't even tell any more.

"Should I stop?" I ask.

"No!" he says and swallows. "No, please. Just—have some mercy."

I grab the vibe again, turn it all the way up, and shove it right up against my clit. I'm half numb and half oversensitive, but this time I rock against him while I get myself off, and Javi shudders in relief.

I don't come hard, but I come with our foreheads together and Javi murmuring "Fuck, yeah, there it is—I love how good this makes you feel" and then we're kissing and I'm shaky and he's pulling us backward until he can lean against the headboard of my bed, hands back on my hips. I brace myself with one hand and clench and roll my hips, close my eyes against the little shockwaves it sends through my body.

"That's *so* good," he says. "Jesus. Thank you."

"You're welcome," I whisper, a purely automatic reflex, and it's kind of dumb but— "I wish you didn't have to go home."

"There's tomorrow," he gets out.

I push against the headboard and move my hips harder, rutting into him. He groans. I think his hands might be shaking.

"To Sprucevale, I mean. I wish you weren't so far."

Javi's eyes are glazed, and he's a flushed, sweaty mess and maybe the most perfect thing I've ever seen.

"I wish that, too," he says, and it sounds like he's cracking apart. "I miss you every fucking day, Madeline, every fucking"—he breaks off for a moment—"*minute*. God, I love the way you fuck me, please, *please—*"

Javi falls apart under me, the muscles in his shoulders standing out as he goes still and incoherent, hands tight on my hips. All I can think is *Holy shit, I did that* as his head goes back and a deep pink flush travels down his neck. He's beautiful and perfect and he's coming so hard it looks like he's getting rebooted, and *I* did that.

The thought makes me wildly, insanely possessive. His eyes flutter open and then his hand is in my hair, pulling my mouth down to his, and I quit thinking for a while.

# FORTY

## JAVIER

WHEN I COME out of the bathroom after we've both cleaned up and I've dealt with the condom, I spend a good ten seconds contemplating the pile of my clothes on Madeline's floor. Then I contemplate her, sprawled naked on top of her comforter.

"You have to go?" she asks, and it's the easiest decision of my life.

"In a minute," I say and get back into her bed. She's easy and loose-limbed, hair slightly damp with sweat, and she curls into me when I tug her over.

"Your ankle all right?" she asks a minute later.

"It's great. Perfect. Unbothered."

"Unbothered?"

I rotate the limb in question. "Slightly bothered," I amend. "But it'll be fine tomorrow."

I told her the whole story of my ankle a week or two ago, when I called her with some wedding-related excuse, like asking whether the tablecloths were white or cream. It's a comedy of errors, more than anything: I tripped going down concrete stairs with a fifty-pound pack on my back and broke two different bones in my ankle. I got one surgery to fix it, but it healed wrong anyway, so they had to re-break it and operate again. The only part I liked was the pain meds, and they ended up being the worst part of all.

"Good," she says. "Are you still getting lunch with your cool friend Castillo from the Marines? Maybe I'll be lucky enough to meet her someday."

I snort, and Madeline starts laughing, her body shaking under my arm.

"*How*," she says. "How did you never mention her first name?"

"I barely remembered it was Amy," I admit.

There's a long pause. I'm idly wrapping her hair around one finger, sliding my big toe up and down the front of her ankle.

"Was it always platonic?" she asks.

I grin down at her. "You mean, did we fuck?"

"Or date!"

"No, it was always platonic," I say, trying not to laugh at the face Madeline's making. "We were in basic training together. She wrote poetry and joined because her parents were too mean and broke to send her to college. I joined because I have daddy issues. We bonded, I guess. And then afterward she...wouldn't let me fall out of touch, basically."

"So I shouldn't be jealous?"

"Not of her, no."

Madeline pulls back a little and narrows her eyes at me. "Is there someone I *should* be jealous of?" she asks dryly.

"Dunno. Are you the jealous type?" I tease. Now I've got my hand on her hip.

"Of course not. I'm a reasonable adult who's in control of her emotions and never does anything irrational."

I raise one eyebrow at her.

"Never," she repeats.

"Too bad. Could be hot."

Her eyes narrow more, and I move one arm under my head, grinning down at her.

"Maybe someone else starts hitting on me, *right* in front of you," I say. "You wouldn't scare them off, just a little?"

"No, I'd trust you to tell them you weren't interested," she says, but she's trying not to laugh. "Like a *grown-up.*"

"Okay, but maybe they don't get the hint," I go on. "You wouldn't tell them *Get lost—this one's taken*?"

"What exactly are *you* doing in this scenario?" she asks. "Are you just standing there, batting your eyelashes?"

"I do have nice eyelashes."

"I'm kinda jealous of *those*, actually."

"I knew it." I pull her in and kiss her again, slow and sleepy. When she pulls back, our legs are tangled together.

"For the record, I wouldn't actually fight someone who hit on you," she says. "But if *you* didn't say *Sorry—I'm taken*, I'd probably get mad. At you. And if someone hit on me, I'd also tell them that."

Someone's probably said something more romantic before in the history of the world, but none of them were Madeline, talking to me in her bed, so they don't count.

"What if we told them after their honeymoon?" I say, my hand on the curve of her waist. "Maybe wait a week so they can settle in, and then..."

There's a brief silence. The backs of Madeline's knuckles brush against my chest. I wonder if she can feel the way my heart flutters whenever she says things like that, the way it flutters when we talk about the logistics of telling our parents. Whenever I confirm that this thing between us, which still feels like gossamer and quicksilver, stolen touches and secret glances, is *real*. Even now, there's a part of me that expects her to wake up tomorrow and realize what a dumb mistake she's made.

"That sounds right," she says, and she sounds faraway. "A month, then."

"Right."

"Don't fall asleep."

"One more minute," I say, and I hope it goes by slowly.

# FORTY-ONE

## MADELINE

YOU EVER HAVE one of those dreams where the real, non-dream world intrudes into your subconscious? Usually when that happens, I'm dreaming that I can't find a bathroom, and when I wake up, I need to pee. Glamorous, I know.

This time, I'm on some *Jeopardy*-like game show. Only, whenever I try to give an answer, all that comes out of my mouth is a buzzing noise. It's maddening and scary in that way that dreams are, and then I finally wake up to warm weight slung over my chest and my phone buzzing away on my bedside table.

*DAD*, the screen says, and it's still dark outside and oh my god, who died?

I answer the phone with "Is everything okay?" and sound just short of dead myself.

"Hi, honey," he starts. He sounds much more awake than me, but he's using his Nervous Voice. "Sorry—I know it's early."

"'Salright." The warm weight shifts, pulling me closer, nuzzles into my hair.

"Have you heard from Javier since last night?" Dad asks. "He never showed up at Paloma's, and we're all a bit worried over here."

Shit. *Shit.* It's morning, or close, and the cause of every-one's worry is currently my big spoon, one hand splayed over my rib cage, his mouth sleepily moving against the back of my neck. I take a deep breath and—

"I should go soon," Javier mumbles into my neck, approximately three inches from the receiver of my phone. "Sorry, I fell asleep. Mmmmm."

Before I can do anything, such as throw my phone across the room, he presses the world's loudest kiss against my neck.

The other end of the line is very, very quiet.

"Was that—"

"Hey, can I put you on hold for a sec? Thanks!"

Javi jolts behind me as I pull the phone away from my face and chant "Fuck, fuck, fuck" while I jab every button, hoping one is Mute.

"Wait. Fuck. Shit," he says. "You were on the phone? *Fuck.*"

I hang up by accident, then fling my phone onto the floor. We're both very, very still for several seconds.

"I'm sorry," he says, his voice still ragged. "I didn't realize you were on the phone. Shit. Uh, was it—"

"My dad," I say, rolling onto my back. "You're missing. Well, you were."

He swallows, and even though it's dark except for the first gray light of dawn and the streetlight filtering through my curtains, I can see the muscles in his throat move. According to the clock on my bedside table, it's 6:34 in the morning.

"Did he say anything else?" He's on one elbow above

me, hair dark and wild around his face. I want to reach out and push it back, run my fingers through it because Javi looks alarmed and soft and sleepy. He looks like he belongs in my bed.

"He said, 'Was that—' and then I panicked and hung up," I confirm.

"You think he knows my voice?"

"Probably, but he definitely just heard a male-sounding person in my bed at six thirty in the morning, so I'll probably end up explaining *something*." I pause and try to think of an alternate explanation. "I could always tell them that after ice skating I went out and picked up another guy, then slept with him? So that's who he heard? And you're still missing?"

Javi frowns the grumpiest frown I've ever seen on his face. It's kind of adorable. "Uh, that's okay. You don't have to."

My phone starts buzzing on the floor. We both glance over, but neither of us moves to pick it up.

"If I don't answer do you think your mom would come over—"

"Yes."

I wait for the buzzing to stop, then stare at my ceiling. When I was a kid, we painted my ceiling dark blue and stuck glow-in-the-dark stars on it. I should do that again.

"We can still lie," I say. "Tell them that you were tired after ice skating, it was late, you didn't want to bother anyone at your mom's house so you crashed here. No big deal. Still a secret."

Javier blows out a breath, then flops onto his back. "We could," he agrees without enthusiasm.

"Or, I don't know." I fold my arms over my eyes. "We could sort of tell the truth, that we hooked up but it was a casual one-time thing, no big deal, won't affect anything going forward? Would that be better or worse?"

Javi sits up, shoves a pillow out of the way, and leans back against my plush headboard. I swear that if I look hard enough, I can see where I held on to the top of it last night.

"Is that what you want?" he asks.

I roll over onto my stomach and shove my face into my pillow.

"I don't *know*," I say and then push myself up. We both fell asleep wearing underwear and nothing else—sleeping fully naked has always felt too weird—so he's in boxer briefs and I'm in panties. I pull the comforter around my shoulders. "I want to not ruin our parents' wedding. I want your mom to not kill you. I want the next two weeks to not be *weird*."

"We were going to tell them anyway," he points out.

"But this wasn't the plan! We were going to have time to figure out what to say, how to deal with it tactfully. They were going to be in a good mood right after getting back from a honeymoon…" I trail off. "I've done enough spontaneous shit in the last six months to last me a lifetime. I'd like to plan *one* important event in our relationship."

"You think it's a better plan to lie to them now and then in a month tell them we lied?" he questions, a little incredulous. "Fuck, I hate lying. I'm terrible at it."

"You lied to *me* the first time we met," I say, and, shit.

He looks at me, steady and serious, like he's hoping the right words will fall from the sky. "I know," he says softly.

"Sorry," I say in a rush. I squeeze my eyes shut against the feeling that I'm really fucking up right now: I know I should be over that, and I *am*, almost, but it's still there. Like a tiny splinter that hasn't worked its way back through the skin yet. "That wasn't fair. Forget I said it. We don't have to lie."

"I never did tell you the truth," he says. His voice has gone low and quiet.

My stomach flips, and I pull the comforter tighter around myself, suddenly cold. A voice in the back of my brain whispers, *How much has he lied, exactly?*

"No?" I sound steadier than I feel.

"I always liked you as more than a casual fuck," he says and shoves a hand into the wild halo of his hair, locking eyes with me. "Ever since—maybe not quite the moment I saw you, but pretty soon after that. Maybe when you said *Madeline, like the little French girl with the nuns*, or when you said you weren't going to dance on the table but that I could? I don't know."

"You almost did," I say, because it's true. He had one foot up there, ready to go, and I had to grab his wrist to pull him off.

"I would have," he says, and now he's smiling a little, like we're sharing a secret. "I was smitten by the time you said *Come back to my place*, you know."

Of course I didn't know, but I don't bring that up now.

"I didn't lie at our parents' engagement dinner," he says, serious again. "I really was six weeks out of rehab, working at a candy store by the boardwalk, and living with my mom. And I really was trying not to make any huge life changes for a while—it was supposed to be a year—because you're supposed to focus on your sobriety and on taking it one day at a time. On learning to function in this shiny new life you've got. It's not supposed to be too exciting or too out of the ordinary. Like, that's the point. Function at baseline for a while. Learn to deal."

Javi grabs one of the pillows, readjusts his legs, pulls it into his lap, and starts wrapping a corner of it around one finger.

"But I didn't tell you that I was already fucking it up. My parents had just split up, my sister was fighting with both of them about her new boyfriend, and my brother had taken that opportunity to come out to our mom. And they were all walking on eggshells around me, and I wasn't really handling any of it. I was supposed to go to meetings and do check-ins, but I was skipping them and lying to my mom and my therapist about it. And I had been talking a little with old friends who were still using, and I was so *bored*."

He's found a loose thread from the pillowcase, and now he's pulling at it.

"I was going to bars, for fuck's sake," he says quietly. "And I'd managed not to drink so far, but how long was that going to last, you know? Even if booze wasn't my big problem, it's not like it helped me make good choices. I'd relapsed twice already, and by then it had started to feel like...that was it, that was my story. It felt inevitable, like it was always going to happen."

I clutch the comforter tighter and try to ignore the cold swirl of guilt and unease in my stomach, the fact that I'm glad he went to a bar so we could meet.

"That's where I was when we hooked up," he says. "And afterward, I was, like, head over heels. Smitten. Down *so* bad. But it would've been the worst thing for both of us. I was already slipping, and I knew that the first time we got into a fight or something, I'd blow it."

Javi sighs, then tilts his head back against the headboard of my bed.

"But I also didn't trust myself, so I lied about being on

vacation. That way I couldn't come clean without you knowing I'd lied in the first place. Not my finest moment, but I couldn't bring myself to say *I like you, but if we date I might relapse*, either. You seemed so together, and I didn't want you to realize you'd just slept with the world's biggest fuckup."

"Javi, there are serial killers," I point out. "You can't possibly be the biggest fuckup."

"I can't even have that?" he says dryly, and I can't help but laugh. He flips the pillow around on his lap, twirling it by the pillowcase. "It worked, though. I didn't see you again, and it helped, I think, for me to remember I could do hard things. It didn't make the rest of it any easier, but I felt a little more like I could get through it."

My phone starts buzzing again, still on the floor, and this time I lean over and manage to snag it with two fingers. I only flail a normal amount. Predictably, it's my dad. I toss it onto the mattress in front of me.

"I should probably answer the next one," I say. "So we just tell them, right? Fuck lying?"

"Yeah."

"I also liked you," I say in a rush once my phone stops. "But first I thought you were just looking for a vacation fling, and *then* I thought you'd lied so you wouldn't have to see me again—which I guess you sort of did—"

"I *just* explained why that was actually romantic."

"And after that, we kept agreeing that everything was super casual and not a big deal, and I just—didn't want to throw my heart out there to get stomped on," I finish and then laugh. "Wow, what if we'd talked about our feelings?"

"Crazy talk," he says. "Blasphemy. C'mere."

He grabs the front of the comforter around my shoulders and pulls me off-balance toward him.

"Wait!" I yelp unbecomingly, my face two inches from his.

"What?"

"Morning breath."

"Jesus Christ," Javi mutters, rolls his eyes, and kisses me.

# FORTY-TWO

## JAVIER

WE TELL THEM THE TRUTH, but there are edits. Telling my mom *Hey, I'm in a romantic relationship with my stepsister* is bad enough; I don't need to start it with *So when I was fresh out of rehab, I picked up a total stranger at a bar and we had sex.*

"Wow," Gerald is saying, sitting opposite me at my mom's kitchen table. "Well, gosh. I had no idea. Since *Christmas*?"

Right. We omitted a few other details, too.

"We were going to tell you after the wedding," Madeline says quickly. "But we weren't sure how you'd feel about it, and we didn't want to do anything to overshadow your day."

"I gotta say, I'm surprised," Gerald says. "And it's a little unorthodox. But stranger things have happened."

"Yes, they have," my mom says, her eyes slicing at me.

"It's not like they're actually related," Gerald points out to her. "Just related by marriage. Or at least, they will be in two weeks!"

Madeline laughs nervously, but she also seems relieved. At least one of our parents has taken this pretty well.

"Who else have you told?" my mom asks after a long pause. She's using her Dangerously Neutral voice, and even though I've been an adult for over a decade, I start sweating.

I give her the list.

She gives me a long, hard look, her hands resting on top of each other on the table, dark red nails and a tasteful diamond engagement ring. Her hair is usually streaked with gray, but I think she's gotten it colored recently because it's the same brownish-black as mine.

I lean back in my chair and look right back at her, horribly aware that I need a shower and I'm wearing the same clothes I wore ice skating. God, I hope there are no sex fluids on me.

"Javier," she says. "Could we speak in private?"

I briefly consider telling her that anything she says she can say in front of Madeline and Gerald, but neither of them really needs to hear the fight I think we're about to have.

"Sure," I say and stand. Before I can follow my mom, Madeline reaches out, squeezes my hand, and gives me a smile. I can't help but smile back.

· · * * ★ ★ ★ ★ * * · ·

"JAVIER, I'M CONCERNED," is what she starts with. We're in the room that was mine for a few years, after we moved here and before I left for the Marines. The sleeping bags and air mattresses are gone, the bed unslept in. I guess that was for me.

"About what?"

"*About what.* What do you think? About you and your stepsister!"

I shove my hands into my pockets and ball them up so I

don't fidget too much because she'll probably get mad at me for that, too.

"You haven't thought this through," she starts. "I know things seem good now, but what if something goes wrong? You'll still have to see her sometimes. You'll still be family."

"Then we'll manage it like adults."

My mom looks doubtful, which is fair, I guess. "Are you going to ask Gerald and me to take sides? Or pretend like nothing happened? What if she cheats on you or something, and you don't handle it well?"

"What the hell, Mom?"

"It's a valid question. These things—"

"Is that really what you think of Madeline?"

"Of course not!"

I want to shout *Then what the fuck?!* but heroically, I don't.

"I'm just asking what will happen if she hurts you and you...spiral," she says, both hands out like she's trying to calm a strange dog. She's using her *I'm an adult and you're an idiot* tone of voice, the one that drove me insane while I was in high school.

"I don't know," I say as reasonably as I can. "Is Gerald the kind of guy who's going to kick me out and change the locks to *help* me get my shit together?"

"Jav—"

"Is he going to be more worried about whether I'm embarrassing him or whether I'm alive?"

"That is *not* what your father thought," she hisses, taking a step closer to me. I'm taller, but she's scarier.

"Sure."

"It's true that he wasn't perfect, but he was—"

"If you say *doing his best*, Mom, I swear to god I'm going

to jump out of that window," I say, lowering my voice and stabbing a finger at the window by the bed.

"Go ahead. We're on the ground floor," my mother says, rolling her eyes. "And you call *me* dramatic?"

"Where do you think I get it from?"

"You haven't thought this through," she repeats, deciding to ignore my window threats. "You're always like this—you see something shiny and interesting, and you *have* to jump in with both feet. What happens when she dyes her hair purple and you lose interest?"

Incredibly, I don't say *I was also super into her with pink hair, actually.*

"You think I only like her because she has blue hair?"

"Don't be like this. You know what I mean. You'll get bored, or she'll do something to hurt you, and everything could blow up in your face. In *our* faces."

I know my mom doesn't trust me. She doesn't trust my judgment, she doesn't trust my willpower, and she's probably still got the good silverware locked away somewhere. I wouldn't know, because I haven't gone looking for it.

She's not even wrong, because God knows I've given her reasons not to trust me. I'd probably tell her she shouldn't, if she asked. I barely know how to trust myself.

When I first got out of rehab, this last time, Bastien came over and we went through this room with a fine-toothed comb. We looked in every hiding space that I could remember. We looked in all the ones I could think that I might use, and we looked in some I'd never thought of. We took furniture apart and pried up floorboards and stuck our arms into vents. For our efforts, we found two pills and an empty baggie, and Bastien flushed them.

A couple of weeks before I helped my sister move and met Silas, I had a really bad day. I don't even remember what was so bad—some shit with the VA, some awful customers at the candy store. I came home, took a whole desk apart, went through even nook and cranny in this room, just in case we'd missed something. We hadn't.

I haven't bothered looking since then. Even when I've wanted to. I know there's nothing to find. I've spent years now prying up the floorboards of my life, foreseeing disaster and doing what I can to forestall it. This whole time I've known that sooner or later, I'll revert to my true self and I'll need every goddamn failsafe I can get once I do.

Only this is more than flushing some pills, isn't it? It's a messy apartment in a tiny mountain town. It's Zorro stepping on my face every morning to wake me up. It's the key to Silas's house and the instruction to use it if I ever, *ever* need to. It's a gold star on Wyatt's kitchen calendar. It's Castillo on speed dial. It's taken a long time and a *lot* of help, but I've been cobbling together a life that I don't want to take apart.

"You know it's been three years, right?" I finally ask.

Her face changes: now she's all pity and concern, like I'm a kid who's just skinned his knee. "You can't take that for granted," she says, quick but gentle. "Just because it's been a while doesn't mean you can let your guard down."

"I *know* that," I say and think *Jesus Christ, I fucking know that*, but don't say it out loud. "I also know that I've made it through worse."

I can tell she doesn't really believe me, and I can't even blame her.

"You could date someone else?" she suggests, changing the subject. "I'm sure there's someone nice in Sprucevale. Doesn't Wyatt have a sister?"

I want to scream, but instead I scrub my hands over my face because I'm a model of self-control.

"I'm not in love with Wyatt's sister, I'm in love with Madeline," I say as calmly as I can.

"Of course you are," she says, at her most patronizing and resigned.

"The fu—what does *that* mean?"

"It means I wish you'd think of someone else before you went and—*got intimate with*—Gerald's daughter! I'm tired of my family being torn apart, Javier!"

I don't have a good response for that because she's not even wrong. Shit happens. Maybe this will all fall apart and it'll be a huge disaster for everyone, and all I can say in the face of that is that I want this for as long as I can have it. I know fighting for something doesn't mean you'll win, but that doesn't mean you don't fight.

"Okay," I say, because I've got nothing else. "I'm gonna go talk to my girlfriend and then go home."

And I leave my old bedroom.

· · ✦ ✦ ★ ★★ ★ ✦ ✦ · ·

AN HOUR LATER, Bastien is holding up a bottle of Tabasco sauce, politely asking the waitress, "Is this the only hot sauce you have?"

She makes an apologetic face. "I can check in the kitchen, but I think so," she says. "More coffee?"

We all say yes. Once our mugs are full and there's another handful of single-serve half-and-half containers on the table, she leaves with a promise of pancakes and bacon, and the four of us are alone in a corner booth.

"This is a good spot," Bastien says, looking around. "Is it really open twenty-four hours?"

"Only on the weekends, I think," say Madeline. "But

they're still open late on weekdays, like maybe one or two? I haven't been out that late in a while—sorry."

I can't quite tell if Shirley's Diner is an actual relic or just cleverly decorated to look like one, but whichever it is, it's working. The wall behind the booth is stone halfway up, and above that there are a million framed photos, none of which look more current than 1985. The booths are bright red vinyl. The tables are sparkly fake-marble veneer. The counter looks straight out of the 1950s. The menu has an extensive milkshake selection.

Best of all, Madeline and I are holding hands under the table.

"Can you get diner mugs?" Madeline asks, holding hers up in one hand. It says *Shirley's Diner: Cookin' it up since 1953* on one side, with a picture of the exterior on the other. "They're always so good."

"They might sell you some if you ask?" Thalia says.

"Not this one specifically—diner mugs in general," Madeline amends. "They're always really thick, and they have a good shape, and the handle is so..." She squeezes it a little, in thought. "Holdable."

Obviously the other three people at the table pick up their mugs and consider this point. She's right: it's a very holdable handle.

"I'm sure you can find them on the internet," Bastien says. "A restaurant-supply store, maybe? They have to come from somewhere."

"How come you never see these for sale to consumers, though?" I ask, still contemplating the mug. I like contemplating the mug. It means I get a break from contemplating anything else. "There's gotta be a conspiracy."

"Maybe there's some trick that makes them only work in

diners," Thalia says, both hands around her mug. "Like, the... shape."

Everyone looks at her for a moment.

"No, go on, the shape," Bastien says. "Tell us why that's—"

"I don't hear *you* offering suggestions."

"I'm not the one who said it was a conspiracy!"

"*Anyway*, I like these mugs a lot," Madeline interrupts, as naturally as if she's been breaking up younger-sibling fights her whole life. "And Shirley's is a great place if you ever need a hangover cure."

Turns out when Madeline and I got to my mom's house at 7:30 this morning, my siblings—and the assorted cousins who were staying there—were in the den pretending they couldn't hear us. Thalia claims they *actually* didn't hear much of the reasonable talk the four of us had at the kitchen table, but no one has made that claim about the fight Mom and I got into immediately afterward.

But I forgive them because as soon as I stormed out of my old bedroom, Thalia and Bastien scooped Madeline and me up and informed us we were getting pancakes and coffee, no parents allowed.

"Well, I see you're going to make us ask," Thalia says, setting her mug down with a *thunk*. These things really are solid. "How'd it go?"

"And what *exactly* did you tell them?" Bastien adds. "I'd like to get my story straight."

"We said we started talking after we met at the engagement dinner," Madeline says calmly.

"Smart." Thalia nods approvingly.

"My dad was kind of reasonable, actually," Madeline goes on, twisting the mug around in her left hand. I squeeze her right, because I can. "There was some *Gosh, I wish you'd told me* and I think he feels bad that he didn't suspect anything, but I'm not bringing shame on my house or whatever."

"I am," I say cheerfully, and lean back in the booth.

"Well, yeah," Bastien says.

"Do you do anything else?" adds Thalia, so I flip them both off.

Naturally the waitress comes with our food in the middle of all this, so we have to pretend like we're adults while thanking her profusely. Madeline doesn't look impressed.

Once she's gone—the kitchen had no other hot sauces, which Bastien accepts with grace—I give them the whole dumb story of my dumb fight with Mom while eating pancakes.

"You should've jumped out the window, just to prove a point," is Thalia's final verdict.

"I didn't want to fuck up the azaleas," I say, dragging pancake through syrup. "And I'd probably have ended up somehow impaling myself on a branch. Then our entire family would have to come outside and see what happened and ask a lot of questions about why Javier jumped out of a ground-floor window. It wasn't worth it."

"Would've been an incredible story, though," Bastien points out.

"You're welcome to jump next time you and Mom get into it."

"I'm a perfect son who would *never* fight with our mother. I don't know what you're talking about. *Ow*, what the hell?" he says, because both Thalia and I immediately pelt him with napkins. Madeline even blows a straw wrapper at him, then looks absolutely thrilled to be abusing a sibling. She's so adorable that I can't help but smile.

"Fine, god, I won't offer you any brotherly comfort," he says once he's done fending off projectiles.

"I don't want your brotherly comfort."

Bastien leans forward over the table, toward Madeline. "I'm sorry that this happened to you," he says with as much sincerity as he seems capable of mustering. "And I'm sorry that *this* guy is the one you fell for, because he puts empty milk cartons back into the fridge and sometimes wears the same socks for two days in a row."

Madeline looks over at me thoughtfully. "Ew."

"I don't put them back empty on purpose, it just... happens," I say. I do not address the sock allegations.

"I don't care why you do it. It's annoying," Bastien says, and Thalia elbows him.

"Javi. Look at me," she says, all sisterly and intense. She's holding a piece of bacon, and she points it at me. "Mom's wrong. Even if you two do have some horrific breakup—sorry—you'll get through it okay. She acts like you're made of glass, which is clearly not true. And if she and Gerald break up because you two break up, that's not your problem. That's on them. They're the adults here."

The youngest person in this conversation is twenty-three, but I don't point that out. Under the table, Madeline reaches down and squeezes my thigh, so I take her hand and lace our fingers together.

"Thanks," I say, rubbing my thumb along the back of Madeline's hand. "I just hate fighting with her. Plus, she's the best parent I've got, so if *she* disowns me..."

"Javi," Bastien says around a mouthful of egg, then swallows. "She's not gonna disown you for dating a nice girl."

Madeline snorts.

"Or her," Bastien amends.

"I just didn't want it to go this way," I admit. "We were

going to tell them after they got back from their honeymoon, over dinner or something. It was going to be very mature."

"And instead, you caused a panic and then got caught in bed together," says Thalia. "Maybe it's the thought that counts?"

"I don't think it is," says Madeline, then flexes her fingers in mine. "Can I have my hand back?"

I hold it a little tighter, because I can. "What for?"

"So I can eat?"

"You've got a hand."

"That's not enough! My French toast is getting cold. Romance can wait."

"Get a room," Thalia says, but I release Madeline.

# FORTY-THREE

## MADELINE

"CALL ME WHEN YOU GET IN?" I ask, my hands shoved into the pockets of my winter coat.

"Yeah, of course," he says. "You'll tell me if anything else goes down?"

"Are you expecting something else?"

"You can never tell," he says, looking askance at his mom's house. We're standing outside, by the driveway. Thalia is already in the passenger seat of Javi's car. She's studiously looking at her phone and pretending she's not paying us any attention. Behind us, the curtains are drawn, but the back of my neck prickles, like all Javi's relatives are watching us from right behind them.

I feel like I'm in a fishbowl. Or, worse, like I'm a panda in a zoo, surrounded by people anxiously waiting to see if I'm going to mate. No wonder panda birth rates are low. This is *extremely* unsexy.

"But I'm glad they know," he says after a moment. "It's easier than lying."

"I'm sorry your mom is mad at you."

"I think Thalia and Bastien are right and she'll come around." His shrug is a little too casual to be real.

"She will," I say, because I want that to be true and because I want the insistent voice in my head that's saying *What if she doesn't, what if you ruined their relationship* to be wrong. I don't think I've fought with either of my parents like that since I was in high school. I can't imagine doing it now. What would we even fight about?

We stand there a bit longer, close but not touching, trying not to feel *observed*. He should go, since he promised to have Thalia back home on the early side, but I think neither of us wants him to leave.

"Hey," he says. "If I'm disinvited from the wedding, can I come as your date instead?"

"Sure, if you're willing to share," I say. "You *know* I already have one."

"Wow, greedy." His voice is pitched extra low. My face flushes hot at *greedy*, and he smirks, leaning in a little. "But I knew that."

"You say that like it's a problem."

"Absolutely not. I like you greedy." There's a flash of teeth on his lower lip while he thinks.

"I know."

That gets a real smile, then a glance at the curtain-covered windows. Right. Pandas.

"I like Ben, by the way. I wasn't sure if I would."

"Great. You can smoke cigars together at the wedding when you're both my date," I tell him.

"You're really into this idea, huh?" he asks, one eyebrow raised. His sister glances over at us, and I laugh.

"They already paid for everything. They're not going to waste money by disinviting you," I say. "My dad reuses Ziploc bags."

"And drives an hour to get her the ice cream she likes."

"Well, that's different. Turns out he gets a little crazy when he's in love."

As soon as it comes out of my mouth, I swear all the normal, everyday, city sounds stop. There's no traffic, no birds, no breeze, no people going about their days. Javi and I look at each other, and it feels like we're in a diving bell at the bottom of the ocean. Then we both look away, and life resumes like a record player starting back up.

"You should go. It's freezing out here, your sister's waiting—"

"Right, yeah, but—I'll call you tonight."

He steps forward and gives me a soft, chaste kiss. The tip of his nose is cold where it touches my cheek, but his mouth is warm and so are the hand he puts on my face and the fingers he slides into my hair. The kiss lingers, and then I've got my hands on his coat. I grip his pockets, both pulling him in to me and trying not to because *everyone is watching*.

I want the bell jar back, right now. I want the world to fade, because this is what we should have and what we've never quite managed to get: the time and the space to be like this. Kissing and nothing more. Lazy in the morning. It's mostly our own fault, but still.

We both pull away before tongues get involved, and Javi rests his forehead on mine.

"I'll miss you," he says. "I always do."

"Always?"

"Yeah." He's too close for me to see his smile, but I can hear it. "Always."

· · · ★ ★ ★ ★ · · ·

IT'LL BE TWO WEEKS. Two weeks from yesterday, actually, and I think Javi is getting in the day before the wedding, so less than two weeks. Thirteen days. That's *nothing*, that's less than a fortnight, that's shorter than winter break at college.

I stand in Paloma's yard for longer than necessary, more time than it takes for Javi and Thalia to drive away. It's February, and February kind of sucks in this part of the South: the sky's a blah gray occasionally mottled with different shades of blah gray, the trees are stark and bare like skeleton hands, the grass is dead and crunchy under my feet. It's cold, but not an interesting cold, like the kind of cold that brings snow, just a shitty cold that feels bad for no reason.

I glance at the house, but I've got my keys in my pocket and I don't really feel like reporting back to the observers about whether the pandas have fucked or not, so I start walking toward my own car.

I haven't gotten ten feet when Paloma's front door opens, shuts, and there are footsteps.

"Hey, kiddo," my dad says, so I stop and turn. He's not wearing a coat, just a button-down shirt and jeans. His hands are jammed into his pockets. It's pretty obvious that he was watching us through a window, waiting for Javi to leave, but I don't bring that up.

"Hey."

"Big morning," he says, which is an understatement. "You got any plans for the rest of today?"

· · · · · ★ ★ ★ ★ · · · ·

HE MAKES COFFEE, and then we sit in the breakfast nook he built when I was a kid. I don't think he'd built anything before and I don't think he's built anything since, but he decided that breakfast needed a nook, so by god, he found plans, bought tools, and made a nook. I helped, mostly by holding tape measures, and I never fully understand what drove him to build a breakfast nook but also, on some level, I get it.

And he's eaten oatmeal while reading the paper in it every morning for at least twenty years now, so obviously he was right about breakfast needing a nook.

"Listen, blueberry," he starts. "I just wanted to talk to you a little without...outside help."

I nod, my hands wrapped around a mug that isn't quite as satisfying as a diner mug.

"Nothing bad," he says quickly. "I admit I was pretty surprised at first when, ah, he was on the phone."

I breathe deep and retain my composure, because while my dad has always striven to be open and chill about this kind of thing, he's an awkward person at heart.

"We didn't mean for him to...stay over," I say, which is the most tactful way I can think of to say *Oops, we fell asleep after fucking.*

"Oh, I don't care about that," he says. "I mean, well, like I said, it was a surprise, but—now that I've thought about it some, I'm less surprised. You two always did seem to get along."

"I'm sorry I didn't tell you."

That gets a scoff and a half smile. "I understand why you didn't."

"We really were going to, after the wedding," I say, something I'm certain I've said twenty times this morning. I look down into my coffee. "We just needed to figure some things out first, and—I don't know, we thought it could wait. It's your big day. I didn't want to steal your thunder."

"I'd like to see you try."

I raise one eyebrow. "What, you got something big planned? Live dove release? Fireworks display?"

"I'm thinking of throwing smoke bombs, then appearing at the altar as if by magic," he says, with some jazz hands around *magic*. I stare at him for a moment too long, making sure that he's not serious because—on the one hand, I can't imagine that, but on the other, if someone could pull together last-minute smoke bombs, it'd be my dad.

"Kidding," he finally says, looking smug. "But I'm pretty excited. You'll have to try a lot harder to ruin it."

"Oh, decline," I say. "Hard pass."

"I talked to Paloma some, after the four of you went out." He takes a very deliberate sip of coffee. "She told me some of her concerns."

I wait, wondering what I'll do if he says *And I agree that this is a bad idea.* I've never gotten into a big fight with him before. I hold the coffee mug a little tighter.

"I don't know Javier that well," my dad starts, evenly and deliberately. "And I can't speak to what he's been through, but I know it wasn't easy. But I *do* know he's every inch as stubborn as his mother. Not a mystery where he gets it from."

"To be fair, I've never met Raul Lopez," I say.

My dad gives my coffee mug a solemn, understated little *cheers.*

"She's still dealing with the trauma, too, you know," he says. "Her ex-husband kicked their son out of the house, and then he went missing for months. She's always going to blame herself. And she's always going to worry about Javier a little more than the other two. It would be bizarre if she didn't. Everyone worries about their children. I worry about you all the time."

"Dad, I'm fine," I say by reflex.

"Of course you are, but that doesn't stop me. I worry about whether you're safe at night, whether you need a new dead bolt for your front door, whether you're eating enough vegetables, whether the people in your life are treating you with respect. I worry about whether you're happy. It's hard to let a child out into the world, even if they're thirty. But once you do, they get to make their own decisions, and your job is to be there for them when they do. I sound like my therapist, don't I?"

That's a lot, and I feel some kind of guilt about all of it, like there's something I've done to make my dad feel this way even with everything he means to me.

"You think this is a bad decision?" I finally ask. I press my hands into the mug even harder.

"No!" he says. "No. It's—well, it's surprising. And I haven't quite wrapped my head around it, to be honest. But I don't think someone who makes you smile that much can be a bad decision."

Then he leans forward, serious behind his glasses.

"And you know our home will always be open to both of you. Any time, any reason."

"I know," I say, because I do. In truth, I've never really thought about it before. I just assumed I could go home to either of my parents whenever I wanted. But I know why he's saying it now, like this. "Thanks, Dad."

"And if he hurts you, I know where they keep the nuclear submarines."

"Okay, *that's* overkill."

"Is it?" he asks with a shrug and a smile.

· · · · · ★ ★ ★ · · · · ·

I DO NOT MAKE good use of my Sunday. I didn't really have plans in the first place—I assumed I'd be doing something family or wedding related, and instead I ditched—and unstructured blocks of time can make me anxious. I spend about an hour mindlessly scrolling *Am I the Asshole?* posts on Reddit and sending the fakest sounding ones to Amy just to get her baffled reactions. I'd send them to Javi, except I think he's on the road for most of the day, and I don't want to bother—

I manage to stop that thought in its tracks. I bite my lip. Then I send Javi a particularly wild post involving a seagull, a toupee, a lobster roll, and an outdoor dining patio.

*Everyone is the asshole,* he texts back two hours later. *Especially the seagull. Call you when I'm home in an hour and a half?*

I change the sheets on my bed, but I keep the pillowcase he slept on last night because it still smells like him and I'm a little bit pathetic. I do some meal prep and some menu planning and some cleaning, but it's an oddly empty Sunday. I left the whole day open for Family Wedding Stuff, then didn't do any Family Wedding Stuff because I don't feel like dealing with them any more today.

I end up getting dinner with Emily because I can't rattle around my apartment any longer and don't know what else to do with myself, then don't tell her anything. I just listen to her talk about her office drama (someone left a mildly salacious printout in the printer, and no one knows who) and her wedding stuff and enjoy someone else's problems for a while.

The whole time I feel wrong-footed, like I lost my balance at some point and haven't quite gotten it back. I try not to resent the casual way that my dad and Amy and Emily all say *we,* but I can't help it. I try not to think about the fact that if things had been different, I could've spent the last three years saying it, too, instead of missing him and hating myself for it.

When he calls, he sounds so far away it hurts. When we hang up, he says "I miss you already," and I say "Me, too," and when I'm alone again in my quiet apartment, I sit on my couch and finally cry about it.

Three years ago, my life didn't look much different. Same apartment, same job—I got promoted a year and a half ago, but I still work at the same place—same friends. I'm pretty sure I've got the same bed sheets and the same coffee maker, and all of that's solid and steady and comforting, but that's not enough any longer, is it?

*Someone who makes you smile that much,* my dad said.

I know what I want, so maybe I should go get it.

# FORTY-FOUR

## JAVIER

WHEN I finally get to Wyatt's after the day I've had, Zorro rushes to the front door, puts his paws on my thighs, and unleashes a *howl*. I can sympathize.

"It was awful here?" I ask, scratching him behind both ears. "No one fed you even once? Your sister bullied you? The sunlight patches were insufficient?"

"He's a liar," Wyatt calls from the next room. "He got plenty of cat treats *and* I busted out some brand-new catnip."

"I don't know who to believe," I tell Zorro. On the other side of the room, a pile of orange fur rises, stretches, and then hops off a cat tree. I scoop Zorro up and hold him like a human baby, fluffy belly facing up, which is a thing he's never let anyone else do. "Did you act right?" I ask him.

"He was a gentleman and a scholar," Wyatt says, coming out of the bedroom. Then he stops short, frowns, and gives me a concerned up-and-down look. "What happened?"

Just once, I'd like to not get read like a book by my friends.

"It's a long story," I say.

"Are you saying that because it's true, or because you're trying to get out of telling me?"

"When have I ever done that?"

Barry, the pile of orange fur, comes up to Wyatt and meows at him, so he picks her up. "I think she's jealous when other cats get attention," he explains as the enormous cat headbutts his face. Her fur and his hair are nearly the exact same shade. "You finally gonna tell me what's up, or do I have to keep making up stories that you're secretly a Soviet spy who's also got an illicit lover in the mafia?"

"I—*what?* There haven't been Soviets for, like, thirty years."

"That's what made it so exciting," Wyatt agrees nonsensically. Then, to Barry: "I *know.* What a life, right? If only he'd tell me what's really going on so I could help. Or at least lend a sympathetic ear."

I'm tempted to tell Zorro something like *All this from the man who claims to not be in love with his best female friend,* but I refrain because I'm a good person.

"My whole family found out that I'm dating Madeline because I literally got caught in bed with her," I say instead, and Wyatt whistles.

He does not, however, look surprised.

"Yeah, that'll do it." He's taking this *very* well. "You have dinner yet?"

· · · · · ★ ★ ★ ★ · · · ·

WYATT, who seems like a magician sometimes, makes us grilled cheese sandwiches that consist of very thin apple slices and at least three types of cheese on fancy bread. I help by not stealing all the cheese before he can use it, and give him the story in the meantime.

"Three years ago?" he's saying as I hand him plates. "That's before you moved here."

"Almost three years," I correct, which seems important somehow.

"Huh." We take the sandwiches into his living room to eat on the couch. I almost feel bad that Wyatt didn't know about the first time I met Madeline, but it's not like I give my friends a list of people I've had sex with. He'd probably know if it had happened after I came to Sprucevale, though. "So, to clarify, you'd been hooking up *before* you got caught in bed with your stepsister this morning."

"Yes, and you don't have to make it sound like a bad porno."

"Then don't make life choices that lead to things that sound like bad pornos," he says and then drapes a string of cheese into his mouth. "Also, Silas owes me twenty bucks."

I stop, sandwich halfway to my mouth, and narrow my eyes. "You were betting on me?"

"He thought you just had a big crush on her. I thought you two had already hooked up."

"You were *wagering money* on my happiness and emotional well-being?"

"Yes. And now I've made twenty American dollars from it."

"And you didn't just ask me?"

He chews slowly, then swallows, giving me a funny look. "I asked you at least a dozen times, my dude," Wyatt finally says. "You had all the opportunity in the world."

"You never *asked* asked."

"Can you imagine how weird a question that would've been if I were wrong?" He takes a bite, then frowns and goes on with his mouth full. "Not that it's weird for you two to get together, but like—*Hey, are you banging your stepsister* is kind of intense, you know?"

"It's a little weird," I admit.

"Gideon used dark magic to turn a snow sculpture into a girlfriend," he says, shrugging. "Madeline's not *actually* related to you, and wasn't created via sorcery, so I think you're good."

"We should stop saying that about Andi before she hears us," I tell him. "Or at least before Gideon hears us. Andi seems like she'd get a kick out of it."

Over Christmas, our friend Gideon went to a remote cabin for a two-week solo trip to be alone and look at birds, because he's the kind of person who does that. He returned with a girlfriend, who he apparently found in the woods. They claim he saved her from a snowstorm. Wyatt and I have drawn our own conclusions.

"I could have pushed harder, I guess," he's saying now, while also fending off a too-interested Barry. "But you're kind of stubborn, and I didn't think you'd tell me if you'd decided you were really serious about keeping a secret."

"Probably," I admit, and we both eat grilled cheese in silence for a moment. Barry continues to pester Wyatt, because he lets her get away with too much. Zorro sits at my feet instead and makes sustained, intense eye contact with my sandwich, because he was raised right.

"You don't think it's fucked up to date my stepsister?" I finally ask, because I want the reassurance. "'Sister' is *right there* in the title."

"Dude, no. You two just met in a nontraditional way. Which will not stop me from making jokes about how you like to keep it in the family, but seriously, who cares?"

"The rest of my family," I point out.

Wyatt shrugs. "They'll get over it," he says, and he's probably right.

· · · ✦ ★ ★ ★ ✦ · · · ·

THE NEXT EVENING, I've got the key in my apartment lock when my phone rings, and my heart soars stupidly.

"Hey, I was about to call you," I say, tossing my stuff onto a chair, where it joins yesterday's pile. "I just walked in the door."

"How was work?" she asks.

"Thrilling," I tell her. "The fast-paced, high-stakes world of auto and homeowners' insurance is second to none."

"Your boss urgently needed more PDFs?" she asks, laughing.

"Always. I keep offering to show him how to do it, but I think he gets a rush from saying *My assistant will get those to you*. I'm not even his assistant, technically."

"Do you ever get to investigate fraud? That could be fun."

I blow out a breath and flop backward onto a couch. Zorro hops up half a second later, *mrrp*ing. "Nah. If someone seems fishy it gets sent up the chain, usually. I get to make coffee, keep a calendar, and look pretty when people come in for meetings." It's a tedious, boring job, but I've had way worse ones. At least for this one I don't have to wear a hairnet. "I'm trying to talk Bill into letting me keep their awful website up to date. Maybe blog about insurance. How are you?"

There's a slight pause on the other end of the line. "I had a thought," Madeline says.

"Yeah?"

Zorro chooses this moment to get on my lap and meow, loudly, in the direction of my phone. "Dude," I mutter.

"Hi, Zorro," she says.

"It's Madeline," I tell him. "You liked her." He puts his teeth on one of my fingers. "Yes, you *did*. Tell me your thought," I say to Madeline.

I can hear her inhale, a little nervous sounding, and I try not to smile. I wonder what she's wearing and if I'm about to find out.

"I didn't get to see you much this weekend," she says.

"I know. I wanted more time, too." I spent some of my lunch break today looking at Google Maps and gas prices, trying to figure out how often I can get out there. I thought about driving down just for Friday night, maybe, but I've got to work at my other job all weekend because it's nearly Valentine's and flowers are in huge demand. Next weekend is the wedding anyway. I'll live. "Twelve more days, though."

"I could come there," she says, and I can practically see her with her hair pulled back from her face as she aimlessly wanders her apartment in giant fuzzy slippers. "I work from home half the time anyway, and no one really cares where I work from as long as I get it done. So as long as your place has internet—"

"Yeah, of course. Wireless. It's cable, it's pretty fast," I say before I can stop myself, like the internet speeds here are something to brag about. "You could really do that?"

"If you don't mind me being underfoot for a couple of days," she says, like it would be some kind of burden on me.

"Madeline," I say as Zorro purrs on my lap. "There's nothing I want more than you under—uh." She laughs again, and I flop my head back against the couch. "That sounded better in my head. I would love for you to come."

"You're sure?"

"Quit *asking* that. Yes."

"Okay," she says, and then pauses, clears her throat. There's clinking in the background. "That's good, actually, because I'm at a coffee shop in downtown Sprucevale right now."

# FORTY-FIVE

## MADELINE

JAVI'S WAITING by the front door to his building when I pull up. I'm barely out of the car when he pushes me against it, his mouth already on mine. It's dark out, winter in the mountains. The lights outside his building glow orange. I sink my fingers into his hair and kiss him back.

"How long can you stay?" he asks a minute later.

"Saturday morning."

"You're gonna put up with me for that long?"

I want to say *Longer, if you'll let me*, but I don't. Four days is already about eight times as long as we've ever been together. "If I can," I say, and he grins. "I was going to surprise you and knock on your door, but I thought better of it at the last minute."

I can't bring myself to show up at someone's door and say *Hey, I'd like to be a surprise guest*. Not even if that someone is my boyfriend.

"What were you going to do if I said no?" he teases.

"You knew I wouldn't."

"Drive back home and pretend I was never here," I

answer, which is the truth. I take a deep breath, my back still against the rear door of my car. "I wanted to be with you after this weekend instead of both of us going back home and not being together again until the wedding, because *that's* going to be crazy, and—I just wanted some time to be a couple. Together. In a normal life where we're not sneaking around or trying to convince our families we're not deviants."

"Speak for yourself," he says, and I snort. It's unladylike.

"Can we go inside? You're not even wearing a coat," I say, because he's in nothing but a button-down shirt and slacks, presumably what he wears to his receptionist job.

"Yes." He kisses my forehead. "Welcome ho—to my place. Mi casa es su casa."

"Wow, he *does* know Spanish," I say, and he steps back so I can open the trunk to my car.

"I took two years in high school," he says, gently shoving me out of the way and grabbing my suitcase. I packed in a hurry, and I probably packed too much, so it's heavy enough that his shoulders flex against his shirt. He sees me notice and smirks. "You ever go to Mexico and need someone to ask for a library, I've got you. I know that, prayers, and all the things my grandma baked when I was a kid. Sorry—my *abuela*."

The inside of his building is more functional than it is *nice*. The floor is still concrete, and the enormous elevator is obviously a freight elevator with paneling put in to hide that fact. In a city, this would be the kind of building that would've been gutted and turned into luxury apartments, the kind that would charge extra for exposed brick and pipes across the ceiling. Out here, though, I'm pretty sure they did the bare minimum required for habitation and then started renting them out.

I didn't miss the fact that he nearly said *Welcome home* before he stopped himself. I don't know if it was a slip, or wishful thinking, or both.

"Hope you like lots of cat fur," Javi says as he opens the door.

· · · ★ ★ ★ ★ ★ · · ·

HIS PLACE DOES HAVE a lot of cat fur, which is fitting because it's also got a lot of cat. Javi gives me a quick tour, pushing piles out of the way, and Zorro watches suspiciously from the top of a bookshelf. He looks like a jaguar waiting to pounce. It would make me a little nervous if he were only the size of a regular cat, and he's the size of at least three.

"Can I give him some treats?" I ask, once my stuff is in Javi's bedroom and I've been fully reintroduced to Javi's apartment. ("This is the fridge, it's got fridge stuff," he said at one point.)

"Oh, that's a good idea." He goes to a cabinet. The second he opens it, Zorro flows off the bookshelf like a black liquid and walks over to Javi, tail held high. "You gotta take them from her," he tells the cat and hands me a plastic canister.

"Hi," I tell Zorro and sit on the floor in a show of...solidarity, I guess. I've never had a cat, and I'm suddenly realizing that I'm not exactly sure how this goes. "Friends?"

I hold out a couple of treats in my palm, and he comes up to me, sniffs them, then sits back.

"You gotta put them on the floor," Javi says, a little apologetic. "He's not a hand-treat guy."

I follow instructions, and Zorro scarfs them down, then looks at me expectantly. I reach one hand out, which he sniffs. After a few seconds, I gently pet the top of his head, and he accepts this.

"He'll warm up to you." Javi crouches down and gives Zorro a vigorous under-chin scratch. "He's still mad that I left him with Wyatt and Barry this weekend."

"How dare you," I say, and Zorro meows in agreement.

· · ✦ ✦ ★ ★ ★ ★ ★ ✦ ✦ · ·

HOURS LATER, Javi collapses on top of me, forehead just below my collarbone, breathing like he's just sprinted here. I wrap my hand around the back of his neck, damp with sweat, and I close my eyes and try to get my own breathing under control.

"I'm glad you came," he finally says.

I'm floating a little, his weight on top of me an anchor, my mind blissfully clear. "Was that a pun?" I manage to ask.

"Double entendre, I think."

"Ah."

Later, in the shower that's too small for adults to share, I let him wash my hair, though I make him use the fancy color-safe shampoo that I brought.

"Oh," he says. "This is what you smell like."

"Is that good?"

He puts both hands on my hair and then rubs his fingertips in, slow and gentle. "I like it," he says, still barely touching my scalp.

"You can go harder," I offer, and yes, I know how it sounds.

He hums, a noise I can barely hear above the water, low and rumbly. "I know." He digs in a little harder, and I feel my shoulders relax. Then he pauses. "Is it supposed to be turning blue?"

"Yeah, some of the dye washes out every time. Your hands won't get stained or anything, don't worry."

"Right." He gets back to it. "Is it weird that I forget this isn't your natural hair color?"

"A little."

"I can't picture you with brown hair."

"Someday I'll get tired of all the upkeep and grow it out," I say, eyes closed, head back. Now that he's not quite so focused on the task at hand, he's really digging his fingers in, and it's *great*. "I'm sure you'll see it eventually."

Javi doesn't say anything for a moment, long enough for me to wonder at what I just said, whether it was too much, too fast. Whether I'm assuming something I shouldn't.

"How long would it take to grow out completely?" he finally asks.

"A year or two? But I still like the blue for now."

"You change it much?"

"When the mood strikes." I shrug. "Every couple of months, sometimes. Once a year, sometimes. It was emerald green this time last year."

"You've still got some in there," he says. "I always thought it made you look like a mermaid."

"I do like to lure sailors to a watery grave," I say, and Javi snorts.

"That's Sirens—get your mythical creatures straight. Mermaids put shells over their tits and look pretty."

"Oh, that's *way* more doable than luring someone," I say, and now Javi's gently rinsing my hair out. I hope he uses conditioner, too. This is nice. "I could have shell tits by tomorrow."

"I could be into that," he says, and I laugh.

· · * * ★ ★ ★ * * · ·

"HERE, YOU CAN KEEP THIS," Javi says the next morning. He's on his way out the door, coffee in hand, bag slung over one shoulder, and he presses two keys on a key ring into my hand. "The square one is the downstairs door. The unicorn is this door."

I blink at them. I'm technically awake, but we were up late last night, so my brain's not fully online yet.

"That's a unicorn," I say of the key with a rainbow-maned unicorn on it. "Wow."

"All yours." He kisses me and then leaves.

· · · · ★ ★ ★ ★ · · · ·

I TAKE walks around downtown Sprucevale on my lunch breaks, just to see how it is. By the second day, everyone seems to recognize me. I know it's the hair, but when the barista at the Mountain Grind says "Hey, welcome back," I don't know if it's welcoming or off-putting. It's not like Virginia Beach is New York, but it's a real city, big enough that I'm just one more person instead of a noteworthy newcomer.

"Madeline?" a woman's voice asks as I'm waiting for my vanilla latte. I turn to see an Asian woman in glasses go from frowning to visibly relieved. "Oh, thank god it's actually you," Kat says.

"If I were a different kind of person, I'd pretend I don't know who you are," I tell her. She wrinkles her nose but laughs.

"I would probably just leave if you did," she admits. "Forget the coffee. There's no coming back from that."

"That happened to me a couple of years ago and it was pretty awkward," I say. "I was sort of dating this guy at the time, and I was meeting him somewhere. I saw someone I thought was him and went up and grabbed his hand. Wasn't him."

Kat shudders. "I feel awkward about it when I try to open the wrong car door," she sighs. "Even when there's no one else around."

"The guy I was *actually* seeing witnessed the whole thing and made fun of me all night," I add.

"Dick," she says, and I laugh.

"We didn't last," I say dryly as the barista calls out her order. I don't tell her that I still dated him for weeks longer than I should have, trying to convince myself that when he did shit like that he was laughing *with* me, not *at* me.

"Can't say I'm sorry about that." She shrugs. "Good riddance to bad assholes."

"Is that how the phrase goes?"

"If it's not, it should be." Kat has this smile that would be a grin on anyone else, but on her it's this secret, quiet thing that feels like a privilege to see.

"How long are you in town for?" she asks once we're outside, strolling back toward her office, sipping our coffee. It's gray and cold and leafless, the same February in Virginia that I know so well.

"I'm leaving Saturday morning," I tell her.

"Are you coming back?"

"Yeah, definitely," I say before I can think about it. It's true, though. "A lot, maybe."

There's that pleased, quiet smile again, and I realize that I like Kat a lot. "If you need a tour guide who'll introduce you to everyone, you can call Silas," she says, offering up her boyfriend's services. "And if you need to know where you can buy a sandwich without ten minutes of small talk, you can call me."

"Do you like it here?" I ask. The question gets the tiniest

eyebrow twitch above the thick frame of her glasses. If she knows why I'm asking, she doesn't say anything.

"I do," she says slowly. "It's definitely not perfect, but yeah. I do."

· · · · ★ ★ ★ ★ · · · ·

BEFORE I LEFT, I didn't quite think this through. I didn't think through how it could be kind of strange to be in his apartment all day, working from home while he's not here. I also didn't actually think though telling my boss on Monday that I was sick and would be working from home the rest of the week when I'm really at my boyfriend's house, five hours away from where I'm supposed to be. Thankfully there are no looming deadlines, but it's a challenge to find an angle for video meetings that don't include an oddity in his apartment.

When I'm not trying to keep Mothman out of frame— harder than you'd think, actually—I'm plying Zorro with cat treats because I'm not above bribery. By the close of business on Wednesday, he's lounging on the table where I've been working.

Thursday morning, when I sit on a couch to drink some coffee, he jumps onto my lap and meows directly into my face. His breath is not good.

"He doesn't even like *me* that much," Javi grumbles from where he's standing in the kitchen.

"Of course he does. I'm just new and exciting." Zorro slams his head into my chin, and I nearly spill my coffee. "Ow, dude. Aren't you supposed to be stealthy or something? Sneaking around in the shadows?"

"I tried to train him to scratch Zs into things, but it didn't work," Javi says.

"Do you not even know the alphabet?" I murmur to the cat. "Embarrassing."

I get another headbutt, but I'm ready this time and my coffee is safe.

"Have you even stolen from the rich to give to the poor *once*?" I ask him.

"That's Robin Hood," Javi calls, walking out of the kitchen to sit next to me. The cat abandons me immediately.

"I thought Zorro was Mexican Robin Hood, kinda? A folk hero?" I'm realizing that my Zorro knowledge consists of a few scenes of black-and-white television, maybe, and that one movie that came out when I was a kid. I'm not even sure I saw it.

Javi laughs, petting the cat, who seems satisfied and oblivious. It must be wonderful to be a housecat: dumb, warm, fed, doted on.

"Nah, he was a vigilante, so more like Mexican Batman. Except also not really Mexican, which I didn't realize until I'd already named the cat."

I tilt my head against the back of the couch and start laughing.

"Look, he was suave, handsome, and spoke Spanish, plus I hadn't seen the show since I was a kid. *Obviously* I thought Zorro was Mexican."

"I can see your confusion."

"You do sneaky murders at night in disguise, don't you?" Javi asks Zorro and gets the world's loudest purr in return.

· · * * ★ ★ ★ * * · ·

MY SCHEME TO bribe my way into Zorro's heart is revealed later that day, when he vomits spectacularly as soon as Javi gets home. It's not my greatest moment, but I made dinner since Javi has class tonight, so I am forgiven.

# FORTY-SIX

## JAVIER

"I KNOW it's late to be asking this question," Madeline says as we get out of the car, "but I thought Beast was a stray he found taking shelter in his cabin at your secret society retreat. How does he know her birthday?"

"It's not a *secret* society," I say. "Obviously."

"You're telling me you've never summoned even one demon?"

"Of course not." I lock the car and offer a hand. "I can get that."

She waves me off. "I promise I can carry brownies. And no demons besides the cats, you mean."

"Zorro slept on *your* side of the bed last night, and you're calling him a demon?"

She grins at me under the streetlight, and I realize what I just said. It feels like something in my chest catches, tugs, and stays anchored. Of course it's her side of the bed.

"I'm just saying are you *sure* you guys have never done any summoning? Because unreachable off-grid cabins erected around a central bonfire sounds...blood sacrifice-y."

"Only if all the times I cut myself or got splinters count

as a blood sacrifice. But I think the only otherworldly figure I ever invoked was *Jesus Fucking Christ*."

"If you say so," she says, all teasing and doubtful.

It's funny, the pieces of our lives that were missing before, the little mundanities, the holes we hadn't known to fill. The way she takes her coffee in the morning, the sound of her electric toothbrush, the way she rolls out her neck after she's been working at my kitchen table for a long time. She paces when she takes phone calls, back and forth in front of the windows, and I wonder if she'd carve a path there if she stayed long enough.

"You should come up when it gets warmer," I say as we're heading up the steps to Silas's townhouse. This morning I got a group text informing me that we'd be celebrating Beast's birthday tonight, my attendance was mandatory, and I should bring a dessert. "It's a really great spot. There's a creek nearby and good hiking. The views are spectacular. And it's so dark at night. And quiet."

We're on Silas's small front porch, and Madeline's just looking at me with the brownies in her hands. She's not quite smiling, but the look on her face is so fond it makes me giddy.

"What?" I ask.

"Nothing," she says, and then, "You really love it out here."

It takes me a second to process that, because I'd never thought of it that way. When I moved here, it felt like a leap into the unknown. Exactly the sort of thing I wasn't supposed to do a little less than a year into sobriety. I'd needed a change—an escape—and this was it. Once I was here it was a puzzle, a half-foreign land, somewhere I stuck out like a sore thumb.

And then, when I wasn't paying attention, it became

home. For all its problems, for all that I sometimes still get asked where I'm *really* from, it's home.

"Yeah, I do," I say, surprised. Then the door opens and Silas is standing there, waving us in.

"Happy Beast's birthday!" he says, then laughs at the skeptical look Madeline gives him.

· · · · · ★ ★ ★ · · · · ·

"FUCK NO," Wyatt's saying. "That place is *haunted* haunted."

"By what? Squirrels? Spiders?"

He sighs. "Ghosts, Lainey. It's haunted by *ghosts* and probably a bunch of worse shit, too. What was that thing in the movie you made me watch last week? It was like a bunch of ghosts mashed up into one thing that also had teeth?"

Lainey looks blank. "A vampire? Why do you keep watching these movies with me?"

"Why do you *let* him watch these movies with you?" I ask her.

"He says he can handle them."

"The movies are fine," Wyatt lies. "It's Santa Claus's Last Chance Christmas Asylum that I've got an issue with."

"It was never an asylum!" she says.

"There's an asylum?" I ask.

"No."

"Yes! A *Christmas* asylum," Wyatt insists.

Lainey sighs. "My aunt and uncle have this idea that they're going to open a bed-and-breakfast somewhere out of the way," she says. "And one of the properties they found is an old sanatorium"—Wyatt makes a noise—"where rich people would come bathe in the hot springs and take the air and get massages, and in theory it would cure their vapors or balance their humors or whatever. And after it was a sanatorium, it was apparently some sort of Christmas-themed attraction, with reindeer and Santa and everything."

"Haunted," Wyatt says again, and Lainey elbows him in the ribs.

"Nobody's making you go," she says. "They're not even buying it."

"They could rent rooms *and* give ghost tours," I say. "Which, by the way, I'm available for."

"There're no ghosts!"

"Lainey. There are *always* ghosts," I say, because I'm right. Everything's haunted if you try hard enough.

"I'll pass your offer on," she says, and then an arm snakes around my waist and Madeline's standing next to me.

"Hey," she says. "What's happening over here?"

"My aunt and uncle might buy a haunted asylum on a mountain," Lainey explains. "Javi's gonna give ghost tours."

"Ooh, fun," she says, and Wyatt makes a face.

· · * * * ★ ★ ★ * * · ·

"SO," I say a few hours later when I catch Silas alone in the kitchen. "Is it really Beast's birthday?"

He doesn't answer me, just laughs, so I lean against the counter and watch him.

"No one can prove it's not," he points out.

I glance over my shoulder, at where everyone is still hanging out in the living room, scattered on chairs and couches. Madeline and Kat sit on the stairs, deep in conversation. It twists something funny in my chest.

"Did you throw your cat a birthday party because Madeline's in town and you wanted everyone to have a chance to come check out Javi's new girlfriend?" I ask him.

Just then, Kat must say something funny because Madeline laughs. Kat looks pleased.

"Of course not," Silas says a moment later, turning back to me. "I threw my cat a birthday party so all your friends would come have fun and make your new girlfriend think Sprucevale is cool."

"Do you think it's working?" I ask.

"She doesn't seem to hate it."

I watch her for a few more seconds, like a creep, until she suddenly looks up and sees me. Then she smiles, and it's this perfect, beautiful, unguarded thing that makes me forget to breathe. Just for a few moments, and then it's gone, she's talking to Kat again, and I'm left feeling like I've walked out of a cave and into the sunlight.

"I can't ask her to move here," I say to Silas, lowering my voice. "I mean, I can't ask her to move anywhere. It hasn't been that long. *Moving* somewhere is a whole...thing."

"Yup."

"And I don't think I can leave." The words rush out of me, too fast. "Here, I've got work, I've got school, I've got a place, I've got you guys. That's not gonna happen again. But I can't ask her to move here."

Silas walks to the counter opposite me and hops onto it, leaning forward on his hands.

"Javi," he says. "You could move anywhere and be okay. You know that, right?"

Two and a half years ago, Silas met me once, then invited me to move to a little mountain town in the middle of nowhere. I've asked him why about a hundred times, and he's never really given me a good answer. *It seemed like the thing to do*, he always says. I'm pretty sure he's telling the truth.

"Yeah," I admit, because I do.

"Good," he says. "Because whatever happens, I think you'll work it out. I like her, by the way. You seem happy."

"I like her, too," I say. "And yeah, I am."

· · * * ★ ★ ★ * * · ·

"I'M NOT GOING to be surprised that it's the skeleton," she says. "I know where we are."

"I wasn't trying to surprise you with Bart," I lie, because I was. I didn't realize she knew her way around that well already. It makes a bubble of something light and stupid swell inside me that she does. "I'm trying to surprise you with Bart's *appearance*."

It's late, and it rained a little while we were at Silas's place. The sidewalk is damp, and all the streetlights reflect back at us. It's quiet here, even though we're in town. There's no highway nearby, no naval yard, no airport. Just the occasional car a few streets over, someone's late-night television, the breeze through the leafless trees. I can even see stars.

"Okay, close your eyes," I tell her and get a skeptical look in return. I parked on the block behind Wells's house, so we haven't seen Bart yet—we came up from the back—but I want her to have the full, very romantic experience.

"You showed me a picture from last year," she points out. "With the negligee and the heart boxers."

"C'mon, trust me."

Madeline takes a deep breath, and then she does.

I take her hand and lace our fingers together. She's uncertain at first, hesitant, but after a few steps she relaxes a little and starts moving normally. I hold on to her tightly, quietly narrating everything (*four more steps to the corner, okay, turn left, there's a crack in front of your right foot so watch out*), and she trusts me.

She always did, I realize, from the night we met. She trusted me more than I trusted myself, spectacularly vulnerable in a way I had to learn to be with her. A way I'm still learning to be. I stare at her now. She's stopped on the sidewalk with her eyes still closed, and I think: I can't believe she thought I was worthy.

"Turn to the left, then open your eyes."

She obeys, her eyelashes flutter open, and then her face lights up.

"What is *that*?" she whisper-shouts, clutching my hand even harder. She's giggling. "Is that—is he Cupid?"

"I think so," I murmur.

"Wow," she says in a tone I choose to believe is *awestruck*. "Javi, are those...wings? And a halo? Why does Cupid have a halo?"

"I wasn't consulted and couldn't begin to guess," I tell her. "Wells and Josie did this one all by themselves." I help out with about half of Bart's costumes, and did the initial setup, but Valentine's Day is special to the two of them. It's very cute.

"This is incredible," she murmurs. "It looks like one of the stop-motion skeletons from *The Seventh Voyage of Sinbad*. Only it wandered through Renaissance Faire first and grabbed some wings."

"I'm not sure it's exactly what they were going for," I admit.

"What were they going for?"

Bart does, technically, look like Cupid: he's got an enormous bow and arrow, a heart for an arrowhead, and a toga wrapped around his bony frame. He has wings that are too small for him and a fake rose gripped in his teeth.

The thing is weaponry, sheets as clothing, and tiny wings have a certain vibe when they're on a picture of a cute, chubby baby. Bart is a twelve-foot-tall skeleton. On him, it's more *nightmarish* than *cute*.

"Less terror, maybe?"

"I feel like he's threatening me with romance."

"Happy Valentine's Day *or else*."

She bumps against me and then leans into my side, our hands still linked. I rest one cheek against her hair.

"Too bad there's no mistletoe," she teases. "How come there's a make-out plant for Christmas but not Valentine's? Seems backward."

It's a great question that I don't have a good answer to. "Maybe on Valentine's, every plant is a make-out plant?"

"Hm."

"I'd forgotten about the mistletoe when I brought you here on Christmas," I admit. "And I was so nervous you'd see it and think I was trying to be romantic."

"I was too busy looking at the mistletoe and worrying that you didn't realize it was there and I was overthinking your motives."

God, we're idiots.

"I did want to kiss you then," I tell her quietly.

"Is there something stopping you now?"

There's not a thing in the world, so I lean down and press our mouths together, under the streetlights and the giant skeleton. Madeline arches up against me, her hands on the lapels of my coat, her body warmth soaking through the layers. It's a quick thrill to be doing this in public, even though it's late. The kiss goes on and on, way past propriety.

When she pulls back, I take her bottom lip between my teeth and tug, gently, just for a moment.

Madeline runs her tongue over the spot and looks pleased.

"I passed the test?" I ask, because it's time. She's leaving first thing tomorrow morning, and my apartment's going to feel so empty.

"What test?"

"The *will this work* test." There's a brief silence. "You were trying to figure something out, weren't you?"

"That's not why I came." Now she's frowning, a few strands of blue hair stuck to her forehead. "I came because I wanted to see you."

"But you were making sure," I press.

"Of what?"

I'm not sure if I know myself. I just know that half the time I feel like boards laid across mud after it rains: mostly fine, but it only takes one misstep and you're covered in muck. I couldn't blame someone for quality-testing first.

"Of me," I finally say, and Madeline stares at me. I start to wonder if I've fucked up, if maybe *this* was the test that I'm not passing—

"I came out here so I could spend time with you." She looks away and takes a deep breath. "That's honestly it. I like you, and I missed you, so I drove my ass out to see you. I wasn't making sure of anything."

I feel tilted, off-balance, part of me whispering *That can't be true*, but I have to believe her. If I love her—if I *respect* her—I believe her.

"I'm really glad you did." It's not good enough, but I don't know what else to say. Being with Madeline feels like all my loose pieces snap into place. Like someone's turned me toward the light and from this angle, my flaws aren't so bad. "You can always come. You can always stay, if you want. I always want you around."

"Always?" she asks, skeptical, but those are all the words I had, so I take her face in my hands and kiss her.

"Always," I say when we come up for air, but I don't let her go. She's holding my coat again, her eyes closed, her lashes against her cheeks. "And don't you dare doubt me."

This time she kisses me, warm and soft and sure, and it feels like the world was made just for us.

· · · ★ ★ ★ ★ ★ · · ·

MADELINE DRIVES away early the next morning, and it doesn't feel like I thought it would. I thought it would hurt, and it does—it *sucks*—but I'll see her in a week, and I know we're both counting down the days. It's easier this way, when I can say *I miss you* and she says *I miss you, too*.

# FORTY-SEVEN

## JAVIER

SUNDAY, my mom calls. I'm at work when she does, elbow-deep in roses, so I let it go to voicemail. When she calls again, five minutes later, Pat sees me check the screen and tells me to take the break I've earned. I throw my coat on, head to the alley behind the shop, and call my mom back.

"I was just leaving you a voicemail." She clears her throat. I can hear the worry in her voice. I'm the world's leading expert at hearing the worry in my mom's voice.

"Sorry—I was at work," I say. It's cold out here, and I'm already pacing the width of the alleyway. I can never stand still on the phone. Especially not when my mom's calling after an argument.

"It's Sunday."

"Blooming Blossoms, the florist," I remind her. "Valentine's is this week. I picked up a couple extra shifts."

She clears her throat. "Well, I was going to call sooner, but I wanted to talk to you when Madeline wasn't there, so you wouldn't be distracted. Gerald said she was visiting."

"She was."

"Was it a good visit?"

395

How long are we going to make small talk for? I know it's not why she called. "It was great," I say. "I really liked having her here. It's been hard that we live so far apart."

"Your father and I had to do long distance a few times," my mom says after a slight pause. "I don't know if you remember—you were very young. He struggled, missing you so much. Not that he would talk about it, of course. But I could tell."

She was younger than I am now. Twenty-five when I was born, a little less than a year into their marriage. I take a deep breath, shove my other hand into my coat pocket, and shut my eyes.

"Yeah, I miss her," I admit, half to prove I'm not my father. Half because, fuck it, it's true. "It's only been a day, and I already miss her."

"You always had the biggest heart, Javi," my mom says, her voice gentle. "I know sometimes that wasn't a good thing."

I don't have a response for that.

"I called to apologize," my mom goes on, and something in me relaxes, something that's been wound tight for a week now. "Well—I called to apologize for saying that Madeline would hurt you on purpose. I know she wouldn't."

"No," I agree.

She takes a deep breath. "And I'm sorry for thinking you couldn't handle something going wrong between you. Of course you could. That was—it was shortsighted of me to assume the worst like that." She clears her throat again, and I think I can hear her swallow. "My memories of your worst days are so clear, and the good ones are so hazy. I wish it was the other way around. Maybe I'd be more inclined to think of them first."

I stop pacing and sit on a cement curb. There's a

chunk missing from one end. "Thanks. I wish that, too." I take a deep breath because it's my turn. "I'm sorry for not being honest. It probably would have solved some problems."

"Maybe," my mom says, which is accurate. I'm not completely sorry for not telling her, but I'm sorry shit blew up so hard. "It's too late now, though. And I admit I understand keeping the secret," she says, grudgingly.

"I don't think you can blame me for that," I say, and she just sighs.

"Don't push your luck," she says, and I smile at the asphalt beneath my shoes. "I'm sorry I reacted the way I did, Javi. I was scared for you, and I should have been happy. Madeline is...she's wonderful. I've thought that since I met her."

I'm thirty years old and my mom's approval still feels like I'm levitating off the ground.

"Me, too," I say. "And—Mom," I start, then stop because I'm not sure I know how to say this next thing, but it's been scratching at me for too long now, an uncomfortable spot between my shoulder blades.

"Javi?" she asks when I'm quiet for too long.

"Thanks for still worrying," I say in a rush, just so I can get it out. "I know I'm kind of a fuckup, and I know I'm the reason for most of your gray hair, but I also know you could have written me off a while ago or given up on me, and maybe that would have been easier for you, but you didn't. So, thanks. And, ah, sorry for making you worry so much. I'm trying to do that less."

There's a *really* long silence, but I can hear her breathing. She clears her throat twice, and when she finally speaks, I can tell she's trying not to cry. Shit. I feel like I'm twelve years old and just brought home the first of many bad report cards. My father was furious, but my mother was disappointed, and that was so much worse.

"I would never give up on you," she finally says. "I'll be worrying about you until I draw my final breath."

"That's not quite what I was going for."

"Well, it's the truth."

There's an ache at the back of my throat, and I swallow it down. "So, I'm still invited to the wedding, yeah?"

My mom scoffs at me, and even over the phone, I can practically see her roll her eyes. "It's already paid for. You think we're going to let it go to waste?"

"I would *never* think that."

"Besides, I would never disinvite you. I'd spend the whole ceremony worrying about where you were."

"Wow."

"Stay where I can see you, Javier Tomás," she chides, then laughs, and as much as I hate getting middle-named, I feel lighter.

# FORTY-EIGHT

## MADELINE

DAD AND PALOMA'S wedding is, by far, the most relaxed one I've ever attended. I guess that's the nice thing about getting remarried in your fifties: you've probably seen enough to realize that it's just one day, and as long as you end up married at the end of it, it went well.

I spend the morning helping Javi put together the flower arch—they got wholesale flowers, and since Javi works at a florist, he put them all together—while Thalia walks around with a clipboard and Bastien, Caleb, and some of their cousins point a lot and move chairs around a little.

The wedding is at an inn toward the southern end of Virginia Beach, right on the water. The room we're using has huge windows that look out over the dunes and the Atlantic. My dad has bragged more than once to me about what a great deal they got, it being the off-season and all.

When the arch is done, we both step back and look at it. It's half greenery and half white or pale pink flowers. Some sort of ivy is wrapped around and through everything, and it's adorned with evergreen branches and pale turquoise berries. It smells like flowers and cedar and looks like it might be the gateway to a fae kingdom.

"That looks great," I tell Javi.

"Thanks. You think she'll like it?"

He's been a little anxious all morning, quieter than usual, so focused he snapped at his sister about a table runner and then apologized immediately. I'm not sure he's eaten yet today, but his cousin Manny went on a McDonald's run a couple minutes ago, so he should be back soon.

"She'll love it," I say and press a palm to the center of his back.

· · · · ★ ★ ★ ★ ★ · · · ·

EVERYONE on the groom's side of the family is ready a full hour before the ceremony is set to begin. There aren't that many of us—my dad, my aunt Susan and her wife Kate, his best friends Burt and Carl—so we sit around the suite and talk about what Virginia Beach used to be like.

Fifteen minutes before the ceremony is set to start, my dad's phone alarm goes off. It says *Get married*. He stops it, puts the phone on the dresser, then slaps his thighs.

"I guess we better go get started," he says. There's some backslapping from his friends and hugs from Susan and Kate.

I wait for them all to file out of the room before I walk over to my dad and pretend to straighten his tie. Suddenly, there's a lump in my throat and my chest feels tight, which is not what's supposed to happen at all.

"You nervous?" I ask him, and he chuckles.

"Not even a little."

"Well, you look good." I give his tie one last pat. "Can't have you going out there with a crooked tie."

"Thanks, kiddo." I've never seen my dad smile quite like that. "And thanks for keeping your old man company all those years."

It's really, really weird to hand your parent over to someone else. Especially when it was the two of us for so long. My mom remarried after a couple of years, when I was still a kid, but my dad's been mostly single this whole time, and we're pretty close.

But my dad's so happy he's practically glowing, so whatever pangs I might be having right now, I can't be sorry he's getting married. Besides, now someone else can be the first line of defense against his fashion choices.

"Yeah, of course, Dad," I say, and then we're hugging, his arms tight around me.

"You're still my number one girl," he says, which is cheesy as hell and makes me tear up anyway. "Always."

"I love you, too," I say and swallow hard, then take a deep shaky breath. "And if she hurts you, I know where they keep the nuclear submarines."

His arms tighten around me.

"No, you don't."

"I can find out."

I get more one rib-crushing squeeze, and then we let go. I'm not crying, but I did wear waterproof mascara.

"Let's go get you married," I say, and we head downstairs.

* * * * * ★ ★ ★ * * * * *

AT THE CEREMONY, I sit between Ben and Javi, in the same row as his siblings; this isn't the kind of wedding that has a bride's side and a groom's side. It's lovely and short and heartfelt, and when I start crying, Ben hands me a tissue and

Javi takes my hand. The flower arch looks great. Paloma and my dad both look like nothing better has ever happened to them.

· · · ★ ★ ★ ★ ★ · · ·

"I'M only dancing with you until they refill the sliders," Ben says, glancing over my shoulder. "They're really good."

"You would abandon me for *meat*?" I ask, trying to look shocked. "A *slider*?"

I may have had a glass of champagne while we took family photos and then maybe another one while they put appetizers out. Javi's been drinking seltzer with lime and swearing up and down that *he is fine*, so I decided to take him at his word. He's off somewhere, talking to a family member.

"They're really good sliders," Ben says with a shrug. "And listen, the list of things I'd abandon you for is pretty long. I'm just here for the food."

"Liar," I say, rolling my eyes. It's a slow song, so I've got one hand on his shoulder and the other in his hand, and we're moving more or less in time to the music. "You like me, and you also like my dad. Besides, no one goes to weddings for the food."

"The free booze?" he asks, raising one eyebrow. "Ooh, try to look attractive—there's the photographer."

"I always look attractive."

"Debatable."

"I should step on your foot."

"You say that like you haven't stepped on my foot five times already," he says, and then we bicker about that until the song ends and we drift off the dance floor. I drink some water and also some more champagne, and I don't hear Javi come up behind me until there's a hand on my back.

"There you are," I say.

Javi looks good, unsurprisingly, in a navy blue suit, with his hair pulled back from his face. His pocket square is bright blue and matches my hair. Ben's matches my purple dress.

"My cousin Sandy wants to know why you're dancing with some other guy and what I'm going to do about it."

I take another sip of champagne. "Oh, easy. That's because he's my date to this wedding and you're not."

"That's what I told her. I believe she was scandalized."

I can't help but laugh, and Javi grins at me.

"*That's* what scandalized her?"

"These people are unpredictable." He curls his hand around my hip as I shift closer. "Wanna make it right and come dance with me?"

By the time we get there, another slow song is playing, something I half remember my dad playing a lot when I was a kid. Javi pulls me in close and holds me tight, and we dance in front of all these people.

"You look good in that dress," he says when we've been dancing for a minute or two.

"Thanks."

"I bet you also look good out of that dress."

"You're *so* creative."

"Oh, so you're critiquing my pickup lines?" he teases, and I shrug. Javi pulls me a little tighter and puts his lips closer to my ear. "Okay, I think that dress would look good hiked up around your waist while you got railed in a broom closet," he says. I bury my face in his chest because I'm pretty sure I'm bright red. "It would also make a great curtain while you sat on my face. Is that creative enough for you?"

"I regret everything," I mutter into his shoulder, and he laughs.

"That's for later," he says. "Right now, I'd rather dance with you."

I move my hand so our fingers are laced together, which is awkward for dancing, but oh well.

"Me, too," I say, and we stay on the dance floor for a long time.

· · · · ★ ★ ★ ★ ★ · · · ·

AFTER DINNER and cake and dancing and more dancing, I need some air. I head out to the deck and sit on a lounge chair so I can stare at the ocean. It's cold, but I'm overheated and it's a relief to be outdoors for a moment, away from the light, the noise, the people, and the wedding-ness of it all.

I'm about to go back in when the door behind me opens and Javi steps onto the deck.

"Aren't you cold?" he asks and sits behind me on the lounge chair.

"I came out here to cool off."

He nods at the unlit cigar in my hand. I forgot I had it.

"You gonna smoke that?"

"Nah. My dad's friend Burt was handing them out. He sort of shoved this into my hand and moved on."

"Your dad's friends are wild," Javi says. "One of them has a story about blowing up a pond by accident? With secondhand SCUBA gear?"

"Sounds right. I'm sure it was some experiment gone wrong. Or right—who knows?"

I shiver, and Javi sighs. A moment later, a warm suit

jacket drapes around my shoulders. I start to protest, but he pulls me back against his chest with his arms wrapped around me, so I don't bother.

"You thinking about something?" he asks.

"I don't know if I'd miss it," I tell him and nod out at the darkness. "The ocean."

Right now, at night, the Atlantic is more suggestion than sight: the lights don't shine much farther than the waves breaking on the sand, and everything beyond that is inky blackness. There are lights to the north, far away, and the scattered constellations of ships out at sea, but not much more.

Its presence is all sound right now, the steady baseline thrum of waves on sand. It's hypnotic.

"I do, sometimes," he says, his chin over my shoulder. "We lived a lot of places when I was growing up but always near the ocean. When I moved, I thought I'd miss it more than I do."

He's going back Monday, the day after tomorrow. We've got a month of visits sketched out: the weekend he has off, the week I can work from home, and it's a start. It's even a good start, mapped out and planned, the way I like to do things.

I can already tell that it's not going to be enough, and for once, it doesn't feel bad to want more.

"We've gotta do something." I burrow back a little into him. I'm still tipsy and my thoughts are hard to grasp.

"I graduate in May," he says, and I can tell he's been thinking about it. "In the meantime, I could look for a job out here—"

"Don't," I say, and he goes rigid. "I mean, I'd rather go there. I think."

'To Sprucevale?"

"That's where you live, yeah?"

Javier *scoffs*. "I can't ask you to move there. It's tiny."

"*Great* news: I just volunteered."

"It's got two stoplights, the only thing open past nine p.m. is the sports bar, and I once got pad thai made with spaghetti noodles from the only Thai place in town."

I consider this. "There's a Thai place?"

"It closed."

Makes sense. One of the big ships out at sea is moving slowly, and I watch it for a moment. "Sprucevale has at least twenty stoplights, the Kroger is open until ten, and the Hollow Hearth has really good biscuits. And they make their own jam. Did you know they make their own jam?" I ask, twisting toward Javi because this is very important.

"Yes, because I told you that in the first place," he points out. I think he's trying not to laugh at me.

"We could make jam."

Now he's definitely laughing, his face in my shoulder. "You want to make jam?"

"Yes. Raspberry. *Wild* raspberry—Gideon said those grow out there. Also, he said that eating stuff I find in the woods probably won't kill me as long as it's not a mushroom."

"How many drinks have you had?" he asks gently.

"Not that many," I say, which is true. "I'm not drunk. Also, I've been thinking about this all week while I was dead sober. You love it there."

"I do." His arms tighten around me.

"We can do a trial run for a month or so, and if it's awful, we'll think of something else."

"You make it sound so easy."

"I know you've done harder things than move. If it doesn't work, it doesn't work. There are other places." I pause, waiting. I'm starting to get nervous. "This is where you say *Yes, I'll do it.*"

He's still quiet, and suddenly I can really feel the cold like a weight, like this was too much, too fast. I close my eyes and make myself wait.

"You could have anyone you want," he finally says. "You could have something easier, with someone who isn't so much work. You know there's nothing after *in recovery*, right? There's no *recovered.* This is it."

I turn my head toward his and nuzzle his cheek with my nose. "Javi," I say as quietly as I can, the ocean shushing beneath us. "Why would I want easy when I could have you?"

He turns me so our temples are pressing together, and I'm still in his jacket in this weird tangle of limbs, and it's cold out but warm everywhere that we're touching. I have the brief certainty that no one else has felt this way in the history of the world. How could they? If everyone felt like this, the earth would explode.

"I love you," he says, and that's all.

"So you'll let me try moving?"

"Please. You knew I'd say yes," Javi says. "All I've wanted for three years is to say yes to you."

"All I've wanted is to ask," I say. "I love you, too."

We kiss out there, in the cold, on the cusp of the ocean. There's salt in the air and ships on the horizon, a slow song playing inside, and waves breaking on the shore, one after another, forever.

## EPILOGUE

### JAVIER

**October**

"I'M A FIRM BELIEVER IN NONVIOLENCE,"
Madeline says, frowning at the chainsaw. "I just want to
state that up front."

"You're not supposed to do actual violence. Just menace
the children."

"I'm not sure I love menacing children."

"That's only because you haven't tried it yet," I say, and
she snorts.

We're currently standing in the former Sprucevale
Middle School, which got a new building two years ago, but
the county hasn't done anything with the old one yet.

Besides rent it out to various organizations, like the
Sprucevale Town Council Events Committee, so they can
use the space for haunted houses and whatnot. Lainey's
parents are very involved, so she's involved, so now I'm
talking Madeline into wielding a chainsaw and chasing children through a room decorated like a haunted sawmill.

Adam, our usual chainsaw-wielding maniac, got food poisoning.

Also, it's a plastic chainsaw. Obviously.

"I just have to hold it up and shout?" she asks. "Do I shout anything specific?"

"*RAARRRRGH* should do just fine."

She nods very seriously, thinking. She looks down at the chainsaw, then to her feet on the old tile floor, then back at the corner she's supposed to pop out of.

"Okay, let me try it again." She gets back into position. I head back to the door and watch as she ducks behind a blood-spattered pile of logs. With the lights on, in the daytime, you can really tell it's red paint, but it looks great at night.

"Wow, this haunted house is so scary," I call from the door. "Guess I'll go into this next room and—what's this? An impeccably rendered old saw—"

"AAAUUUGHHHH!"

Madeline runs out from her hiding spot, chainsaw wielded overhead.

"I'M A ZOMBIE LUMBERJACK! GRRRRAAAAAAH! Stop *smiling*—that was scary."

"No, that was perfect," I agree. She pokes me with the chainsaw. "I'm serious! With the lights and the sound effects and the makeup, people will be terrified out of their minds."

"What do I do if there's some teenage dickhead who's not scared?"

"Just keep cackling. There's always someone. Shout anything that comes to mind. Tell them their parents know what they do on the internet."

"That's way too mean."

I raise one eyebrow at her. "What were *you* looking at on the internet when you were fifteen?"

"None of your business," she says, primly sweeping her (now purple) hair back over one shoulder.

I check the door to the room, then sidle forward. "You could make it my business." I grab the front of her overalls.

"How much do you know about the television show *Supernatural*?" Madeline asks, batting her eyelashes.

"Sounds kinky."

That gets a laugh. "You have no idea."

I file that away to bring up again later, and in the meantime, I give her a quick, chaste kiss on the lips. "Want to try it with the lights out and the sound on?"

Madeline heads back to her hiding spot, and I hit Play on the boom box in the corner. Sprucevale Horror House is volunteer-run and funded, so the budget is shoestring and the technology is outdated. The haunted sawmill's soundtrack is on a CD set to loop for four hours, and after I start it up, I mess with the settings a little. As if I'm going to get good audio quality from a piece of equipment someone's aunt bought in 1995 and kept in her garage for thirty years.

Just as I'm finishing up, the door to the room opens and someone walks through. It's dark in here, except for the hellish red lighting and some fake fire. There are several huge (cardboard) blades spinning and loud buzzing and screaming echoes through the room.

"Oh, wow," Wyatt says, looking around. "This is—"

"AAARRRGGAUUUUUGHHH!" Madeline comes out of her hiding spot screaming, chainsaw overhead. The lighting makes her look like a demon.

Wyatt *screams,* throws his arms over his face, tries to take a step backward, and trips over his own foot.

"Oh, fuck!" Madeline yelps, tossing down the chainsaw. "Shit, I'm so sorry. Are you okay?"

"I'm great," Wyatt says, sprawled on the floor. "You're good at that."

I silence the soundtrack and come over to them, but Madeline's already helping Wyatt up, so I hit the lights.

"I thought you were Javi," she's explaining. "We were practicing. I heard the door open, so I thought it was him."

"I'm not afraid of plastic chainsaws," I tell him.

"One, fuck you," he says, but he's grinning. "Two, Lainey asked if I'd do a walkthrough before we open for the weekend in a couple hours, see if anything needed fixing. You good?"

"Better than you," Madeline shrugs.

"Wow, both of you," he deadpans. "For that, I'm gonna go change the soundtrack in the coal mine to the Backstreet Boys CD my mom found in a box."

"You wouldn't *dare*," I gasp. Wyatt raises his eyebrows with a *try me* kind of look.

I spent two weeks decorating a hallway to look like an abandoned coal mine, complete with fake skeletons half-stuck in fake rocks. It's really good.

"Maybe the Spice Girls," he threatens.

"Who?" I ask, and Wyatt laughs.

"How do you not know the Spice Girls?" Madeline asks, gesturing with the chainsaw. "Girl power? Union Jack minidresses? I always liked Scary Spice best."

It sounds...vaguely familiar?

"Scary Spice was the best," Wyatt confirms, then shrugs at the confused look I give him. "I have an older sister. *Anyway*, do you guys need anything in here, or are you good?"

"We're good," Madeline says cheerfully. "Thanks for the confidence boost."

Wyatt grins and rolls his eyes. "Yeah, anytime. Glad I could help."

He heads off, and Madeline tosses the chainsaw into the air, letting it flip end over end before she catches it again with so much ease you'd never know she wasn't a chainsaw juggler.

It is, god help me, fucking hot.

"You still willing to do my makeup?" she asks.

· · · · · ★ ★ ★ ★ ★ · · · · ·

I'M one of the tour guides, so after the haunted house opens, I only see Madeline when she's a chainsaw-wielding maniac, covered in fake blood. By the end of the night, she's pretty into it; when I take the last group through her room, she shouts "I'll use your bones as fertilizer!" when they leave.

"Bones as fertilizer?" I ask later, when we're grabbing our stuff and heading out, both of us still in full costume.

"It's good for plants," she says. "Um, in *Minecraft* anyway. If you put bone meal on a tree it'll grow faster."

"Dork," I tease as we walk into the parking lot. It's deep autumn here in the mountains, chilly out, winter close at hand.

"You like it."

"Yeah," I say and take her hand as we walk to my car.

· · · · · ★ ★ ★ ★ ★ · · · · ·

WHEN WE GET to Wells and Josie's house, the first thing we see is Bart in full Halloween regalia. This year he's in Grim Reaper garb, complete with a black cloak, a scythe in one hand, and a decapitated zombie head dangling by the hair from the other. Gravestones adorn the rest of the front lawn, along with skeleton arms breaking through the earth. Jack-o'-lanterns line the front porch.

There's a group of people gathered in front of it, all looking and pointing up at the roof, where there seems to be a very small fire.

"I don't think this is responsible homeownership," I say to Wells, who's standing there with his arms crossed. He's wearing a...Hamburglar outfit? With green hair?

"You'd be surprised," he says, still looking up at the roof. On closer inspection, it turns out that the very small fire is actually a candle, somehow still burning amid the wreckage of a jack-o'-lantern.

"Is that supposed to be up there?" Madeline asks.

It's a legitimate question, given Wells's decoration proclivities.

"No. Teenagers," says Gideon, who's also standing there. "This was the only one they got, luckily."

"Dickheads," mutters Wells.

"I think it was supposed to roll off and smash," Josie says. "That's what I would've...uh, meant to happen. At least they didn't toilet-paper Bart."

"Do people really do that?" Gideon asks. He grew up in the country, so he looks surprised when everyone answers yes.

"It's really annoying to get out of trees, and if it rains before you can pull it down, it's a lost cause," I explain. "It turns into paper sludge that sticks to everything, so it's basically there forever."

"We did it once to the vice principal's front yard," Josie reminisces. "And we were gonna egg our math teacher's car, but Diane Beaufort was working the corner store that night and she wouldn't sell us any."

"Did you get caught?" Madeline asks, half-thrilled and half-scandalized.

"Not that time," Josie answers, giving us a reckless little grin.

"We put a bunch of lawn flamingos in the principal's front yard as our senior prank," Madeline offers. "Well, *I* didn't. I wasn't cool enough to get invited to senior pranks. But some people did."

"Where's your ladder?" Gideon asks, getting us back on track.

Wells sighs. "I lent it to someone. Best I can do tonight is a stepladder."

"I bet we could put a stepladder on a chair or something —" I start, but Gideon gives me an incredulous *look* that cuts me off. "Or we could definitely not do something that dangerous."

Laughing, Madeline pats my arm.

"I'm brainstorming," I tell the group. "What about a rake?"

"A rake would probably work," Gideon agrees.

· · · · ★ ★ ★ ★ · · · ·

INSIDE, the party is crowded but low-key. There's a cauldron filled with apple cider, a ton of cookies, and several plastic pumpkins filled with choice Halloween candy.

"Josie was saying that neighborhood expectations are very high around here," Madeline sighs, poking through candy until she comes up with a full-size Twix, then opens it and offers me half. "They have to get the big candy bars, or the neighbors will talk."

We're still in our haunted-house costumes. She's in overalls and a tank top, hair in branded pigtails, fake blood everywhere. It even looks like it's dripping from the scar on her forehead, which is a nice touch. I'm a dead circus ringmaster, complete with a loud jacket and my face painted like a skull. Not a Dia de los Muertos skull, just a regular one. I did a very good job, though.

"I thought the neighbors already talked about Bart," I say, biting off a piece.

"They do," she confirms. Madeline and Josie hit it off the instant they met, the first time Madeline and I came over for dinner during the summer. "But it turns out Eugene—the one who *really* hates Bart—has been a pain in everyone's ass lately, so there's a growing portion of the neighborhood who are in favor of the giant skeleton."

I take another bite and glance around, making sure no one can hear me.

"What the *fuck* is going on with small towns?" I ask, and she laughs. "They've been fighting about decorations for two years now. There are *factions*."

"Have you ever read the letters to the editor in the paper? They are *unhinged*," she whispers. "Last week someone wrote a very strongly worded one about graffiti on the Main Street bridge. There was *one* graffiti tag, and it got removed within a day."

I'm trying to think of a bridge or underpass in Virginia Beach that doesn't have graffiti on it, and I can't. It's a city. People spray-paint things. It's part of the charm, I swear.

"Do you hate it yet?" I ask her and cover my sudden nerves by taking a sip of apple cider.

"What do you mean, *yet*?" She pokes me in the side. "Quit expecting me to change my mind. I'll tell you if I do, but so far, I find the factions and the letters charming."

It's too good to be true, right? Madeline loving this town, loving my friends, loving my cat, loving *me*. There are still times, late at night when I can't sleep, when I think I'll wake up from a long dream and be on someone's filthy couch in Richmond, already thinking about another fix. I can't possibly be here, at a Halloween party where there's cider and cookies and "Time Warp" playing in the background. I can't possibly have a girlfriend who moved across the state to live with me. She can't possibly be happy about that decision.

But then Madeline wraps an arm around my waist, and the song changes to "Thriller," and Wells and Gideon come through the front door proclaiming victory over the roof jack-o'-lantern, and it is. It's all true somehow.

· · · · ★ ★ ★ ★ · · · ·

"YOU HAVE TO HOLD *STILL*," she says, which is dumb, because I *am*. I've been holding still for several minutes now while she slathers some Crisco-like substance on my face. It's gross, but it does get the makeup off.

"I can do it myself," I say, moving as little as possible. I'm sitting on our bathroom counter, in my underwear, with her between my legs.

"You miss spots."

"I don't."

She ignores me, swipes more Crisco onto my nose, then steps back. "Rub that around real good, then get in the shower," she orders me.

"You gonna join me?"

"No, because you actually have to get clean."

"What if I got clean and *then* dirty?"

"What I like about you is how creative you are," she laughs. "Clean and then dirty. Groundbreaking."

I pull my hands off my face. They're now covered in Crisco and face paint.

"You didn't say yes or no to getting dirty," I point out.

"Ask again in ten minutes," she says and starts the shower for me.

· · * * ★ ★ ★ ★ * * · ·

MADELINE CLEANS the fake blood off, then joins me in the shower, which is pretty big and surprisingly good for fucking in. I'm not saying it's the main reason we picked this house—it's also got three bedrooms and a garage that I turned into an art studio—but we did take the fuck-size shower into consideration.

· · * * ★ ★ ★ ★ * * · ·

AND IT'S GOOD—IT always is with her—but it's afterward, when the water is losing heat and I'm pressed against her back, skin warm and slick, my forearm braced across her chest, that always breaks me a little. She relaxes into me slowly, one hand against the shower wall. Her breathing echoes. It's warm and wet and slippery, and in this state, it's a little hard to tell when I end and she begins. I don't mind.

After another moment, she takes my hand, raises it to her lips, and kisses each knuckle softly. She does it a lot, I've realized: sweet kisses, featherlight touches. Soft hands in my hair. Madeline treats me like I'm breakable, sure, but more importantly she treats me like I'm too precious to break.

"Love you," she says when she's kissed the final knuckle.

Sometimes I can't believe this is what I have to settle for: *I love you.* There has to be something better, something bigger, something planet-sized that could explain the way this feels. I haven't found it yet, though.

"Love you, too," I say, and she turns in my arms. I shut the water off and hold her tight as the cold creeps in.

"It's late." She kisses me on the tip of my nose. It makes me feel like I'm made of dandelion fluff, sunny and light. "Bed?"

It's our bed, in our house. I've never had a thought I like better.

"Bed," I agree, and kiss her on the forehead.

**THE END**

# ACKNOWLEDGMENTS

No one tells you this when you get the handbook on novel writing, but a book is actually a group project. (Also, there's no handbook. Sorry if I just disappointed you.) Half the time the other members of the group don't know they're doing a project and have no clue they're being graded, but without them the whole thing would crumble.

So, a huge thanks to my group, who didn't always know that this would be on the test. There's Julia and Theresa, who have never stayed on-topic even once; Becca, an angel of calm serenity and patience who seemingly never tires of reminding me how to write books; Kate and Kat and Andrew, who have known me practically since the first time I googled "Self-publish romance novels?" a decade ago. Also, a huge thanks to Daniela and Patricia for their sensitivity reads (and for generously doing them at the last minute).

Given Javier's ADHD, it only seems fitting to finally mention the musical artist Tmsoft's White Noise Sleep Sounds. The track "Mining Pump Sound" is nearly perfect: just melodic enough to stay interesting, but still relaxing, world-shushing white noise. I've never seen a mining pump in real life, but I'd know one if I heard it.

Thanks to my husband, a Renaissance man who makes me both bookshelves and book spreadsheets, and thanks to my kiddo, who makes sure my days are never boring.

And finally, the cats in this book—Zorro and Barry—owe

a debt of gratitude to Sinbad, who we lost earlier this year. He was the smartest and most dignified orange cat I've ever met, and I miss him terribly.

# ABOUT ROXIE

Roxie is a romance author by day, and also a romance author by night. She lives in Los Angeles with her husband, cat, child, and a stack of used notebooks that may soon become sentient.

Want to be the first to hear about new releases and free extras? Sign up for her newsletter!

www.roxienoir.com
roxie@roxienoir.com

Made in United States
Cleveland, OH
14 March 2025

15037683R40249